CW01663345

Rivers Apart

Nora Rose

Michael Terence Publishing

First published in paperback by
Michael Terence Publishing in 2020
www.mtp.agency

Facebook Nora Rose
Instagram @books_by_nora_rose
Twitter @BooksbyNoraRose
Email booksbynorarose@aol.com

ISBN 9781913653828

For my husband,
the home where my heart lives.

With love

Nora Rose

x

Contents

1

Monday

She knew, standing in the doorway of her living room in her London flat staring at what lay in front of her, that her life was never going to be the same again.

***

"Why are you being so difficult?" Max asked, "Have I not always been there for you? Don't I always back your crazy half-arsed ideas?"

Nate rubbed his forehead as if in pain, "Max," he said, "you know how important you are to me, it's not that I don't trust you it's just that I need to be in control, I do the hiring and the firing, it's always been that way."

Nate Rivers was ruggedly handsome, his dark hair always looked a mess swept over and uncared for but somehow it worked, short at the back, it fell carelessly over his face which had him running his hand through it, his unshaved stubble another of his trademarks that made the mostly frustrated housewives tune in to any television show he was currently producing and starring in.

Nate had been successful most of his life, he took every knockback as a tool to strive harder and higher than before. He was a Michelin star chef with three to his name and eight awarded to his restaurants. His small business empire consisted of ten restaurants in both the UK and the States. He went from a sous chef to a world-class chef within a period of six long years. He deserved it; he had worked hard, relentless in his hunger for success, he had let nothing stand in his way.

"Nate," Max sighed, "I have never asked anything of you before, I need this favour and I need you to trust me." Max was nearing fifty, his thinning hair and round, portly shape screamed years of overeating and drinking. Max had met Nate early in his climb to stardom. Twelve years his junior, at twenty-five, Max had immediately liked the cheeky young lad, now thirty-eight he was one of the most recognised reality TV personalities of his time. Max had been by his side through it all.

"OK! OK! Stop chewing my balls off for God's sake." He knew he would end up relenting, as he trusted Max with his life, it was just such an unexpected request.

Rivers Productions was Nate's baby. The team was currently based in a hotel on White Meadow Lake in the state of New Jersey. It had been unimaginatively named 'The Inn on the Lake'. With a population just under 9,000, Nate loved the location. His make-shift office overlooked the lake and it was, just as the tourist brochure had said, 'one of the most picturesque places in the Garden State'.

They had taken over the hotel, an-old style country lodge and, set well away from the main street, it was both beautiful and quiet.

Max's behaviour was intriguing Nate. There was an empty desk in their office, beside his desk and opposite Max's where Nate's previous assistant producer, also known as a PA, had once sat before managing to fall pregnant and deciding to go home to the UK. But Nate had been in no great hurry to fill the position, preferring to take his time and find the right fit for the team, so when Max had announced he had hired someone and she was on her way from London, it had perplexed Nate.

"Have you called your wife lately?" Max asked Nate.

"Don't do that," Nate replied,

"What?" Max said, doing his best to sound wounded.

"Change the bloody subject!" Nate retorted throwing his hands in the air. He knew Max had a point. His wife Sarah lived in their home in the Surrey Hills on the outskirts of London. His once carefree life had turned into a kid, marriage, followed by twins. It kept Sarah happy and kept her at home freeing him up to follow his dreams.

He knew he was selfish. He'd only married Sarah as it seemed the right thing to do at the time. Both of them were young when Sarah became pregnant with their eldest son Mike, who was now sixteen. Their marriage had become more of a business deal in the last few years, with Nate never home and Sarah having no interest except reaping the benefits of a very comfortable and financially secure life. It seemed to work for them even though she felt the need to constantly nag him.

Nate had never strayed from home, well almost never, there was that one time he drank too much and, in the company of a famous and notorious womanising rock and roll star he almost ended up going home with a groupie. He chuckled to himself remembering that night; he had not drunk Tequila since.

The truth was Nate could have any woman he wanted. He was not only handsome but also charming with it. He had been brought up in a strict but secure family and he didn't care much for cheap sex or one-night stands. All they would bring him was 'a story in the tabloid trash and a divorce!' he heard his father telling him time and time again over the years. He was probably right. 'Best to be safe than sorry, son.' He would say with a wink and a grin. Sometimes, Nate missed his dad.

It's not that he didn't love Sarah but, in truth, he had fallen out of love with her not long after they were married. She did not share his interests or dreams. It was a shame, if things had been different maybe she would be by his side now. It didn't help to dwell but Nate always felt as though he had missed out on having a lover and a partner, but she was more interested in coffee mornings with friends than business ventures with him.

"So, let me get this straight, Max, you've hired a girl from London without seeing her résumé, to be my PA as a favour to a friend of yours?"

"It's not that simple," he replied, "look, like I said before, she needs someone to give her a break and I wouldn't ask but I've known Dominic since school, that's a long time, and he says it's really important to him."

"But it's not him who's working for me is it? This girl…" he said waving his hand as if looking for the word.

"Evie," Max said.

"Evie, who is she to him that it's so important?" Nate was shaking his head, he felt like he was going round in circles.

"Nate, all I know is that she needs a new start, Dom says she's like a daughter to him which, believe me, means for whatever reason she is important to him. I think he likes the idea I can look out for her, which is probably all the reason is." He sighed, "look, if it doesn't work out and she's useless or whatever at least I can say to Dom that I'd tried to help. Who knows, it may even be the best thing that's happened to this company in a long time!" he declared grinning, as he knew Nate wouldn't go against him at the end of the day. He had never let him down before.

"The shit I have to put up with," Nate said, still shaking his head as he walked out of the room.

In truth Max knew very little. Dom, his long-time friend of old was a police detective at New Scotland Yard. Max had never known him get personal on a case and did wonder if this Evie was his girlfriend who he was trying to keep away from home. Dom had been a player in his day but Max thought he was happily married but then really, is anyone truly happily married? Not being married himself it was something to ponder on. He knew he was putting Nate in a difficult position and just hoped this Evie could do the job but more importantly be able to get a handle on Nate.

Nate was a fair but firm boss. He was liked by his co-workers and tried to always look at things from another's point of view. He knew Max would not do anything to put his business in jeopardy but it bothered him not knowing any back-story on this woman. He literally knew nothing. Nate would usually do extensive research before hiring someone for a job, especially for one as important as his PA, he was concerned.

***

Evie's eyes were closed. She was thinking of the friends she was leaving behind. She held back the tears, this wouldn't be forever after all, that's what the detective told her. She was fond of Dom, he had been there for her from the start and she wondered if she would have made it this far without him.

As the pilot's voice came over the speaker asking the crew to prepare for landing, Evie thought of the irony, she had always wanted to go to New Jersey, it had been on her bucket list to see Bon Jovi in concert in their hometown. She smiled to herself, maybe it wouldn't be so bad after all. She was still apprehensive though as she had heard that Nate Rivers was obnoxious, big headed and arrogant. "Christ," she muttered, how was she going to work for a man like that. A bloody chef she mused, how the hell was this going to work? Hopefully she would be home again soon and this would all be behind her.

***

Nate was standing in the reception area of the hotel, hands on hips, he was engaged in conversation with his personal make-up artist, Tina. "I'm not having Botox," he told her grinning at her persistence. "I don't have that many wrinkles!" he protested.

"It's for prevention, Nate!" she retorted, "I can't make you look handsome forever with just make-up!" He laughed. This conversation happened quite frequently. He knew everyone on TV had Botox at one time or another, but he felt sure at thirty-eight he wasn't there yet. He turned away as Tina started to engage in conversation with some other poor victim.

That was when he saw her for the first time. She was standing in the doorway of the hotel gripping a small shoulder bag with what looked like a gym bag on the floor next to her. She was looking around nervously chewing the inside of her cheek.

Nate's stomach dropped and turned over, it was like he had just reached the top of the big dipper before falling down the other side of the rollercoaster ride. He rubbed his chin with one hand feeling his stubble, regretting being too lazy to shave today. She was beautiful.

Evie, at thirty-two, was a natural blonde. Her hair cascaded over her olive-skinned face in waves, her hazel eyes complemented the tone of her skin. She was slim in build but curved in all the right places. She was aware she was probably a mess after the journey. She felt grimy, that feeling of being in too close proximity with people on a plane. She desperately wanted to shower. She made her way to the reception desk and waited for the receptionist to acknowledge her. Her name tag said she was called 'Leanne'. Evie squinted at the middle-aged woman and saw the once beautiful face before the years of cigarettes and sunbathing had taken their toll.

"Miss?" Leanne said again, "can I help you, dear?"

"Sorry," said Evie, "yes, I think you're expecting me? Evie Grey, I'm due to start work here for Rivers Production."

"Hello," Nate said, he wasn't even aware he had moved yet he was standing next to her at the desk. "I'm Nate," he said holding out a hand to her. He felt like Forrest Gump.

"Hi!" she said tucking her hair behind one ear and holding a hand out to shake his. She smiled trying to look better than she felt. She was surprised when she saw him. He didn't look like the scary picture she had painted, quite the opposite, he was extremely handsome, he looked like he worked out but just enough to stay toned, and he had chiselled features that reminded her of the likes of Brad Pitt and Rob Lowe. His bright blue eyes shone and contrasted against his dark hair. He was very easy on the eye, but looks could be deceiving.

They shook hands.

Holding her eye, Nate was unaware he still had hold of her hand. "Oh sorry," he chuckled almost nervously. "Welcome to The Inn on the Lake," he continued, "how was your journey?"

Evie was tired but this was her boss for the next however-long of her life so she lied and said, "Great thanks."

"Good," he said, "Leanne, can I have Miss Grey's key? I will show her to her room." Leanne reached behind her picking key 13 off the rail and handing it to Nate.

"Oh wow!" Evie smiled, "an actual key! How quaint!"

Nate chuckled, "Yeah they are not quite on the modern system here yet. Leanne, can you get Miss Grey's bags sent up to her room please," he said picking up her gym bag.

"Oh, that's it," Evie said, "I travel light."

"Light?" Nate said with a quizzical look. "My wife packs more than this in make-up!" he declared genuinely surprised. "Leave in a hurry?" he said, only half joking.

She laughed nervously as she replied, "Yeah kind of. What I haven't got I can pick up, after all, what girl doesn't like shopping!" He smiled, thinking to himself, what girl doesn't pack half her wardrobe? This woman was a complete mystery.

They rode the lift to the second floor in silence. Walking down the corridor to her room she said, "I just wanted to thank you for this opportunity."

He unlocked the door, opened it and stood aside for her to go in first. "I didn't exactly have much choice," he said. "You have a lovely view over the lake," changing the subject. He put her bag down on the bed and faced her. "Why don't you get settled in and then join me in the bar and I can introduce you to whoever is about." It wasn't a question.

"Great," she replied.

It was the best shower she had ever had. She felt the grime of the last few months washing away down the plughole. 'You got this,' she thought rinsing the conditioner out of her hair.

It was 6pm local time when Evie finally made an appearance. After showering she had lain on the bed and drifted off. She slept heavily for the first time in a long time.

Nate was leaning up against the bar laughing amongst a small group of people. He lifted his wine glass to his lips and looked up over the rim as he saw her. She was searching the room with her eyes when they met his and she smiled. His stomach was back on that rollercoaster.

He stood up straight putting his glass down and holding an arm out towards her. "Evie," he said, "come and meet the others."

She walked up to him looking even more beautiful than before.

This was unlike him. He was confused that his body seemed to be acting like someone else was in control. Maybe he was unwell, picked up a bug, that would explain his stomach. As she glided over and stopped in front of him he could smell the hotel shower gel on her, she wore it like a veil of a hundred roses.

"Hello," she said.

He introduced her to the group. "This is Evie, she is my new PA."

Everyone said hello and she heard a wave of names rush in her direction, so she laughed and said, "I'm sorry if I don't remember all your names but I'm sure I will get to know you all well." She was polite and well spoken.

"Right, go away you lot," Nate said waving his hand, "go drink somewhere else Evie and I have business to discuss." The group dispersed into their own smaller drinking parties.

"What would you like to drink?" Nate asked searching her eyes.

"I'll have the same as you please," she said.

"Good choice," he said, then turning to the barman, "two glasses of the Pinot Noir please." He gestured towards the bottle on the shelf.

Evie glanced up at it, "La Crema Monterey Pinot Noir," she said, "very nice."

He chuckled, "Did you not think I would have good taste in wine?" he teased. She smiled and accepted the drink.

"Cheers," he said as they held their glasses in the air. "Welcome to New Jersey." At that point Max turned up and joined them.

Max smiled at her and said, "Hello Evie, I'm Max, it's great to meet you." Evie stared at him, put her glass down on the bar and walked towards him. Before he knew what happened she had her arms around his neck and hugged him tightly.

"Thank you," she said holding back the tears. She didn't know why she was being so emotional. She was tired and the last few months had caught up with her.

"Oh, my dear," Max said as he patted her back.

She stepped back to look at him.

"You are most welcome. I have some money for you as well, to spend as you wish, I understand you came with very little."

She smiled and said, "Yeah I kind of just decided to get out of Dodge."

"Don't blame you, a change is as good as a rest, so they say," he said smiling. "I will catch up with you in the morning my dear." And with that he left.

Nate felt like he had gatecrashed a party. "I didn't get a welcome like that!" he protested. Evie laughed.

"Can you tell me what is going on?" he continued.

She looked at him and he felt his stomach about to take another ride when she said, "That's for another day and it's going to take a lot more wine."

She was a curiosity but he decided not to push it any further for the moment. He was on his second red wine so he decided to try and drink a little slower, he wanted to keep his wits about him in this new alien territory he found himself in.

"Are you hungry?" he said.

"Starving," she replied.

"You should have said, let's eat." And with that he picked up her drink along with his and headed towards a table in the corner of the room next to a window overlooking the veranda and lake.

They looked through their menus in silence. In truth Nate didn't need to look, he knew the menu inside out. He had been known some days to head into the kitchen and cook for himself.

"Have you ever eaten in one of my restaurants in London?" he asked.

She replied, "I haven't actually," looking back at her menu trying to hide her face. If this had been a proper job for her she would of course have made sure she had eaten in his London restaurants and indeed researched the rest. But this wasn't a job she cared for. The premise was OK, but the job content was debatable.

"Oh," he said, trying not to sound disappointed, "well my flagship restaurant, Wild Rivers, started as a grill famous for its burgers, of course most of the recipes are my own," he continued proudly, "but I do let my chefs have a say and have their own dishes." He stopped. "Why are you looking at me like that?" he said.

"Like what?" she replied, not realising until he mentioned it that she was indeed staring at him.

With that, a waiter came over with his pad and asked, "What can I get you both?" Nate motioned to Evie to go ahead.

She had dreaded this moment. She held her menu up and pointed to the dish she wanted. "Erm, this please," she said with her finger.

"Vegetable Pattie, do you want fries or chips with that?"

"What are the chips cooked in?"

"Vegetable oil ma'am," he said.

"Great, chips please." She smiled as if all was well with the world and looked up at Nate. He was staring at her with a quizzical look on his face.

"Evie," he said slightly bemused, "are you a vegetarian?"

"God no!" she said and he started to relax, "I'm a vegan." Nate nearly choked on his mouthful of wine. "But I don't knock vegetarians because obviously they are making a difference but you know, I don't get it, why choose not to eat animals but still support the torture and murder of the dairy industry?" she shrugged and pulled a face. "It's just weird." She picked up her glass to take a sip and he was staring at her with his jaw open. "What?" she said.

Nate looked at the waiter and said, "I will have the same please, thanks," and shooed him away. Evie was perplexed that he had chosen the same meal but said nothing. She waited for him to compose himself, inwardly she was enjoying that feeling of making him feel uncomfortable but outwardly she just deadpanned.

To Evie, the Nate Rivers of the world were the enemy. A prestigious chef making a living out of exploiting animals. She would not in a million years have wanted to work for such a person but what choice did she have? Dom had told her not to say anything. "For God's sake, Evie," he had said, "don't try and convert the man or talk the way you talk to him."

"What do you mean?" she had protested, definitely wounded by his comment.

"You need this escape. This is a cover for you, you can't be in that world right now, and it's for your own good. Just smile sweetly and tell him it won't interfere with your job."

His words echoed in her ear as she realised what she had just said to Nate. Hmm, she thought, must try harder. She tried not to giggle; after all, Dom was right, this was serious.

"I'm guessing from that statement you are not plant-based for health?"

"No," she said, feeling mean now for enjoying his original discomfort, after all, so far he had been nothing but kind to her.

"I am most definitely vegan for ethical reasons."

"Ethical," he said, nodding his head as if in a daze. Could this day get any more bizarre for him?

"Animals, environment and health," she said. "I know it's not ideal, but my job won't be affected, I won't let you down I promise."

He wondered what the hell Max had got him into.

As if reading his mind, she said, "Max doesn't know. Dom was worried I wouldn't be a suitable candidate for the job."

He smiled seeing the irony and said, "Well in truth you're probably not, I guess I should just feel lucky it wasn't a marketing position."

She looked at him trying to keep a straight face but it was impossible and they both laughed.

Nate didn't really have much time to process the information as she quizzed him on his wife and kids thinking it was a safe subject. "Three kids!" she said, "poor woman."

Nate looked surprised, he was finding that was happening a lot recently. "Don't you want kids one day?" he asked.

"No!" she said as if he was mad.

"I thought that's what every woman dreamed about, husband, house, kids…"

"Not this one," she said. "I will be too busy."

"Saving animals," he teased.

"Yeah," she smiled. She was so amazingly beautiful; he was gutted, as this would probably be the first and last time they ate together.

Dinner came out and they both dug in. Evie was famished by now and knew she needed to soak up the wine quick before she got loose tongued and said too much about her life.

"This is very nice," Nate said genuinely enjoying his meal.

She laughed, "You sound surprised?"

"Well I don't usually choose the vegan option," he said.

"Just wine?" she teased.

"Wine?" he was confused.

"The wine you're drinking is vegan," she said, "one thing I do know is which red wine is vegan or not. It runs through my veins on a daily basis!"

He looked serious. "That's very interesting."

"What? That red wine runs through my veins?"

"No," he said with that don't-be-daft tone. "Red wine, never even crossed my mind about alcohol being vegan or not."

"It's a landmine I can tell you," she said, "you wouldn't believe the shit they put in…" She stopped. This is what Dom had meant. Time to zip it, Evie, she told herself. Instead she said, "This is lovely, Nate. Thank you."

They made small talk throughout the rest of the meal, keeping to safe subjects like discussing local attractions and things to see and do. Neither wanted dessert but Nate suggested a coffee on the veranda. She had planned to go up to bed after this and catch up on some sleep but she found herself saying yes, and what was most strange to her was the fact that she actually wanted to spend more time with this man, and for this evening not to end.

They sat on the veranda, both on the same bench, sitting facing each other. He looked at her so desperately wanting to know everything about her. He knew if not for the detective going to school with Max that their worlds would never have collided.

He was berated by the vegan movement, as were all his peers. He understood why, he had feelings, but it's always been the same, why should things change now. He had publicly said some things before that didn't make him popular with vegans but he was fed up with the constant barrage of insults. Why were they always so rude and in your face? Telling him he should change his ways as if he was responsible for the whole thing.

Right now he didn't care about anything but the beautiful mystery in front of him. Resting his head in one hand on the back of the bench he mirrored her position. He didn't want to walk across the minefield but he found himself asking her why she chose to be a vegan.

She smiled at him and said with passion and sincerity "I love animals, I just love them. They are no different to children, more vulnerable even as they cannot talk. I mean, each one is a sentient being like you and me," she put her hand on her heart, "they all have a brain, a heart, a nervous system. They all feel fear, pain, joy and love. They all smell death and are frightened when…" She stopped talking as if she forgot what she was saying. The truth was she was back there watching, remembering the cries, the pain, she shook her head and shuddered. Those were images that would always haunt her.

Nate was mesmerised. "Evie," he said carelessly reaching out and tucking her hair from her face behind her ear, a gesture so familiar as if he had known her forever. "You are a beautiful person, not just on the outside." He had seen her passion and he had seen her weakness. Empathy was a killer.

He wished for the first time in his life that he was anything but a chef, right now, in this moment. But that was all he knew and loved. His feelings were confusing him; he didn't want to say anything that might upset her, even though he had the arguments and comebacks, he didn't want to anger her. At least not on their first meeting. Instead he said, "A nightcap?" as he waved at a waiter through the window.

"Sure," she said smiling, "but then I must go to bed."

"OK, two whiskies straight please," he said winking at her, "to help you sleep."

They drank their whisky and made their way to the lift. Evie was feeling light headed and wished she hadn't had that last drink. They travelled the lift in silence again until they reached the second floor. Nate held the button. "I'm next one up," he said, holding the door for her.

"Thanks for tonight," she said, "see you in the morning."

"It's been entertaining," he said smiling. He had this overwhelming urge to reach out and touch her face, he must have drunk too much. He stepped back not actually trusting himself at this moment. She started to walk off and he said, "Evie wait." She turned and met his eyes, he held her gaze for what seemed like an hour before he finally said, "Don't worry about starting early, get some rest and shake off the jet lag." He smiled at her as the doors closed and she disappeared from his sight.

Evie went to her room, stripped off and lay on her bed thinking about the evening and pondering her new boss. She couldn't wait till the morning to see him. Hmm, she thought, that must be the drink talking as she shut her eyes and drifted off.

Nate was standing in his room staring at his reflection. God, maybe Tina was right, maybe he did need Botox. What was happening to him? He went to his fridge and pulled out a bottle of whisky and poured himself a double. Looking in the mirror again he said to himself, "Nate, you're in serious trouble." And with that he sat on his bed and drank.

2

Tuesday

Evie woke with a start. "Shit!" she said, jumping out of bed and into the shower. She knew Nate had said sleep in but it was nearly 11am. She had wanted to make a good impression as she was unsure how the land lay after last night. She knew she had drunk too much, but you know, sometimes shit just happens. She smiled, she liked Nate. She hoped sober Evie also liked him; it would make this time a lot easier.

Nate was up early as usual. He never slept past 7am, always awake before his alarm went off. He was sitting at his desk, back to the open window that overlooked the lake.

Max laughed out loud holding his portly belly when Nate recounted the events of the night before. "Oh dear, oh dear," he chuckled, "this is going to be fun."

"Fun?" Nate said, nodding his head in sarcasm, "Fun? You got me into this Max!" he said pointing his finger at him. "Remember it only works until it doesn't! If she has to go then so be it."

Max muttered something inaudible under his breath and walked out of the office still chuckling.

Nate hadn't meant what he said, he wanted Evie around. He couldn't remember the last time he had met someone who didn't hero-worship him to his face. He was surrounded by people like that whenever he left the confinement of the hotel. It was refreshing to meet someone who he really, at this point, had no idea what opinion she had of him. He rubbed his stubbly chin, wondering why it mattered so much to him.

Half an hour later there was a knock on the door. Nate hadn't realised the door was shut; he had always had an open-door policy. "Come in," he said as Evie came through the door. "Morning," she said smiling at him.

"Good morning, did you sleep OK?" he found himself asking her.

He was hoping that whatever took hold of him yesterday would have sorted itself out today. She was wearing blue skinny jeans that hugged her figure and a white sweatshirt that hung off one shoulder. There was no bra strap visible yet her breasts were in the right place. Her nipples were showing through her top. He saw her and took it all in with one glance. He felt sick. Anxious even. Maybe he was having some kind of panic attack or maybe he should consider going to the doctor and getting checked out. His mind was trying to work out if he might indeed have an underlying health problem when he realised she was talking to him. "Nate?" she said with genuine concern. "Are you OK? You look pale."

He gathered his senses and replied, "Yes, maybe a bit too much whisky last night." She smiled at him and he grinned back. "Have you eaten?" he found himself asking. "Did they cater for you OK?"

She smiled as she replied, "Yes thanks, I'm fine, I missed breakfast but I had some protein bars with me from the journey." She put her hands in the back pockets of her jeans, rocking on her feet she said, "So err, what is it exactly we do here?"

He looked at her with total bemusement and said, "Oh my God, you have no idea what the job even entails?" She started chewing the inside of her cheek, a nervous habit she had picked up. He saw and his face softened, he found her so endearing, the constant churning in the pit of his stomach since she had walked into the room was something that had not gone unnoticed.

Currently Rivers Productions was working on a show that would start filming in the coming months. Nate wanted to help others, he had been determined and driven when he was young, but there were not the same resources for the youth of today. It was a different world. He had decided it was time for him to do something about it. He had wanted to open another restaurant but instead of being high-class dining he wanted it to be more casual, more appealing to everyone. He had decided to search for young adults who were training to be chefs, but needed a break. He knew the system was different over here. In the UK you had to be a trained chef to work in most establishments but in the States, they pretty much hired anyone who said they could cook, in more places than Nate would care to admit. If it was a success then

Nate was hoping he would be able to do a similar show back home in the UK and open a similar eatery in London.

As Nate finished explaining his plans, Evie looked on intrigued. It was a good idea. After years of practice of self-survival in a cruel world, Evie had learned how to listen to things, ignore the bits she didn't like and replace them in her mind with the kinder option. For example, eating with carnivores had always been tricky and even though now she would no longer sit at the same table with people who ate animals, in the early days she would pretend that their food was vegan so she could cope with social gatherings. She would just have to do the same when it came to dealing with the cooking aspect of the show, if she was still here at that point.

She had been glad Nate had ordered the same as her last night because she would have had to have compromised herself. She knew she would struggle while she was here but she knew needs must and she needed this escape.

"It sounds great," she told him.

"We are still in the early stages," he replied. "Lots to do and to be honest I need someone to be there for me," he said gesturing towards her. "Answering my phone and emails, checking on my social media, arranging my life really, and helping me make sense of it. Is that something you think you can do?" he asked.

Evie had briefly mentioned to him that she had been a PA in London for a company but she had not mentioned names or experience. He was going in on this blind. "Evie, you will be handling some sensitive issues and also some of my personal life will be laid out, you will have to sign a confidentiality agreement of course, there is no question about that."

Nate had prided himself in staying out of the tabloids and keeping his private life private. He and Sarah had done a spread in *Hello* magazine after the girls were born but otherwise that was it. He disliked the tabloid press. They were so intrusive and did not care who they trampled all over to get a story.

"Sure," Evie said, "I mean I don't know how long I will be here but I guess it's OK." This was all so odd for him. Here he was letting a complete stranger take the reins to his life to do a favour for an old school friendship of a friend. He must be mad. The only good thing was he had been struggling to keep all his social media up to date while making his own appointments, amongst other things. He was tired and needed help organising his affairs.

In his room, Max was on the phone to Dom. "Yes, yes, she's here, she's fine and I have got $3,000 cash to give her to see her right for a bit, she brought nothing you know!"

Dom knew Evie was travelling light. She had been so scared that last time she had called. He had gone straight over to her flat and helped her throw a few things in a bag and leave.

She had stayed in a safe house for the following week while Dom organised everything. Max had been a godsend, coming through for him as usual. Max had been the fat kid at school and was picked on relentlessly, but Dom had taken pity on him and that pity had turned into a life-long friendship that Dom could now not imagine being without.

Dom had sorted out a temporary identity for Evie, keeping her first name as it was. She was not allowed any contact with anyone from her life. He had given her a new phone that had two numbers in it, his and Max's. When Evie had asked how long she would have to be in hiding for he had simply shrugged. "You know I will do everything I can to catch him," he had said, "we will get him, Evie, I promise." He had hoped for everyone's sake it would be soon, as this guy really scared him.

Nate had two phones, one he kept on him all the time which was for family and close friends and then another which was for everything business. He gave Evie the business phone and told her the pass code. "Get familiar with it," he said. "You'd better take my personal number as well, in case you need me of course."

"I'm honoured," she joked, as she tapped in the number on her phone, that he was telling her. His phone rang, he went to answer it. "That's me," she said disconnecting the call, "in case you need me." She deadpanned, laughing with her eyes.

Evie was pleasantly surprised that seeing Nate this morning had made her smile. She told herself she was too old for crushes even though she didn't mind admitting that she liked the way he looked at her. She wasn't in a relationship, thankfully, with what was going on in her life right now. She hadn't been, and wasn't, looking for a boyfriend, being quite content with her life the way it was. Until 'he' had come along and changed everything.

Evie had been working for the Animal Liberation Movement (ALM) back home. She hadn't lied to Nate; she helped with their public relations and marketing campaigns, her job was often stressful and heart-wrenchingly painful. She had come off all social media and had no contact with anyone in that world at the moment. Dom reassured her he would make suitable excuses for the time being. It wasn't unheard of that working for causes such as the ALM could result in being over stressful and employees and volunteers alike would sometimes go AWOL. Evie had seen enough heartache to last a lifetime. If she could press a button and delete her worst memories as easily as she had deleted her social media pages she would in a flash. She wished on some level that she was still ignorant of the pain and suffering humans inflict on animals on a daily basis, and that she could go back to living in ignorant bliss. She was used to the stupid statements from people such as, "you should care more about the murdered children in the world! They are more important!" The truth was she did care. Of course she cared. If she could identify every child killer and take them down of course she would but that was not something she had any power of changing. Her food choices were.

People were waking up to the error of their ways and she was helping to change a lot of people's mindset when it came to animal welfare, the environment and health. And now here she was, working for a company that makes its money out of the very thing she had spent her life trying to change. She felt wretched. She was fooling herself that she would cope. Then there was Nate. She had hoped sober Evie would see him for what he was, the enemy, but the truth was she liked him… worse she was attracted to him. She couldn't think about all that now. She had to focus. She had been sitting at the desk to the right of Nate's, looking at him run his hand through his hair and watched as he sat back in his chair and stretched his arms out above his head. She felt a stirring. She couldn't even go there. Not only was he married but he was also an animal eater. She could never be with a man who didn't feel the same way as her on the animal front. Never.

Without warning Nate jumped up and said, "Have you looked around the grounds yet? Of course you haven't, you haven't had time," he said answering his own question. "Come on, the lake is beautiful." It was mid-June and it was a beautiful warm day. Nate held the door open for her as they stepped outside. He steered her off the main driveway following a path around the back of the hotel towards the lake. It was stunning. Surrounded by trees on three sides, the hotel sat perfectly amongst the surroundings overlooking the beautiful scenery.

"I want to show you something," he said and took her hand and pulled her off the path between the trees. She laughed at his excitement and she felt like a kid again playing hooky from school. They came out the other side of the trees and hidden out of sight from the hotel was a small boat shed and a jetty heading out onto the lake. There was a small clearing with a burnt patch of grass. "I guess kids hang out here sometimes," he said, nodding towards the patch. "Sometimes, when I need time to think I come and sit here on the jetty and just take it all in."

"It sure is tranquil," she said, "I can understand why you come here."

"Yeah, it's my secret hideout, I always wanted one as a kid," he said with a half smile.

She searched his face, looking at him curiously. "It's not so secret now," she said looking at him questioningly.

He smiled looking at her before looking away across the lake. "Everyone needs somewhere, Evie, I know you're a long way from home and maybe when you're ready you will tell me what's going on with you, but if you ever feel like you need an escape I'm happy to share my spot with you." He folded his arms across his chest and looked at her.

"Is it a timeshare?" she joked.

"Smart-arse," he replied. "Come on, I'm hungry. Let's get lunch."

Back at the hotel he led her into the restaurant. One side of the room a buffet table was set out. "Breakfast and lunch are always served buffet style," he told her. "Head chef, Lucas, likes to do a different theme each day of the week. There is a vegetarian section, as there is with breakfast, but I have spoken to Lucas and he will be adding vegan options."

She smiled and said, "Great, thanks."

He motioned towards a table for eight which currently only had two people sitting at it. Tina, his Botox-mad make-up artist and Daryl, who worked in wardrobe. They were deep in conversation like two giggling school kids.

"Guys," Nate said, "this is Evie, say hello I will be back in a minute. Play nice." With that he turned and headed off to the kitchen leaving Evie standing by the table.

"Come sit, sweet thing," said Daryl, who's name was much to macho for his persona. "Come sit next to me," he said tapping the seat next to him. Evie knew she was going to like him from the start.

When Nate came back out of the kitchen carrying two plates of bruschetta with salad he found the three of them as thick as thieves all laughing. "Well this is good to see," he said putting a plate down in front of Evie, sitting next to her with his own.

"What's this?" Tina said, "personal service?"

Evie shrugged and said, "Looks delicious, thanks."

Nate looked at Tina, "Yes, Tina, I'm playing nice with the new girl. OK? Happy?" he said with that pretend exasperation that had him liked amongst his team.

"Evie's a vegan," said Daryl, "I heard Nate this morning giving orders to Chef Lucas."

"My God, you get everywhere, Daryl," Nate joked, slightly embarrassed that he might have been overheard giving Lucas instructions on menu ideas for Evie. Evie and Tina Laughed. "Well it looks good whatever it is," Tina said to Nate, "where's mine?" she teased.

"You lot are impossible," he said picking up his last piece of bruschetta and standing up. "Excuse me," he said, "I'm off to sit with the grown-ups." With that he winked at them and moved across to another table with a much older occupancy.

He had a feeling that Tina and Evie would get on well together, and Daryl was gay so Evie was in safe hands. Not that if Daryl wasn't gay she wouldn't be in safe hands but for some reason it made him feel better knowing she wasn't going to be hit on by him. Not that it should matter to him, but it did. It would be good for Evie to make some friends. He somehow felt responsible for her.

Nate was sitting with Cassie, a middle-aged woman who most certainly used Botox on a regular basis, so Tina told him. Cassie was in charge of location, from finding the hotel for them to use as a base and any location needed for the shows. She was good at her job. "Hey Cassie," he said, sitting down.

"What is that?" she said, looking at his lunch. "Don't tell me you are on a diet?"

"I've put on a few pounds recently," he replied, "it doesn't hurt to eat healthily now and then."

She turned her nose up at him, "Nathanial, you without your steak sandwich just doesn't bode well."

He didn't like it when people called him Nathanial, that's what Sarah always called him when they argued. That's what his mother had called him when he was being chastised as a child. Neither good memories.

Changing the subject, he said, "How's it going with Max?"

Cassie blushed, she wasn't aware it was public knowledge. "I should have known Max would have told you," she said in her most hoity voice. Nate laughed, stood up and kissed her head affectionately, and with that he left.

When Evie returned to the office, Max and Nate were in a full-blown debate over sponsorship for the new show. "Ah, Evie my dear," said Max, "Dean Harper, we were debating the pros and cons of asking him to sponsor us. What do you think?"

Dean Harper was huge in the industry. A famous movie producer, he knew everyone who was worth knowing. At sixty-five he didn't look a day over fifty, thanks to the best doctors and plastic surgery money could buy. A one-time down-and-out, he had lifted himself out of the depths of despair and never looked back, except once. He had hired the best private detective and tracked down his stepfather of six months in his sad childhood and had a bullet sent with love straight through his child-molesting brain. Money was king. He was untouchable and unrecognisable from that scared little boy who had run away, and now owned half the Hollywood world.

"He's a great choice," Evie said, "he's certainly got money and if he's not interested in our show then he may know someone who is," she shrugged. Nate loved the way she had referred to it as 'our show', it pleased him for some reason.

His phone rang. He looked at the caller ID and stood up, "Excuse me," he said and left the office.

"How are you settling in, dear?" Max asked Evie. "I hear you've met Daryl," he said raising his eyebrows playfully.

Evie laughed, "So far so good, everyone I've met seems to be really nice, it's just I feel like I'm on holiday, displaced, I want to be of help here but it's all so different from the surroundings I'm used to working in. I don't want to let you down," she said looking at her feet like a child being told off.

"Oh, my dear girl," Max chuckled, "it won't take you long to get to grips with what we do here. Just keep smiling and always ask for help if you need it." He squeezed her shoulder and sat down at his desk. Evie sat down as well and opened the laptop on her desk. Twenty-three new email messages, she had better check those.

"Speak of the devil," she said to no one. Max had left and Nate had just returned.

"Who me?" he asked quizzically as he sat down.

"Dean Harper, you have an email from his office," she said looking at the screen. "Apparently he is having a 'gathering of friends' at his Manhattan penthouse and requires your presence," she said raising her eyebrow in jest. "Didn't know you were his type," she joked, knowing Harper's preference was men.

"Easy," he said, "that man would eat me alive!" They both laughed. He looked at her as his stomach danced somersaults.

Harper's soirées were famous for the crème de la crème of the industry. The truth was, Harper had been a good friend to Nate in the early days when Nate was fresh-faced and slightly cocky, he had been approached by Harper after the opening of his first restaurant in Downtown Manhattan. Harper had asked him to cater for one of his famous parties and Nate's food had been a hit, along with his cheeky persona, they soon became friends. Nate hadn't been to his New York restaurant, Rivers Rush since last week. Truth was he, like Harper, was a desperately private person that only came out and acted the part when needs must. Harper's parties were some of these times.

"His parties are great for getting all the talent together and a lot of deals are done over cocktails and whisky, they are also one of the only places that no press are allowed and it's strictly personal invitation only, total privacy guaranteed," Nate explained to Evie, who had come over to his desk and was resting on the edge of it facing him.

He looked at her and she smiled, "Well?" she said, "Do I accept for you?"

Nate felt a warmth rush through him as he looked up at her from his seat and said: "Yes, and tell them it's plus one." With that he stood up and excused himself.

Jesus what has happened to him? He had never been so attracted to another human being in his life. It felt like electricity running through him and he didn't know how to deal with it. He must be overdue a trip home. Maybe he should go and spend some time with Sarah and the kids, impractical at this stage of pre-production as it was. He rubbed his head with one hand the other on his hip. It had been Sarah that called him earlier, he was pleased to speak to her, catching up on the kid's gossip and then there had been some bullshit about him never being home and guilt-tripping. Women! He needed to sort himself out fast and get back on track.

Nate took out his phone and went to his favourites and speed dialled Harper. He answered on the third ring. "Nate, my old mate," he said in his best English accent.

"How ya doing?" Nate said in his best Yankee accent. They both laughed,

"It's been too long," said Harper. "Have you replaced me already?" teasing Nate as always. Nate sucked in his breath, "Uh-oh!" said Harper "what's troubling you, my old friend?"

Nate looked ahead gazing out his window that overlooked the lake one floor above Evie's. "It's big," he said to Harper, "and not a trouble I have had before."

Harper was delighted, he loved to be the confidante that a straight man went to, even though he found it somewhat amusing. He loved Nate, he was a true friend. It wasn't often you met the man of your dreams, even if he came in the straight package that was Nate Rivers.

Nate trusted Harper implicitly and the feeling was mutual. They had shared many secrets and laughs over the years, enjoyed gossiping and drinking brandy out of ridiculously large glasses.

"Maybe someone has paid her," Harper said matter-of-factly after Nate had finished telling him about his rollercoaster ride.

"Paid her? Are you serious, Harper? I mean seriously is that really the best you can come up with?" Harper laughed.

"For the great Nate Rivers to be in knots over a woman then she must be a pro of some sort." He continued, "In all my years of knowing you, Nate, you've never been interested in playing away from home."

Nate cut in, "But I've never been very good at playing at home either," he mused. Nate had said he was bringing her to the party and although Harper was in two minds about introducing a newbie to the scene he was curious to meet this woman.

"Keep it in your trousers," Harper said as Nate rang off.

Nate returned to the office where Max had just given Evie an envelope filled with cash as an advance on her wages.

"Thank you," she said. "I'm going to ask Daryl to come shopping with me if that's OK." Nate smiled. "You don't need our permission," he said.

"Why don't you both go out tomorrow morning," Max suggested. She looked at Nate for affirmation and he nodded to her smiling. She was so endearing, confident, and yet somewhat unsure.

The rest of the day disappeared in a rush of calls and Evie was exhausted. "Your phone never stops," she said to Nate, genuinely surprised.

"Tell me about it," he said after putting his phone down. "Have you made plans for dinner tonight?" he asked nonchalantly.

"No," she said, "to be honest I hadn't given it much thought."

"I tell you what, I'm cooking for you tonight, as you haven't even been to one of my restaurants," he said with mock chastisement. "I think you should at least taste my cooking."

She smiled. "I'd love that," she replied, meaning it and looking forward to it.

"Great!" he said. "See you in the bar at six." With that he turned and left.

Evie hugged herself smiling. What was it about this man that had her excited? She wanted to get to know him more and that surprised her. She felt like she was letting her morals down on one hand but she deserved a break, didn't she? She had felt happier since being here than she had done in a long time. Even before 'he' came along and chased her away from her real life.

She hadn't realised how down she had been feeling these past months with everything going on back at home, she now realised how unhappy her life had actually been. She picked up her two phones and headed up to her room. She was still wondering what it would be like to kiss Nate as she got into the shower.

Nate was in the bar chatting to the barman when Evie crept up behind him. He turned round startled and he looked at her and said, "Hey, beautiful." Shit had he said that out loud?

Evie blushed and said, "Hey," enjoying the way he was looking at her.

He snapped out of it and said to the barman, "Two glasses with that please." The barman handed him a bottle of red and two glasses. He grabbed the bottle by the neck and turning the glasses upside down he took them between his fingers and said to Evie, "Come on." And marched off towards the kitchen.

Service was slow tonight, a lot of the crew being stir crazy had found various fast-food joints and bars local to the hotel. Nate felt good that he was helping contribute towards the local economy. The kitchen was clean and tidy, it wasn't like this when they had first arrived and Nate had done his absolute nut when he saw the standard of hygiene. "Chef," he had said pleadingly to Lucas, "what the hell is this? Come on man." With the help and guidance Nate was so good at giving he had helped turn around this once shabby kitchen into a modern-day cuisine within a matter of days.

Lucas and his sous chef, Nancy, were busy down one end of the vast kitchen cooking an order for a table of four. Nate walked in and waved and said in a loud voice, "Evening Chef." They both looked over and waved back and went back to what they were doing.

"They are used to me coming in and cooking, it's not that I don't like their food but I enjoy cooking, without creating food I'm nothing," he said very dramatically. Evie stared at him, not sure if he was being serious or not when he nudged her, laughing, and said, "Pour the wine, woman, it's dry in here!" She laughed at him while she poured them both a generous drink. Nate was in the fridge, "I sent the pot wash out to get me things earlier so I'm hoping he's got everything I asked for."

"Sounds intriguing," she said as she picked up her glass, enjoying the full-bodied flavour of the wine she drunk. "What are you making?" she asked genuinely curious.

"Ah," he said, "well, I kept the ingredients simple, I thought I would make you a pasta dish, kind of a bolognaise but with home-made sauce." Evie's stomach growled, it had been a while since she had had the chance to cook a good old home-cooked meal and she was looking forward to this one.

Passing her some tomatoes and chillies to cut up he started blending the mushrooms in short pulses so they were small pieces like mince. "Even the biggest meat eater wouldn't tell the difference once it's flavoured," he winked. She smiled at him; she was confused how she felt. He seemed so genuinely caring, yet she couldn't get past the fact that the industry he was in was not one she cared for.

They chopped food, drank wine and laughed. While they waited for the food to finish cooking, Nate recalled some tales from the days he used to sous chef and some of the sights he saw in the kitchen. "I'm telling you," he said, "I didn't eat out for a year after working in that kitchen." He pulled a face and said, "Worst experience ever. It was then I knew I was going to have the best kitchens, the best standards." He looked at nothing nodding his head, "Yeah, those days made me who I am."

The food smelt delicious and, as Evie poured more wine, Nate dished up the pasta. It smelt amazing and Evie couldn't wait to eat. They stood at the counter they had been chopping up on leaning against it eating casually. It was the best food she had had in recent memory, having lived off fast-food and microwave dishes this was a treat.

In London, especially, it was easy to eat kind. There was a huge plant-based society along with those like her with a lifestyle-choice preference, she was used to being able to grab take-outs and eat on the go. She couldn't remember the last time she had a date but this was the closest thing. Being with Nate in the kitchen, she forgot her worries, she forgot her lifestyle choices and his and realised she was enjoying the company of this man a lot and she liked the carefree feeling that engulfed her.

After they ate, Nate put the dishes through the washer and suggested another bottle of wine on the veranda.

Sitting on the veranda Evie said, "You know half the problem is that the nice restaurants, such as yours," she said gesturing towards him, "is that they only have two or three vegetarian choices and possibly one vegan dish, if you're lucky. Zizzi's, for example, has a complete vegan menu." She had earlier Googled his restaurant to familiarise herself.

He looked at her thoughtfully. She continued, "Imagine, you could be a market leader, creating a menu to cater for everyone, it would bring in more diners." She shrugged, "I don't know, it's just a thought."

He searched her face tipping his head to one side he said, "Maybe you will be good for business." He held her eyes and that roller coaster ride took him over and he felt his stomach turn over, "Evie…" he said, not getting to finish his sentence as Daryl and Tina came bounding round the corner.

Seeing Evie and Nate they came over and sat down.

"What's up?" said Tina. "What are you crazy kids doing?" she asked with her normal exuberance. "We've just been to Bar 60 in town," she continued without waiting for them to answer. "Brilliant," she said, "you should come next time, Evie."

"Maybe once I've been shopping for some clothes," Evie joked pulling at her sweatshirt.

"Let's get drinks," Daryl said. Nate got up and excused himself. Five minutes later Evie received a text from him:

'Off to bed, been a long day.

Thanks for a lovely evening.

N. x'

She was surprised how disappointed she was. She replied:

'Thanks for dinner;

I've had a great evening too.

See you in the morning. x'

They carried on drinking for another hour before they finally decided to call it a night.

3

Wednesday

The following morning after breakfast with Daryl, Evie headed off to the office. Nate was sitting behind his desk, he looked up and gave her a warm smile and asked her how she was.

"I'm looking forward to going shopping with Daryl," she said, in truth she was looking forward to getting out to a town. The week before her arrival she had been cooped up in a safe house on the outskirts of Surrey. It had been a very long week. Evie was just grateful Dom had been able to act so quickly getting her out of the country. She hated looking over her shoulder every day, an action she had got used to, now a habit.

Daryl came bounding in the office, "Ready darling?" he pronounced in his campest manner possible.

"I'm just coming, be there in a minute," she replied looking back at Nate. "Thanks for this," she said to him smiling.

He looked at her as she turned to leave, "Oh, Evie," he said, she turned round and he continued, "you'd better pick up a dress or something for Harper's party." He had returned his eyes to the paper that he was reading and pretended to study it so as to not meet Evie's eyes. She cocked her head quizzically at him and said, "I assumed the plus one was Max?"

Nate looked up, "Max thought it would be a good idea to take you," he lied, "thought it would be good to take a fresh face to get a different perspective, for business of course," he stated trying to sound matter of fact.

"Huh," she said, trying to work him out. "OK, awesome!" she drooled in a bad American accent. He laughed and told her to get out before he changed his mind.

She turned back and said, "One thing," he looked up at her waiting. "Long and sophisticated or short and sexy?" she asked referring to his dress-code request.

"Short and sexy," he said, not missing a beat as he felt a warm rush throbbing through him and he was grateful he was sitting behind his desk as he grew hard.

"Short and sexy it is," she confirmed turning away from him and leaving the office.

Evie had texted Nate asking if it was OK to stay out longer with Daryl as he wanted to show her some of the sights. Nate figured that as there was not much for Evie to do, she might as well stay out and have fun.

'Maybe catch up later for a drink if you're not too tired.' he had texted her. She texted him back saying she would love to.

They stopped at a fast-food joint and grabbed a burger. "I don't know how you eat that shit," she told Daryl as he bit in to his beef burger.

"It's delicious!" He declared looking at her veggie burger, "better than that," he snorted. She punched him playfully in the arm and changed the subject.

They returned to the hotel, bags in arms, exhausted from a day out with Daryl she was keen to get showered and catch up with Nate. They went to her room and Daryl helped her hang up her clothes. "You're so lucky," he said in a bitchy tone, "you have a figure to die for." She shuddered, if only he knew how close she had come to danger because of how she looked. Feeling her mood change she thanked Daryl for the day and his help and ushered him out so she could shower.

She felt better after she had showered, washing away the negative memories and feelings as she pondered on what to wear now she had a bit more of a choice in her wardrobe. She settled for a casual white blouse that tied at the front showing off her midriff and it fell nicely between her breasts showing a teasing of her olive skin and complimented her skinny jeans. Daryl was right, she did have a figure to die for. Wearing her hair loose, she wore little make-up but still wondered if she was over dressed.

She texted Nate to ask where he was: 'I'm on the veranda', he texted back, 'I've got wine just need you'. She felt a strange sensation in her stomach, like she was nervous but excited at the same time. She looked in the mirror; unsure if she looked OK, what was wrong with her?

She headed through the main entrance of the hotel, rather than walking through the bar, and went round to the back of the veranda where Nate was sitting looking out at the lake. "Hey," she said.

He saw her and said, "Hey," as he tried to sound casual and not at all overwhelmed by her beauty. He hoped his body would not betray him again. "You look lovely," he said standing up and gesturing for her to sit down. They were sitting in the same place as last night, it was quiet and they were alone.

"Most the crew have headed out," she said. "Daryl told me earlier it's Carly's birthday and they were heading to a club." Carly worked in wardrobe and was not so keen on Evie. Evie had felt her animosity and asked Daryl what her problem was.

Daryl had shrugged and simply said, "Jealous much I guess."

Evie had been through too much to worry about high-school bitchiness.

They both seemed nervous. Nate poured the wine and said, "To you and a new wardrobe."

She laughed, "Wardrobe!" she exclaimed, "Cosmetics, make-up, shoes, oh, and of course a dress."

He blushed. She must know what effect she was having on him, surely? "Are you OK?" he said. She had been sipping her wine but she took a huge gulp and finished the glass. He smiled at her and said, "Talk to me," as he poured her some more wine.

"It's just something Daryl said to me earlier, it reminded me of him." She had almost spat the word out.

"Who? Evie, please, talk to me," he asked again facing her. She nodded and sighed.

Evie was well known in the animal liberation world. Having spent the first half of her life in ignorant bliss of the plight of animals. She had happily been brought up on the old lie that meat and dairy were good for you. Ha! If only society had been more educated. She didn't really blame the older generation, but today, in 2020, there was no excuse. All the medical and scientific facts were available. Animals and fish were eaten to get the protein that they had been fed or ate as part and parcel of their natural diet. Killing all these creatures was unnecessary and unhealthy. The leading cause of heart disease is animal cholesterols. It wasn't rocket science. The facts were there. Just like the tobacco industry. We had successfully been lied to and duped into thinking we could only get certain proteins from eating flesh. Lies made up to line the pockets of the most evil industry in the time of man.

Worst of all was not just the mass murder of these sentient beings but the conditions they were kept in on the factory farms and the misery of the dairy cows, but that was another discussion. Evie was trying to explain to Nate how and why she was where she was at this point of her life.

She had started getting messages on Messenger through her Facebook page from a man who's profile said he was Liam McKlusky. His profile picture was of a cute looking boxer dog. Evie's Facebook page was a platform for her activism and she had many followers, as her profile was public. She had set all the correct settings to keep her private information private and to be honest she had not given security much more thought.

She had checked out Liam's profile before replying to him. He came across quite normal from the few things he had posted. He had asked her if it was possible to meet and discuss a few things to help him along the right road to a kinder life. Evie sometimes got messages from random guys, usually activists themselves asking for dates. She had always been polite and had never had any trouble. She declined and sent Liam some useful links such as Veganuary, Challenge 22 and LIVEKINDLY, links she always used to introduce newbies to help them make a transition to a more ethical lifestyle choice. She didn't believe in frightening people away with graphic images of the true plight of the animals, she believed re-education was the answer, along with making plant-based food more readily available and affordable.

Liam had continued to message, first it was a message a day and then it progressed until she was getting such a barrage from him that she had no choice but to block him. That, she had hoped, was the end of that. It had been a couple of weeks since she had blocked Liam when she started to get an uneasy feeling of being watched. She couldn't quite put her finger on it but something wasn't right.

That was when she received her first black tulip. A single black tulip had been delivered to the ALM office addressed to Evie. There was no note and she, like others, just brushed it off as someone with a crush too shy to approach her. If only. She received a black tulip a day for a week. Curious, she stopped the delivery guy and asked where they had come from. Giving her the name of the florist he worked for, she called them up but to no avail. Someone had left an envelope of cash through the letterbox with instructions, which had now been thrown away.

Walking home from the pub one evening with some friends, Evie had said good night to them as she turned off down the road to take her home. She was not more than a few yards away from them when she felt a gloved hand over her mouth, while being manhandled down a side ally. She had tried to scream, but his hand was too tight over her mouth and then she felt the blade in her back. "Make a sound and I'll stab you," he had said in a low gravel of a voice. She was terrified but went with him as he dragged her backwards off the street.

Nate was on the edge of his seat. "My God, Evie, you must have been so frightened," he said covering his mouth and chin with his hand. He looked at her, she looked so vulnerable and scared it pulled at his heart as he refrained from reaching out and holding her.

"It wasn't the best day," she said dryly.

Nate suddenly realised where this was going. "Oh no, please tell me he didn't…" he said, feeling a hot anger leave the pit of his stomach ready to explode.

"No, no," she said, shaking her head at him. "Nothing like that, he just wanted to scare me, to let me know he could get to me if he wanted to."

Nate relaxed a little realising his whole body was stiff, he took a deep breath and said, "More wine?"

He finished the bottle off and waved it at the waiter, who returned momentarily and replaced it with a full bottle. She looked at him. "I need this," he said, "go on, you were saying…" Her heart tightened as she watched him drink, she hadn't told anyone other than Dom what had happened before but on some level she wanted Nate to know, she wanted him to know everything about her and she didn't understand why.

Her masked assailant had had her face up against the wall standing behind her with a knife at her throat. At this point she knew she had not been paranoid those last weeks and she had been followed. "You should learn some fucking manners," he had growled at her, pushing the blade against her skin. "You can't just block people out of your life." He continued, "I gave you a chance and you blocked me?" he questioned.

Realising this must be Liam she said, "Please, let me go."

He laughed and said, "I know everything about you, Evie, you will learn your lesson the hard way." He pushed her harder up against the wall, "Just remember I'm watching you at all times. I'm always watching." And with that he knocked her head against the wall, as she collapsed he left.

She had been concussed and she couldn't find her phone, it had been in the back pocket of her jeans. She looked around, seeing double and her vision was blurred by the blood from the cut on her head, she couldn't see it. She had stumbled out of the ally and straight into a couple that were heading home. They had helped her by calling the police and an ambulance for her. It was at the hospital that she first met Dom. She was sitting on the edge of the bed in a room away from the wards. She had considered how lucky she had been as she guessed this room was probably used for examinations after a physical attack. She shuddered not quite knowing how she would have reacted if he had tried to rape her. She was still considering this when there was a rap on the door, and the man who came in with a uniformed officer introduced himself as Detective Dominic Anderson.

The detective was well built and in good physical condition for his age. He had a hard face with soft lines that contradicted each other. He was apologetic that this had happened and reassured Evie that everything would be done to catch this guy. She had explained that this wasn't a random attack and filled the detective in on the past few weeks. He took notes in a small notebook that he pulled from the breast pocket of his jacket. He looked like one of those old-fashioned detectives you see in old movies. He took her statement and asked if she wanted to call anyone. Evie was worried that if Liam was watching her he could find where her friends lived. She remembered her phone. "I don't suppose you found it did you?" she had asked hopefully.

"We are still checking the area but so far no, sorry. Did it have a passcode on it?"

Evie said it did and felt slightly reassured by the detective that Liam would not be able to access it.

Dom offered Evie a lift somewhere but she really just wanted to go home so he said he would take her. He drove her to her flat and helped her out the car. Taking her key, he opened the door and took her inside. He did a check of the windows and back door and was happy that they had not been interfered with; as he turned around he stood on something and from the yowling he realised he had stood on a cat's tail. "Shit, sorry," he said, as Evie scooped the beautiful black cat up in her arms.

"Barnaby baby," she had said tickling the cat's chin.

"Chances are he was just out to scare you, some sick scumbag," said Dom as he gave Evie his card and wrote his mobile number on the back. "Call me, anytime!" he said looking at her like a father leaving his daughter at university for the first time. "I mean it, in the meantime I'm going to cross reference this guy to other cases and see what I can dig up, lock up behind me," and with that he was gone.

"Shit," said Nate.

"Yeah," said Evie.

What she hadn't realised until later was that the detective had actually driven round the block and pulled up a few houses down from where she lived and waited in case the guy had decided to make an appearance. He had another unmarked car parked out back. He hadn't wanted to worry Evie but he couldn't bear to feel responsible should something happen to her on his watch.

The next few days were unproductive. Evie looked over her shoulder every five minutes, searching desperately to spot anything unusual. How was she ever going to feel safe unless he was caught? She used Uber to get anywhere now and she didn't stay out after dark. A week had gone by and the detective had dropped in to see her after calling ahead. He had found no matching cases or anything with any slight resemblance to hers. She was gutted. She was tired; she hadn't been sleeping well, understandably.

"I will stay in touch," the detective had said.

"Thanks, I appreciate it." She knew he had tech looking into her social media pages. They had tried to track her phone straight away but after no luck they had got onto the service provider to cut it off.

Evie was at her desk, head in her laptop working on a dairy exposé article. "Evie Delany?" a voice called out across the office.

She raised her hand and said, "That's me," looking up at a teenage boy.

"These are for you," he said giving her six black tulips tied together with string. "He said to tell you that you won't be so lucky next time," said the boy.

"Who said that?" she asked.

"I dunno, some guy gave me £20 to bring these up to you."

Evie already had her replacement phone out and was dialling the detective's number. "Don't move!" she said, pointing at the boy, then gesturing another guy in the office over. "Jerry, keep your eye on him, don't let him leave."

The detective had shown up within fifteen minutes, "Where is he?" he said bouldering into the building.

"I ain't saying nothing without my lawyer," the kid declared, having watched too much TV. "Pipe down you're not in trouble," Dom told him as he bagged the tulips and the £20 note, much to the boy's disappointment. He had worn a baseball cap and dark clothes, he was white, five foot eight and was just a 'normal looking guy' the boy told Dom.

Taking him off to the station for further questioning, Dom looked back at Evie and said. "Be vigilant," as he held his finger up towards her. Evie hadn't realised how stressed she was until she started crying. Not being able to stop she was ushered into a separate office. Her boss had told her to take some time off, maybe she was right but where would she go and what would she do? They were no further forward in finding out the identity of the Black Tulip, as he had been nicknamed in the office; Liam's Facebook page led to a dead end.

Nate was sitting listening to her, he felt useless. She had been through so much and he couldn't bear the thought of her being frightened.

"Anyway," she continued, "it all went quiet for a few weeks, until one day I came home to find a parcel on my doorstep." She shuddered as she recalled what happened.

She had called the detective and he told her not to touch it. It was unmarked except for her name, which had been written on the box in thick felt tip. She had gone inside and put the kettle on while she waited. Thirty minutes later, Dom and a police squad unit turned up at her door.

"It's not ticking," she joked. Dom told her to go back inside while he checked it out. Happy it wasn't an explosive devise he carefully opened the box. He wasn't ready for what he saw and he fell back mouth agape.

The uniformed officer came over, "Sir?" he said.

"Don't let her see this," Dom instructed. "Get this box back to the yard," he said stepping backwards.

Inside the flat he sat her down. She stared at him unemotionally until he had finished. She got up and called out for her cat. "Barnaby, come on good boy," she said picking up one of his mouse toys and holding it.

"Evie," Dom had said gently, "he's gone."

She pulled herself away from his outstretched arm and demanded, "NO! I need to see for myself."

Dom had no intention of letting her see her dead cat. Forensics had later shown that the cat had had his throat slit and hung upside down to bleed out. This was how pigs were slaughtered; this had been a direct dig at Evie and her liberation work. Barnaby's eyeballs were missing. Dom had not wanted to tell her the graphic detail.

She collapsed on the floor crying uncontrollably. Dom got down on the floor with her, not an easy job at his age and stiff old bones. He had hugged her until she stopped crying and there were just small audible sobs. Dom helped her up. He must have got Barnaby on his way out or back into the flat.

Evie realised at some point Nate had moved closer and his hand was covering hers. She looked up at him, his face was full of concern, and he squeezed her hand.

It had been difficult keeping the story away from the press, Dom did not want any details getting out and he hated the nickname 'the Black Tulip', he did not want the press sensationalising what was happening. This was someone's life, after all.

Evie had new locks installed at the insistence of Dom. He talked to her on a daily basis checking in on her whenever he passed. It went quiet for a couple of months. Evie could not replace her beloved Barnaby so she settled down to life by herself spending her days crusading and her evenings locked up behind her doors drinking wine and watching movies.

It had been a day pretty much the same as the last, it was raining and the Uber had brought Evie home. She was so tired. She longed for a decent night's sleep. She went up the steps to her door and put the key in the lock. She turned back and smiled and waved at the driver, who always waited for her to go in before driving off.

As she opened her door she noticed something on the floor in the hall. It was a black tulip. Everything told her to get out, to run, but she was walking slowly forward. She opened the living room door, which she never closed, and sitting on the table was a vase with six black tulips, a small ring-size box next to it with a bow on and note which simply read, 'forever mine'. Her hands were shaking as she reached for her phone and speed-dialled Dom. "Evie?" he had said when she didn't speak,

"Help," she almost whispered, "please help me," and the phone went dead.

Dom had called it in and was driving so fast he nearly spun out twice. By the time he got to the flat the uniforms were already there. "Where is she?" he had demanded as a uniform motioned to the bedroom. He bounded in; Evie was on her bed hugging her knees rocking back and forth.

"He's been all through the house, Sir," said the uniform, as Dom went to Evie's bed, sitting next to her. "Every drawer, every cupboard, he's left black tulips everywhere, that's not all, Sir," he continued widening his eyes and motioning with his head, "probably best you see for yourself." Dom left the bedroom and went into the living room. In the ring box were Barnaby's once beautiful eyes.

That was it; Dom helped her throw some things together and took her to the station. From there she was sneaked out and taken to the safe house.

She felt the sting and knew the tears were coming. Not wanting Nate to see, she got up and walked over to the veranda rail, crossing her arms across her chest she stared wistfully out at the lake. She felt him behind her, he was so close she could feel his breath on her hair. She didn't dare move, not trusting what might happen next she realised she was holding her breath.

"Evie," he said softly as he put one hand on her shoulder and the other around her waist holding her arm, she leant back on him as he wrapped his arms around her and hugged her from behind. He said softly, "you know I would never let anything bad happen to you, you're safe here with me." He hugged her and kissed the side of her head.

Now Nate knew the enormity of the situation he was worried about her safety at the hotel. "No one knows I'm here," she said turning around to look at him.

He smiled at her uncertainly. "I can get security," he said.

"It's not a problem," she looked at him, she felt a little light headed, she couldn't think of anything except kissing him. They stood face to face, her breathing was uneven, and he was searching her face with his eyes. Did he feel it too? Was he resisting or did he feel sorry for her? She was so confused.

"Evie," he said, tucking her hair behind her ear, he went to say something but was interrupted by a raucous noise coming from the hotel lobby. Taking her by the hand as if afraid to have her out of his sight he turned and headed towards the noise.

In the lobby a very drunk Daryl and Carly were having a full-blown shouting match at each other. Tina had come running in after paying the taxi outside. "Oh shit, I'm so sorry, Boss," she said towards Nate.

"What the hell is going on?" Nate said, leaving Evie standing in the doorway.

Carly shouted pointing a finger towards Daryl, "That bitch saw me chatting to the hottest guy in the bar and came over and pushed his gay little way in!" she seethed.

"Darrrrrling perlease!" Daryl responded, "he wasn't interested in your tight little ass now was he, hmm?" And with that Carly launched herself at him.

Nate jumped in and stopped the fight. "For God's sake, guys! My ten-year-old girls are better behaved than you," he said, referring to his twins.

Daryl covered his mouth with his hand, "I'm going to throw up," he said through his fingers.

"Come on," said Evie, looking at Nate while heading towards Daryl, "let's get you to bed." She put his arm round her neck and headed towards the lift.

Nate nodded towards her and said, "Let me know all's OK." Before turning to Tina with his arms folded across his chest waiting for an explanation.

It was late when Evie finally texted Nate; 'You still awake?' she had typed.

Her phone rang in reply. "Yes," he said, "is he OK?"

She laughed, "Yeah, gross but OK. He's going to have a headache in the morning."

"Serves him right!" Nate replied.

"I'm going to stay with him a bit longer before heading to bed," she said.

"OK, see you in the morning."

"See you in the morning," she echoed.

With that he rang off.

4

Thursday

He had been parked outside a florist. He looked around thinking what a shitty place this was. Why would anyone want to live in New Jersey? He took another bite of his cheap burger from the golden arches. Even the food was shockingly disgusting. He knew fast-food joints were not the best but why did a McDonald's here taste worse than in the UK? What was that about anyway? Everything here sucked. His motel was shitty, stained sheets and yellowing wallpaper from years of tobacco. Yeah, he hated it here. But he had to come. The girl was here. He had hired a car when he arrived at the airport. He used cash, no cards. He had one emergency credit card, which had the same name as his passport and driver's licence. Frank Porter. He spat the last bite of his burger out of the car window and quickly washed the remains down with a strawberry shake. Jesus Christ, he needed a shower. He wanted to go back to London.

***

The morning after the night before, Nate walked into breakfast and saw Evie, Daryl, Tina and Carly all sitting together chatting quite calmly. Thank God for that he thought. He didn't think he could handle any more drama this week. "Morning all," he said trying not to favour Evie with his eyes. "Everything sorted?" he said with his hands on his hips looking from one to another.

"Yup."

"Yes, Boss."

"Yeah, sorry."

"Good. Don't embarrass me again like that," and with that he walked off to get some food. Choosing to sit at a different table to them he joined Max and Cassie. "Still eating the healthy stuff," Cassie noted as he sat down to join them.

"I am, don't mock, I feel better than I have in days," he replied.

Sure, Cassie thought, raising an eyebrow at Max who winked and looked away. "Nothing to do with that pretty young lady over there then?" she teased motioning her head towards Evie.

"My God, man, you're actually blushing!" Max said.

"Stop it, both of you, don't be so crass." He ate his breakfast without saying another word.

***

Frank had a job to do and he wasn't going to stop until it was done. He had followed the girl as she shopped with her strange little friend. He had nothing against gay guys, he just didn't understand why some of them had to act so camp. What the fuck was that about? What has this world come to? he thought, a world where boys can be girls and girls can be boys or whatever the fuck they wanted to be! It was just fucking weird if you ask him. This political correctness bollocks had gone too far. As for that binary bullshit, just what the fuck? If you had a dick you're a guy, it was all bullshit to him. What a world, fucked up and self-destructive.

"Ah shit," he said out loud as he shook his head.

He had some good pictures on his phone he had taken of the girl yesterday. Phones as they were now meant he didn't need to carry the extra luggage of his long-lens camera, another thing of the past he thought shaking his head. Pretty little thing that she was. He'd like to get down and dirty with that, he thought, readjusting his ball bag. She was mighty fine. He would enjoy taking her down. Timing was everything. For now, he would slip back to the seedy motel he now called home and await further instructions.

***

Nate had been at a meeting with his USA head chefs. He held monthly conference meeting to make sure everyone was on the same page, operations were running smoothly, any problems identified and, of course, menus were amongst the topics of conversation. Nate was actually the only person physically in the room; the other four chefs were in little boxes on his laptop. Technology was awesome, Nate thought. He could attend meetings without leaving the comfort of his room if he wished. Of course he visited all his restaurants on a regular basis, but when filming it was never as easy. He was finishing off the call and he had asked head chef, Conray, to stay on for a quick word.

Conray had been head chef at Nate's New York Restaurant, Rivers Rush, for two years. A Michelin star chef himself, he had amazing talent. Nate had asked in his initial interview why he did not want a restaurant of his own. Conray had replied that he would end up like Nate, running a business and not doing what he loved. Nate couldn't argue with that and knew Conray was destined to become a world-class chef one day.

Nate loved helping people. Having struggled himself with no one giving him a break he knew how disheartening it could be. Don't get him wrong, if you get knocked down and stay down then you are not ready for this industry. Only the fighters survived.

Early in his career when he was head chef making some other rich person richer, he had struggled holding onto the job and a wife. He started work at 6am to be there for deliveries and he was the last to leave in the evening after checking and double-checking that all the chores were done. One thing he couldn't stand was the lack of organisation and mess. He had very high standards and, in truth, it was one of the reasons his restaurants worked so well. He had mentored and taught many a chef in the past, some had gone on to become household names, and others had not lasted. It was a difficult business.

Nate knew the world was changing whether he liked it or not. Plant-based eating was a real thing. With people like Lewis Hamilton and Arnold Schwarzenegger getting together and introducing the new concept of plant-based food fuelling the superior athlete with their documentaries like *The Game Changers*.

He had watched the Netflix documentary; it was funny, serious, and had changed a lot of people's perception on the way they ate. With Hamilton opening his own chain of meat-free burger bars, Nate knew he couldn't afford to be left behind. If he wanted to stay on top he had to move with the times. The truth was he could not bring himself to eat meat in front of Evie. It made him feel uncomfortable, he wasn't sure why. He had been accidently vegan since Evie turned up, except for that delicious steak sandwich he might have had when she was out shopping, he actually felt pretty good. Whether it was the diet or being around Evie he wasn't really sure.

He told Conray he wanted him to produce a vegan menu that would be trialled at Rivers Rush. Conray had been excited, which pleased Nate. An excited chef meant outstanding food. He couldn't wait to see what he would come up with. "And Conray, I'm coming over later today, I'm bringing my PA who eats plant-based food, so can you make us a couple of dishes to sample please?"

"Sure, Chef, no problem," said Conray.

"Thanks, Chef, see you later." And with that Nate ended the call.

***

Meanwhile back in London Dom was struggling. The forensic team had been over Evie's flat and had only found a partial print. It wasn't enough to search the database that the scumbag might not even be on. Dom was frustrated. "How? Please explain, just how do you break into someone's home, touch everything and leave no DNA anywhere?" he said across the office. His younger counterpart Eddie said, "This guy's a ghost. Nothing."

"A ghost? How?" Dom said, exasperated.

"Sir, you can look up anything on the Internet these days," said a uniformed policeman who was helping with the search.

"Jesus!" Dom exclaimed, "we must have a lead somewhere, OK, go back over the last five years, widen the search, we are looking for anything with a similar MO, stalking, tulips, knife attacks check them all out, we are missing something."

Dom didn't want to call Evie if he didn't have any positive news for her. Max had said she was getting on with everyone and Nate had taken a particular shine to her. He wasn't sure what to make of that. Rivers was married and Evie most certainly didn't need to be in the limelight. I'm getting old he thought; maybe time to retire. Not a chance. He knew as long as the Black Tulip was loose, he would never rest.

***

Evie had been going through Nate's social media to get a feel about the things that were posted. There was Twitter, Instagram and Facebook. Facebook was linked to Twitter so that was cool. Instagram was mainly pictures of food. She would have to liven this up a bit. Dull as dishwater she muttered to herself. She wondered if she was the only one who saw pictures of meat and wanted to call animal abuse helplines. She chuckled at herself, when had she become so serious? She had felt relaxed since arriving; she had found she wasn't so uptight. Coming off social media was the best thing she ever did. She hadn't realised how bad it had been for her mental health until she stopped.

Evie was torn. There was a part of her that never wanted to go back to social media or her life at ALM. She had walked around for so long hating people for their choices, only being friends with people from her world. She felt she was betraying the animals by not fighting for them every day, but she was also so much happier away from it. Her head hurt.

Evie had been a member of the Save group. They would hold vigils outside the slaughterhouses. Sometimes the owners would allow the trucks carrying the miserable animals to stop and receive a short moment of kindness, some water shared from bottles amongst the dehydrated babies. It was awful. Most the time the animals were kept dehydrated so they did not make such a mess in the kill room. The whole procedure was inhumane. Those faces she saw, the eyes she looked into pleading with her for help. How do you come back from that? How do you sleep again without it being the first and last thing you think about? What did it mean last night when her last thought was of Nate. God, she needed to get out, she couldn't think straight. She stood up grabbed her bottle of water and headed out of the door.

Nate had wrapped up the call to Conray and decided to FaceTime Sarah.

"Hi," he said, as her face appeared on the screen, "how are you?"

Sarah was in her workout gear. "I'm good," she replied, "I've just got back from a workout."

"Back?" he questioned.

"Yes back, Nate, from a workout with friends at the gym. Is that OK with you?"

He hated it when she took that tone. "I'm only asking as I had a gym installed for you last year, I just assumed you would use that." He answered defensively. Jesus when did it stop being fun. He rubbed his forehead and asked after the kids.

"Mike's been a little shit, he plays up all the time," she said with blame in her tone.

"What's he done?" Nate asked.

"What hasn't he done! I'm fed up with clearing up after him, he's old enough to look after himself!"

"Sarah, he's still a kid!" Nate said finding himself jumping to his son's defence.

"He's just like you," she retorted, "thinks he can waltz in whenever he feels like it and do whatever. I'm over it, Nate! He needs disciplining and you're never here to do it!"

He rubbed his head again. "Sarah, don't blame him for my mistakes. Look, I will talk to him, put him on."

"Well I would if he was here, off with his mates smoking weed probably," she snorted. "Don't blame him," he muttered under his breath.

"What? What did you just say?"

"I said get him to call me when he gets home. How are the girls?" With that his two beautiful mousey-haired bubbly twins came running into the room.

"Daddy! Daddy!" they said to the screen. "I came top in the class for a math's test, Daddy!" said Trudie,

"I started netball!" said Florence. He laughed; he missed the kids so much when he was away. "Well that's brilliant, my angels," he said smiling stupidly at the screen. He chatted away for a further ten minutes before Sarah shouted out it was time to say goodbye to their father.

"I love you both," he said, blowing a kiss at the screen.

"We love you too, Daddy," they both said in unison. God they were great. His kids were his biggest achievement. He hoped he wasn't missing too much precious time with them.

Feeling warm and fuzzy from seeing his kids he was grinning away to himself when he entered the office. Max looked up. "What are you so happy about? It unnerves me," Max said to him narrowing his eyes.

"Trudie got top marks and Flo has started Netball," he said. "My girls," he beamed proudly. Max smiled. If he knew nothing else about Nate other than his love for his children, it was all he needed to know.

"I worry, Max, you know, being the absent father, what I'm missing, you know?"

Max didn't know. He loved the girls, he was Trudie's godfather but not having kids himself he was clueless. "Look they seem well rounded kids, get them over here for a holiday." Max was thinking a bit of space between Evie and Nate wouldn't be a bad thing either.

"It's not practical, Max, there is school and if they are here I would be busy anyway. Forget it," he said waving his hand in the air dismissing the discussion. "Where's Evie?" he asked.

"I'm not sure, she said something about the lake."

Noticing Max's tone change slightly he said, "Why don't you and Cassie join Evie and me for dinner tonight, I'm going to take her to Rivers Rush to sample some plant-based options. It would be good to have your opinions as well." Successfully having made Max feel important again and thinking it wouldn't be bad to have a chaperone so things don't get cosy, he left to go and find Evie making a mental note to call Conray to let him know it was now a table of four.

Nate was guessing she had gone to the secret hideout. Wow, that seemed like it happened weeks ago. It was such a weird feeling but he felt as though he had known Evie forever. He was right, she was sitting on the side of the jetty dangling her feet in the lake.

"Penny for them…" he said, as she smiled and looked up at him. He felt that wave rush over him and smiled back. "Can I join you?" he asked.

"Please," she said, motioning for him to sit next to her.

"Are you OK?" he asked.

"I am," she replied not really knowing if she was or not.

"I thought I'd take you, Max and Cassie to Rivers Rush tonight to try some vegan options for the menu," he said.

"Really? That's great, I can get some pictures of the place in action for Instagram." She was pleased he had listened to her about the menu options.

He laughed, "OK, whatever you say, that's your job now." He smiled at her, nudging her arm. "Hey you sure you're OK?" he said, aware that neither of them had spoken about what was said the night before. "I'm here for you," he continued. They looked at each other and Nate thought, yup, right thing to do bringing chaperones tonight. Even if they didn't know that was their role. "Leave about 6pm," he said, as he got up and left her to her thoughts.

At Rivers Rush, Head Chef Conray was delighted Nate was coming to dine. He had mentioned to Nate in the past that they needed more vegetarian options on the menu. Not being a fan of processed food, he was not keen on all these meat replacements, preferring his food to be fresh and healthy. Conray was Jamaican and his talent for creating dishes was outstanding. Being brought up on an island where Rastas believe the human being is a natural vegetarian and meat is unnatural to the human body, and, with others also following strict vegan eating regimes, basing it on the human physiology and anatomy, they also consider dairy to be unnatural for human consumption. He didn't want to label dishes as vegan or vegetarian, as meat eaters tend to see these symbols and skip past the item on the menu without even glancing at it. He was all for the healthier option, having grown up in a world where natural living was freely taught, he knew the rest of the world needed to catch up with the tiny island of Jamaica.

He had told the restaurant manager, Louis, that the boss was heading in tonight and Louis had immediately clapped his hands together to get everyone's attention. "OK, staff meeting, everyone in the restaurant now," he had demanded.

Louis was in the middle of a separation from his wife. She had finally given him the ultimatum, her or the job. She knew it was a lifestyle more than a job, it's not like she didn't know what life was going to be like. She had hoped that after a few years working for Rivers he would have made enough money to settle down to a less demanding role. The fact of the matter was, Louis loved his job. He loved the hustle and bustle of the busy restaurant. Yes, the tips were amazing as they attracted the richer clientele, but it was brushing shoulders with celebrities that dined at the restaurant that he really loved. He was sure his wife would come round eventually.

"Right, I want this place so clean and tidy I could eat off the floor!" He demanded of his staff. He knew Rivers had exceptionally high standards and he had no intention of displeasing his boss. "Chef!" he shouted over to Conray, "All good in the kitchen I'm assuming?"

"Don't worry about us, Louis, you get your shit together and leave us to ours," Conray shouted back. The kitchen staff all laughed. They were a good team but there was always that small rivalry between front and back of house. It kept everybody on their toes.

The car was waiting for them out front. Evie and Cassie came down in the lift together; Evie was wearing a gunmetal grey halter-neck top along with white skinny calf-length trousers. Her high-heeled open-toed shoes showed off her Bright Lights nail varnish on her toes, a burnt orange colour that complemented the silvery grey of her shoes and top. Her hair was swept off her face, except for the two wavy curls that fell each side of it; it was twisted and tied up at the back showing off her neck.

Cassie had taken it all in with one look. What she would give to be that age again and have a metabolism that still worked. Cassie was envious but not in a mean way. Standing next to Evie, she felt like a frump.

Evie looked at Cassie's dress, which was black and designed for the larger woman to hide all the wrong bits. "I love your dress," Evie told her.

"Thank you, dear," Cassie said. "You're a kind liar," she smiled warmly towards Evie. Evie looked down at her toes then back up at Cassie, they both laughed as the elevator doors opened.

Max and Nate were chatting in the lobby. Nate had one hand in his trouser pocket, his jacket held over the shoulder with the other. He had almost shaved, but was aware Evie had not yet met clean-shaven Nate. What if she didn't like him? He had laughed out loud when this thought went through his head standing in front of the mirror contemplating his look earlier. He had a smart shirt on but the top two buttons were casually undone. This was the first time Evie had seen him in anything other than jeans and casual tops. He was devastatingly handsome. As the doors opened, Max and Nate had stopped talking and took in the two women as they stepped out of the lift. Nate felt a stirring of excitement and his stomach somersaulted. As they walked over, stopping in front of the men, Nate said, "Ladies, you both look beautiful, shall we?" as he gestured to escort Cassie.

Max offered his arm to Evie who said, "Why thank you, kind sir," to Max as they left the lobby and headed out to the car. She had not missed Nate's look of appreciation when he saw her.

Max sat in the front with the driver, Gus, who suffered the same misfortune as Max in the overeating department. Knowing he would take up more space then the others Max had headed straight for the front seat. Nate had opened the door for Cassie to slide in and waited for Evie to follow. She smiled at him and got in the car. He smelt the soft aroma of jasmine, as he followed her in, sitting next to her with their legs touching he had felt giddy. Hold it together, he said to himself as his mind tried to think of anything other than the beautiful woman sitting next to him.

The doorman was straight over to open the car door when they stopped out front of Nate's restaurant. It was an impressive place. The front had tinted windows so passers by could not see in. Another doorman was standing outside the entrance, underneath the canopy on a red carpet, opening the door and standing aside as his boss and three guests entered the building. Nate said, "Thank you," nodding his head.

"Enjoy your evening, Sir," the doorman said nodding back.

Inside was modern and well lit. The kitchen was visible and you could see the chefs working and cooking. It was like nothing Evie had seen before. She liked the fact you could see the kitchen. The tables were evenly spread with ample room for the diners to relax and the waiters to move around without having to continuously bump into people. The first thing that truly hit her was the smell. It smelt divine. She was cross with herself that it was probably the flesh cooking that smelt so good. She hadn't become vegan because she didn't like the taste; it had been an ethical choice. This reminded Evie how weak the human race was and she chastised herself.

A good-looking, well-dressed man came over and shook Nate's hand. "Mr Rivers, Sir, it's such a pleasure to have you dine with us tonight, please follow me, I have of course reserved the table you requested."

Nate hadn't missed the way Louis had looked hungrily at Evie, he shook his hand and said, "Thanks, Louis."

Walking through the tables almost everyone was saying hello to Nate. He stopped and shook a few people's hands thanking them and telling them to enjoy their meal. A US senator waved Nate over to his table.

"Rivers," he said standing up to shake Nate's hand.

"Evening, Senator, Mrs Trials," he said nodding his head towards the senator's wife. "You look lovely as usual," causing the senator's wife to blush and giggle. Nate certainly had a way with people, Evie noted; she hadn't missed the looks on the women's faces as they walked the floor. They all wanted Nate to notice them.

Stopping at their table, Nate pulled out a chair for Cassie and then for Evie, who he sat next to her. Ushering Max to sit opposite Evie, he sat opposite Cassie. "Max are you happy for me to order the wine?" he asked respectfully.

"Sure thing, Kid, whatever, this is your shooting match." He smiled affectionately at Nate. Nate ordered a bottle of red and a bottle of white. Evie knew she didn't have to worry; both would be suitable for her.

He was at his usual table, which was set back from the crowd and had a good view of the restaurant while keeping some privacy. He had sat the ladies with their backs to the other diners. On the way, in the car, he had suddenly worried about the consequences of Evie being in such a high-profile place. Caught up in the madness he hadn't even considered it. He called Louis over and said quietly to him, "No pictures tonight if you're asked." Louis nodded wondering who the beautiful woman sitting opposite Max was, and wondering if Mrs Rivers would approve.

Nate didn't like to go into the kitchen during service, he knew it was a crucial time and he didn't need the chefs worrying that their boss was looking over their shoulder. Conray had seen them arrive. He waited for them to get comfortable and he went out onto the floor to greet his diners.

Hands behind his back he nodded and said hello to everyone. "I have made you some of the most wonderful dishes tonight, I sincerely hope you enjoy," and with that, he left.

Wine was poured and the conversation was flowing. Max was keeping Cassie and Evie amused with tales of Nate in his early years. Nate was trying not to stare at Evie, he was smiling at her, enjoying seeing her laugh even if it was mostly at his expense. Max had explained the situation to Cassie and had given her strict instructions not to ask questions. Max was still surprised that a woman with Cassie's good looks would be interested in a fat old fool like him. He knew it wasn't money, Cassie had buckets of the stuff after divorcing her director husband. Husband number three he thought he remembered her saying. He found it hard to believe that she actually found him attractive. He had tried to lose weight but it had been so boring. Cassie looked across the table at him, noticing the way he looked at her she knew he was self-doubting himself. She reached across the table and surprised everyone by taking Max's hand and squeezing it before letting go and leaning back as if nothing had happened. Evie and Nate looked at each other and smiled before Evie lowered her eyes. Old people were cute sometimes she thought.

Louis approached the table followed by two waiters. "We have here hemp and pumpkin salad, chipotle and capsicum hummus with crudités, spicy mango and grilled avocado salad and jackfruit nachos, please enjoy."

The dishes had been placed in the middle of the table for everyone to try.

"Wow!" proclaimed Evie taking her phone out to take pictures for Instagram, "Those look so good!" Not standing on ceremony she dug in causing Nate to laugh.

"What's a jackfruit?" said Max. "I mean salad and fruit, I'm not dieting!" he said looking pained.

"Try it, Maxy," Cassie said as she took a mouthful of the pumpkin salad. "This is divine," she continued, still chewing but covering her mouth with her hand.

"Oh my God," said Evie, rolling her eyes after tasting the hummus.

"This jackfruit taste like meat," Max said, confused. "It has the same texture. How is that even possible?"

Nate was delighted. Conray had not let him down. Having tried each of the dishes himself Nate excused himself and broke his own rule heading back of house into the kitchen. He went in and said, "Chef!"

Conray looked over surprised to see Nate in the kitchen, he hurried over. "Everything OK?" he said, worried.

"On point, Conray, delicious, I mean seriously, just amazing," he said, as he turned and left as quickly as he had arrived. Conray stood starting at the door.

"So you're plant-based, Evie, is that correct?" Cassie asked ignoring Max's request to not ask any questions.

Evie wanted to say she was a vegan, plant-based was a diet, and veganism was a lifestyle. She looked at Nate who was looking at her worriedly. She didn't want to embarrass him, she smiled and replied, "Yes that's right, I don't believe eating meat is healthy," she couldn't help but add. Who was she? Had she really just put a man before her beliefs? There was time to beat herself up later; right now, she was looking forward to the mains.

She hadn't even noticed the bottles of wine being replaced, all she knew was her glass was never empty. She could get used to this she thought, fast-food joints and fake meat seemed like someone else's life a decade ago, not her own life less than three weeks ago. It had been a while since she had done anything back home except work and return home. She thought of Dom and wondered if she should call him, she had not yet spoken to him except a quick text to say she had arrived and was fine. Noticing Evie drift off somewhere else, Nate interrupted her thought by asking her if his restaurant was anything like she had imagined.

"It's quite stunning, Nate, I saw pictures on the website but the atmosphere is something else," she said sincerely. Nate was pleased.

Louis marched back over, sweeping his gaze over the table before nodding to the waiters to approach. Starters were cleared, cutlery replenished and water poured to cleanse the pallet. Shortly after, the mains arrived. There was a selection of dishes including, roast sweet potato tagine, biryani with coriander chutney, roast beetroot mash, double cooked rosemary chips, and aubergine katsu, there was also a Greek mezze of kofta, tabbouleh and baba ghanoush. It was outstanding.

"And there is no meat in any of this?" Max asked for the third time.

"Max, just eat the food," said Nate.

They ate, Nate was yet again impressed. Conray had done him proud. Even Max had to admit he loved the food, "But I wouldn't have ordered it had I had the option of a good old rib eye steak." He stated, matter-of-factly.

Evie's favourite course was next, desert. She was a sucker for anything chocolate or lemon. She looked at Nate, a sparkle in her eye, she was glad he wasn't sitting opposite her otherwise she knew the temptation to touch him under the table would be too much after this much wine. How many had she had now? She had lost count. When desert came, she was not disappointed. They each had their own plate this time with bite size samples. Each plate had baked strawberry cheesecake, a mini banoffee meringue, a chai spiced cookie, a peanut butter crackle slice and a good old chocolate brownie. A mouthful of each but enough with all the various flavours. Conray had most definitely earned the right to be where he was.

The restaurant had thinned out. They had coffee and whisky and chatted about the upcoming show before deciding to call it a night. In the car on the way back to the hotel Evie nudged Nate and, smiling, she motioned her head towards Cassie. Nate leant forward and saw Cassie's head back, fast asleep. He chuckled. He rested his elbow on the door, looking out the window his chin in his hand. With his other hand he searched for Evie's, found it and held it. She couldn't breathe properly, she was sure he would notice. He moved his thumb backwards and forwards affectionately over her skin. She had no idea that he was feeling the same nervous electricity. They didn't look at each other.

Pulling up at the hotel, Nate jumped out of the car and stood aside for Evie to follow. He had moved round and opened the other side for Cassie before Max had even made it out his seat belt. "Oh, was I snoring?" Cassie said, realising she had just woken up.

"Too much wine for you, my lady," Nate joked, offering his hand to help pull her up from the car. Everyone had eaten and drunk so much that a nightcap would have been a stupid thing to suggest, but Nate desperately didn't want to say goodnight to Evie. He knew he had drunk a lot, he knew he would regret it if he embarrassed himself in front of her. Sober-Nate would go to bed. Drunk-Nate knew he had to do the same. They all rode the lift together. Stopping at the second floor, Evie took Cassie by the arm as she tried to locate her key from her purse. With Nate standing in front of the doors to stop them closing, Evie helped Cassie out as she brushed past him. She turned back and said, "Thank you, Nate," smiling warmly. God, he wanted to touch her so badly.

"Yes, thank you for a very pleasant evening," Cassie said waving at Max. "Night, Maxy," she crooned.

Max waved back saying, "Night, my lovely."

"Night," Evie said looking at Nate.

"Night, Evie," he said, stepping back to let the doors close. He felt deflated.

5

Friday

Evie hadn't seen Nate all morning. She was at her desk looking through the applicants that had made the shortlist for Nate's show. She scrolled down the page of the laptop wondering how he was going to choose which ten to take part. They were all between the ages of eighteen to twenty-eight and all had suitably sad backgrounds and could do with the kind of break Nate was offering. She was so confused right now. There was a part of her that wanted to stay in New Jersey and be a part of Nate's team. Why couldn't it be a vegan programme so she could really get behind it and enjoy being part of it? She couldn't stop thinking about Nate. She felt guilty on so many levels, he was married, he had kids, he supported the exploitation of animals, but he was also kind, sensitive and so damn handsome. He just had this way about him and he wanted to do good and help others better themselves and the electric pull between them was torture.

Evie felt as though she had known Nate for so much longer than the reality. Tomorrow was Harper's party and also marked almost her first week here in the States. What was it about him? She had never felt like this before about anyone and it unnerved her not being in control of her own feelings. Damn hormones, she thought.

Nate had woken up early as usual, he wished his body clock would take a day off and let him sleep past 7am, just once. He had skipped breakfast, instead dragging Max into town for a diner-style fry-up.

Max laughed when he had realised Nate's intention. "Oh, my boy," he chuckled, "these are quite some lengths to go to not to be seen enjoying a cooked breakfast." He was watching Nate soak up the last of his egg yolk with his bread. "You want to talk about it?" he said trying to adopt a more serious approach.

"Max, I just don't know what to do," Nate said. "I can't eat normally in front of her."

"To impress her?" Max asked.

"No, it's not that, I just don't understand why it bothers me," he said with genuine confusion.

"Are you questioning your own morals maybe?" Max suggested.

"No, I don't think so, I mean don't get me wrong I am dead against factory farming, which is why I have the suppliers I do. I know all the animals are outdoor reared and treated well, I don't feel guilty," he said feeling guilty.

"Well maybe it is about the girl after all. Nate, I've known you a long time, you need to be careful, you're a married man with kids and Evie can't be pushed into the limelight of a scandal, so many lives depend on what happens between you two." He thought that was a good speech and hoped it came across fatherly.

"Yes, Dad," said Nate, leaving Max feeling proud of himself. "I'm not going to mess around, you know it's not my style, but I've also never experienced these feelings, either, which confuses the hell out of me." He rubbed his forehead before putting his face in both his hands. "I don't know," he said looking up at Max, "I just don't bloody know." He asked for the bill after checking Max had finished. Truth was, Max had been eyeing up the apple pie that sat behind the glass at the counter but said nothing as, after all, he could do with losing a bit of weight not putting it on. "I've just got one stop on the way back to pick up something," Nate said as he started out the door.

Nate was quiet on the drive back to the hotel. He had taken one of the hire cars that they had for the crew's general use. He had felt a lot better since cutting down the amount of meat and dairy he consumed. When he had watched the documentary *The Game Changers* he had laughed at the section where three volunteers had their erection duration and hardness throughout an evening's sleep monitored after eating meat and then another day after eating plant-based food. It had been so funny; the guys in the documentary had been like giggling schoolboys waiting for their test results from teacher. It had been unanimous that all three performed better in both departments after eating plant-based food This had intrigued Nate greatly and he wondered what validity it actually held.

Nate's sex life wasn't great. He was away from home so much he was used to taking care of himself as and when the need arose. He and Sarah were very infrequent, but that was marriage, right? Sarah was an attractive woman, she would always turn heads with her mane of brunette hair and winning smile. She cost him a fortune in anti-ageing beauty treatments, manicures, pedicures, facials, God, how much did one woman need? He had created a lifestyle for her to enjoy while he was out busting his balls making the money. Maybe it was time the tables turned, he thought. Ha! She wouldn't last five minutes in the real world and he would go mad stuck at home with the kids and coffee mornings.

Evie was real, down to earth, well her earth at least, where all animals were sacred, he thought. She had a quality to her that he couldn't quite put his finger on. She was sincere and he admired her passion for fighting the cause she believed in. Would they ever work as a couple? It's not even a question worth pondering, he thought. She was an animal liberator and he was a world-class chef. Their worlds should never have met. They should not have been put in this situation. Yet they had and they were.

Max excused himself when they got back to the hotel. Having overloaded on breakfast at the diner, he needed to go to his 'private office' in his room to 'think for a while'.

Chuckling at Max as he walked into the actual office, he saw Evie sitting at her desk staring at the screen. She was so engrossed with what she was looking at she jumped when he spoke to her. He laughed and said, "Sorry, what you looking at?"

Evie had her hand on her heart and looked at him, "Jesus Nate!" she exclaimed, "are you trying to kill me?" He looked at her and, having realised what she had just said she quickly came out with, "I was checking out the applicants, it's going to be a difficult choice for you." Nate knew he would struggle with this job, he hated to think of not giving someone who really needed help the chance, but he was doing what he could.

"Maybe we could go through them together?" he suggested. "I wouldn't mind some help." Evie was excited at this prospect, that she might actually be responsible for causing someone's life to change. He saw this reaction and his heart swelled. "Great," he said, as his phone started to ring.

"Mike," he said, as he answered. "What happened to calling me yesterday when you came home?" he questioned his son. "What do you mean you only came home now? Where have you been?"

"Dad, chill out. I was at Dan's house, you can call his mum if you want," he said, knowing his dad would never do such a thing and knowing his mum had already called to check her son wasn't lying. "I needed a break from the girls," he said, making Nate laugh, as Nate knew he was referring to his mother and sisters.

"OK, OK, fine, so what's with the weed?" Nate continued.

"OMG she didn't tell you that!" Mike said. "Mum's so hung up about drugs she's ruining my life, Dad you have to talk to her!"

Nate listened to his son for a few minutes before saying to him, "Son, listen to me, I was your age once, I know what goes on in a sixteen-year-old's mind and I trust you to take care and be safe. I need to know you're setting a good example for your sisters but most of all I need you to stop aggravating your mum so she stops chewing my balls off about your behaviour." He was firm but friendly, Evie liked that. "Yes, I'm fine, I know, I love you too, OK, bye for now, bye," and he rung off. He looked skyward before looking at Evie and said, "Kids!" They both laughed.

By the time Max put in an appearance they were talking through the applicants. So far they had agreed on all of them. Max sat down and said, "Come on then, what've we got?" They spent the rest of the morning discussing who should make the second interviews.

Nate decided to skip lunch, as he still felt bloated from this morning's overindulgence, leaving Max and Evie to head off to the restaurant together. Evie had been really helpful with the applicant choices. Between the three of them they had chosen a good solid selection of young men and women for the second interviews.

Evie had jumped out of her skin earlier when Nate came into the office, largely because of what she had been looking at. She had minimised the box with the applicants and had opened Google and found herself searching 'Nate Rivers'. She clicked on images and saw pictures of him and Sarah. She felt her stomach turn over in waves of jealousy. She knew no great detail about Nate's marriage except that he didn't seem to spend much time with her. Sarah was stunning. Brunette, with a gorgeous figure, especially for a woman who had had three kids. They made a very attractive couple. She had been reading about Sarah when Nate had walked in and startled her. Quick to close the search down, instead maximising the applicant page, she had made a mental note to delete the search later. She was gutted. She had built up a picture of an unattractive wife at home with the kids. She had not expected Sarah to be gorgeous. And why not? She had asked herself. Jealousy was not an attractive feature, she wasn't going to do any more Googling, and it didn't make for a pleasurable outcome. She had felt guilty and was a little ashamed of herself. She had welcomed the work distraction.

"Where's Max?" she said entering the office. Nate was standing by the window looking out across the lake, he turned and smiled at Evie, they looked at each other and Nate signalled to her desk with his head. Evie walked over and looked. Sitting on her desk were two bars of Nomo vegan chocolate. One was creamy chocolate and one was caramel and sea salt.

She looked at them, eyes wide, mouth open in amazement. She looked at him and said, "How did you know?"

He laughed and said, "I overheard you telling Daryl about the best chocolate in the world and how much you missed it."

"Where did you find it?" she asked, still taken aback.

"Aha," he said, tapping his nose with his finger, delighted by her reaction. He had picked it up earlier from a confectionary store on his way back from breakfast after spending the early hours of the morning finding out where it was sold. Evie went over to him and flung her arms around his neck, he put his arms around her completing the hug. "If I'd known this was the reaction I would get, I'd have bought more," he joked.

She had never been this close to him, holding him, smelling him. One hand went to the back of his head as she said in his ear, "Thank you." She slid her other hand down his face touching his cheek. He held her hand to his face as he leant his face into her hand, he was mesmerised. He felt as though he was drowning in her eyes and he couldn't surface to breathe. Evie felt the pull, it was like an electric magnet was holding them together. As her other hand came down to his chest he took hold of that as well and held it.

"Evie," he barely managed to make any sound.

As she looked at him, searching his face, she wanted to kiss him so badly; they were so close he could feel her breath. He let go of her hand and touched her face, he knew his body was going to let him down and he pulled away, looking at her as she stepped back.

"I'm sorry," she managed, "I didn't mean, I mean I did but..."

Nate looked at her and interrupted, "Evie, it's OK, it's my fault, I just wanted to... I can't explain it's just..."

And with that, Max came in the office, seeing them both standing together he said, "Is everything all right?" Worried there might have been a development he should know about. "Of course!" Nate said, returning to his desk trying not to look at Evie in fear his expression would give him away to Max.

"I need to check something," Evie said, and left quickly.

"What was that about?" said Max.

"Nothing, Max, Evie is just missing home that's all," he said and returned to his screen.

Evie had gone up to her room, lying on her bed she had cried with frustration. What was happening to her? She had gone and embarrassed herself to Nate. She knew he could feel it too and she knew it had been unfair of her to touch him the way she had but it hadn't been premeditated it had just happened. How was she going to face him again? she thought. She picked up her phone and called Dom.

"Evie?" he answered with a worried tone. "Are you OK?" He waited a beat then said, "Evie?"

"I'm here," she said, sniffing, "sorry, Dom, I just miss home, I don't belong here with these people."

"It won't be forever Evie, you need to hang on in there, we've had a small breakthrough, nothing concrete which is why I haven't been in touch," he paused, she waited. "There's been another report from a woman filed that we found from over two years ago. It happened in Wales and wasn't on our database, we only found it by accident, I've had the uniforms call round the police stations in our vicinity and a policeman that used to be based in the Welsh department remembered a similar case, so we are getting the paperwork sent over, if it's the same guy and he used to be based in Wales, it could give us a clue how to find him now." That was a lot of information for Evie to take in at once. "Oh right," she said, which surprised Dom, he thought she would have been much more excited.

"Evie, I don't know what's happened, what can I do to help you?" he said.

"I'm sorry, Dom." She quickly pulled herself together knowing that her self-pity was selfish as she knew Dom was working round the clock to help her. "I just got homesick, I'm fine, really, thank you, you know I appreciate everything." She hoped she sounded sincere because she meant it. Dom told her not to worry she would be home before she knew it and with that he was gone.

She went into the bathroom and washed her face, she sat back on her bed knowing she needed to go back downstairs when her phone went off. It was a text message from Nate: 'Hey, beautiful, you had nothing to apologies for earlier,

can we grab a drink later? N. x'

She was smiling, it hadn't been just her after all, and she knew Nate liked her, she knew how she felt but did he feel the same? She decided to get up and get on. Let's see what happens, she thought, as she texted him back saying that she would love to and she was fine.

She headed back downstairs to the office where Nate and Max were sitting talking about religion. "All I'm saying, Max, is that religion is one of the biggest reasons for war. You can't deny it."

"Uh-oh," said Evie, "what have I just walked in on?"

"Money or religion? Which is the bigger evil?" Max asked her.

"Ha," she said. "Difficult one, I'm going to say money," she declared. "Yeah, definitely money."

"Reason?" said Nate.

"Well 200 million animals are slaughtered a day for food around the world. Food is a money machine," she shrugged. "That's against an average of 150,000 people who die every day around the world, 100,000 of those are old-age related so I guess some of the other 50,000 are because of war which is usually down to religion, and health issues."

Max looked at Nate, Nate was frowning at Evie, "I mean, I'm going to say you know these figures and they are factual?" he asked.

"Yup, Google it," she said.

"Oh my," said Max. "Those are pretty grim numbers, really that many animals?" he questioned.

"Oh yes, and that's just land animals. Let's not forget the wild and farmed fish either, that brings it to more like 3 billion animals killed each day. That is roughly 72 billion land animals a year and 1.2 trillion aquatic animals killed every year." Facts and figures on the murder of innocent animals was something she was far too aware of.

"That's unbelievable, I had no idea so many, I mean I have never actually given it a thought before," said Nate.

"Remind me not to invite a vegan into the conversation," Max said.

Evie smiled at Max then looked at Nate who was staring at her. "I'm shocked at those numbers," he told her.

"Welcome to my shitty world," she said dryly, sitting down.

At 4pm Nate said he had had enough for one day and was heading over to Rivers Rush as they had requested a managers meeting with him. He was pleased for the excuse to get away from the office for a bit. He had been truly shocked at what Evie had said about the number of animals that were killed daily. She saw him as contributing towards this, which he knew inadvertently he was. "Shit," he said out loud to himself. He was in the car heading to his restaurant and he thought about earlier when Evie had hugged him, he didn't want her to think he didn't care but he seemed to have lost any self-control around her and he didn't really understand how it was possible for his own body to betray him.

He had pulled away because he was embarrassed she would notice but if he hadn't then what would have happened? Would he have kissed her? The truth was, he didn't know. Yes, a distraction at the restaurant was much needed.

***

It had gone 8pm and Nate had texted saying he was needed at the restaurant and wasn't sure what time he would be back. Evie was in the bar with Daryl and a few others having a drink and a laugh. She was tired, it had been a long day so when Nate texted her again and said he would be back around 11pm, she messaged back saying she was headed to bed and catch up in the morning. She wasn't sure if he was avoiding her and didn't want to come across as needy by saying she would wait up for him. Nate was disappointed. He had hoped she would wait up but realising maybe it was better this way instead of calling her when he got back to the hotel, he went straight to bed.

6

Saturday

Dom had been working relentlessly. Once the file arrived from Wales he sat down to go through it with a pot of coffee. It was similar, the photo of the woman showed she was of similar build and looks as Evie. This creep obviously has a type. It had started with someone following her, escalating to text messages. The victim had had no idea how he got hold of her phone number so all the male contacts in her phone had been checked out and crossed off as suspects. Next came the black tulips at work, same MO, cash with instructions left at the local florist. But as fast as it had all started, he had disappeared. She had not seen anyone and he had not been identified. Case closed. Bloody typical, thought Dom, no follow up with the victim or searches for similar cases by the lead detective. Damn! He thought, at least he had the address and contact number for the woman so he decided the best thing would be to go and see her for himself.

***

Saturday at last. Evie was glad that she had the distraction of Harper's party that evening. She called for the lift wondering if Nate would like her dress. The doors opened and he was inside, he smiled, "Morning, beautiful," he said as she stepped in, the doors closing behind her.

"Morning," she said, already lost in his eyes.

He took a step towards her, put his hands on his hips and said, "I'm sorry about last night, I missed not seeing you."

She held his gaze, it was intense. She wanted to reach out to him, he was so close she could smell him and it was making her feel giddy he smelt so good. They were still standing together looking at each other as the doors opened at the lobby.

"After you," he said, gesturing for her to go first. "Join me for breakfast?" he asked.

"Sure," she smiled, as they both walked over to the vegetarian and vegan section. It hadn't gone unnoticed by her that he always respected her eating preferences when they were together. This unfortunately made her want him more.

Over breakfast he asked her if she was ready for the party tonight.

"I'm curious," she said. "I've not been to many parties let alone one filled with people I know from the TV."

He laughed and said to her, "Believe me they are just people with oversized egos and oversized mansions and some have very little substance other than that."

She looked at him and he looked at her and said, "I'm looking forward to spending the evening with you."

She looked away and looked back to him, "I can't wait," she said quietly. Nothing else needed to be said.

Daryl had said he was going to help her get ready and Tina, not wanting to miss out, wanted to help as well even though Evie had insisted she was doing her own make-up but she didn't mind help with her hair. Nate had laughed when she told him how excited they were getting. "I think they wish they could come too," she said,

"Maybe a bit of jealousy going on," Nate had half-joked. He usually went to these parties alone but no one seemed at all bothered by the fact Evie was going with him this time.

"Do they think something is going on between us?" he asked,

"Nah, well they have never said anything to me if they do." She was lying, of course they had asked her, she had made some half-baked excuse that Nate was a family friend, that seemed to have sufficed.

"Shit," Nate said. "I need to pick up my suit from the dry cleaners." He was not one to get other people running about after him.

"Why didn't you tell me? That's what I'm here for. Hello PA…" she said. They had gone to the office.

Nate laughed and said, "I told you I needed help, I can't even help myself by hiring you to help me." He smiled as he walked over to her and kissed her on the cheek without even thinking. "See you later, we leave at 7pm." With that, he grabbed his keys and left, seemingly totally oblivious to the fact he had just kissed her. It had, after all, seemed so natural.

Evie was nervous. Last week she was fighting for animal rights, this week she was attending the party of one of the most famous celebrities in the world. Not only that, but she was going with a world-class chef and the place would be packed with actors and TV personalities. She was meant to be keeping a low profile but she wouldn't miss this for the world. She was looking forward to being with Nate away from the hotel and the crew. It hadn't seemed odd that he kissed her on the cheek, which in itself was strange. She had no idea where the evening would take her but she couldn't wait.

Resisting the urge to drink the champagne (not typically vegan) that Daryl had brought, she was having fun with Tina and Daryl while getting ready. "You must take pictures of who's there," Daryl said.

"I can't," said Evie. "It's a private affair remember? We are trying to find backers to sponsor the show, not take selfies with film stars. I mean I'm gutted, don't get me wrong, I can't imagine not getting a selfie with Brad Pitt if he is there." This caused them all to giggle like teenagers preparing to have a sneaky drink.

"Just have fun, girl, and bring us back gossip!" said Tina. "Nate has never given anything up," she continued, admiring her boss's resilience to her constant asking.

Evie was wearing a strapless bra and matching thong set. "OK, let's get you in that dress," Daryl said taking it off the hanger.

"Oh my, oh my," Tina giggled. "You're gonna give the boss a heart attack wearing that!"

Daryl looked at her with disdain. "No, darling," he purred towards Tina, "all she will give him is a hard-on, this dress is every wife's nightmare!" he proclaimed, holding it up against himself looking in the mirror.

Evie laughed at them both. "You guys it's just a dress, I'm going to be brushing shoulders with the rich and famous, I need to look the part," she said, taking the dress from Daryl and stepping into it carefully.

"Oh, you look amazing," Tina said with a slightly jealous tone in her voice.

"Doesn't she?" said Daryl, all pleased with himself as he had successfully managed to persuade Evie to be brave and go red instead of black, that was so last year. It was a stunning dress, it was a sweetheart off the shoulder mini dress; it clung to her body showing off every curve. The deep sweetheart neckline plunged low showing off her cleavage and neckline. It accentuated her whole body, showing off her perfect figure, leaving just enough to the imagination. Standing up, it stopped above the knees but when she sat it showed off her thighs. She wore high-heeled strappy shoes; her toenails varnished the same deep red as her dress. She had a French polish on her fingers and she wore no jewellery. Her hair cascaded down her back, swept back at the sides showing off her sensual neck. She looked amazing. She looked at herself in the mirror and all she could think was that she hoped Nate liked it.

Nate had picked up his suit and headed back to the hotel to make a few calls. Had he really walked over and kissed her? Man, he thought rubbing his chin. He had kissed her cheek before he even realised what he had done. Trying to not make it a thing, he had just walked out and not looked back. Inside he was cringing. He couldn't wait to take Evie out tonight and he was looking forward to having a partner with him to show off. It should have been Sarah, he thought wistfully but even so he had never felt like this about her as he did Evie. Was he having an early midlife crisis? Could all this just be written off as that? He didn't think so, he knew he had to either put an end to it now or he would pass the point of no return and it would be too late. He sighed, his relationship with Sarah was stagnant, and his relationship with Evie was electric. One way or another he knew he would have to make a life-changing decision at some point and that terrified him.

He looked at himself in the mirror in his room. He wore silvery grey trousers; he couldn't abide the fashion of trousers ending at your calf, no socks, just shoes. He was thirty-eight not eight, preferring a more traditional look of trousers that covered your socks. He had a stylish white shirt that had no top buttons showing off a teasing of his chest. He had a firm body and was in good condition. Did he look OK? he wondered, as he picked up his jacket and flung it over his shoulder. It would have to do. He wasn't out to impress anyone after all. Was he?

It was a quarter to seven, He chugged down the glass of whisky that he had poured himself and headed for the door. On the way down in the lift he decided he would wait outside with the car for Evie. Seeing Gus out front he went out and joined him. He texted Evie to let her know where he was and she had texted back saying she was on her way.

He was chatting to Gus when he realised that Gus was not listening, his eyes were on the hotel door. Nate turned and saw Evie standing there and his mouth fell open. He looked at her and was speechless. Gus nudged him and said quietly out of the side of his mouth, "lift your jaw off the floor brother." Nate quickly closed his mouth. He was at her side before he knew it and offered his arm, eyes wide, he knew he was staring at her. He walked her the few steps to the car trying not to look at the flesh of her olive breasts where the dress line ended. Gus was waiting, holding the door open. She said, thank you, to Nate and Gus as she got in the car. As Gus shut the door and Nate headed around the car to get in the other side, Gus looked at him with wide eyes, he didn't need to say anything, Nate heard it in his head, "you're in trouble brother," Gus had told him with his look.

Sitting in the car, Nate looked at Evie and said, "You look absolutely amazing, Evie."

She had seen the way he'd looked at her and knew he meant it.

"You're looking extremely handsome," she returned. As soon as she had seen him she knew she was going to have to watch how much she drank. Gus couldn't help keep looking in the mirror and taking in his boss's obvious discomfort with the beautiful woman beside him.

"Is there anything I need to know?" she said, noticing Nate looking at her thigh.

Looking at her, smiling, he said, "Harper is a bit full on, but he's going to love you." He smiled at her. He couldn't wait to show her off.

They arrived at a tall building in the middle of New York. Nate had jumped out and run round to get Evie's door, offering her a hand to get out. "Thanks, Gus," he said, putting his jacket on and doing up a button. The doorman opened the doors of the luxurious complex and, once inside, Nate took Evie's hand and they walked towards a lift in the corner of the lobby.

"Evening, Mr Rivers, ma'am," the porter said, calling the lift.

"This goes straight up to the penthouse," Nate told Evie. "I mean, I say penthouse it's the whole top floor of the building. There is a courtyard in the middle with a pool and bar, it's quite mad." Evie was wide eyed listening to him. He noticed and said, "It will be OK," squeezing her hand. Another couple had turned up and they exchanged hellos before the four of them stepped into the lift. Evie stood in front of Nate and she could feel his breath on her shoulder, he moved slightly closer and he closed his eyes as he took in the beautiful aroma she wore. He touched her shoulder with his finger tracing an imaginary line down her arm. The doors opened. They had arrived.

The room was vast, open-plan living at its finest. There were people everywhere. Waiters were walking around with canapés and drinks; there was a fully operational bar in the corner of the room. A few people turned to see who came out of the lift but mostly people were engrossed in conversation. Evie took it all in trying not to look out of place. She saw faces she recognised and tried not to look in awe. A waiter headed towards them offering them a glass of champagne. "No thanks," Nate said taking Evie's hand and heading to the bar. He knew he was safe here, this was the place that you could bring your mistresses or toy boy; all secrets were safe in here. At the bar Nate nodded at the barman and said, "Special request please." Immediately understanding the barman reached behind him and turned back with what look liked an extremely expensive bottle of red wine.

Evie didn't catch what Nate said, but the barman nodded and said, "Yes Sir, vegan."

Evie realised Nate must have prearranged the wine for her, she took the glass Nate offered to her and said, "Thanks Nate, you think of everything."

"Nate!" Harper's voice echoed through the room as his old friend wound his way through his guests. He hugged Nate with one arm holding his drink with the other.

"Dean, my old mate, good to see you," he said. "Can I introduce you to Evie?"

She smiled and said, "Hello, Mr Harper, it's a pleasure to meet you."

He looked her up and down and replied, "Darling, you look divine, I can see why our mutual friend is having troubles," he purred looking at Nate. "She's so polite and what a cute little accent, Nate, mingle, catch up later." With that he blew Nate a kiss and disappeared back the way he came.

Nate looked at her and, shaking his head, said, "Told you, full on."

They walked the floor stopping to talk to people who knew Nate or wanted to know him. Evie had men and women staring at her, she hoped she didn't look like a hooker.

Nate looked at her, "You look gorgeous, Evie, the women are jealous and the men want to sleep with you," he told her when she voiced her concern. "Not just the men either," Nate laughed as he saw a well-known lesbian TV host eyeing her up and down.

Evie looked about and saw someone who got her attention. "Nate is that Lloyd Baxter?" she questioned, noticing the award-winning action-hero actor surrounded by people.

He looked over and said, "Yeah, I guess it is." He knew Baxter was a ladies' man, devastatingly handsome, he worked out every day to keep his body muscular and firm.

"Can you introduce me?" she asked.

Nate felt a stab of jealousy cut through him. Had she really just asked to be introduced to the womanising handsome actor? He was gutted. "Sure, why not?" he sighed, taking her hand and moving through the crowd. "Lloyd," he said pushing his way through.

"Rivers," Lloyd said, stepping forward to shake his hand. Taking Evie in with full appreciation, holding out his hand he asked her, "And you are?"

"Evie," she said, letting him take her hand and kiss it.

"It's a pleasure," he said, looking at Nate wondering who this foxy little chick was to him.

"So I guess you're a fan," Lloyd said smugly.

"Sure am," said Evie. "I just want to say, thank you for all you do, I respect your work so much."

Nate was taken aback; he hadn't pegged Evie as a groupie. He had his hands on his hips looking at her. She hadn't taken her eyes off Lloyd; she's smitten he thought.

"What's your favourite movie?" Lloyd asked, convinced it would be one where he spent most of his screen time scantly dressed.

"Movie?" she said, confused, before realisation dawned on her, "Oh sorry no I haven't seen any of your movies, I don't really enjoy those macho kind of things." She waved her hand in front of her face as if to say, 'Silly'.

Nate's mouth hung open for the second time that night in disbelief at what she had just said. He looked at Lloyd and Lloyd looked at him as Evie continued, "What I should have said is thank you for all you do using your platform to spread the word of the plight of the animals." Lloyd got that 'aha' look over his face, he immediately dropped the arrogant actor part and took her hand. "A fellow liberator," he said, talking low and sounding completely different.

Lloyd Baxter and his brother had been brought up vegan by their hippie parents. Witnessing the horrific murder of a family of deer while on a camping trip, a sight he would never forget, was the start of the family's complete lifestyle change. Having grown up in a world where veganism was taboo, Lloyd had always stayed true to his belief. In his private time and away from the public eye, Lloyd would split his acting time with attending animal Saves. He had always kept his animal liberating ways and friends separate from his film career in an unforgiving world where it had still been wrong to be openly gay.

How times had changed. Lloyd was well known in the vegan activism world where his privacy had always been respected.

In 2018 when vegans and animal right's activists burst into the forefront of the world news, he had decided to use his platform to spread the word of the evil of men. Being a famous, much sought after actor, he had no repercussions to care about. He started a trend that was going to change the world forever. Celebrities and sportsmen alike followed suit. By 2019, and with the likes of Extinction Rebellion, not only was veganism and plant-based eating the topic of conversation, but also it was on the verge of changing people's perceptions forever.

Looking at Evie completely differently Lloyd said, "What are you doing with him?"

"I am here you know," Nate said angrily.

Evie touched Nate's arm. "He meant a chef, what am I doing here with a chef," she clarified as Nate relaxed a little. To Lloyd she said, "I'm working from the inside out," she laughed. "Nate's brilliant," she said, looking at him, "he has been looking after me."

Reading the situation loud and clear, Lloyd said to Nate, "So do you think we could encourage you to the dark side?" he asked jokingly.

Ignoring Lloyd, Nate said to Evie, "Are you OK for a minute I'm going to see Harper?" With that he left her talking to the handsome actor animal activist. He needed a drink.

He found Harper and, seeing his face, Harper ushered him into his office down the other end of the floor. "Come on," he said, "let's open the good shit."

His office was huge with a balcony leading out overlooking the city below. On one side of the office were old books and records, a collector's fortune; on the other side, pictures framed the wall of Harper with everyone and anyone in the who's who of show business. He had a large oak desk with an expensive bar behind with some of the finest whiskies and brandies money could buy. Harper poured them both a drink, handing a glass to Nate who flumped down in the seat opposite Harper's desk.

"She's with Lloyd," Nate said when Harper asked.

"What! You left the poor girl with that womanising scoundrel?" he asked totally bemused. "Not only a scoundrel but a fucking animal activist hero in her world," he said, shaking his head. He was feeling sorry for himself. He didn't stand a chance against that sort of competition.

"Hang on a minute," Harper said, as he left the room shutting the door behind him. Nate stood up and went out onto the private balcony. He looked out over the city.

Harper spotted Evie deep in conversation with Lloyd so he pushed his way between them and said, "Sorry, darling, I need to borrow you," and whisked her away. He took her hand and guided her out of the room towards the other side of the penthouse.

"Where is Nate?" she said, still disbelieving that he had dumped her like that.

"He's in my office, darling, last door on left." With that he turned around and walked away from her.

Hmm, that was strange Evie thought but she was interested to know why Nate had left her. She opened the door and looked around the office in amazement, wow, how the other half live, she thought shutting the door as she looked for Nate. She found him on the balcony. He had his drink balanced on the rail he was leaning on.

"Hey," she said, as he jumped round immediately pleased to see her.

"Evie," he said as his stomach turned over.

"You left me," she said.

"You looked like you were doing OK," picking up his drink and taking a gulp.

"What's that supposed to mean?" she looked at him confused.

"I can't cope with it," he said putting his drink down.

"With what?" she replied feeling the magnetism and getting drawn into his eyes.

"I'm jealous, Evie, and I have no right to be, I'm a married man, I have no place to say who you can and can't see but seeing you with Lloyd, knowing you could quiet easily go home with him, I'm just jealous," he said, looking down at his feet not wanting her to see the pain in his eyes.

She walked over to him, he looked at her and she said, "You don't think I feel it too?" Their faces were so close, she brushed her cheek against his, he lifted a hand to her face as he closed his eyes, he was spinning, she pulled her face back looking at him imploringly as he leant forward, mouth slightly open, and kissed her. She felt a wave of urgency come over her as she pushed him back until he was up against the wall. He was kissing her face, her neck then back to her mouth searching for her tongue. He ran his hands down her back resting on her bum cheeks, he squeezed as he pulled her body against his still kissing her. She could feel him up against her, he was so hard, she slid her hand down his chest reaching for him as she rubbed him through his trousers.

He stopped kissing her as he rolled his head back against the wall, eyes closed and said, "Oh Evie," as she brushed her lips over his neck still rubbing his manhood, she was driving him insane.

"Evie, please, you have to stop," he said between shuddering breaths, "I can't control myself."

She looked at him as she started undoing his trousers. Before he had a chance to object she was down on her knees and she had him in her mouth. He had his hands on his head, tipped back against the wall he said, "Oh my fucking God!" He thought he was going to explode as he said, "Evie, I'm coming, I'm ahhhh…" He felt the warm rush charge through his body and leave him. She waited until it was over and he had stopped shuddering before she worked her way back up to face him. He looked wrecked. She smiled at him and he smiled back, "Evie, you just blew my fucking mind," he said.

She touched his face and said, "Silly, that wasn't your mind I blew." He looked at her, they both laughed and then he kissed her again and held her close. "There is no one else, Nate," she said, running her fingers through his hair, he stroked her face and with no warning they heard someone enter the office.

Quickly tucking himself back into his trousers he pulled her close and put a finger to his lip to say, shh.

Harper entered his office; surprised not to see Nate and Evie he helped himself to a glass of the good stuff and left again. Nate picked up his drink and offered it to Evie, "You may want this," he said smiling. She took a gulp of whisky and gave it back, coughing, as it burnt the back of her throat. "Come on," he said, let's get out of here. He took her hand and they headed back towards the party.

They walked through the main room and headed to the lift, Nate texted Gus and told him they were on their way. They stepped into the lift and Nate barely waited for the doors to close before he grabbed Evie pulling her towards him he kissed her with urgency. His hands crept down her back reaching below her dress, he felt her bare cheeks beneath his hands, he groaned into her mouth as he lifted one of her legs slightly, rubbing his hand down and up her leg, he'd never wanted anyone the way he wanted her. The lift made a ting sound and they both jumped, straightening themselves as the door opened and they stepped out.

Gus was waiting for them with the car, he opened the door and they both slid in. Gus got in the front and, looking in the mirror at his boss, he asked if they had had a pleasant evening. Evie looked out the window trying not to smile as Nate nodded and said wryly, "It was OK thanks." He reached across the seat reaching for Evie's hand to hold.

Saying goodnight to Gus they headed up the steps to the hotel lobby. It was late enough for the bar to be closed but there were still a few people sitting in the bar area. They went straight to the lift and got in. They didn't speak as Nate pressed number three, missing out Evie's floor. She was suddenly nervous, or was it excitement?

He looked at her and said, "OK?" She smiled at him in response as the lift doors opened and they got out. He looked left and right to check no one was about then took her hand and they walked quickly to his room. He opened the door and she stepped inside. It was identical to hers. He shut the door, took his jacket off and threw it over the back of the chair. He went to her; standing in front of her he searched her face as his hands found the zip of her dress. Undoing it slowly, Evie stepped out of it and stood in front of him. He was breathing heavily as he looked at her, he could see her reflection in the mirror and saw she was wearing a thong, looking back at her face she stepped forward and started to unbutton his shirt. He stopped her and turned her round so she was facing the mirror. He traced a line with his finger from her shoulder down her arm, both of them watching in the mirror. He undid her bra letting it fall to the floor, her firm breasts not moving, her nipples so hard when he touched them she felt a fire flash through her. He moved his hand down to her navel admiring every inch in the mirror. He traced a line at the top of her thong enjoying watching her struggle to stay composed. He slid his finger under the material of her thong as he touched her she groaned and he held her tight as she slightly opened her legs and he slipped his finger between the soft skin. "You are so wet," he said, as she turned back round and he picked her up and walked her to the bed.

Laying her down, he stood up ripping off his shirt and undoing his trousers, she pulled him down to her as he kissed her his hands searching her body. He made his way down her body kissing her; he brushed his lips over her erect nipple as she wiggled beneath him, moaning. He worked his way down until he reached her thong, pulling it down and off he looked at her on his bed naked, he was breathing heavily as she opened her legs and he fell to his knees kissing and licking her most sensual part of her body.

"Oh my God," she moaned. "Nate, I need you, I want you inside me now," she demanded, as he took her to the edge of orgasm with his tongue, he stopped and stood up, taking the rest of his clothes off. He straddled her as she took hold of him and guided him into the softest part of her body, looking at her, watching her until he couldn't take it any more, he held himself inside her as she shuddered, they came together. Nate had never experienced anything like this before as he held her, watching the pleasure on her face, he kissed her so tenderly and she held him tight as another wave of ecstasy tore through her, he held her close until she was done. He brushed her hair out of her face and they looked at each other. He rolled off her and said, "Come here," as he slid beneath the sheets with her and held her against his chest. They both fell into a deep contented sleep.

7

Sunday

Nate's alarm went off at 7am and woke him up. He had slept through the night. Evie was still in his arms and he kissed the top of her head.

"What time is it?" she said through a yawn.

"Early, sorry I didn't think to turn my alarm off." Lifting her head from his chest she looked up at him and they both smiled.

"Oops," she said.

"Oops indeed," he echoed, frowning at her mockingly. She touched his face and kissed him. Nothing had ever seemed more natural in the world.

Nate was pleasantly surprised he was woken up by his alarm instead of his usual wide-awake at 6am. The first thing he had thought about was Evie and he had kissed her head waking her up. She was so beautiful, last night had been amazing. The second thing he thought about was Sarah. That feeling was not so amazing and he felt an anxious knot in his stomach. Then Evie kissed him reaching for him with her hand she mounted him and rode him slowly and deeply, taking him back to the edge of heaven as he watched her face and her perfect breasts as she moved on top of him. All he could think about was how to make this feeling last forever as he released himself inside her, she came down to his face kissing him.

As they lay in each other's arms looking at each other like love struck teenagers, Evie said, "I need to go, I can't get caught sneaking back to my room still wearing last night's clothes." Nate hadn't even considered this. "I don't want you to go, though," he said, meaning it.

She stroked his face and said, "You have too much to lose," and with that she got out of bed.

He sat up and watched her get dressed. "You are so sexy," he said, feeling a stirring.

She went over to the bed and sat down, "So what do you all usually do on a Sunday?" she asked. He shrugged.

"The crew all have the weekends off unless we are filming," he said. "How about I sort us out lunch at the boat house?"

"Sounds perfect," she said picking up her underwear, "text me." She kissed him and went to the door. Opening it a tiny bit she peeked out and the coast was clear. Oh well, she thought, time to do the walk of shame, and closed the door behind her.

Back in the UK, Sarah was sitting at the breakfast bar in the kitchen of her mansion in Peaslake. Nestled in the Surrey Hill Area of Outstanding Natural Beauty, it had been their family base for the last ten years. Sarah loved it; she had redesigned and refurbished the once shabby house to bring it up to her taste of open-plan living. There was a games room, an indoor pool and jacuzzi, a 'Man Den' with a bar, an outdoor pool and out house. It was immense and impressive. Sarah had good taste and designed a house perfect for entertaining and socialising. She had wanted to live near her parents who had a house in Dorking. Nate was away so much it made sense to live close by so they were on hand to help.

Sarah loved the limelight and recognition of being Nate Rivers' wife. Nate was so introverted, he loved what he did and being successful coupled with his drive to help others achieve was commendable, but he never really liked being the centre of attention. If only she had had his skills and the roles were reversed. She resented Nate. She knew it was unfair because she had made it easy for him to work away in the earlier days. She had had the excitement of the new house; the refurbishment and then the twins had come along keeping her busy and occupied. Now, she was bored. She knew she couldn't leave the kids and she didn't want to take the kids out of school and move them around following Nate wherever he went. Their relationship had become boring. Phone calls were always centred on the kids and when he was home he irritated her. There was barely any physical contact between them except on birthdays and anniversaries, the obligatory wham bam thank you ma'am. He used to be fun in bed but it had become a chore and she had become so used to pleasuring herself she hadn't even missed sex. What had happened to them? She loved him still but they had grown apart. She had to find a way to reconnect. She wasn't ready to give up just yet. She liked being Mrs Nate Rivers and all the privileges it brought her, she would fiercely protect her marriage.

***

Dom had made the journey from London to North Wales. He hadn't minded the drive as it was nice to get out of London and head to the country. Carrie Jones lived in a small village called Beddgelert, in Snowdonia National Park. She had worked at the Bryn Llewelyn Hotel as a receptionist. It was a busy hotel all year round, as tourism in Wales never stopped. The retired community, referred to as the silver tops, would visit whenever the schools were open, always avoiding the school holidays. Dom had booked a room at the hotel deciding the force could pay his expenses, it would be a long drive there and back in one day. He had called ahead as a curtsey to the local PD and had spoken to Ms Jones who had said she was happy to chat but doubted she could be of much help. Dom had decided he would get a better idea of this creep if he could somehow trace his steps back. We will see, he thought, as he turned the radio up and started singing along with Dolly who was working nine to five.

***

Evie had got back to her room to find text message after text message from Daryl. She messaged him saying that she had just woken up and she would catch up later. She stripped out of her dress and got in the shower. As she closed her eyes letting the shampoo run off her hair she thought about last night. Just remembering that moment on the balcony when they first kissed was turning her on. She hadn't set out with the intention of sleeping with Nate had she? It seemed like a natural progression of their relationship. What the hell did that even mean anyway, he's a married man, what was she thinking? But that was the point, wasn't it? She hadn't been thinking about anything other than herself. She would apologise to Nate. She knew it couldn't happen again, he had a family. It was unfair of her to have put him in that situation. It was decided then. So why did her decision make her feel so sad?

Nate had jumped in the shower when Evie left. He got out and looked at his naked image in the mirror. He was looking good. He had been unbelievably surprised that he had sustained three decent hard-ons, well four if you count the one in the car on the way to the party. He chuckled, life in the old boy yet he thought. His phone rang. It was Sarah.

"Hey," he said, trying to sound casual, "what's up? It's early."

"Hey," she said, "nothing much just felt like hearing your voice."

This was weird, Nate thought, very out of character for Sarah. "Is everything OK, Sarah? Are the kids OK?" he asked, starting to worry a little.

"Jesus, Nate, I'm your wife! Why does there have to be something wrong for me to call you?" she said and started to cry.

"Sarah, has something happened?" he asked, this was such strange behaviour for her.

"No, Nate, I'm fine, I just miss you."

"Since when?" he said, "you've never said you miss me, why now?" He was actually pissed off. He had just spent the night with the most beautiful person and now his wife wanted to play needy. Perfect fucking timing. He was rubbing his forehead,

"When will you be home?" she asked.

"I wasn't planning on a trip home for a while, Sarah, we are right in the middle of things here. I've got second interviews to do, it's just not practical."

Sarah sighed. "OK, I will come to you," she said.

"What? No, Sarah, I don't have time for this. I will get my assistant to look at my diary tomorrow and see if I can get home for a few days, OK?"

Feeling pleased with herself that she had successfully got him to agree to come home, she replied, "That's great, Nate, I can't wait to see you. Love you, bye." She hung up.

Nate stood there with the phone still up against his ear, he couldn't remember the last time either of them had said those words to each other.

***

Frank had followed the fat black driver as he left the hotel with the girl. He followed at a distance through the busy network of roads that led to the skyscraper building they stopped at. She certainly seemed to be dressed to impress, he thought, as she got out the car. He had snapped some pictures. He Googled what the building was, it appeared to be very expensive apartments and after a chat and a couple of hundred bucks to the doorman, Frank found out who lived up top and that he was entertaining. Interesting he thought. He waited in his car until he saw the fat black driver pull out front again and open the door for his rides. They hadn't stayed long, he thought, following them back to the hotel. They both looked as if they were really into each other. He laughed. "I'm going to put a stop to your little games, young lady," he said out loud, still visualising Evie in that little red dress as he drove back to his motel.

Evie had received a text from Nate:

'Hey, beautiful, 12pm the hideaway. N. x'

She smiled feeling the excitement build up. She wondered what Nate's take on last night was. She knew she had to put a stop to it, it couldn't happen again. She put on her jeans and a baggy off the shoulder top, her hair was loose and she felt revitalised. She went off downstairs to see if she could find Daryl. She would tell him some cock and bull about something to feed his gossiping ego. She knew what had happened between Nate and her last night must never come out. Seeing some of the guys, including Daryl, in the bar she went over. She told them everything about nothing. It was nearing 12pm so she made her excuses and left.

Sneaking off the path towards the clearing by the lake she saw Nate standing looking out. Her heart turned over. She walked over to him, standing on a branch that snapped he turned around and saw her. He broke into a smile and before either of them knew what had happened they were kissing. They stood there facing each other, touching arms around each other and he said, "Hope you're hungry." Taking her hand and pulling her away towards the edge of the lake. Nate had packed a proper picnic even down to a blanket on the floor to sit on. He had sandwiches and salad, some chocolate brownies and fruit and of course a bottle of red wine and two glasses.

"This looks amazing," she said as they sat down.

He poured the wine and they chinked glasses.

"What shall we drink to?" she said, completely forgetting her pre-prepared speech on the reasons why it was a one-time thing. Who had she been trying to kid?

"Happy endings," he said, gazing in her eyes. "After all, we all deserve them don't we?"

She looked at him and took his glass from him, putting them both down she leant forward and kissed him so tenderly and he stroked her face looking at her with complete adoration. He had forgotten about the call from Sarah and the picnic he had prepared as she took her top off exposing her bare breasts. He undid her trousers and pulled them off leaving her naked and vulnerable, standing up, he stripped off his t-shirt and trousers. As his tongue found hers she took hold of him guiding him into her. Knowing they could be caught at any point didn't seem to be a thought. At that moment it was only them and nothing else mattered.

They lay naked on their backs on the blanket holding hands. "We are going to have to be careful," she said as she started laughing.

"Why?" he said rolling over on his elbow to look at her.

"Well," she said, "we are both butt naked lying by a lake for anyone to come along and find us." She scrunched her nose up at him.

He kissed her, stroking her navel. "Hmm, I've never seen another living soul down here to date but you are probably right," he said, as he stopped stroking her and made to get up. "Where do you think you're going?" she said, taking his hand and placing it between her legs.

"I see how it is," he teased, as he leant forward to kiss her breasts and his fingers found the spot that made her wriggle and moan.

They got dressed and, both famished, they ate and drank Nate's picnic with a new-found hunger.

"Mmm," he said, "licking the melting chocolate off his fingers, "you taste pretty good, I mean for a vegan." He looked at her with eyebrows raised.

She laughed. "Thinks he's funny," she said nodding. "OK, OK, you wait," she laughed. He refilled their glasses. "You know I was talking to Lloyd last night?"

"How could I forget?" he said, holding his arms up like an action hero.

"Stop it," she giggled at his fun making. "I had a really good talk to him and I think he might be interested in sponsoring the show. He thinks it's a really good idea to help the under privileged."

"Ah, Evie, my secret weapon," he joked.

"Be serious, Nate, this could really work."

"How? Why would he want to fund me with a cooking show?" he said genuinely confused. "I mean the guy is against anything meat."

"Have you considered... Nate, now please just hear me out," she said, holding her hand up to stop his protests. "Have you considered making the show plant-based, take it in a whole different direction." She sounded excited.

"Evie," he said.

"No wait, Nate, listen, you're helping underprivileged young adults, while advocating for our planet, showing people how to eat healthily and showing compassion and kindness, it will be a complete first."

He thought about it, she was chewing her cheek; this made his heart melt because he knew how passionate she was and how important this was to her but it was his reputation and career on the line. "Evie, I just don't see it marrying in place with the concept. I need to think about this I can't just turn my world upside down." She looked disappointed, he didn't like that so he said, "Look, I will think about it. I promise." He leant forward and pulled her into his arms. She sat back against him, his head on her shoulder as he kissed her cheek.

"OK," she said, "thanks." In his arms she felt safe for the first time in a long time.

***

Dom checked into the hotel Carrie had worked in. He called her and invited her over for a drink with him and an off-the-record chat. Carrie had left working at the hotel after she started receiving the black tulips, choosing instead to follow a life-long ambition to teach and was currently a teaching aid for the local junior school. She had accepted Dom's invitation more out of curiosity than anything else.

Sitting in the hotel bar Carrie immediately liked Dom. He was not like the other policemen who really seemed disinterested in the whole thing.

"Carrie, I can't tell you how lucky you were to escape the interest of this creep," Dom told her, sipping his pint of Welsh beer. Carrie was petit and very pretty. She looked twelve even though she was in her mid-twenties.

Sipping her tonic water, she asked Dom about the details of Evie's case. "I can't tell you anything, Carrie, I'm sorry but just know, and please trust me, you got off easy."

Carrie ran over the basics of the file again and told Dom nothing he had not already got from the file.

"The thing is," Carrie said, "why did he just stop? He just disappeared."

This is what had been troubling Dom, was he using Carrie as a test subject or was Evie Carrie's replacement? He just didn't know. He had asked to see all employment records for that period from the hotel and the hotel had been only too happy to help.

"I hope you find this guy," Carrie said, "before he does something crazy."

Too late, Dom thought. Too bloody late.

Having not got anything new from Carrie and after exhausting the employment files, Dom gave up and retired to bed. He wished he hadn't drunk that last pint; he would be up in the night to pee. Goddamn the old bladder, he thought, as he left the bar for his room.

***

Sarah was pleased with herself. She had successfully managed to get Nate to agree to come home. She would farm the kids out for the first night back and, with the sexy lingerie that she had just ordered, Nate would be unable to resist her. If her plan worked she would give him a night to remember sealing the deal and hopefully bringing him home where they could then concentrate on working together as a team. She wanted her name out there with his. She was hungry for adventure and she would let nothing stand in her way.

***

Evie had kissed Nate before heading back to the hotel. She had said she would meet Daryl and Tina for a drink in the bar before dinner. Nate kissed her back and said, "See you later?" Evie smiled at him.

"Of course," she said, not really wanting to leave him.

She went into the bar and joined the others who were already drinking. Later on she saw Nate arrive at the bar. He came over with a drink and said, "Hi gang, are we all OK?" The response was unanimous and he left them to it.

He was shortly joined by Max, followed by Cassie. Nate leant over and said something to Max who then came over to Evie and her drinking buddies and said, "Sorry kid, the boss wants to do a run down on last night," he shrugged as he said it.

Evie feigned exasperation, made her apologies and headed back to the bar where Nate and Cassie were chatting. "Hi Cassie," Evie said, genuinely pleased to have been pulled away to join Nate.

"Hello, luvvie," Cassie replied. "I think the boss wants a meeting," she said raising her eyebrows towards Nate. Nate smiled but both Cassie and Max did not miss the intimate look passing between Nate and Evie.

"Sorry," Nate said, "to pull you away from your friends. But I thought it was important to discuss some of the new options for the show that have come to light." Looking towards Evie she smiled with genuine excitement. "So, shall we all have dinner together and talk over food?" Nate suggested. They headed off to the restaurant choosing to be away from the crew who always ate in the bar.

Nate said to the waiter that he wanted four vegan dishes for mains much to the horror of Max. "Oh Maxy," Cassie said, "I've been doing some research and there is actually something in this health thing with plant-base eating, it would be worth trying it." She had been concerned about his recent shortness of breath.

"Don't fuss me, woman, I'm perfectly healthy," he said, trying to believe his own lie.

Nate looked at Evie and said, "Evie, tell them about your discussion with Lloyd Baxter." Stopping dead in her tracks Cassie said, "Evie, you got to speak with Lloyd Baxter? Oh my gosh how utterly dreamy." Causing Nate and Evie to laugh. Max was not impressed.

Evie explained the conversation she had had with Lloyd. "You're not seriously considering this, Nate, are you?" Max said.

"It's genius," said Cassie. She had chatted to Evie about the benefits of plant-based eating and after checking out the World Health Organisation's recommendations and indeed on heart, diabetes and stroke websites she had found that eating plant-based food was the recommended way forward for good health. It had always been there but heavily hidden behind the lie that meat was good for you. "It's the way forward, Nate," Cassie said, I know I made fun of you but looking at the research actually I am all for plant-based eating."

Evie had a way of adapting to her audience's weakness. With Cassie it had been Max and the strain on his heart from overeating all the wrong things. Evie was a hundred per cent vegan for the animals but having learned along the way about the health benefits it had left her angry. She had seen Cassie's weakness and worked it. Giving Cassie independent website information, recommending films to watch such as *What the Health*, *Earthlings*, *Dominion* and *Forks over Knives*, to name a few. Cassie was able to draw her own conclusions after doing her own research. The truth is there for all to see. Built-in perceptions from childhood were the real killer.

Nate had Googled Lloyd Baxter and his animal activism this afternoon after his rendezvous with Evie. Deciding he needed to be objective, he had checked the facts out. He was surprised at what he found. Lloyd would attend Saves, which from what he could gather was when vegans would wait outside slaughterhouses, giving the animals water before they were sent off to die. Lloyd had been on the front lines. Nate had been disturbed by the numbers Evie had previously given him on the amount of animals slaughtered daily, and had looked into that as well. He had been astounded at what he found. He found that the RSPCA and Red Tractor certified slaughterhouses meant literally nothing. Their rules and guidelines allowed horrific death to the animals and it had made him feel physically sick. He used to believe that all animals were killed humanely but after what he read about what happened he realised that the word was made up as an excuse for man to kill. He had found nothing humane about slaughterhouses. He heard Evie's voice saying to him, "If slaughterhouses are humane, then why don't we take pets there when it is their time?"

Nate was struggling. He didn't know how to feel. So much had changed for him in such a short amount of time. He didn't know what was up or what was down anymore. The only one thing he knew was the way he felt about Evie and he didn't know how to deal with that.

Max was dead against any idea of change. "No, Nate, it will finish you!" he scolded. "You can't afford to lose your fan base. You make people question their eating habits it won't help you! Evie, I'm sorry I mean no offence, you're entitled to believe whatever you want but the world is not ready for this kind of change! You will ruin Nate if you carry on down this road!" With that he excused himself and headed off.

"I'll go after him," Cassie said getting up. "For what it's worth, Nate, I think it deserves looking in to further,"

"Well that went well," Nate said.

Evie put her hand over his and said, "Whatever you decide, the fact that you have seriously considered what I said means more to me than you will ever know." She let go of his hand as the food arrived. They ate in silence, both having lost their appetite.

"Let's have a coffee on the veranda," he said to her as he asked the waiter to send it out. They drank coffee, Nate asked her if she had attended Saves.

"Yes, it's heart-breaking. Looking in someone's eye knowing you can't save them," she broke off.

He moved closer to her and said, "Will you spend the night with me? I liked waking up with you."

She looked deep into his eyes wanting him to hold her. "Yes," she said, standing up, "can we go now?"

They got into his room and he poured them both a whisky. "It's Monday tomorrow kid so I expect you to be at work bright and early," he jested. She smiled taking the whisky. He took his clothes off as she watched him and got into bed. "Join me," he said, as she put her drink down and stripped naked. She slid into bed next to him as he took her hand and placed it on his solid manhood. "What the hell have you done to me, Evie?" he said as she started moving her hand up and down. "I've lost all self-control."

She lowered her face to his and started kissing him.

8

Monday

Setting the alarm for 6am, Evie kissed Nate and crept out of his room. He hadn't wanted her to go but they both knew they had to be careful that she was not seen heading back to her own room. Was this going to become a habit? So much for a one-time thing but if no one knew then no one could get hurt, she thought to herself trying desperately to rationalise her actions.

Max had called Nate and requested a private meeting with him. "Private as in you don't want Evie present you mean?" Nate stated as he joined his friend on the veranda for coffee.

"Nate, I'm not stupid, please don't take me for a fool, I've known you a long time. When did you start sleeping with her?" he asked.

Nate rubbed his forehead, had he really thought he could hide his relationship with Evie from Max?

"Since the party, not long," he said looking across the lake rather than looking at Max.

"It's not too late to end it, Nate. She's not a permanent fixture here you know this. She isn't going to hang around here once her life in the UK is sorted. Jesus man you're thinking with the wrong head!"

Max was in despair. Was Nate really going to let his business go to hell along with his marriage and reputation for this girl? "I feel responsible," Max, continued, "I brought her to you, you should never have met. She will be the end of you, Nate." Nate looked at him but said nothing. Did Max really think these weren't thoughts going through his own head? He knew what he was risking more than anyone. The constant anxious feeling in his stomach told him that.

"The thing is, Max, forgetting Evie for a second, I have learned things about the world we live in that just don't sit right with me. I don't know how to process anymore. I'm so confused." Nate rubbed his forehead again.

"Look," Max said, "you're not stupid, what did you think happened to the animals? You must know on some level that you can't humanely kill someone who doesn't want to die."

Nate looked at him and frowned. "Someone Max?" he said completely taken aback. "Did you hear what you just said? I guess Evie is brushing off on you too."

Max had copped an earful from Cassie last night on his health again and he was getting fed up with the constant talk of changing the way he was. He was happy, it was his body. "Just because I don't partake in the conversation doesn't mean I don't listen and form my own opinions," he snapped back. "I just don't want to see you end a perfectly good career because you're trying to impress a chick."

"Evie is not a chick," he said protectively. "And she's never pushed her views on me either. You need to have a little more faith in me if you honestly think I would turn my life upside down to impress a woman. I'm disappointed in you Max." That last comment stung Max. Nate got up, "I've got work to do," he said and walked off.

Evie was in the office running through emails when the work phone ran. She answered. "Hello Rivers Productions, how can I help you?"

The voice on the other end of the line said, "With whom am I speaking?"

"You're speaking to Evie, Mr Rivers' assistant, how can I help you?" she repeated.

"This is Mrs Rivers, I wasn't aware Claudia's position had been filled," Sarah said.

Evie almost dropped the phone; she was talking to Nate's wife, why the hell would she call this phone and not Nate's mobile?

"Erm, well I'm sorry about that Mrs Rivers, Nate is not actually here at the moment can I get him to call you?" she said confused.

"No. Have you sorted out dates and flights for him to come home yet?" she demanded, "He said he would get his assistant to sort it out today."

Evie felt like someone had just kicked her in the stomach. Her head was spinning. "Again, I'm sorry Mrs Rivers but I've not seen Nate today yet, so this is the first I'm hearing of it." She wanted to cry.

Sarah sighed a very long meaningful for-God's-sake sigh. "Well let me fill you in, Evie, you did say Evie right? I need you to look at my husband's diary and find a few days when he can come home, can you do that?" she said patronisingly.

Feeling the full effect of the words 'my husband' and her tone, Evie had formed her opinion of Sarah, rightly or wrongly she was not a fan. "I will speak to Nate when I see him and do what I can. Anything else?" she said.

"No. Let me know as soon as," she said, ringing off.

Evie was furious. Who the hell had that woman thought she was talking to like that? She couldn't say anything to Nate, as she didn't want him thinking that she was petty and jealous. She put her face in her hands, why did she feel so wretched?

Nate came in shutting the door behind him. "Hey, beautiful lady," he said, stopping when he saw Evie's face. "What's happened? Are you OK?" he said, suddenly worried.

"I just had your wife on the phone," Evie said. Nate's face turned white. "She wanted to know when you were going home and the flight details."

"Oh," was all he said.

"How long do you need to be home so I can look in the diary?" she asked.

"Evie," he said, "I'm sorry, I was going to tell you now about my conversation with Sarah."

"You don't owe me any explanation about anything, Nate," she said in a very business-like tone.

Nate knew she was pissed off. He was going to tell her that he needed to go home for some reason but he just hadn't as yet. "It will just be for a few days, I need to catch up with the kids before filming starts." He went over to her and pulled her up out of her chair. He tucked her hair behind her ear and stroked her cheek. He could feel her softening as her body relaxed and she smiled at him. "That's better," he said leaning forward and kissing her. He wrapped his arms around her and she hugged him back. She couldn't stand the thought of him kissing another women but she was the other woman not Sarah. This was going to be harder than she thought.

Sarah was mad. Why had Nate not told her he hired someone else? She knew his last PA went and got herself pregnant and ran off home in shame but Nate had said he wasn't replacing her. Evie sounded young. Hmm, she thought, suddenly feeling threatened at finding herself talking to a girl rather than Max, who she had expected to be covering the phones. She made a note to ask Max about her at another time. First she wanted her husband home. She had a plan to carry out and besides she could check Nate's phone as she had already made a mental note of his passcode. It wouldn't be the first time and it wouldn't be the last she thought pleased with herself.

***

Having not found any new leads in Wales, Dom had driven back to London. He was sure he would have found an employee or a guest from the hotel culpable of the crime. All the employees were still in their same job apart from Carrie, and no guest stayed longer than two weeks and they all checked out. He was baffled. The timeline between the end of Carrie's stalking to the beginning of Evie's was less than a month so the perp must have had previous knowledge of Evie, or did he come across her by accident? They had kept a car on Evie's London home but nothing. There had been no more black tulips at work so whoever this was knew Evie was in hiding. Maybe he acted too quickly, maybe he should have kept her here and used her as bait. Jesus Dom, he thought, that would have been too risky. No, he was going to have to think of something though. Evie couldn't stay in the States hiding forever.

***

The man whose driving licence said he was Frank Porter had been entertained the night before by a $20 hooker. Having seen Evie in that dress he had gone home and masturbated to the picture on his phone. Not feeling satisfied he had told the seedy motel owner to sort him out a whore. He had fun that night. He knocked her about a bit to get himself in the mood, what he really wanted to do was put his hands around her dirty little neck and wring the life out of her. He had managed to refrain; after all it wouldn't help him to draw attention to himself when he still had a job to do.

***

Nate and Evie were both at their desks. "Evie, can you get in touch with Baxter's agent and see if you can organise a meeting for me with him please."

Evie looked up surprised. "Really? That's great, of course, I mean I have his cell number if you want to call him direct."

"Of course you have," he said shaking his head in jest trying not to show the jealousy that he actually felt at the thought of them being in contact.

She laughed. "OK, I'm going to call him and organise something for you, also you need to let me know about the dates for going home so I don't double book you," she said, trying to sound casual and OK with the whole thing.

Evie rang off from Lloyd after he had called her back in response to her voicemail. Nate had heard her end of the conversation and felt better having heard her use a professional tone with him rather than a familiar one. "Well that's great, tomorrow it is," Evie said all excited. "I must let Cassie know, she will want to meet him." Evie was thinking out loud, wondering what effect that would have on his old friend Max who had not as yet put in an appearance.

Nate was pleased. "OK, yes, that's good news, I can talk with him and think about what to do at the weekend," he said looking at his diary. "Can you book me a flight back to London Thursday evening leaving Sunday so I'm only away a few nights?"

Evie felt the excitement of the last conversation disappear. "Oh, OK sure, but that's two night flights you will only have a couple of evenings at home," she said.

"More than enough time to catch up with the kids," and deal with Sarah, he thought, although not voicing this. Evie was a little relieved. He wouldn't actually be gone for long and she knew it was important for him to see the kids. She didn't want to think about him sleeping in the same bed as Sarah.

The phone rang and Evie picked up, "Rivers Productions, Evie speaking." Nate looked at her and smiled, she smiled back listening. "OK, aha, yes, totally understand. Can I call you back in ten minutes please? I need to track him down and check his movements for the week, great bye." She rang off and looked at Nate.

"Who was it?" he said intrigued by her side of the conversation.

"That was Stanley Morgan's office," she said.

Stanley Morgan was one of the biggest chat show hosts in the States. He had a reputation with the ladies, which the long-suffering Mrs Morgan did not seem to outwardly mind. I guess when you are a billionaire you stop worrying about monogamy, Evie thought. Stanley was used to having the rich and famous on his talk show, everyone wanted to be on it. He had had actors, politicians, even presidents on his show. He always delivered the entertainment. Sitting on his couch was the only showbiz couch you needed to sit on to be someone. Evie supposed he was the equivalent to the likes of Jonathan Ross and Graham Norton in the UK.

Dean Harper had been lined up for the show that was to be filmed on Wednesday and aired on Saturday Night. Harper had pulled out last minute promising Nate as his replacement. Nate was surprised Harper hadn't been in touch since the party and chastised himself for not checking in on his old friend.

"It's good, right?" Evie said feeling he should be a bit more excited.

"Well yeah, but I'm still upside down about the show. I can't promote it until I've decided the format, it's just a bit premature," Nate said.

"It will be fine, you can mention the premise of the show, you don't have to go into detail now, focus on the underprivileged aspect." She was right, he didn't have to talk food, and the coverage would be handy, it's just that he hated these things, but needs must.

"OK, sign me up, so let me get this straight, tomorrow Lloyd, Wednesday Stanley and Thursday fly home. You better line up the second interviews next week then." God he was going to be shattered.

Max came into the office as Evie was booking Nate's tickets home. This seemed to cheer Max up as he thought maybe something he said had hit home.

"Ah," he said. "Yes, good idea, you must be missing your wife terribly." Nate glared at him but Max chose to ignore it. Nate looked at Evie who was staring at the screen chewing the inside of her cheek. He shouldn't have asked her to book the ticket, that was unfair of him he thought.

"All done," she said, "I've sent you an email with the details."

"Thanks," he said.

Evie, unaware of Nate's earlier conversation with Max, went on to fill him in on the plans for the week ahead.

"Lloyd Baxter?" He looked at Nate and shook his head. "Excuse me," Max said getting up and walking out the office.

Nate texted Sarah and gave her the details of his flight. He had said he would get a taxi home so he will see her early hours of Saturday morning. He would have preferred to have stayed and watched the Stanley Morgan show with Evie but the thought of Sarah surprising him by showing up one day was too stressful. He would go home, do his duty and come back. At least that would keep her happy and he would be able to see the kids.

Nate left the office to phone Harper. "Nate my old mate," Harper said.

Not really being in the mood to play along Nate said, "Sorry to run out of the party the other night, and thanks for the Stanley Morgan show. How come you don't want to do it?"

"I'm still recovering from the party, darling," Harper said. "Some of us have only just finished partying."

Nate chuckled at his comment. "I didn't keep it in my trousers," Nate told him.

"Neither did I, dear boy, woke up with four young men in my bed," he boasted.

Nate laughed out loud, "No lectures from you then?"

It was Harper's turn to laugh. "I am quiet ashamed of myself, who am I to tell you off for your indiscretions. Are you happy?"

"She makes me happy," Nate replied.

"Then be happy, we all deserve a little bit of fun, I am a firm believer of what they don't know can't hurt them," he said. "I liked her by the way, pretty and smart."

Nate realised he was smiling as he said, "Yeah she sure is. Thanks, Dean, speak to you later." With that he rang off. He couldn't wait to be alone with Evie.

The second interviews would take place at Harper's studio on 53rd Street. They would be filmed, and the successful applicants would have snippets from their interview on the show. The first interviews were done by a team of Nate's researchers. He sat and watched the chosen fifty candidates and knocked the selection down to twenty-five. A hard decision helped by both Max and Evie. Twenty-five interviews were going to take all week to film and Nate knew it was a long gruelling task for all involved. He texted Evie.

'Fancy going to the movies with me tonight?'

'In Public?' she replied.

'In my room, I will bring popcorn.'

She smiled at his reply feeling the stirrings of excitement. 'It's a date', she sent back.

'8pm. Nx.' He walked back into the office where Max and Evie were working. He didn't dare look at her, instead whistling to himself as he sat down and looked at his screen.

Evie had dinner with Daryl and Tina in the bar and they exchanged some laughs and talked about the upcoming interviews. Everybody loved it when filming started as they got to go to different locations and the vibe was intense. Nearing 8pm, she made her excuses and headed off to Nate's room. 'I'm on my way', she texted him.

'Door's open', he replied.

She checked no one was looking before going inside and locking the door behind her.

Nate jumped up off the bed, going over to her he scooped her off the floor spinning her round before putting her down and kissing her. Smiling she said, "Hey, handsome"' He stroked her hair and kissed her again lingering on her lips. She felt that feeling come over her and she started to feel giddy as he parted her lips and found her tongue. He groaned as she pressed herself up against him so she could feel if he was ready for her. She pulled away and started to undo his trousers. There was a sudden urgency between them as they pulled their clothes off, falling onto the bed he held her arms above her head as he entered her and they were moving as one. There was a rush of pleasure from them both as he went in deeper and deeper until she put her arms around him holding him tight as if she was frightened to let go.

They lay there until he said, "I'm squashing you aren't I?"

"A little bit," she said, as he kissed her nose and rolled off her.

"Wow," he said, lying across the bed next to her.

"Wow," she agreed before eyeing the popcorn. She rolled on her side to look at him and stroked his chest. "So, what are we watching?" she asked curiously.

"Anything you want," he grinned at her. She put his t-shirt on which fell down past her bum and grabbed the remote control. Lying the wrong way on the bed she started going through the movies.

"No chick flicks!" he shouted out from the bathroom. He had put on a casual pair of trackie bottoms he lounged around in and opened the wine. They settled on *Hidden Figures* a movie based on the true-life events about a NASA supervisor and a black mathematician who calculated flight trajectories during the space race and the prejudice she faced.

They sat up on the bed drinking their wine and eating popcorn watching the film. It was inspiring and they both enjoyed it. When it was finished they carried on drinking and chatting. She had asked if he wanted her to attend the meeting with Lloyd in the morning but he declined saying he would feel ganged up on. She laughed at him and leant forward, she kissed him. She looked so young and vulnerable in his t-shirt.

"Have I told you how sexy you are?" Nate said. She looked at him and noticed the bulge in his trousers grow.

"Take them off," she demanded and he did exactly as he was told. Taking his t-shirt off as she mounted him, sitting up face to face he had hold of her bum cheeks as she moved with him slow and deep. Nate had never experienced anything like he had with Evie ever before. He felt as though he had discovered a dormant part of himself. He liked it.

Later on, as they lay holding each other in bed Nate said, "I don't remember life before you. I feel like I finally have a purpose."

She held him tight and they both fell asleep.

9

Tuesday

Evie followed her now usual routine of leaving Nate's room early so as not to be discovered. "See you later," she said, as she kissed him and left. Nate showered and dressed wondering what the day would bring. Evie had asked him to keep an open mind when meeting with Lloyd. He was more concerned about Max, he needed to put things right between them, he didn't like this bad feeling that had grown. And then there was Sarah. He had all that to face this weekend and he was dreading it.

In the office Evie was organising the itinerary for the following day and the chat show. Max was at his desk. He looked up at Evie and said, "You are going to ruin him if you continue down this route."

She looked up at him and replied, "I'm not going to pretend to be someone I'm not. I have asked nothing other than he investigates different options he could take."

"Jesus, Evie, really? You've got him spinning out of control. For Christ's sake he's a world-class chef!"

"You can have world-class chefs cooking plant-based food you know!" she replied angrily back at him. "I would never do anything to hurt Nate!"

"Except ruin his marriage!" Max cut in. This stung Evie like a slap in the face. "I may be old but I'm not stupid!"

"Max!" Nate said, standing at the doorway. "Enough!" They both looked at him not knowing how much he had heard. "Evie," he said, more calmly "Could you please go and find Tina and let her know I will require her presence for the show tomorrow and ask Daryl to pick me something suitable to wear please." She nodded and got up from her desk. Nate moved aside from the door to let her pass and then he shut it behind her.

"What the hell, Max?" he said. "I mean I know you're trying to protect me but don't ever go at Evie like that again," he said it firmly and Max knew he meant it. "You brought her here so you have no grounds whatsoever to judge her. She is who she is, and yes, she's come from a different world to the one we know but that doesn't make her world wrong and ours right! Wake up, for Christ's sake, the world is changing and we need to change with it." Max looked at him and nodded.

"You're right, OK, so let's say you do this venture and make it plant-based, what about your other restaurants?"

"What about them? I am planning on introducing a vegan menu in all of them; we can then attract the whole market. I can't see how it's going to be a problem to have one plant-based restaurant off the back of this show. With people like Lewis Hamilton opening up plant-based joints why should we not join in? There is a target market," Nate said.

"And what about you?" Max asked.

"What about me?"

"I haven't seen you eat properly since the diner," Max retorted.

"And I haven't felt this good in years. I can think better, clearer, and I feel good Max, you should let Cassie help you try and eat more sensibly, I promise you will be so much more healthy."

"Don't you bloody start, Nate or I'm off, it's bad enough Cassie going on at me. I don't need you as well." Nate held his hands up as if to say, OK.

"And Sarah?" Max continued.

Nate sighed rubbing his forehead. "I'm seeing her this weekend, OK, I haven't been happy for a long time and we do need to sort things out, I know. Can you just leave it and let me deal with it in my own time? But in the meanwhile, you need to apologise to Evie."

Max sighed, he was fighting a losing battle; he had done all he could, if Nate wanted to self-destruct there was nothing he could do. "Yeah sure," he sighed as Nate opened the door before sitting at his desk.

Nate texted Evie and told her she could come back when she was ready, which she did. Max apologised, as did Evie. Calm restored in the office, Nate could get on with his research before he met with the action hero activist.

Evie greeted Lloyd with Nate at the entrance. Lloyd arrived in a blacked-out Land Rover Discovery 5, which Nate expected had all the mod cons inside. He had a driver and two security guards flanking him.

"Evie," he said, holding his arms out to her, much to Nate's annoyance.

"Hi," she said, hugging him back like they were old friends. "It's good to see you again," she said, stepping back for Nate to shake his hand.

"OK," Nate said, "Do you want to do the fan thing inside as they are all waiting and then we will chat?"

Lloyd laughed heading up the stairs to the lobby, "Fan thing always," he said, loving the limelight. "Lead me to them, Evie," he said, as they all went inside.

Nate was looking at Evie shaking his head, which made her laugh. He was watching Lloyd revel in the attention from the crew; selfies were taken by the dozen. Evie came over and stood next to Nate. He had his arms folded across his chest and, still watching Lloyd, he said to her, "I don't get it I mean he's not even that good looking."

Evie laughed at him and walked away, it was her turn to shake her head. After the initial excitement was over Nate led Lloyd through to the set-up conference room where there was a selection of beverages and nibbles, all vegan of course, Nate reassured him.

"So, Lloyd, thanks for making yourself available so quickly," Nate started.

"No problem, Nate, anything for that Evie of yours, how's it going with her by the way?" he said, leaning forward and winking.

"Going? No nothing like that you've got it wrong, she's my PA," Nate said defensively.

"Oh sure," Lloyd said. "I have quite a few PA's," he added, winking again at Nate.

Nate sighed; he guessed he didn't have to like the guy. "Anyway, moving on," Nate continued, "I've done extensive research and I agree the world is moving in a 'cleaner' direction and I think it's time for Rivers Restaurants to evolve."

"Nate, that's awesome buddy," he said, once again dropping the arrogant actor persona. "The planet is dying and people are starving, did you know that, Nate? Did you know that the crops that are grown to feed livestock, the same animals we then eat to get to the protein from that crop, could actually feed the world's starving people? Instead we have the livestock that pollute the planet, that we then murder to eat, while the third world starves. It's fucking insane man. Transportation is less than half the gases emitted by land livestock, we are literally killing everything."

Nate listened. He did know, he had researched figures and statistics. He agreed with Lloyd on one thing, it was fucking insane.

"People like you are major contributors to all this. Until you sit down and figure it out," Lloyd said, tapping his finger on the table with every word. "The moment we put a piece of animal, be it flesh or secretion, in our mouth our body starts fighting it. This clogs the arteries; cholesterol levels go crazy – hello heart disease. Who gets rich, Nate?" he said, on a roll. Nate just looked at him and shrugged. He was mesmerised at the transformation of this man. "The cardiovascular surgeon, he gets mega rich, the meat industry, they get rich, the dairy industry, man, they get fucking rich, pharmaceutical companies, oh boy those motherfuckers," he said, leaning closer to Nate and speaking quieter like it was a secret, "they get rich, Nate, feeding you all those drugs to fight the diseases eating animals causes." He leant back, eyes wide and nodded his head. "Yeah man they all get rich, you get sick, planet gets sick but this is the part most people forget, an innocent baby was tortured and killed."

"Baby?" Nate said, now genuinely confused.

"Let me break it down for you Nate, a cow can live for twenty years, killed at eighteen months, chickens can live up to eight years, killed at eighteen months because they are spent. Did you know chickens can recognise people? Pigs, I love pigs, Nate, they are as intelligent as a toddler, did you know that they are more intelligent than dogs, huh, yeah bet you didn't know that, twelve years is old for a pig, but at five months they are gone, lambs the same." Nate's head was spinning. "Now the dairy cows, four years is the average a dairy cow can stand the pressure on her poor body and mental state. Mothers make milk for who? Their babies of course. It's not rocket fucking science." Nate understood now why Evie liked this guy. "So mums been interfered with, by humans, kept pregnant all her short life, had her babies taken from her at birth, who are murdered for veal, she is mentally fucked, physically tortured every day of her sorrowful life before she's dragged off and murdered herself because she is spent." He sat back. "Sorry man, it just gets me so fucking mad, they've taught us from birth, love one – eat another," he said, shaking his head. "Speciesism, Nate, fucking speciesism!"

Nate wasn't sure who 'they' were but he understood what Lloyd was getting at. "It's fine," Nate said, "I understand completely." The truth was he was still trying to take everything in. "If you're happy to be our backer and sponsor we will do this completely plant-based. But I want to focus on the health aspect rather than anything else, I need to tread carefully, there will be a lot of people who won't understand my decision."

"The thing is, Nate, I'm happy to back you, but to me you seem like you just want to see how the land lies, you've got to understand this isn't about revenue, if you're doing this just to capture the vegan market as well as the carnivores then you're doing it for the wrong reasons."

"Hello, McDonald's!" Lloyd sighed. How much more did they want from him? "I have to transition my position slowly," Nate said. "I can't just go all in, it's not viable, I will go bankrupt overnight, let me do this my way, help me to make plant-based eating the way forward for my business." Nate knew, financially he did not need Lloyds money, but having him associated would bring audiences in.

"OK, I made my mind up at the party anyway after talking to Evie, so yeah, let's do this. Call my people and let your people talk it out. In the meantime, is Evie available to date then?"

"No," Nate said firmly "She is most definitely off limits." Lloyd just laughed.

Evie was like a cat on a hot tin roof. She had heard Lloyd speak at protests and knew he could be full on. She was worried it would put Nate off. She hoped Nate wouldn't let her down, if he did this, it was going to be a huge deal. Nate walked into the office where Evie was pacing around her desk. She looked up, "So?" she said. Nate looked sullen and Evie's face dropped.

"Thanks for considering it, Nate," she said, meaning it. When the smile spread over his face and she realised he was teasing her, her face lit up and she threw herself at him hugging him so tight he thought she was going to break him. "Thank you, thank you," she said, as she looked at him. "Did you get on OK with him?" She was genuinely curious.

"He's fucking insane, man," Nate said, trying to mimic Lloyd.

This had Evie in stitches, "Yeah he is pretty full on."

So it was done, this was going to bring a whole new dimension to the interviews and candidates. They would have to be prepared to change their way of thinking and cooking now that the show was basically taking out the largest and most traditional ingredient. It was exciting for Evie but Nate was scared. He had not done this for Evie, whatever anyone said, she had made him aware of things he had taken for granted and the choices had been his. He wanted a better world for his kids and the way we were heading something had to be done. He was ashamed of the human race for the way animals were treated like a commodity, a thing not a living being. He now knew he was a large contributor to their suffering, thanks to meeting Evie and Lloyd. This did not make him feel great but he wasn't ready to let go and change his life completely. One step at a time he thought.

Nate briefly filled Evie and Max in on the conversation. Evie knew they were getting the very much-watered down version for Max's sake and it made that little feeling in her stomach twist with emotion for him. She couldn't believe she was going to be part of this and she couldn't tell anyone. How ironic was that she thought. Nate had said the format of the show was to stay secret until it aired. That was going to be tough but it was doable. Tina knocked on the door and, as she walked in, said, "Boss, we need you, I need to check your face and Daryl wants to talk wardrobe."

"Bloody hell," he said, "here we go, pretty me up. Great."

Evie laughed and said, "Come on, let's go get you sorted for tomorrow." She led the way out of the office followed by Tina and Nate.

Nate decided he needed some time alone to prepare for the chat show. He knew Stanley Morgan asked poignant and sometimes controversial questions and he needed to be ready. He made his excuses and left the crowd that had gathered at the bar.

Later on, he texted Evie asking her to join him for dinner in his room. He had asked Head Chef Lucas to bring up the food, as he knew no questions would be asked and discretion kept. Chefs had their own kind of respect for each other he thought wryly. Nate sat at the small table eating his food and Evie was cross-legged on the bed facing him eating hers. He kept smiling at her, she looked so adorable.

"I'm nervous," he said, when he finally put his fork down, wiping his mouth with a napkin. "Of what?" Evie asked, putting her own plate aside and giving him her full attention.

"He is going to ask me awkward questions," Nate continued.

"Who? Morgan? Like what?" she was looking at him with a curious look.

"Like he's going to be interested in my views about Trump, I can't say what I really think, half the audience love him!"

Evie laughed, "Oh boy," she said, "you are nervous, OK, look you can fudge over questions like that."

"How?" he asked.

"Erm well, just say, you know, he's the president, and you're sure he is doing whatever he thinks is best for the country, be diplomatic. I mean anyone who voted for him isn't that smart so they won't realise you're being diplomatic and everyone else will know that's exactly what you're doing so win win."

He smiled. "I need one of those ear things and you can tell me what to say," he said, only half joking.

"You will be OK, Nate, I promise. You've got this. I have complete faith in you," she said, getting up and clearing the plates. She went over to him and sat on his knee. She kissed him. It was so nice having someone who supported you and listened, he'd never had this from Sarah. He hugged her and said, "You should leave some clothes here then you wouldn't have to sneak off so early in the mornings."

She looked at him and said teasingly, "That would be really cool, it's like we are almost living together."

"Careful," he said, "I might take away some of your privileges." He stood up, pushing her off his knee.

"What privileges?" she asked, as he was stripping his clothes off.

"Come and join me in the shower and we can talk about it," he said, disappearing into the bathroom. She stripped and stepped into the shower behind, him putting her arms around him she kissed his shoulder. He took her arm and turned round so they were facing each other. He looked at her before kissing her, enjoying taking in every curve of her body. He was so hard, he picked her up and held her against the wall, kissing her, second attempt he entered her, "They make it look so easy in the movies," he said, causing her to laugh.

After they showered they settled down and he poured them both a drink. Getting into bed, they watched the news to catch up with what was going on in the world before falling asleep. They were both shattered. They slept through to the following morning.

10

Wednesday

Frank had been keeping a close eye on the hotel. He had seen the butch actor arrive. He bet he could kick his ass in a fight. He had wondered what would bring him here. Judging by the girl's reaction to him they appeared to be friends. Hmm, that was an interesting development. Later that same day, having caught up with the little snitch that worked in the kitchen, he found out all he needed to know. People would sell their own mother for a buck in this country, he thought, wishing people back home would be as easy to bribe for so little.

***

As Evie never made it back to her room to get a change of clothes before she got into bed last night she had to get up early and leave. Nate didn't like it; he had been serious about her leaving clothes in his room. He had even offered to stay in her room but she seemed quite happy. He couldn't imagine falling asleep or waking up without her by his side.

Evie had told Gus they would need the minibus to go to the studio so he had been out in the morning polishing it. Gus took pride in his job, he had worked for Nate a long time and he liked his boss. Nate would take Gus everywhere he went, as he was not married and had no kids he loved the lifestyle his job gave him. If it was just the two of them, Nate would always sit in the front choosing to chat to Gus rather than sit in the back and be chauffeured. Gus liked Evie; he saw the way the boss looked at her. Whenever he had driven Sarah and Nate she would always belittle her husband and never showed him the respect he deserved. Yeah, he was definitely team Evie.

Having decided on what to wear for the chat show, Daryl had got Nate's trousers and shirt pressed. He wanted Nate to look the best version of himself possible. His boss wouldn't comply with the latest fashion so Daryl had a fight on his hands trying to get his boss into the trousers he had chosen. He settled for what Daryl called old-people's trousers, causing Evie to laugh, but Nate looked good in a pair of casual jeans and white casual shirt so Daryl couldn't complain.

Taking his boss' clothes, along with a spare change, just in case of a wardrobe malfunction, he handed them to Gus to pack neatly in the van. Tina had her make-up bag ready having made sure she had the right foundation for Nate's skin tone.

"Do I really have to wear that stuff?" he had complained knowing he was fighting a losing battle.

"The studio lighting will make you look pale and pasty, so yes." Tina was used to having to fight her boss.

It was mid-morning and time to go. Nate jumped in the front of the van with Gus while Tina, Daryl, Evie and Cassie sat in the back. "I'm surprised Max didn't want to come," Cassie said, blissfully unaware of the situation.

"Never mind, Cassie, at least we will have fun." Evie smiled, she was excited, she had never been to a chat show before let alone be backstage. When they arrived at the studio Gus dropped them by the studio door.

"Thanks, Gus, if you park up and head upstairs just tell them you're my security and you can get into the VIP section. Eat as much as you like," Nate said, walking towards the door. These places always put on a good spread for the guests and their entourage.

"Thanks, Boss," Gus called out, "and good luck."

Nate waved without turning round.

It wasn't as glamorous backstage as Evie thought it would be, which pleasantly surprised her as she had chosen to wear skinny jeans and a tight-fitting Bon Jovi tour t-shirt. A small round woman greeted them and showed them to Nate's dressing room. "Leave your stuff here," she said, "and you can head upstairs to meet the others, eat, drink, etc. I just don't advise you to drink too much before going on stage."

She aimed that at Nate who smiled and simply said, "Thanks."

"Right let's go mingle, see which other victims are here." Nate said, starting to feel his nerves resurface. Cassie was out the door and ready to brush shoulders with anyone famous she could find.

Evie looked at Nate, she could see he was working himself up again. "Go ahead, guys, we will be up in a minute," she said, closing the door after they had gone. "It's going to be fine." She smiled and went to him. She touched his arm, "Just remember, I'm here, there is no need to be nervous."

He stepped towards her taking her in his arms he kissed her. "Where would I be without you?" he said, looking into her eyes.

"Probably somewhere in your comfort zone," she said, causing him to laugh. "Come on I'm starving, let's see what there isn't for us to eat," she laughed leading him out of the dressing room.

Upstairs there was a canteen-style area with complimentary food and drink. There was not an overwhelming selection of vegan food but they found enough salad to keep them going. "This is what I mean, you see," Evie said to Nate and Cassie. "There are no plant-based meals, it should be part and parcel of any eatery in this day and age. Lifestyle choices, health and intolerances even. It shouldn't be a thing that you always have to phone up and arrange before going somewhere, it should automatically be on offer."

"Are you hangry?" Cassie said, making fun of her.

"Of course I am!" Evie said, laughing. "It's OK though, I've packed some protein bars just in case, Nate are you OK? You want me to get you a bar to eat?" she asked noticing he hadn't touched his salad.

"No, I'm too nervous to eat." He looked at Cassie and said, "Repeat that to anyone and I will deny it."

She laughed, "Good luck, I'm going to mingle." And she left them.

Stanley Morgan came over and shook Nate's hand. "Hi Stanley, hope you're going to go easy on me," Nate said.

"Never," Morgan said, shaking his hand roughly. "Any no-go areas?" Stanley asked?

"Wife and kids," Nate replied. "I don't want to discuss my private life. It is off limits."

"Got it. And who is this?" Stanley said, staring at Evie's boobs.

"Those are my breasts, if you want to look a little higher you've found me, hi I'm Evie," she said, not liking this man at all. Nate had to choke back the laughter at Evie's comment. Luckily Morgan seemed to take no offence. "Hmm, sassy isn't she?" he said to Nate staring at Evie.

"Sassy and unavailable." Evie excused herself and walked off to find Daryl.

"Oh my God," she said when she found him. "That Stanley Morgan is a total wanker!"

"Darling, you don't know the half of it, he's a total odd ball on the sex front, I've heard people in his circle say he's a freakoid! Stay away is my suggestion." Evie was only just starting to learn about the television industry. From what she could gather the people you saw and respected on the TV were completely different in real life and any oddities they had were accepted amongst the showbiz scene and kept quiet. God, she thought, this is how the Jimmy Saviles of the world got away with things for so long.

On the Stanley Morgan Show there were three other chat guests and an Indy band Evie had never heard of. There was Evangeline Paradise, a very famous actress who had made her name in the pornography world before taking Hollywood by storm. She was stunning, plastic but stunning.

"Are they real?" Evie said to Daryl about her boobs.

"No, darling perlease," he said. "If they were real they would knock her out. Those puppies don't move."

Evie was no expert but it had fascinated her. "Did you know her boobs were fake?" she asked Nate, genuinely amazed.

He laughed at her naivety and said, "You are so adorable, Evie."

"Do guys find that attractive?" she said, not realising she was cupping her own boobs.

"Stop that," he laughed when she realised what she had done she looked around nervously to see if anyone had noticed. He leant forward and said quietly to her, "You have the most beautiful perfect breasts that I have ever seen." She looked at him and half-smiled as she knew from his expression he was fighting a hard-on.

There was a politician who was going to be up against Trump so maybe Nate's fears would come true about his line of questioning, and there was an NFL football player. Evie came up to his waist and, mouth agape, he had laughed at 'the pretty little lady down below'.

"It's all good, Boss," said Tina, "There is no competition here, you're by far the most interesting person."

Nate smiled, "Thanks, Tina, that makes me feel so much better."

Evie laughed and said, "Well Nate is on last so let's go get him ready and watch from the wings." With that they all headed back to his dressing room.

"I can get changed by myself, you lot can wait outside," Nate said, walking into the dressing room. He heard the door shut and turned around. Evie, Daryl and Tina were all standing in his room arms folded looking at him. "Brilliant," he said, "fucking brilliant, where's Cassie? Wouldn't want her missing out on the peep show." Evie had to hold back a laugh.

"Nate, take your t-shirt off and sit down so I can do your make-up and hair," Tina demanded. Nate had forgotten he always has hair and make-up done first when he is wearing a shirt. "Hmm," he said, taking his shirt off.

"Oh my, oh my, what a fit bod!" Daryl said dramatically, waving his hand in front of his face. Evie saw the look on Nate's face and left the room quickly before she burst out laughing. Poor Nate, he was right out of his comfort zone and Evie knew exactly what he needed.

She came back five minutes later with an expensive bottle of whisky and a glass. "Look what I persuaded the barman to give me," she said, all proud of herself.

At this point Nate didn't care what she had done to get it. "You angel," he said, taking the glass from her and drinking it like water.

"Hey, take it easy, Chef," Evie said to him genuinely concerned.

He looked at her and said, "I like it when you call me Chef."

She frowned at him, as did Tina and Daryl.

"OK, no more whisky," she said.

"Let's get a look at you," Tina said as she turned the chair round. "Perfection, you're welcome and thank you to my adoring audience." As she curtseyed and blew kisses to the fake crowd she was acting to.

Nate looked at Evie and said, "Do I look like I'm wearing make-up?"

Evie considered her answer before she said, "Yes, but it won't notice on set. Tina is right you need it. Besides, I saw that politician a minute ago and he's way done up more than you."

Nate spun his chair back round looking at himself in the mirror. "So much hairspray," he said, trying to run his fingers through it.

Daryl looked at Tina and Evie, "Ladies," he said, "can you please leave and let the men work."

"Men?" Nate said, looking at Daryl and raising an eyebrow.

The girls left and Daryl feigning anger said, "Darling, let me do my work please." He fetched Nate's trousers. Five minutes later Daryl opened the door and the girls came back in smiling. "Daryl, Cassie has got us all seats in the audience," Tina said,

"The show is starting in five, so why don't you guys go ahead, I'm going to watch from the side with Nate, keep him calm," she said, raising her eyebrows towards them. Laughing they left, wishing Nate good luck as they went.

"Alone at last," Evie said to him, "You look gorgeous, I promise, you have nothing to worry about." Her heart was ready to explode, this was the first time she had seen the vulnerable insecure Nate and she found him quite endearing. "I won't kiss you because of your make-up," she said, straight faced. "Come on let's go watch."

He looked at her and touched her cheek. "Evie," she looked at him, "I'm glad you're here with me."

The politician had argued some serious points against Trump, and Morgan had tried to rattle him whenever he could. The NFL player talked a lot about himself and how great he was. The audience seemed to agree. Evangeline came out to wolf whistles. She was flirtatious and dirty and Morgan loved it.

Evie looked at Nate and said, "Go get them," as she adjusted his shirt collar.

Morgan said, "Please give a huge round of applause for the culinary mastermind, Nate Rivers."

The audience cheered and clapped and there were also a few wolf whistles.

Nate walked onto the set smiling at the audience and saying thank you as he sat down next to the plastic actress. She was moving her shoulders and pushing her boobs towards him flirtatiously. Nate looked uncomfortable and looked at Stanley instead. Bitch, Evie thought.

"So, Nate, it's great of you to join us tonight."

"It's lovely to be here again, Stanley, it's been a while."

"It has but I ate in your downtown restaurant a few months ago, I was entertaining some friends, and your manager, Louis, is it?"

"Yes, Louis, that's right," Nate said, looking a bit more at ease.

"Yes, Louis said it was on the house, courtesy of Mr Rivers."

"Yes, I fired him the next day." Nate deadpanned. The audience laughed.

"Not really," Nate continued, "he called me and of course it's always a pleasure to have you at my restaurant."

"Well thanks, Nate, we all sure had a delicious meal, yes, Evangeline did you want to say something?"

Evangeline was still thrusting her fake boobs towards Nate. Evie wanted to throw something at her. "Yes, darling," she purred leaning over and stroking Nate's leg, "I wonder if I came to your restaurant would I get a free meal?"

Nate looked at her weighing up his options. "It's always possible," he said, deciding to play it safe.

"Hey, what about me?" the politician said, feeling left out.

"No," Nate said to the audiences delight and laughter. "Most defiantly not."

The politician decided to laugh along rather than be laughed at.

"So, Nate," Stanley cut in, "are you team Trump?"

Here we go, Nate thought. "I don't tend to keep up with politics too much these days," Nate was stalling for time trying to remember to be diplomatic.

"So, do you think Trump has been good for the county or would you prefer to see the opposition in place?" he said, gesturing to his other guest.

"I think the president is running the country to the best of his ability and I am sure if the opposition wins next time," he said, gesturing towards the politician, "then they will run the country to the best of their ability."

"Very diplomatic of you, Mr Rivers, sitting on the fence a little bit there I see, how very British! How about telling us about your new show coming up in the autumn?"

Great, Evie thought. Nate looked at Stanley and said, "I am going to be giving ambitious underprivileged young adults the chance to compete to become the kitchen staff in a new restaurant we will be opening. These guys may not have been given a great start in life, one of the candidates served time and can't get a break, you know I want to give back to the community." The audience clapped and Stanley was nodding his head,

"That's very commendable of you, and these young adults will be fully in charge of your new restaurant when it opens?"

"There will be guidance available every step of the way, they need to fight hard for their roles, it's going to be tough for them," Nate said.

"So, I understand you are a practising vegan now, is that right?" The audience laughed thinking this was a joke, Evie's face dropped.

Nate looked at him suddenly on guard. "I'm not sure I follow," Nate replied cautiously.

"I've heard on the grape vine you've been eating plant-based food for a while now, is that true?"

"Yes," Nate said. Evie wanted to run out and hug him.

"You wanker," she muttered under her breath referring to Morgan.

"So you've stopped eating meat totally?"

"I have cut animal-based products out of my diet, yes."

"Is this a permanent thing or are you just experimenting? How will this affect your show?" he was bombarding Nate, but the audience was on the edge of their seats waiting for a reply.

"For the foreseeable future I don't see myself eating animals, if there is a way to live that doesn't bring pain or fear to anyone else then why wouldn't I live as kindly as I can. As for my show and my restaurants, I guess you are just going to have to wait and see. Is there anything else you want to know because I need to go and find some decent plant-based food. Your food here is shockingly bad."

Stanley looked at him, leant forward, and shook his hand. "You heard it here first folks, Nate Rivers is plant-based, watch this space and now, here to play us out with their latest single, is Turnout City."

The audience all cheered, and music started playing. Nate stood up and said to Stanley, "What the hell was that?"

"I asked you if there was anything off limits," he said, waving a finger at Nate.

"Where have you got your information from?" Nate demanded.

"Oh come on, Nate, I'm not giving my sources up. But I guess one of your people is easily bought." He laughed, slapped him on the shoulder and said, "See you next time buddy and bring that hottie back as well." He walked off the stage leaving Nate trying to compose himself.

Nate followed along with the other guests after smiling and waving at the audience. Tina, Daryl and Cassie found Evie. "What the hell?" Cassie said, "how did he know what goes on in the hotel?"

"I don't know, let me go and see Nate, go to the bar I will come and get you in a bit," she said, heading to Nate's dressing room. She went in closing the door behind her. Nate was standing with his hands on his hips staring in the mirror.

He saw her in the reflection but didn't turn round. "How did he know my eating habits?" She looked at him. "I mean someone has given him information?" he said to her.

"I don't know, something has gone wrong along the line somewhere but we will get to the bottom of it. You said animals."

He turned round confused and looked at her. "What?" he said.

"You said animals. Not food not meat but animals, you referred to them as someone not something," she said, staring at him. He cocked his head and his face softened and she went to him throwing her arms around his neck, he hugged her.

She pulled her head back and, searched his face, said, "Nate I…"

He put his finger to her lips, "Shh," he said, "I know, me to."

"So much," she said.

"So much," he repeated and locked in each other's eyes they started to kiss. She knew at that moment that she was going to spend the rest of her life with this man.

***

In the minibus on the way back to the hotel, Gus was listening to the girls in the back going over what had happened. Gus looked at Nate and said, "What's that shit all over your face, Boss?" Knowing it would wind Nate up he laughed at his own joke.

"Laugh it up, Gus," Nate said in good humour. He had been furious before Evie came in and saw him. He wasn't going to let it lie though, he was going to get to the bottom of how Stanley Morgan found out he had been eating a plant-based diet.

"I mean I'm not a vegan," he told Gus, "I'm not even properly plant-based, I'm trying." He continued, "But whoever is giving out information is in a lot of trouble."

Gus knew his boss was serious about his privacy and whatever happened in team Rivers stayed in team Rivers. "Boss, it's got to be someone on the hotel staff. Our team is good, you know it and the newest member," he said, nodding his head towards a giggling Evie in the back, "well there just ain't no reason for her to do something like this."

Nate had not considered Evie, but Max had crossed his mind. No, he trusted his guys, Gus was right.

"You want me to ask a few questions, do some digging for you?" Gus said.

"Yeah, yeah if you could, Gus, that would be great. Thanks." Nate was enjoying listening to Evie laugh; she was so much more relaxed these last few days. That moment in the dressing room, when he knew what she was going to say but even though he felt it he didn't want them to say it. It would make the problem real. It would go beyond a fling, midlife crisis or whatever the hell you wanted to call it. It couldn't be real otherwise he would have to admit his marriage had failed and he wasn't ready to face that reality.

Back at the hotel, Cassie went off to find Max and fill him in, and the others went to the bar. "Gus, come and join us," Nate said. Gus parked the car up and followed them into the bar. "Drinks on me," Nate said.

Tina looked at him and said, "Err, drinks are always on you they are on the business expense tab!" They all laughed.

"Oh yeah," Nate said, laughing at his own stupidity. It had been a long day he was tired.

An hour later everyone was yawning. "Right, I'm going up," Evie said.

"Me too," Tina said.

"Me three," said Daryl.

"I need to wash this shit off my face," Nate said. They all got up and headed for the lift. Getting off on the second floor they all said good night to Nate. Evie went to her room, got a change of clothes and sneaked back down the corridor to the stairs climbing to the next floor up. Nate's door was ajar and the shower was running. She locked the door, stripped off, and got in the shower with Nate who smiled and kissed her. They were both shattered. By the time she came out of the bathroom Nate was in bed, she took her towel off, hanging it up to dry, she got into bed. He rolled over to face her and she felt a stirring, she reached for him, he was hard and ready for her. "Evie," he said, totally besotted with her,

"Shh," she said, putting her finger to his lips, she then disappeared under the covers and as he felt her take him in her mouth he forgot everything that had happened earlier and they were the only two people in the world.

11

Thursday

Having turned his alarm off, Nate woke with a start, checking his phone he said, "Oh shit!" He put it back down and searched under the covers to find Evie and snuggle back down. "What is it?" she said sleepily as she cuddled up to him.

"It's 8.20," he said. "I guess we slept in."

Evie shook her self awake and pushed herself up to look at him, "We'd better get up or everyone will wonder why we are both late." He knew she was right.

"I'm going to shower, stay in bed," he said hoping she wouldn't. Not disappointing him, Evie stepped sleepily into the shower with Nate. Smiling he kissed her as he started to feel the excitement growing, he knew it would be a little while before they were ready for work.

Max was in the office when Nate and Evie walked in. "Afternoon," he said, the sarcasm not lost on Nate.

"Morning Max," Nate said cheerfully, he wasn't going to let anything dampen his spirits this morning.

"So, Cassie filled me in about yesterday, how are you doing after that?" Max asked, he might not agree with the direction Nate wanted to take the business but he certainly still had Nate's back, no matter what.

"It was intense for a bit, Max. We need to find out who has been talking and why." Nate had an uneasy feeling, he wasn't used to having mistrust about his people. Hopefully, Gus would do some digging and find out if any of the hotel staff had talked.

"Hmm," Max replied, "Do we need to get everyone together and have a chat?"

"Not yet," said Nate, "leave it till I'm back from the UK, let's see if there is any press about this after the show airs."

Evie suddenly realised that Nate was flying back home today and she felt sick. Would he sleep with his wife? She couldn't think like that, who was she anyway to think like that? Last night in the dressing room she had felt with such clarity that she was going to spend the rest of her life with him, how was that even a possibility when he had a wife and kids? She felt horrible. She knew she had to put on a brave face today.

Nate sat at his desk and sighed. He was also thinking about his weekend trip home. He didn't want to go. He didn't want to face Sarah and the kids after what he had done. He felt so guilty. He had taken his marriage vows seriously, but thinking hard he had always wondered if he would have married Sarah had she not been pregnant. The twins had been planned. He had not wanted any more kids but he relented to keep Sarah happy and busy, not that he could ever imagine life without Trudie and Florence now, his darling girls. How could he go home and pretend everything was the same? Would Sarah expect him to sleep with her? He had thought he was physically inept sexually but now, after Evie, he knew it was his mental state that had dulled his most intimate relations with Sarah and most certainly not his physical state. He couldn't help but smile a little thinking back to his morning shower with Evie that had led them straight back to bed, still wet and soapy. He had to stop thinking about it he could feel his body ready to give him a replay of his morning's hard-on.

Evie looked over and saw Nate, he looked at her grinning like a teenager and she knew exactly what was going on. She shook her head at him and smiled.

"I will get coffee," she said, getting up and leaving quickly as she thought she was going to start laughing.

Max was clueless about the situation. "Good idea and bring pastries if they have any," he shouted after her.

After lunch, Max had had enough for the day and decided he was going to take the afternoon off.

"Are you OK, Max?" Nate asked, as this was out of character.

"Yes, I'm fine, just tired I need a rest," he said with annoyance.

Nate looked at Evie and said after Max left, "I'm worried about him, at first I thought it was because he was mad at me and didn't want to be around me so much but I think there is more to it."

Evie could see the genuine concern and said, "Don't worry, I will have a chat with Cassie and see if I can find out what's going on with him."

He smiled at her. "I like you having my back, Evie."

She smiled at him, "Fancy meeting me at the boat house?"

"When?" he said, as she was getting up,

"Oh, about five minutes." She turned away from him and headed out of the door.

Five minutes later they were standing by the lake looking out holding hands. He turned to face her as he tucked her hair behind her ear he said, "You're changing my life Evie." He had never felt such a strong bond with another person before. "What will you do this weekend?" he asked.

"Oh, you know me," she joked, "I will be out gallivanting with Daryl." Knowing that she would probably stay inside her room with the TV and a book.

He pulled her in close and hugged her. They stayed like that for a few minutes before he said, "It's getting on, I need to leave for the airport soon." He lifted her chin up with his finger and kissed her not wanting to leave.

"Text me to let me know you've arrived safely," she said. "Then don't worry about me, enjoy time with your kids." She couldn't bring herself to say 'family'.

He hugged her again. "Come on," he said, as he took her hand and they headed back to the hotel.

They went into the office so Nate could pack up his laptop. He didn't need to take anything else. "Laptop, phone, chargers, passport, ticket is on phone, yeah, I think I have everything," he said, looking around. Max hadn't put in an appearance so he asked Evie to let him know if all was OK after she spoke with Cassie.

Gus appeared at the door, "Any luggage, Boss?"

"No, I'm good thanks, Gus, I'm just coming." Gus left and Nate hugged Evie again. "See you later," he said.

"Safe journey," she replied as he walked out the door only letting go of her hand at the last minute. She followed him to the car and watched him get in the front with Gus, he looked back at smiled, she waved and then he was gone.

***

Frank had known that Nate was heading back to England today so he knew he was no longer a concern as he was out the way. She looked sad, he thought, as he pulled a face to no one as he watched her standing outside the hotel waving to lover boy. He chuckled; she was in trouble now she had no one to look out for her. Frank had compiled quite an album on his phone of photos of them both. He couldn't decide which of them would be more fun to destroy. Pretty girls had never looked twice at him; they were all whores who deserved exactly what they got. He thought about the whore he had slapped around the other night, licking his lips. Nate was a typical good-looking man that had ladies falling at his feet, unlike himself, he thought. Life was cruel, you had to be crueller. He would stay at the hotel and keep watch on her. He hoped she would go out, it was boring sitting in the same place for so long.

***

Inside the hotel Evie texted Cassie asking her if she wanted to get together for a drink. She had told Daryl she had work to do and declined the invitation to join some of the crew on their Thursday night trip into town. She sat at the corner table in the bar she had sat at with Nate her first night here. That seemed like a lifetime ago already. Cassie was sipping her gin and Evie had her usual glass of red.

"I'm worried about him," Cassie said to Evie. "He hasn't been himself, he's breathless a lot of the time and he is tired all the time."

"Has the crew's doctor seen him?" Evie asked.

"Oh yes, don't you worry I had him on the case, much to Max's disapproval of my interfering!" she said. "He told him he needs to lose weight, he needs to go and be checked out properly, I mean he's been borderline diabetic for a while, he's just so stubborn." Cassie sipped her gin. "Anyway, how are you doing?"

"Me? Oh, I'm fine," she lied. "Feel a little lost without Nate here," she confessed.

"Yes, well, the two of you have been pretty inseparable," she said, giving Evie the you-know-what-I-mean look.

"Is it that obvious?" Evie asked.

Cassie laughed, "It's the looks that give you away, I was your age once you know, I remember those looks of passion, now it's only looks of concern waiting for the next problem that needs a doctor." She wondered when it had all changed.

Evie looked at her, "Max will be OK, I will speak to Nate when he's back and get him to make Max get checked out properly. Even if it means flying him home to do it."

"Thanks, Evie, I know it's been a struggle for Max, he's, like, you know, he just doesn't know how to deal with the situation."

Evie nodded and sipped her drink. Nate would be at the airport now she thought, in the VIP section sipping whisky. "I wonder what it's like to fly first class?" she said to Cassie.

"Oh, my dear, it's marvellous!" she said, clapping her hands together. "If you stick around you may get to try it one day,"

After a bar snack with Cassie, Evie headed upstairs. She went to Nate's room and let herself in. The maid had been in and the room was fresh and tidy. She wondered what they must have thought of the damp bed from this morning's fun. She walked over to the chair and picked up his shirt, she held it up and smelt his distinct scent. Hugging the shirt, she felt like she was going to cry. For God's sake girl pull yourself together. He's gone home for a few days he's not dead. She left his room and headed back to hers. She sat on the end of her bed and cried. She couldn't remember the last time a guy had made her cry. Her phone rang, it was Nate.

"Hey," he said.

"Hey," she said, trying not to sniff.

"Evie, what's wrong are you OK?" hearing in her voice she had been crying.

"I'm fine, just watching a sad movie," she lied.

"What movie?" he questioned.

"You know, err, that Patrick Swayze one where he dies," she said, it was the only sad movie that came to mind.

"Oh, don't be sad he sees her again before he goes forever," he said, knowing she was lying. He felt like shit. She was crying because he was going home. It seemed crazy he found himself in this position. "I'm at the gate, waiting to board. I thought I'd just hear your voice again before I turn my phone off." Tears were welling up in her eyes again. "So I will speak to you when I land."

"OK." Was all she said, not trusting herself to sound in control.

"OK," he said. "Bye for now."

"Bye," she said, and rang off.

Nate was standing at the window looking at the plane. He felt lost, he couldn't stand the thought of Evie being upset but what could he do really? He sat down and put his head in his hands. "Mr Rivers, Sir," he looked up, it was a member of the cabin crew. "Would you like to follow me we are ready to board you."

Evie sat at the end of her bed and continued crying. She was so pissed off she felt like this. She stripped out of her clothes and jumped in the shower. She put on some clean underwear and put Nate's shirt on, switching on the TV she channel-hopped settling on a true-life crime documentary, she poured herself some wine and tried not to think of Nate.

***

Sarah was nervous. She had sent the kids to her parent's house for the night and asked them to keep them until she called. She intended to greet Nate when he got back in the morning in her new underwear and drag him off to bed. She had envisioned a passionate encounter followed by declarations of love. The kids would come home in the afternoon and they would spend the evening as a family. It was going to be perfect. She would tell him that once this show was done he needed to stay home and keep everything UK based. She could start making a presence for herself with him backing her, she fancied herself as a daytime presenter. It was her time to shine, Mrs Nate Rivers.

***

Max knew he was in trouble. He was terrified about seeing a doctor. He knew he was overweight and he knew he ate the wrong food but he had a sweet tooth, what was he to do? If he were told he was diabetic it would be a catastrophe for him. How could he possibly change his eating habits after all of these years? He knew he needed to change his ways but the truth was he didn't know how. Cassie had offered to help him but he didn't need a woman clucking over him. There are plenty of people in this country that are more overweight than me, he had told Cassie. He knew that was a childish argument but she had cornered him. Cassie had also suggested they take a trip back home and see Max's own doctor but Max didn't want to leave production at the moment, he was worried about Nate and felt he needed to be here.

He was glad Nate had gone home at least. Sarah had called Max asking who Evie was and he had said he had recommended her. He felt terrible for not telling her the truth about their relationship but he had always had Nate's back, he wasn't going to stop now. He hated feeling in the middle of it, he was both their friends but he would always protect Nate. He was the closest thing Max had known to a son. He wondered how different his life would have been if he had met Cassie at a much younger age, would they have married? He was extremely fond of Cassie, he would go as far to say he loved her but he was a bachelor at heart and couldn't bring himself to say it to her. She was undemanding and he had liked that quality until she became fixated on his eating habits.

Evie had successfully managed to re-educate both Nate and Cassie, even though Cassie still had some dairy products and Nate had had the odd bit of forbidden food here and there, in general they were both trying.

"You don't have to do it all in one day," Evie had told Cassie, "just cut out things here and there, start replacing cow's milk with soy, you can gradually change your habits."

Evie herself had first become vegetarian after a lot of soul searching. She didn't drink milk anyway; from a young age she just had a weird feeling about it. She had hated the smell of butcher shops and they seemed unnatural to her, she would refuse to go in. Looking back, she knew she should have always been a vegan. She didn't blame the older generation, after all they grew up with war parents and you ate what you were given and you were grateful.

Evie heard herself say on several occasions that if by her stopping eating meat it would make a difference then of course she would but at that point in time she knew very little about the vegan movement and had said she could never be a vegan.

After becoming vegetarian she started to consider other things like toothpaste and cosmetics. She had a sudden understanding that she couldn't explain. It was almost as though someone had flicked a switch. If she didn't want animals to be killed for her food then why was it OK to have them to be used as test subjects. She had soon discarded all her cosmetics and only bought vegan products.

Evie had headed out to the country with some friends and passed a field of cows, looking into a cow's eyes she realised that she had made a difference, she was different, she looked at the animal differently, she had no guilt, she hadn't realised that she had guilt until she didn't have it anymore. Her friend had told her on average a vegan saves 100 animals from slaughter a year and not only that but it also reduces the impact on the environment as animal agriculture has a major impact on climate change. Being vegan dramatically reduces your carbon footprint. She learned about the environmental repercussions of animal agriculture and she had been mad. Delving deeper, she was exposed to the true practices of dairy farming and, after witnessing that it was industry standard for male baby chicks to be ground up alive, Evie had found that actually it wasn't hard at all to become vegan. She later found out about the health implications and the lies that had been told to normalise eating one animal and pet another. Speciesism had become an accepted normality.

It had been easy with Cassie, she was already thinking about eating healthier and she was ready to listen. She was already on the edge; Evie just helped her to topple over. Max had proved to be a harder nut to crack.

Gus was quiet on the drive to the airport with his boss. He had been a silent observer most of his life and was used to people forgetting he was there. Having heard many a scandal over the years on the back seat of his cars, he wasn't sure which would be more profitable, blackmail or writing a book. Maybe one day he would write his memoirs. He would have to change people's names so he didn't get sued.

He had observed the man parked at the end of the drive, and had been keeping an eye on him. He had also noticed the car follow him on more than one occasion. He had considered telling this to his boss but as yet he had no evidence this guy was doing anything wrong. Maybe a fan, maybe a reporter, he had considered both. When he had heard about what happened on the talk show last night he had a sudden recollection of seeing Alex, the kitchen porter, leaning in through the car window talking to the guy. He had decided he needed a chat with Alex. He was guessing a pot washer's salary was minimal and could understand the desire to make some extra money but not at his boss's expense. Nate had been good to Gus and Gus was loyal. He would see his boss safely to the airport then do some investigating.

Evie was sitting on her bed staring at the screen. She hadn't really taken in much of anything that had been on the TV. It's all shit anyway, she thought. Her phone rang. It was Nate. "Hey, beautiful," he said, making her smile.

"Hey, handsome," she replied. "Shouldn't you be in the air by now?"

"Yeah you'd think," he said, sounding frustrated. "They boarded us then delayed us. Bloody great!" he sounded fed up.

"Oh, that's no good," she said, hoping she sounded sincere. "Hey, I spoke to Cassie earlier."

"Really? What did she say?"

"She's concerned, she said Max had seen the crew's doctor but you know, Nate, I think maybe you need to get him to his own doctor, persuade him to take some time off."

Nate listened, not sure if he should be more concerned than he had been.

"I mean it's just better to be safe than sorry," she said. Someone knocked on the door. "Hang on, someone's at the door."

"Ordering room service young lady?" he asked.

"No," she said, smiling in the phone, "it's probably Tina." She opened the door.

Nate was standing in front of her, phone still to his ear.

Her mouth fell open as she lowered her phone, she said, "But. You… I don't… how…?" he looked at her as he lowered his phone, puffy red eyes from crying, she was wearing his shirt with only a few buttons done up, she looked at him confused. She stepped back making room for him to come in and he closed the door behind him. She was still staring at him like she wasn't sure if he was real or not.

"I forgot something," he said a bit sheepishly.

"Oh?" she said.

"You. I forgot you, they say home is where the heart is and you have my heart, Evie, however much I try to kid myself, you have my heart, you are my home. I love you and I don't want to leave you again. I'm sorry I shouldn't have gone." She was trying to take it all in. "I love you," he said again, putting his bag and jacket down.

She had tears running down her cheeks and he went to her and wiped them. "I love you too," she said, "so much."

"So much," he repeated before kissing her. He picked her up and took her to the bed, he put her down and undid the buttons on his shirt she was wearing. "This looks good on you by the way," he said.

"Oh yeah," she said, slipping the shirt off revealing her perfect breasts.

"Oh yeah," he said. As she sat on the bed he took his t-shirt off followed by his jeans. She could see he was more than ready for her. He got on the bed and kissed her tenderly. "I love you," he whispered in her ear. "I want to make love to you."

She was so turned on and still giddy from what he had said she slid her hands down to remove his briefs, he jumped up taking them off as she removed her panties and then he was inside her, slow deliberate motions both of them feeling the intensity of the moment.

"I'm all yours, Evie," he said, as he moved his hips slowly and meaningfully, he was looking straight into her eyes. "This is all yours," he said, moving deep inside her. "I'm all yours," he said, and the explosion took them both over as they experienced the next level of love making.

Lying in each other's arms later, Evie said, "What about Sarah? She's going to be expecting you home."

Nate sighed. "I texted her and said that we had been held up on the interstate due to an accident and I missed the flight. I said I would call her in the morning."

Evie sat up and Nate did the same. "What are you going to do?" she asked.

Nate actually had no clue, he had been at the gate about to board the plane when he realised he just couldn't get on. He had never before felt such a strong feeling of knowing exactly what he wanted. "I just don't know, Evie, I need to tell her, I don't want her finding out from someone else, she doesn't deserve that. But I need to do it face to face, I just don't know," he said in frustration.

Evie didn't know how to help him, she knew how much Nate loved his kids but he had never discussed Sarah with her before.

"What will the kids think?" Nate said, as if reading her train of thought. "They are going to hate me for leaving their mum. Especially when they find out there is another woman involved."

Evie felt terrible, "I'm so sorry, Nate."

"No, don't say that," he said. "This is not on you, this is all me. My marriage has been a farce for years, two people going through the motions, I just never had a reason to stop and question it before I met you. Which, by the way, is the best thing that ever happened to me." Turning to face her, he kissed her.

She kissed him back not really feeling much better. "I love you," she said.

"I love you," he replied. "I'm going to have to do some explaining here as well in the morning."

"Cassie knows about us," Evie said. "She called me out earlier saying it was obvious the way we looked at each other."

"I wonder who else knows?" he said. "Oh well, it is what it is now, there is not much we can do about it tonight, let's get some sleep, it's going to be an interesting day tomorrow." They lay back down and cuddled up together. Yes, he thought, this is exactly where I'm meant to be.

12

Friday

Nate hadn't been wrong; it turned out to be an interesting day indeed. He had texted Gus in the morning telling him he was back at the hotel. He asked him to come to Evie's room. Gus knocked on the door and Nate let him in.

"You OK, Boss?" he asked, he could hear the shower was on which confirmed his suspicions that his boss was playing away from home. He was surprised, though, that Nate was not trying to hide it.

"Gus, I know you've been loyal to me over the years and I'm sorry to have put you in this position but I have lied to Sarah and told her I missed my flight due to an accident on the interstate." Gus listened. "It's possible she will call you to check and I understand if you don't want to lie and I won't hold it against you."

"I've got your back, Boss," he said, meaning every word.

"Thanks, Gus, I do need to go home and see her and tell her the truth but I don't want her finding out before I get the chance to tell her face to face." Gus understood completely, Nate was a good man, who had done the wrong thing for the right reasons, he felt sorry for his predicament.

"There is something else as well, Boss, that I need to discuss with you but maybe we can do it when you're alone, I don't want to spook Evie."

Nate was immediately alert, "What, did you find something out?" The shower stopped, "OK," said Nate, "I will catch up with you later." He touched Gus's shoulder and looked at him and said, "Thanks, Gus." Gus knew his boss meant it.

Stepping out of the shower, Evie had heard Gus and knew Nate was chatting to him about last night.

She waited until she heard the door close and she stepped into the bedroom. "OK?" she asked.

"Yeah, Gus is cool, I just need to deal with Max and Sarah now."

Evie started to get dressed. "I will leave you alone to talk to her," she said, getting dressed. He hugged her before she left. "Good luck," she said, giving him a worried smile as she left.

He decided to phone Sarah instead of FaceTiming her he didn't want her seeing his guilt. She picked up after the second ring.

"Nate," she said, narky.

"Hello Sarah," he said, "sorry," was all he managed to say.

"Did you really miss your flight or did you have no intention of coming home?" she asked.

"I missed my flight, I'm sorry, I will see if I can book one for next weekend," he said, thinking that will give him the chance to do the interviews and figure out how to tell her it was over. "I have to do the interviews next week as we've already booked the studio and it's not fair to mess everyone around."

"Fine," was all she said.

"Fine? That's it? No arguments?"

"Fine, let me know your arrival time. Bye." And she was gone. Well that was weird he thought.

Gus had driven back to the hotel last night and headed to the kitchen for a sandwich and to have a nosey around. Alex the pot wash was at his station stacking dishes and pots and putting them through the washer. Gus had taken his sandwich and sat on the veranda round the back of the hotel where the kitchen staff exit was. He ate his sandwich and waited.

Half an hour later he saw the chefs starting to leave, Alex was usually last. Gus left the veranda and stood out of sight waiting. When Alex came out Gus followed him. Alex walked along the drive to the road. Gus followed keeping against the verge using the shadows of the trees to stay out of view. He saw the car, he had thought it was a Buick and he was close enough now to see he had been right. Alex went over to the car.

Gus couldn't quite hear the whole conversation but the gist was Alex wanted more money to continue trading information. There had been some heated words and then the window was up and the car drove off. Gus decided not to approach Alex just yet. He wanted to catch him red handed.

Evie was in the office when Max came in. "Morning, Evie," he said, wondering how she was holding up with Nate having gone home.

"Morning, Max," she said, not wanting to be the one to tell him. Five minutes later Nate walked in.

"Morning, Max," he said, to Max's total surprise.

"Nate? What are you doing here?" he asked in disbelief.

"I missed my flight, Gus did his best to get me there on time but the traffic was just so bad." He lied hoping that bringing Gus in on his story might make it more believable. Nate had every intention of telling Max the truth but Sarah had to know first.

"Oh right," said Max. "That's a shame," he said, not really knowing what to think. "Never mind I guess."

Nate smiled and said, "I'm rebooking for next weekend if possible." This seemed to please Max so Nate left it there.

Max had decided not to say anything; he knew Evie already knew, as she didn't react when he walked in. It was up to them, he had decided not to get involved.

***

Sarah was livid. How dare he lie to her. She had searched the Internet and found no mention of an accident on any interstate. Did he think she was stupid? She made her decision; she booked herself on 15.20 British Airways flight to New York. She would arrive at 6.15pm local time. She had no problem getting a seat in first class. The kids were already at her parents so she threw some clothes in a small suitcase as hand luggage and left for the airport. She would show him, she thought. In the back of the taxi she spoke to her mother and told her of her intention. Her mother had asked her if surprising Nate was really a good idea but Sarah was not having any of it. He had forced her hand to carry out her actions.

***

Frank was pissed off with the pot wash, Alex. Who the hell did he think he was demanding more money? He didn't need him now anyway; the plan had changed. He had missed Nate's return last night as he had left after Alex's demand for more money. The dirt bag, his days of extra cash were over. Frank had his pictures, he had everything he needed. It was all going to come crashing down around her pretty little ears soon, he thought with delight of Evie in that pretty little red dress she had worn. Oh yes, she was in trouble now.

***

Nate was in the bar with Evie and a few of the crew having a lunchtime drink. Gus came in and caught his eye. Grabbing a couple of bottles of beer from the waiter Nate took them over and motioned Gus outside.

"Here you go," he said, handing Gus a beer then he leaned on the balustrade of the veranda. They both took a mouthful of beer before Gus said, "I believe it's Alex in the kitchen selling information." Having decided with his boss's return that maybe he should fill him in.

"Alex? Really? Who's he selling information to?" he asked, relieved it wasn't a member of his crew.

"I don't know that, I thought maybe a reporter but why would a reporter leek info to Stanley Morgan's people? He'd want to keep the story for himself surely?" Gus said. Gus was right but if not a reporter then who?

"It must be a reporter," Nate said. "I mean I can't imagine why he would pass info like that on but maybe it's to do with my competitors?" Nate questioned. This was so strange. "Who would benefit? This is beyond me. OK, keep an eye on Alex, see if he meets up with this guy again tonight and if so approach him after and confront him."

"Sure, Boss," said Gus. "I'm on it," he said, finishing his beer.

Nate was perplexed. He couldn't think of anyone or any reason for someone buying information. "I mean we are assuming it's all to do with the show because he gave the information to Stanley Morgan," he told Evie as he recounted his earlier conversation with Gus.

“That’s so strange,” she said. “It doesn’t make any sense.”

“I just don’t know, Evie, someone is out to sabotage the show for whatever reason. Let’s keep this between us for now and see what else Gus can find out.”

Evie agreed that was the best way forward for now.

“What with Sarah’s reaction and this, I just don’t know what’s going on.” He had told Evie earlier about Sarah’s strange behaviour but, not knowing the woman, Evie had just shrugged. “I just don’t know, Nate.” Which she knew wasn’t much help. She had squeezed his hand and smiled at him, he had smiled back as they got lost in each other’s eyes for a brief moment.

Nate had asked Evie to give him some space in the office so that he could talk to Max. Evie made her excuses and went off to find Daryl and Tina.

“Max, can I talk to you for a minute please.”

Max looked up from his desk He never knew these days what Nate might hit him with next. “Go on,” Max said, on guard.

“Max, you have been the closest thing to a father to me since Dad died and you know I care about you very much.”

“But…” said Max.

“No but’s, Max, I’m concerned about you that’s all. I know Cassie is as well and Adam told me he came to see you and has recommended you get a full once-over.”

Max was annoyed. “The doctor has no right to talk to you about my medical condition,” he said.

“Max, come on, we are just worried about you that’s all this is, please humour me.”

“OK, say what you need to,” Max said, deciding he was fighting another losing battle.

“I want you to go home, take Cassie and have a break, book in to see your doctor and get checked over. Please Max, I need you around, you have always been here for me, please let me be here for you.” Nate was sincere. He loved Max.

Max sighed a very long and meaningful sigh. "I had already decided that maybe I should go home and get an MOT," he said, Cassie had worn him down. "I don't feel right and I need to do something, I know."

Nate relaxed and smiled at him. "I'm so pleased, you mean the world to me Max, you do know that don't you?"

Max looked at him, he did know. "I know, kiddo, you mean the world to me too." Nate was so relieved; he had thought he was going to have a battle on his hands. With that Max said, "Right, well, I think I'm going for a siesta so see you later." With that he was gone.

"It was easier than I thought," Nate told Evie. "I'm just glad he's taking it seriously at last."

"Nate," she said.

"Hmm,"

"I think I'm going upstairs for a siesta," she said, looking at him with mischief in her eyes. "Oh," he said, raising an eyebrow at her as she stood up.

"I will be in my room in you want me."

"If I want you," he laughed. She bent over and whispered in his ear

"Five minutes, my room I will be naked, waiting," and she was gone. He could feel his body was responding and she had barely had a chance to strip before he was on her as they both let their bodies take over.

Lying on top of the bed, still naked, holding hands, she turned her head to look at him.

He looked back at her and said, "I hope you never stop looking at me like that." She went to him and kissed him.

"I love you," he said.

"I lovc you," she repeated.

"I'm starving," he said.

"That's because you had a liquid lunch," she reminded him smiling. "Come on, quick shower and let's go eat," she said, jumping up and heading to the bathroom. "Now you've said it, I'm starving too!"

He followed her into the shower.

***

Sarah had landed and was through passport control quickly and easily. One of the perks of being Mrs Nate Rivers. She left the airport and walked the small way across to the airport hotel. "Mrs Rivers," she said at reception, "I've booked a room."

"Ah yes, Mrs Rivers, here is your key card, would like to be shown to your room?"

"No, that's fine, do you have anything for me?" she asked.

"Let me check for you, oh yes, sure we do," she said, handing her a padded A4 size envelope. "There you go, and you have a nice stay now."

Taking the envelope, she smiled. "Yes, I think I'm going to," she said, in a tone that made the receptionist frown as she walked away.

Up in her room Sarah kicked off her shoes and went straight to the minibar to find herself a drink. Pouring a gin into a glass she sat on the bed and opened the envelope. She took out the file inside and started reading. It made for very good reading. She sat for an hour looking through, stopping once to order room service. She knew what she had to do. She showered. It was 9pm local time and she decided she would leave surprising Nate until the morning. She had been up half the night waiting for him to call, she hadn't slept in the last forty-eight hours. A good night's sleep and she would make her grand entrance.

In the bar, Nate and Evie were demolishing a bowl of chips. Daryl and Tina soon joined them. "Hey hands off!" Nate said to Tina as she grabbed the bowl of chips. Giving up he went off to the kitchen and came out with two more bowls. Cassie joined them.

"Did Max tell you we had a chat today?" Nate asked Cassie quietly.

"Yes thanks, Nate, he said I can go ahead and book flights home. I will have a look in the morning."

Evie, overhearing said, "I can do that for you, Cassie if you like?"

"Would you dear? That would be marvellous. First class off course."

"Of course!" Evie said.

Nate put his arm around Evie and kissed her cheek. "That's what I love about you," he said. Cassie looked at him and he quickly stepped away from Evie causing her and Cassie to start laughing.

"You are going to have to tell Sarah sooner rather than later," Evie said. "You are forgetting we are not meant to be public knowledge."

Nate was annoyed with himself. "It's just so natural," he said, "I can't help myself."

Daryl came over and put his arm around Evie, "Oh perlease you two. As if we don't know! You think we believed that cock and bull story," he said, feigning anger. "The only people you two have been kidding is yourselves."

"Oh," said Nate, trying not to smirk.

Evie laughed and said, "Oh well, I guess that's that then." Nate laughed, he knew he shouldn't this was serious but he was happy, for the first time in a long time he was content.

They stayed in the bar drinking and laughing until late. How were any of them to know that life would never be the same again?

13

Saturday

It was late when Nate woke up. "Argh," he said, pressing his palm against the pain in his head. "Who spiked my drinks?" he moaned.

Evie came out of the bathroom and handed him a glass of water and a couple of paracetamol, "Mine too," she complained. She had showered and was dressed.

"Where are you going so early?" he asked.

"It's nearly 9am, Nate."

"Shit we missed breakfast."

She laughed at him. "Come on get in the shower and we can go and get some toast or something."

"Ah, bacon, eggs, sausage, fried onion and tomato, mushroom, beans and toast," he said with a silly grin on his face. "That's what I fancy," he looked at her staring at him trying to look angry. "Woops I mean toast is great," he said, covering his mouth like a naughty schoolboy. She leant over to kiss him he said, "Stop! I think I might smell like a badger's arse."

She laughed and kissed him anyway. "Shower! Now!" she demanded as he jumped up and headed to the bathroom.

"Hey, what happened to my clothes? How come I'm naked? Did you take advantage of me last night?" he said, stepping into the shower. Evie laughed.

Nate reappeared ten minutes later clean and fresh and headed straight over to give Evie a damp hug. "I love you," he said.

"I did not know that," she said, teasing him as he tickled her sides. "OK! OK! I love you too," she said, as they became serious and kissed. She could feel his towel moving.

He stopped kissing her and said, "Uh-oh."

She pulled his towel away and said, "Sit down." As he sat on the edge of the bed she got on her knees and took him in her mouth. He lay back on the bed moaning as she did her magic with her tongue and mouth.

"Oh my fucking God!" Nate said, as he released himself in her mouth. She climbed on the bed next to him, he touched her face, and neither of them said a word. They didn't need to.

They headed downstairs and, as they came out of the lift, Nate stopped dead in his tracks. He went ashen. "Nate what's wrong?" Evie said, looking to see what had his attention. It was Sarah. She was standing in front of them with her arms folded across her chest.

"Hello, Nate," she said, before looking at Evie and giving her the once-over. Evie felt very intimidated and moved on the spot. "Evie," Sarah said.

"Mrs Rivers," Evie acknowledged her back.

"Sarah, what on earth are you doing here? Where are the kids?"

"I left them home alone, Nate, where do think they are?" she said, with sarcasm in her voice. "Why are you here?" he said.

"I need a reason? Oh OK, how about my husband lied to me about coming home so he could stay and screw his pretty little assistant!" she said, challenging him in front of whoever was around. Evie's mouth fell open. Sarah wasn't as attractive in the flesh than she had been in the photos Evie had seen of her. But anyone with an ugly personality looked ugly even if they had the most stunning of looks. "Would you mind terribly, dear, if I have a word in private with my husband?" She emphasised the 'my'. Evie just stood there dumbfounded.

Nate walked over to Sarah and took her arm. "Don't talk to her like that," he said, trying to pull her into the office.

"Take your hands off me you son of a bitch," she seethed. He let go and walked off into the office. He stood by the door waiting for her to join him. Giving Evie one last look-over, she followed Nate into the office and slammed the door behind her.

Evie hadn't realised she had been standing so tense until her body relaxed. Daryl and Tina came running over to her. "Did you hear?" she asked.

"I think the whole hotel did," Tina said, looking around at the audience Sarah had managed to gather.

Daryl had her arm. "Come on darling," he said, pulling her towards the bar. Evie's eyes welled up, seeing this, Daryl changed direction and led her outside.

"What the fuck do you think you're playing at?" he said, going behind his desk to put some space between them.

"Me, Nate, me? Are you fucking serious?" she yelled at him. "How long have you been screwing that little slut?" she demanded.

He pointed his finger at her trying to control his temper. "Don't talk about her like that," he said. She was nodding her head.

"I see how it is, you think you're in love with the little trollop." She had expected him to be defensive but she had also expected him to be apologetic.

This wasn't going as planned. "I was going to talk to you, Sarah," Nate said, trying to calm down a bit. It had been such a shock seeing her but she shouldn't have gone after Evie like that.

"Talk to me?" she questioned. "And what? Ask for my forgiveness?"

"No. I don't expect you to forgive me. I know I have broken us," he said, looking at her, "and I am truly sorry."

"At least you haven't tried to deny it, I would have thought you would have."

"No, Sarah, I am not denying anything."

"How am I meant to take you back and trust you after this?" she said, looking at him.

It suddenly hit Nate, she did not believe for one second that the marriage was over. She was expecting him to beg her forgiveness and then spend the rest of his life making it up to her. He put his hands on his hips and looked down at his feet. This was going to be worse than he had expected.

Outside, sitting on the veranda with Daryl and Tina, Evie was in a state of shock. "Oh my fucking God," she said. "What the hell just happened?"

"Well," Daryl started ready to tell her when Tina punched him.

"It was rhetorical you idiot," she said, looking at Evie. Evie knew everything that had been said between her and Nate and she believed on one hand that he was going to leave Sarah and be with her but now, she was here, and Evie felt very insecure.

"Where would I go?" she said out loud, "I can't go home." Tina and Daryl looked at each other confused.

"Honey, you're not going anywhere," Tina said, starting to worry a little about her friend. Cassie came crashing out of the front door. "What happened?" she exclaimed having come late to the party she had missed the confrontation.

"Well," Daryl began, delighted to be able to go over it again.

After filling Cassie in she said, "Evie, are you OK?"

Evie looked at her and smiled. "Yeah I'm OK, I guess we all have to just wait and see what happens next."

"I am truly sorry, Sarah, I didn't mean for you to find out like this. You have to believe me I never wanted to hurt you."

"Hurt me?" she questioned. "What about the embarrassment you have caused me? What about the disrespect to our children?"

Nate looked at her. "This has nothing to do with the kids."

Sarah glared at him. "Nothing to do with the kids? You have slept with another woman, you have made a mockery of our marriage and our family!"

He wasn't really sure what else to say to her and he was desperate to go and find Evie. "It's over Sarah," he said quietly.

She looked at him, realising for the first time throughout this that she didn't actually have the control, she said, "You can't leave me, and there will be a scandal!"

He laughed. "Oh Sarah, is that all you're worried about? What will the neighbours think?"

"Are you mocking me?" she said, eyes wide in disbelief.

"No, I'm telling you as it is. You care more about the way people perceive your family than you actually care about your family," he said, feeling more in control of his emotions now. "It's over, Sarah. I don't want to be your husband anymore."

She felt dizzy, she could feel it all slipping away and for what, some little slut? "No, Nate. I will never give you a divorce. You owe me, I've looked after your kids and home."

"But you never looked after me!" He cut in, causing her to snap her head back. "What about me Sarah? You stopped being my anything once Mike arrived. You were a mother and nothing else."

"Are you really blaming our son for your short-comings as a husband?" she said in disbelief.

"No, I'm blaming you. I'm blaming me. I don't want to be married to you, Sarah. I want a divorce."

"You will never get it, I will make your life hell," she seethed at him.

"I think you should go now," he said calmly.

She looked at him. No, she thought, this isn't the way this happens. She needed to compose herself. "I'm going to go back to my hotel. I expect you to join me before the day is through." With that she turned and left, slamming the door behind her. She walked out head held high when she saw Evie. "Are you happy you slut!"

Daryl gasped and said, "Really!"

Evie stood up so she felt she was on the same footing and looked at Sarah in defiance holding her own.

Nate came out with Gus. He had his hands in his pockets. "That's enough, Sarah!" She looked at him. "Gus will take you wherever you need to go," he said, as Gus moved forward. As if it wasn't enough that he had humiliated her by sleeping with the slut he was standing up for her in front of everyone. "Go home, Sarah. Just go home."

She held her head high feeling the flush of anger in her cheeks.

Gus walked up to her and said, "Mrs Rivers, it would my pleasure to take you wherever it is you want to go." He looked at her and she nodded as she followed him to the car and he opened the back door for her.

Nate stood looking at the car until it had driven off. He then turned his attention to Evie. "OK everyone, the show is over, come on, get back to your weekend." Getting the message, Cassie ushered Tina and Daryl away leaving Nate and Evie. He walked over to her and held her close. "I'm so sorry," he said, "I'm so very sorry."

Hugging Evie, he asked if she was OK.

"I'm OK, Nate, what about you?"

He looked at her and said, "I'm still starving shall we go and get some coffee and toast?" He kissed her nose and smiled, she smiled back. Nate's phone rang it was Cassie. "Hmm?" he said, answering. Cassie was screaming at him down the phone, she was hysterical. "Cassie, Cassie!" he said firmly. "Slow down I can't understand a word you saying."

"It's Max," she sobbed, "I can't wake him."

Nate ran into the hotel followed by Evie. "Call 911, get an ambulance here, hurry," she called out as she followed Nate up the stairs too impatient to wait for the lift. Nate took the stairs two at a time to the third floor. Max's door was open and Cassie was running in and out of the door.

"Nate!" she screamed at him, "hurry!" Nate disappeared into the room; Evie had had trouble keeping up with him. When she got through the door she was gasping for breath. Nate was trying to resuscitate Max.

Evie looked at Cassie and went to her. "What happened?" she said, putting her arm around Cassie.

"I came in to tell him what had happened, I thought he was asleep when I left earlier!" she was sobbing.

Evie let go of her as Tina came in and took her place. "Get her out of here, Tina and get Daryl to wait for the paramedics," she said. Tina nodded and started to lead Cassie away. Nate was still giving Max mouth-to-mouth and pumping at his heart.

Evie got hold of Max's arm. "Nate," she said, "Nate!" she said louder, "there is no pulse." Nate shook his head. "No, he's going to be OK, where are the paramedics?" he said. She knew he would not stop trying to save his friend.

What seemed like an eternity later two paramedics came running in. "OK, Mr Rivers, we can take it from here," said the male paramedic while the female paramedic was checking for vital signs. "How long has he been unresponsive Mr Rivers? Mr Rivers." The paramedic said more firmly.

"Er, I don't know I've been here what, ten minutes?" he said, looking at Evie for confirmation.

"Yes, about ten minutes, he was discovered about five minutes before that," Evie said.

"OK, stand aside," the male paramedic said. The crew doctor, Adam, came running in reeling off possible problems as the paramedics listened.

"OK, stand back everyone, let's shock him. Ready, clear." Max's body twitched but nothing happened. "Again, clear!"

"No pulse he is still unresponsive." The female looked at her partner and said, "Rick he's been down too long. He's gone."

Nate looked at them and said, "You can't stop."

Evie went to him, "Nate," she said, "come here." She put her arms around him to hold him as he cried. He pulled away from Evie and went to the window running his hands through his hair. He looked out, it was a beautiful day, and it had started so perfectly back in his bedroom this morning with Evie. Then there had been Sarah, now Max what else could go wrong he wondered.

Turning his back to the window he slid down to the floor with his back against the wall, head in his hands. Evie went to him and knelt in front of him, she put her arms around him as he sobbed.

The paramedics were clearing up and had signalled dispatch to send the coroner. Someone had covered Max with the bed sheet and the crew doctor, Adam, was talking quietly with the paramedics.

Tina was standing at the door wide-eyed, she covered her mouth with her hands as if trying to hold in a sound then said, "Oh no!" Cassie followed her in.

Cassie went over to the bed and stood looking at the sheet that covered her Maxy. Nate got up and went to her. "We were too late, we should have seen this sooner. We were too late. We failed him," she said with emotion.

Nate hugged her. "I'm so sorry, Cassie, I'm so sorry," he said, as they both cried. Evie went to Tina and they hugged, both were crying as well. She knew Nate would blame himself for this.

The paramedics waited around until the coroner came to take Max's body away. They had told Nate that there would be an autopsy to find the exact cause of death, although the suspicion was he had either had a massive stroke causing heart failure or his heart had just given up on its own. Nate followed Max's gurney out of the hotel to the unmarked van. The coroner reassured Nate that the news would not get out until he had made a statement to the press and notified the family.

"How long before I can take him home?" Nate asked.

"It will be a few days, Mr Rivers, we will let you know but I can tell you high profile cases usually get priority." He shook Nate's hand and he watched the van drive away. First Sarah, now Max.

The crew had gathered in the bar and there were many tears. Evie came over to Nate as he walked in and said, "You need to say something." He nodded.

"It looks like it was probably a heart attack," Nate started. "I know everyone was very fond of Max and this just breaks my heart," his voice started to crack and Evie went to him and held his hand. Looking at her he continued, "Please keep this to yourselves for now, I need to notify his brother and I need to contact the London office who will release a press statement. That's all for now, look after each other." He looked back at Evie and said, "Where is Cassie?"

"The doctor gave her a Valium and she's gone to lie down, Tina is staying with her." He nodded his head and squeezed her hand.

"I need to phone his brother." He left her and went into the office, shutting the door behind him.

***

Sarah said nothing on the way back to her hotel. She waited for Gus to open the door for her; she didn't acknowledge him as she disappeared inside. Piece of work that one, Gus thought, glad to get rid of her out of the car. She headed straight up to her room and flung herself on the bed and cried hysterically. How could this have happened? She would never willingly give him a divorce; she would make his life hell. She would take him for everything; she would make access to the kids difficult. Maybe she could shame him into coming back to her. It was all that slut's fault. She opened the minibar and drank.

Gus drove back to the hotel thinking that the day couldn't get any worse as he passed the black van leaving the hotel. Nate and the hotel manager had been standing watching it drive off. By the time Gus had parked he just caught the tail end of Nate's words to the crew. Nate didn't even see him as he walked straight past him to get to the office.

"Evie," Gus said, "what's going on?" As Evie told him, Gus's eyes started to well up with tears. She hugged him and then left him to go check on Cassie.

***

Frank had been watching the whole episode outside. He used his binoculars to get a closer look at the woman that had appeared earlier and was now being driven away by the fat black driver. Interesting, he thought. He wasn't sure whose body had been on the gurney but he knew it wasn't Evie, it was too big. He would catch the pot wash, Alex, as he left later and find out what had happened. It's all kicking off today, he rubbed his hands with joy. The best was yet to come.

***

Evie joined Nate in the office; she brought a plate of sandwiches and a pot of coffee. "You haven't eaten all day," she said, pouring him a coffee.

"I just don't have an appetite anymore."

"You have to eat, Nate," she put the plate in front of him and he suddenly realised just how hungry he was.

"Thanks," he said, picking up a sandwich.

"How did it go with his brother?"

"He was gutted, they hadn't been in touch for a while, it makes you realise life is too short to be unhappy." He put the sandwich down pushing his chair back he motioned her to sit on his knee. "I love you so much, Evie, the thought of losing you, I just don't know what I would do."

"Hey, I'm not going anywhere," she said, stroking his hair. "I love you. We will get through this I promise." She kissed him.

"How is it out there?" he asked, raising his eyes towards the door.

"Pretty sombre. Most have either gone into town or up to their rooms. What are we going to do about next week? Are we still interviewing?"

Nate thought about this and let out a big sigh. "No, we need to postpone, I will get the London office to deal with it. We will take a two-week production break under the circumstances. I need to get Max back to the UK, and we need to bury him. The coroner's office confirmed he would be ready to leave by the end of next week if natural causes are sited on his autopsy, which we know they will." Evie nodded.

"OK, so what happens? Does the whole crew take two weeks?" she asked.

"Yeah, everyone has two weeks to go home or do whatever. They can stay here if they want, it's totally up to them. I suspect most will go home and catch up with family, some will want to attend Max's funeral." He looked down and shook his head. "I just can't believe he's gone," he mumbled. Evie's heart turned over, she didn't know how to comfort him. What was she to do now? She couldn't go home, as she had heard nothing from Dom except that he had nothing. She would have to stay here until Nate got back.

They made the calls they needed to organise the next couple of days and emailed and messaged the crew. It would be public knowledge back in the UK as from the following morning. "I guess we better book our tickets as well, we should go on the same plane as Max," he said.

She made her decision then and there. Screw it, she was going home with Nate. No one knew she was with him so she could keep a low profile and she needed to say goodbye to Max. She wanted to be with Nate at Max's funeral. "OK," she said, "as soon as we know when he is being released I will book Cassie and our tickets."

"And Gus's," Nate added.

He didn't know what he would have done without Evie. She was his strength when he had lost his. He thought about Sarah and the horrible names she had called her. Then he suddenly thought. "Shit, Sarah! I need to let her know." He tried phoning her mobile but it was switched off. Surely she couldn't have got a flight back already. "Shit," he said, ringing off and dialling another number. "Hello Mum," he listened and said, "Mum I've got some bad news," and he told her of this morning's episode. "Mum, there is something else as well, I've left Sarah. There is someone else." He closed his eyes and almost chuckled, "No Mum, there is someone else for me." He knew his mum would be in disbelief but he also knew she would support him no matter what. "Yes Mum, very much, you will like her. I'm sorry to give you all this in one call but I need you to be ready for anything that happens next in the tabloids." Asking her to let the rest of his family know what was happening he then hung up and, looking at Evie, he said, "One more call." He called Sarah's dad. He simply said he couldn't get hold of Sarah, explaining what had happened to Max he asked him to let the kids know before they saw something about it in the papers or on TV.

"I think I want to go upstairs now, will you join me?" She didn't need to answer as they went to the lift.

Lying on the bed holding each other they had both cried as they talked about Max. Emotionally shattered they fell asleep.

Waking to the pain of hunger, Evie ordered room service for them. They turned the TV on as a distraction. Watching CNN slate Trump, they ate in silence. Neither of them really enjoying the food, finding it hard to swallow. Evie called down to the bar and asked for a bottle of red to be sent up. "We should drink to Max," she said.

He laughed and replied with humour, "Evie you will drink to anything." They both laughed. Nate sighed, it felt good to laugh but it felt wrong under the circumstances. The wine arrived and they raised a glass to their friend.

Nate suddenly had a realisation. "Oh shit, Evie, what happens about you going back home?" Evie shrugged. "I thought about it earlier, no one knows I'm here with you so as long as I keep my head out of the limelight I don't see why it won't be OK."

Nate thought about this realising as soon as word got out about Sarah and him all eyes would be on Evie. "We need to let your detective know our plans. I can hire security as well."

Evie kissed him. "Stop worrying it's all going to be fine. I promise."

He kissed her back as he started to take her clothes off. He needed her, he found comfort holding her body next to his as they made love, ending the day in each other's arms, and he held her tight and didn't let go.

14

Sunday

It was Sunday morning and they had no reason to get up. They wouldn't hear anything about Max until tomorrow at the earliest. Nate had woken and looked at Evie. She smiled and he smiled back, a brief glorious moment before it hit him and he remembered yesterday and it all came crashing down on him. Evie held him tight. "We need to check on Cassie," she said, worried about her.

"Yeah we do." Nate sighed as he made to get up.

"We should go for a walk around the lake," he suggested. "Get some fresh air, it will do us some good." Evie thought it was a great idea. They got dressed taking it in turns to use the bathroom. He stopped her as she came out and pulled her close, holding her, he tucked her hair behind her ear and kissed her. "I love you," he told her. She would never get bored of hearing him say those words to her.

"I love you," she said, stroking his face.

"Come on let's go and see how everyone is," he said, grabbing the room key.

Down in the lobby Nate looked over to the reception desk and said good morning. He remembered yesterday morning when he had seen Sarah; he shivered and shook the memory off.

Evie smiled towards the desk and Leanne smiled back. "Ooh," she said, suddenly remembering, "you had a delivery Miss Grey it's on your desk."

Evie looked at Nate and shrugged, "Thanks," she said, heading to the office.

Nate was standing waiting for her when he saw her backing out of the office very slowly. "Evie?" she didn't respond. "Evie what is it?" he said, making towards her. She turned her head and looked at him, her eyes were wide and her face had lost all colour. Leanne stood up looking concerned. Nate reached Evie and took hold of her as she started to lose her legs. He ended up helping her to the floor instead. He stroked her hair and got up to go into the office.

On her desk lay a single black tulip.

He felt like that moment in a movie when the character goes small and the camera pans out. "Oh my God," he said, turning out of the office and heading back towards Evie. Gus came out of the lift and looked confused at the scene in front of him. "Gus! Stay with Evie, Leanne who delivered the tulip?" he asked, back at the desk. He was so agitated, his hands were shaking and Leanne was stepping back from him looking really concerned. She had seen more action in this lobby in the last two days than in her entire time working at the hotel.

"It was Sid," she said, shrugging, "He works at the florists in town, he said it was a weird request but the instructions said to make sure it went on her work desk." Leanne was hoping she wasn't in trouble; after all it was her who took it and placed it on the desk.

Nate's world was spinning out of control, he looked back and Evie was just sitting on the floor head in her hands with Gus crouched down beside her rubbing her back as if she was sick.

"Leanne, get the florist on the phone," Nate said, not sure what to do.

"I can't, it's Sunday they will be closed," she said, helplessly.

"Gus, take Evie up to my room and stay with her," he said, taking his key out of his pocket and handing it to Gus. Gus nodded and scooped Evie up in his arms like a child and headed to the lift.

"Wait!" he shouted before the doors of the lift shut, he went to Evie who was still in Gus's arms. "Where's your phone darling," he said softly to her. Gus put her down as she started to move and she took her phone out of her back pocket. "Stay in the room, stay with Gus." She nodded; she still hadn't said a word. The doors started to shut and Nate stepped out.

"Should I call the police?" Leanne asked.

"Not yet, I need to make a call," he said, heading into the office. He looked at Evie's phone, her contact list consisted of him, Tina, Cassie, Max, Daryl, Baxter and The Detective. Nate felt his heart turn when he saw his name had a heart next to it. He checked the time in the UK; he called Dom who he assumed was The Detective. Shit! He suddenly remembered Dom and Max had been school friends. He hoped Max's brother had called him.

"Evie?" Dom said with concern as he answered his phone. Nate was quiet on the other end not really knowing where to start.

"No, it's er, Nate, Nate Rivers," he said.

"Mr Rivers? Why are you on Evie's phone? Is she OK?"

"Yeah, I mean no, I mean she's safe, she's in my room with Gus."

Having no idea who Gus was and in total confusion as to why the chef Nate Rivers was calling him he said, "With all due respect, Mr Rivers, what the fuck is going on?"

Nate inhaled. "He's here."

"Who?"

"The Black Tulip, he's found her, he had one delivered this morning."

"You know about the Black Tulips?"

"Yes, Evie told me, no one else knows so it has to be him because I know it's not me, he must have found out she was here somehow." He felt like he was rambling.

Dom tried to get his thoughts together. "OK, so let me get this straight, Evie has told you what is going on and no one else knows?"

"Yes."

"And she told you why?"

"She loves me."

"She loves you?"

"Yes, and I love her and we are together now, it's a long story, well it's actually not but whatever, we are together that's the point, I mean she told me before we got together but…"

"Mr Rivers," Dom cut in.

"Nate," Nate replied.

"Nate, slow down, have you called the police?"

"Not yet, I thought I would call you first."

"OK, good, don't call the police. If you call them she will have to explain everything and she will be stuck over there. Let me think," he said, scratching his head. "OK, can you get her back to the UK?"

"Yes I can, we were coming back next week anyway, she was going to let you know."

"Why were you coming back without talking to me first?"

Nate felt awful, Dom didn't know about his best friend and neither Evie nor he had even thought to call him.

"Dom," he said, taking a softer tone. "It's been a rough couple of days here, I'm sorry, I should have phoned you yesterday."

"Yesterday? Mr… I mean Nate, you're not making any sense whatsoever!"

"It's Max. They think he had a heart attack. He died yesterday morning."

The phone went quiet at the other end. Dom cleared his throat and said, "Get the both of you booked on the next flight. Don't take luggage just get yourselves out of there, discreetly if possible. Text me your flight details and I will have an escort meet you."

Nate was nodding his head trying to take it all in. "OK, there will be three of us though. I'm bringing my security," he said, deciding to give Gus a new title.

"Fine. Stay in touch and look after Evie."

"I will of course." Nate rang off. He searched flights and found one for that evening. He booked three tickets first class. He packed up his and Evie's laptops along with Max's. He went out to reception where the hotel manager was waiting for him. Nate told him there was nothing to worry about and it had been a misunderstanding. Remembering someone on the staff there was a snitch, and for all he knew the Black Tulip could have been the guy in the car talking to Alex. He needed Gus with him. He knew what he looked like.

Nate went up to Cassie's room and knocked on the door. He put the three laptops down on the table. "I'm going to leave these with you for now. I have to take Evie back to the UK but no one can know."

"Is this to do with her stalker?" Seeing the surprise on Nate's face she said, "Max told me, only that she had a stalker, what's happened?"

Nate filled her in very briefly, if Max trusted her then so would he. "I need you to stay here and bring Max home. I'm sorry I won't be here for you."

Cassie smiled. "Nate, look after her, hang on a second," she went to a handbag and picked out a set of keys. "These are my house keys, I will let my housekeeper, Molly, know that you are coming and to get the place ready for you. You are more than welcome to stay as long as you need." Nate hugged her and took the keys.

"Thank you, Cassie. Thank you." He let go of her hand and went up to find Evie.

***

Dom was still reeling from the call with Nate. Max was dead? He just couldn't get his head around it. His oldest friend was dead. He stood up. "Shit," he said out loud. "Shit shit shit!" He kicked his filing cabinet in frustration, not satisfied, he grabbed it and pulled it from the wall sending it crashing to the ground. He kicked it again for good measure. Frustration out, he needed to concentrate on Evie. How had the bastard found her? There would be a time to mourn his old friend but today he had to concentrate on the living. He grabbed his coat and walked out of his office, slamming the door so hard the glass rattled. As he walked past his assistant's desk, who was staring at him having seen his display of vandalism. "Jeannie," he said, as he walked past her desk, "my filing cabinet is broken, I need a new one." With that he left.

Dom called the task force together for a briefing. He filled them in and assigned a car and two of his most trusted men to go to the airport to meet them. "I want them met off the plane and escorted here," he said, pointing to the desk. "As soon as I know the flight details I will let you know. We need to get the safe house ready. I want every plane's passenger list that landed in the last two weeks in New York. Check everyone!"

"But, Sir, that will take ages," one of the uniforms said.

"Well you better get on with it!" Dom yelled. After giving his orders he went to see his superintendent to brief him.

"I just can't figure out, Sir, how he found her."

"No, it's worrying, Dom, but now this celebrity, Rivers, is involved we can consider this the potential for a high-profile scandal," Superintendent Myers said. "If you need more men let me know."

"Yes Sir, thanks, Sir." Dom left to help with the flight manifests.

***

When Nate got to the room he knocked and said, "It's me." Gus let him in.

Evie was sitting on the bed hugging her knees. "She hasn't said anything, Boss."

"Thanks Gus," he said, going to the bed and sitting down. "Evie," he said, as she looked at him. Her eyes were wide and she looked like she hadn't slept for days. She looked at him as he touched her face. "I've spoken to Dom he is going to meet us at the airport, I've booked a flight for you Gus and me." He looked over his shoulder at Gus and said, "I hope that is all right but I'd like you with us?" Gus nodded. Nate looked back at Evie and continued. "A flight back to the UK this evening. We will only take hand luggage so just pack the essentials OK?" She nodded. "Gus, we need to organise a ride to the airport without anyone knowing. How are we going to do that?"

Gus looked wistful, "If we take the minibus it will be less obvious. We could all hide out in the back and get Gary to drive us. He takes the van out weekly so if we are being watched he will probably be ignored."

"OK great, remind me again, who's Gary?"

"Boss, the sound tech dude, you know that."

"Yes, sorry, you're right, there is just so much going on in my head." Evie got up.

"I'm sorry," she said.

"Hey, you don't ever have to say that to me. Ever. I'm just so glad I didn't go home and you were all alone when this happened. I'm going to fill Gus in on what's been going on OK?" She nodded. Nate briefed Gus and Gus filled Evie in on his investigations with Alex while Nate threw a few things in a small carry-on bag. "Gus, if you want to go pack and talk to Gary I will take Evie to get her stuff." He handed his bag to Gus and they all left the room.

Gus packed what he wanted in minutes. He took his and Nate's bags and gave them to Gary when he found him. He told Gary that Nate was worried Sarah may leak his affair to the press so they needed to go and stay somewhere else for a while.

Gary loved the idea of being involved in a paparazzi screw. "Awesome, dude," was all he said, and he fist-bumped Gus. Gus was quite proud of his quick thinking but he hated it when white guys fist-bumped him. It's a brother thing. Having received his instructions, Gary took the bags to the minibus and threw them in the back. He then drove it round the back and parked it in front of the staff exit. If no one was around it would be a clear run for them to climb in the van without being seen.

Evie threw a few things in the small bag she'd arrived with. It had seemed like such a long time ago, almost a lifetime, so much had happened it seemed impossible it was only a couple of weeks. Nate was looking out of the window as if he was keeping watch. She went to him and said, "I'm ready." She smiled and he hugged her close. "Do you know we have only known each other for two weeks?" she said.

He looked thoughtful. "Wow, I feel like it's been forever," realising he had turned his life upside down in that short time.

"I know I feel like I've always known you, it's as if, it will sound stupid, but it's as if we've met before, maybe in another life."

He looked at her and smiled. "Maybe," he said, kissing her nose. "Maybe we weren't humans, maybe we were cows."

She laughed at him. "You would have been a bull, I'm the cow." He smiled at her again, he was relieved that she seemed to be coming out of her previous state of shock.

"I know how lucky I am to have you, Nate."

He squeezed her hand and said, "Come on we will be safer in the VIP lounge of the airport than here."

She looked at him wide eyed, "You mean I'm actually going to fly first class?"

"Yup, but don't get too excited it's not as great as they make out. It's the leg room that wins out for me, come on let's get out of here," he said, as he picked her bag up in one hand and he took hold of hers with his other.

Downstairs Nate gave the bag to Gary and then both he and Evie went into the bar. "One for the road?" she said, surprised he had gone into the bar.

"No, Cassie is in the corner," he said, nodding his head in that direction.

They went over to her and she said very quietly to them, "Stay safe, if you get the chance to text me, let me know you're OK." Cassie was trying not to cry.

Evie touched her arm and said, "Will you be OK?"

Cassie was overwhelmed with the events of the past day but she reassured Evie not to worry. "Once we are gone can you speak to Daryl and Tina for me?" Evie asked feeling bad that she had not said goodbye to her new friends. Cassie again reassured her and they headed out towards the back staff entrance.

Gus appeared and signalled them to come. They got in the van and the three of them stayed low. Gus struggled to get in the footwell due to his size, opting to lie across the seats instead. "I gotta lose some weight," he muttered to no one.

Gary jumped in and started the engine. Driving down the driveway of the hotel Gus asked if Gary could see a Buick parked at the end, he couldn't, Gus had to refrain from looking himself. "Drive to the end of town and stop there. Are you sure we are not being followed?" The plan was Gary would stop, Gus would take over driving and Gary would walk back to the hotel.

"Chill, man, it's cool," he said, stopping. Before he got out he said, "Take it easy, you guys, later." And he jumped out heading back the way he came on foot.

Gus sat up and headed to the driver seat. "Might as well stay where you are for another five minutes, let me just check I ain't being followed." Obeying Gus they waited until he said the coast was clear and they sat up at last.

"We should land around 5.30am," Nate said, once they were settled in the VIP lounge. There were not many people in the lounge and the flight was not full. Nate tried Sarah again but her phone still seemed to be switched off. "Well I've tried to let her know about Max." He sighed, what a whirlwind the last couple of weeks had been. He realised why Max had been so concerned about him, he barely knew Evie yet he had left his wife and had become a non-meat eater. It was insane. He chuckled as he thought of Baxter, 'it's fucking insane, man,' he had said and he was right. "I knew, you know."

"Knew what?" Evie asked.

"The first time I saw you standing in the lobby. I knew something was different, I just had a feeling life was going to change I guess I didn't realise how quickly it could all happen."

"Any regrets?" she asked worriedly.

"God no!" He squeezed her hand. "I have no doubt in my mind that we are meant to be together."

She was relieved. "I don't want to go back to that safe house, it was horrible."

Nate looked at her, "We can stay at Cassie's, she has a secluded house in Ockham, and it's only half an hour from my house and no one will expect us to be there. Dom can always leave his men with us." She liked that idea. "If this Black Tulip guy has found you in the States, the probability is that he has followed you out there, he won't know for a while that you've come home." Nate knew he was speculating but it made sense. Leanne had told him an envelope of cash with instruction had been put through the florist's door just like in the UK. "We are a step ahead of him, Evie, we can get to Cassie's and stay hidden as long as we need to." He reassured her.

"I just want this to be over." She leant her head on his shoulder and they waited.

Gus had been sitting at the bar. It was his first time in first class and he was going to make sure he made the most of it. It wasn't long before they boarded and Evie was taken aback by the space in the cabin. "Wow," she said. Nate smiled at her and looked at Gus.

"I can actually fit in these seats," Gus chuckled, deciding he could get used to this style of travel.

15

Monday

As it was a night flight the cabin crew fed them and dimmed the lights. Reclining back in the spacious comfy chair, Evie closed her eyes and slept. When Nate woke her to tell her they were landing she was surprised that she had slept the whole journey. "Stress can do that," Nate commented having barely slept a wink, choosing to channel hop instead. Gus had slept and freshened himself up with the complimentary wash kit he was given and thoroughly enjoyed pampering himself in the spacious bathroom. Having done the same, Evie felt better for cleaning her teeth and brushing her hair. "You look lovely," Nate said, as she sat back down.

After the plane had taxied and stopped, the captain came out and introduced himself to Nate. "Mr Rivers, Sir, it's a pleasure to fly you and your guests today, I have had instructions from the tower that the three of you are to remain on the plane until the rest of first class has disembarked."

"Thanks," said Nate, "and thanks for a smooth journey." He shook the pilot's hand with gratitude.

They didn't have to wait very long until the cabin was emptied of people and two ununiformed police officers arrived. They introduced themselves as Brodie and Harris. "Welcome home Mr Rivers we will be escorting you to the station to meet up and be briefed by Detective Anderson." Nate looked at Evie and shrugged.

"Dom Anderson," she said to him.

"Oh, OK great," Nate was eager to get off the plane.

"Follow us," said the younger of the two policemen who had introduced himself as Brodie.

It was a squeeze in the back of the unmarked Audi, in fairness they had not known that Gus was as big as he was. Arriving at the underground car park of Scotland Yard they were all keen to stretch their legs. Leaving their bags in the boot they headed upstairs to the task-force room. As they looked around the room there were photos and information all over the boards telling the story they knew so far of the guy now known as The Black Tulip. There were pictures of another girl who had similar features to Evie. "Who is that?" she asked, pointing at the pretty young girl.

"That's Carrie Jones the only other victim we have been able to find so far," said Eddie, a young officer assigned to the task force.

"Evie!" Evie turned around as she heard her name and saw Dom heading into the room. She went to him and they hugged.

"Detective," she said, he chuckled at her insistence of referring to him as the detective.

"You look well, was your journey OK?" he said, as he shook Nate and Gus's hands.

"Fine thanks, I slept through most of it."

Nate looked at Dom, he still felt guilty that he had been the last to know about Max. "I'm so sorry about Max," Nate said to him.

Dom waved his hand away and replied, "There will be time for all that later, let's concentrate on getting you guys sorted out."

Having filled Dom in on Gus's roll, Dom asked him if he could work with a sketch artist. Gus was thrilled he could be of help. "OK, I will have one sent to the safe house, let's get you guys settled in."

"Actually," Nate cut in, "we are going to stay in Ockham at a friends house. There is no way this creep can know we are there and chances are he is still in the States."

"We are monitoring all flights back to the UK now," Dom replied. "But it would be safer all round if you stay at the safe house."

Evie cut in, "But can't your men stay with us anyway? The place we want to stay has security cameras, it's secluded and very private. No one would be able to creep up unannounced." She was pleading with her eyes and Dom relented.

"I tell you what, we go and check it out and if I'm not satisfied we are going straight to the safe house, OK?" They all agreed.

Evie and Nate went with Dom while Gus chose to ride in the back with Brodie and Harris. "You guys got guns?" Gus asked.

"Yes Sir, we are the firearms unit," Brodie replied. Harris was driving following his guv'nor in front.

"You had to use it before?" Gus continued, Harris laughed.

"You really security Gus?" he asked.

"No Sir, I'm the driver, but I want to help protect Nate and Evie," he said so sincerely that the two men in the front looked at each other and smiled.

"We don't use them unless it's last resort," Brodie said. "But don't worry if we need to use them to protect your people we will not hesitate." This reassured Gus, he knew he was prepared to do anything he had to do to help but he also knew that he was a large overweight hulk of a man that couldn't move fast if his life depended on it. He was going to ask Evie to help him with his eating habits. He didn't want to end up like Max and he quite fancied the idea of a new role as security to Nate Rivers.

In the car in front, Nate and Evie were filling Dom in on the events that led them to where they currently were. "He must be back in New Jersey surely?" Nate said, "I mean if cash was dropped off at the florist?"

Dom had been thinking about this also. "Unless he has an accomplice," he said flatly. This was something that had not been considered as it seemed such a one-on-one crime but it was a possibility.

"But it's not about gaining anything other than terrorising people. It doesn't make sense that two people are involved," Evie added.

Dom was also doubtful but said, "It's a possibility that needs looking into but I think you're right, it's doubtful. Hopefully Gus can provide a decent sketch of the perp that we can get out and check the database."

"That's assuming the guy in the Buick was him and not something to do with sabotaging me," Nate added.

"We can't hide forever," Evie said, as they pulled up to the drive leading to the house.

"Wow," Evie said, sitting forward, looking ahead. The black gates were open for them and there was a long drive down to the house named Harringdon Manor. It was a mansion. It was nestled among trees and there were various outbuildings. Having lived in London most of her life, Evie was completely taken aback by the sheer size of it. "What on earth does she need a house this size for?" she said to no one.

Nate laughed, "It was husband number four, he was a director and producer and a security freak. Cassie said she didn't see the point of selling it after he died, as she didn't need the capital. She has a live-in housekeeper who has an annex to herself. Pretty awesome, huh?"

Evie was still in awe as they pulled up and stopped outside the entrance.

The driveway ended in a roundabout with a water fountain in the middle. "This is like the outside of the house Tommy Shelby owned in *Peaky Blinders*," Gus said, eyes wide and excited.

"Peaky what?" Dom said, looking confused.

A tall well-dressed woman appeared at the front door. "Hello, it's a pleasure to meet you all. I'm Molly and I'm the housekeeper here."

Nate went over to Molly and said, "Thanks, Molly, it's lovely to meet you, can you show the detectives the security measures please, they need to know we are safe here."

"Oh, you are most certainly that if it's the outside world you are hiding from. If you would all like to follow me I will show you round." Obligingly they all followed. Walking through the hall there was a grand staircase sweeping up in a curve that led up to the second floor. The kitchen was bigger than Evie's entire flat. There was an island in the middle with tall chairs around it. On one side of the room was a comfy area with two sofas and a TV the size of a double bed on the wall. Leading out of the kitchen was a seated area in the garden overlooking the well-kept grounds.

"The other side of downstairs is a large entertainment room that leads to the outdoors, and then to the indoor, pools and bar area. I have stocked food and wine, Cassie was very insistent on that and I believe I have met your eating requirements, however, I have left the details here on the table for online shopping. If you come through to this room I can show you the security." Molly was very professional and Evie wondered if she ever got drunk.

"Through here you can see from the screens that all aspects of security are taken care of. I have shut the gates now you have arrived and any visitors will need to buzz in and be passed before they open."

Looking around the room at the TV monitors Dom was impressed.

"This is brilliant, I'm assuming the windows and doors are all securely alarmed?"

"Oh yes, Sir, this is one of the safest houses in the country. It was owned previously by a foreign diplomat for his stays here. Unfortunately, he was assassinated in the Middle East hence it is now in the ownership of my current employer." Walking out of the room she continued, "Everything you need to know security-wise is in there. Upstairs are eight guest suites, which are all ready for use. The only door shut upstairs is the master bedroom which is Cassie's rooms and off limits. She said you could use her study, which is the other door over here if you needed it. I am available twenty-four hours; just pick up the intercom and press 1. Please feel free to let me know if there is anything I can do to help. So you know, the gardeners come on Tuesday and Thursday and the pool man is due next week. They will all need to be buzzed in or turned away as you require."

"Thank you, Molly," Evie said. Molly dipped her head and left. Gus had never met a housekeeper before and was in total awe.

Everyone looked at each other. OK, where to start," Dom said, scratching his head. "Brodie, Harris, check out the security room and do perimeter checks of the house. I want the pair of you to stay here for now. I'm going back to the office so work out how to let me out, I will get a uniform to bring the sketch artist over to work with Gus." With that Dom said his goodbyes and left.

"Let's go and get settled in," Nate suggested, grabbing his and Evie's bag. "Come on, Gus I've got a feeling you will enjoy the size of these beds," Nate joked as they headed upstairs. They checked out the rooms, Gus settled for one overlooking the front of the house while Evie and Nate opted for one at the back with a balcony overlooking the pool.

"I could get used to this." She smiled leaning out over the balcony, "Is your house like this?" she questioned.

"Hmm," he said, not really wanting to disappoint her, "you could probably fit my house in here three times."

"So, it's still pretty big then," she laughed. "What are you going to do about Sarah and the kids? You better let them know you're home."

"I doubt Sarah will let me see them unless I go over and I'm not sure how wise moving about would be at the moment," he replied, genuinely not sure how to deal with the situation. "I will try calling Sarah again after we've showered and had something decent to eat," he said, going over to her, he tucked her hair behind her ear and kissed her.

***

"But I don't understand, Cassie," Tina was struggling. "So, Evie, Nate and Gus have gone home but no one knows?"

"Exactly." Cassie shook her head, "She didn't want to go without seeing you but she had to for her safety."

Daryl was taking it in. "Are they coming back?" he asked.

"I don't know anything other than I am waiting for Max to be released and I will be flying him home, you guys can stay here and chill or go home until we know more." Cassie was so tired. She just wanted to go home and lay Max to rest. "The official line is a two-week production break for Max's funeral but that might change depending on the situation." Cassie wanted to lie down. "I need to rest, can you keep the gossip to yourselves, though, please?"

Daryl and Tina assured her they would and Cassie disappeared to lie down.

"Holy shit," Daryl said, "she kept all that quiet."

"No wonder she always avoided talking about herself," she said, getting her phone out to text Evie.

Frank had resumed his position at the end of the drive and caught Alex on his way to work. Ever hopeful, Alex went over to him licking his lips thinking big bucks were coming his way. "What's going on down there?" Frank asked.

"I want more money for any more information," Alex said, feeling in a position of power.

"I tell you what, Alex, you tell me what is going on in there and I won't pay that ugly little slut of a wife of yours a visit, by the way your kid is ugly as well."

Alex just stared at him.

"You fucking piece of shit," Frank said, and spat out of his car window. Scribbling his burner cell number on a scrap of paper he said, "Call me as soon as, punk."

Alex took the number and watched him drive off. Alex knew there was only one thing he could do and that was to give the creep what he wanted.

Inside, the hotel was bustling with news of the production break due to the untimely death of Max. It appeared that a lot of the crew had decided to go home or tour round a bit to see the country. Alex knew he needed to find something out and quick. He went to the reception desk and found Leanne. "Hey darl," he said, "does the lord and master need his usual vegan meals tonight? Chef is asking," he lied.

"No thanks, Alex, they have gone to stay somewhere else for a while, something to do with hiding from the press. Not sure if they will be back until after the funeral in the UK." Alex nodded and walked back through the kitchen and out the back to make the call to the creep.

"Interesting," Frank, said. "So where are they staying?"

"I don't know that but I know the fat dead guy is being flown back to the UK at the end of the week for the funeral that Rivers will be attending. That's all I got now leave my family and me alone." He hung up. Frank was furious, no one hung up on him, if he had the luxury of time he would have dealt with his ugly slut of a wife, but he had a bigger agenda.

***

"I've got a text from Tina," Evie said, as she sat up at the kitchen island drinking coffee and eating a sandwich.

"So what is this?" Gus asked turning his nose up.

Evie laughed, "Oh Gus, if you want to be healthy you have to start to love all those things on your plate."

Nate laughed as Gus pushed the salad he had made him around his plate. "What does she say?" Nate asked.

"She's checking we are OK, she says Cassie is coping but looks awful, she's asking about the funeral and that her and Daryl would like to come, apparently a few have booked to come home and pay their respects."

"That's good to hear, I'm glad. Tell Tina to ask Cassie to book her and Daryl seats back with her, I will feel happier knowing she's not flying home alone."

Evie looked at him and smiled, "You're always so considerate, Nate."

Gus looked up wide eyed. "You wanna tell my stomach that?" he said, with a piece of avocado on his fork. Nate and Evie fell about laughing.

Nate went into the security room and took two plates of sandwiches, "You guys are welcome to help yourselves to anything, you know that, right?"

Brodie and Harris both thanked him and he left. "He's all right, you know," Brodie said.

"My wife seems to think so," Harris said, making Brodie choke on his bread. "I asked her if she had heard of the guy and she went all gushy fanning herself with her hand! 'He's so dreamy'," he said, imitating his wife. Brodie laughed out loud and spat what remained of his mouthful out.

"He's a good-looking guy I will give him that and his girlfriend isn't half bad either."

"Do you think his wife knows?" Harris said.

"Well if she doesn't I guess it won't be long, with everything that is going on. That's their problem ours is to keep them safe."

Harris agreed and continued eating his sandwich and wondering if he should grow some stubble.

Nate went outside through the kitchen doors and tried Sarah again. She picked up. "Jesus Sarah, you couldn't call me back?"

"What do you want, Nathanial?"

"Are you home? Have you spoken to your dad?" he asked.

"Yes, and yes. I'm sorry about Max, that's shit. Are you coming home?"

"I'm in the UK now but I'm not coming home. I'm staying at a friend's."

"You're with her?"

"Yes, but it's complicated."

"No it's not, you have chosen to be with her over your family."

"No, that's not true, I want to see the kids."

"Then you will have to come here."

"I can't at the moment but I will soon I promise."

"What's going on with you? What was with that interview on the Stanley Morgan Show?" Shit, he had forgotten all about that.

"It's a long story, which I will explain, please give me a few days and I will come over. Just don't tell anyone I'm back for now, it's important, Sarah."

"Whatever, Nate." She hung up.

Nate rubbed his head. He called his head office in London. They had organised a press release for Max and so far there had been no mention of a backlash from the Morgan Stanley Show, even though there had been some chatter on his social media. Nate asked to be kept posted on any developments. He went back inside and said to Evie "Have you checked my social media? I wondered what was being said about the chat show."

"Shit, I forgot," Evie was cross with herself and went up to their room to find the work phone. "Oh, I'm so crap it's not even charged," she said, heading back into the kitchen and plugging it in. "Let me look at your phone," she said, and Nate handed it over.

He had his social media loaded on his phone but he wasn't great at checking it.

"OK, so yeah, Twitter, Morgan's people have tweeted a link with a bit of your interview, they have started a poll, those for plant-based food and those against. Hmm, it's 60/40 against plant-based at the moment, that's a good percentage for Americans, I mean I'm assuming this is just… ah, no wait, yeah it's all over Twitter being debated."

"Good or bad?" he asked feeling a little sick.

"Well, it's out there now so let people do their thing. You let HQ know the situation so they are prepared for anything and I will Tweet some positive things about plant-based eating, it will be fine, Nate, besides if it blows up in our faces we can buy a desert island, fill it with animals and live happily ever after,"

He looked at her. "It really is that simple for you isn't it?"

She went to him and put her arms around his neck. "As long as we have each other we will get through anything." She kissed him and Gus coughed.

"Hello? I'm still in the room," he said.

"Sorry, Gus, did you want a kiss to?" she said, going over to him and before he could protest she had kissed him on the cheek. "Thanks for looking out for us," she said.

"You can't tell but I'm blushing," he said, rubbing his cheek.

Evie laughed as Brodie came out of the office. "Sketch artist will be here in ten," he said, putting the kettle on.

Eddie had been assigned to take the sketch artist over to the house. Eddie was twenty-eight and reasonably scrawny. "I have one of those metabolisms that overworks," he often found himself telling people, embarrassed by his appearance. He was a uniform but, Dom, having liked his initiative to volunteer for the task force had allowed him to take his role as if he was an honouree detective and wear his own clothes. Eddie had taken a while to decide what to wear; he wanted to look professional, as this could be the boost he needed to work his way up the ladder. He was fed up of being a uniform. Driving an unmarked police Audi, he rolled up to the gates of Harringdon Manor, he put the window down and pressed the buzzer. Harris answered, "State your name and business?"

"It's me, Eddie Thompson."

"What's the code word of the day?"

"What? Er I don't know, code word?"

"I'm just messing with you Davies get your ass in," he said, opening the gates for him. The sketch artist, Joe, was chuckling, Eddie was pissed off, people needed to start taking him seriously. One day he would be all their bosses. He pulled up to the house.

"Quite a place," Joe said, getting out the car.

Brodie met them at the door. "Come on in, kettle's just boiled."

Tea and coffee made, Joe sat down with Gus in the snug area of the kitchen. Harris was showing Eddie the security room and explained a bit about his role in protection, the kid seemed eager to learn and Harris felt bad he had made fun of him at the gate. Brodie was learning about plant-based food from Evie while Nate excused himself and headed back outside to try and call Mike.

Mike answered straight away. "Dad! WTF, Mum is pissed with you!"

Nate rubbed his head. "What has she told you?" he asked.

"Gramps told us about uncle Max. Sorry, Dad," Nate knew the kids were fond of Max but he hoped it wasn't going to affect any of them too much. "She said you've left home, you've got a new girlfriend and you're an SOB. That's what she said but it's not true is it? You are coming home?"

Nate felt so anxious. "Mike your mum and I have been having problems for a while, yes I have met someone I want to be with and I will come home but not to live." Silence.

"You know I'm coming to live with you, right? I'm not staying here with the girls!"

Nate chuckled at his son's outlook on the situation.

"Dad, when can I see you?"

"Soon I promise, I need to sort a couple of things out then I will be over. Look after the girls."

"Sure, Dad. Love you."

"Love you," he said, and hung up.

Eddie and Harris were in the kitchen talking to Evie and Brodie. "I'm going to need to go home soon and see my kids," Nate said.

"I can take you," Eddie said.

"Hang on let me check with the guv and we can go from there," Brodie said. "But not today we need to wait and see how the land lies."

Nate nodded. Talking to Mike had made him feel the need to see him as soon as possible. Joe came over with Gus and showed them the sketch. It looked like an average middle-aged balding man.

"I need to get this back to HQ ASAP," Joe said to Eddie.

"OK, let's go," he said, heading for the door followed by Joe with his sketch of Frank.

***

Frank got a call and booked himself on the first plane out of town. He couldn't wait to get home and away from this shitty place. How had they tricked him and left? They were already back home and he was still here, the fuckers. They would get what's coming to them soon. He threw his clothes in his bag and left the seedy motel. Yeah, he wasn't going to miss that place either.

***

Dom was delighted with the sketch. "This is brilliant work, well done." He disappeared with the sketch to enter it into the database, he came back and said to Eddie, "Get this sent to the airports. We need to know if this man enters the country."

"On it, guv," Eddie said, as he hurried off with the sketch.

Back at the mansion, Evie and Nate had opened a bottle of red and were preparing dinner for everyone. Gus had gone for a lie down, Brodie was outside checking the perimeter and Harris was playing solitaire on his phone in the security room.

"This is nice," Nate said, "you and me cooking together, drinking fine wine."

She looked at him, "I love you so much, Nate."

He went to her and took the knife out of her hand and picked her up and spun her round. "I love you so much, Evie," he said, putting her down.

She laughed at him, "I'm looking forward to meeting your kids someday."

It was his turn to laugh, "Good because it sounds like Mike has given himself custody of me!"

She pulled a face. "Well you know these weed smoking kids these days," she ducked as mushrooms came flying her way.

"Unless he is prepared to share he is most certainly not doing that sort of thing with me."

"Of course not!" she said, lobbing the mushrooms back at him. She poured more wine and rang Gus's mobile to tell him food was ready. As the five of them sat around the kitchen island drinking wine and beer, they ate their pasta dish chatting about everything and nothing. It felt like a gathering of old friends.

After clearing up, Nate and Evie excused themselves for an early night. They had a TV in their room and they were missing the normality of life before they left New Jersey. Taking a bottle and their glasses they headed up. They cuddled on the bed while watching a bad movie. Nate kissed her cheek, then her neck as she moved to accommodate him. He felt her breasts through her sweatshirt as he started to take it off. He worked his way down to her jeans and pants, standing at the end of the bed looking at her lying there naked as she touched her breasts and moved a hand over her navel. He stripped and he was kissing her naval working his way back up to kiss her as she opened her legs and they both moaned as he made slow purposeful love to her.

16

Tuesday

Frank had left on the first flight he could catch. He hated travelling by plane, for some reason he always ended up sitting next to a fat person who squelched over their seat and invaded his space. He couldn't abide obesity, there was absolutely no need for it. He sat in his window seat and was shortly joined by a woman and her kid. Shit, what was worse than fat people on planes… fucking kids. The kid was lucky, he sat and watched cartoons when he wasn't sleeping and was no trouble. Decent parenting that was the key. He struck up a conversation with the mother. He found out where she lived, who with, her best friends name and where she worked. And people were worried about their information being on the Internet! Ha! Frank got up to go to the toilet and cornered the pretty crew member, seeing her trouble, a steward came and asked if he could help. Frank sniffed and went back to his seat.

"Thanks, Brian, I don't get a good feeling from him, he's kind of creepy," the pretty flight attendant said, shuddering.

"I recognise him from somewhere," Brian said. "Don't go near him, I will deal with him, I just need to speak with the captain." Brian disappeared.

***

At Harringdon Manor all seemed peaceful. Brodie and Harris had taken it in turns to watch the security screens while the other one slept on the sofa in front of the amazingly huge TV.

"I need a change of clothes," Brodie said, heading out to the Audi to get his bag. He always kept a wash kit and clothes in the boot as did Harris as they never knew when or where they might be somewhere that wasn't home. Checking out the upstairs rooms he opted for a smaller room, as he only wanted the bathroom really. He showered and changed. He could get used to this type of lifestyle. Brodie was in his mid-thirties and single. He was known for his bad temper and had had a couple of domestic abuse allegations against him. However, they always seemed to disappear and the problem would go away. The perks of the brotherhood of the force. He had no record. Since he had been at Scotland Yard he had managed to control his temper. He found if he stayed single he didn't get angry. It's bloody typical he thought, I have to stay single to stay sane.

Brodie had come from a difficult background. He had watched his dad beat his mum up on a regular basis. The last time he saw his dad punch his mum was the last time he saw either of them. At seventeen he had left home. He had tried to intervene as he got older and bigger but he was not a match for his dad and however much he had pleaded with his mum, she wouldn't leave. Brodie had made the decision he was not going to sit around and watch his dad beat the life out of his mum anymore and he left. Never looking back, he had heard that his mum had finally succumbed to the cruelty of his dad who had then taken his own life in a show of 'remorse'. Brodie was angry. He joined the police to make the world a better place. He wanted to get scum like his dad off the streets and behind bars. He had been horrified with himself the first time he struck a girlfriend. The second time it happened he realised that he must have the same illness as his dad. It had to run in the family. Brodie had known he needed help and had confided in the guv'nor. Dom Anderson had admired his honesty and his obvious desire to get over his childhood trauma. Brodie had agreed to fortnightly counselling; a perk of the job, and Dom partnered him with Harris.

Harris was the polar opposite to his partner. Happily married with two children, he loved his job and took pride in upholding the law. His wife had supported him and now enjoyed her role as stay-at-home mum. Dom had never seen Harris lose his cool. He was always the joker and everyone who met him seemed to like him. He was the people-person of the outfit. Brodie had been unsure in the beginning if he would get on with Harris but had been pleasantly surprised by his partner's easy-going attitude to life. They had been partners for three months and it was a happy work marriage.

***

Brian, the male attendant had requested to see the captain. "I think we have the man the police are looking for, I checked his name against the passenger list. Frank Porter."

"OK, good work, I will radio ahead and let them know we have him. Tread carefully with him. Who is he sitting with?" The captain asked.

"A child and his mother, they seem to be getting on fine."

"OK, don't alert her just keep your eye on the situation. We are landing in two hours." And with that the captain disappeared leaving Brian to handle the situation out back.

***

"We've got him!" Dom shouted as he stood up from a desk in the task-force room. "Eddie, with me, we will meet this son of a bitch as he gets to passport control. The rest of you find out everything you can about a Frank Porter." Eddie was delighted. He could feel this was going to be something big in his life, something his mum would be proud of him for.

Dom organised two patrol cars as backup before heading into his office to call Brodie and tell him the good news. Brodie told Harris and went into the kitchen where Evie, Nate and Gus were debating the film *The Game Changers* that they had sat and watched together. It had been the easiest way to explain to Gus about healthy eating and strength. "I had no idea so many athletes were plant-based eating," he said. Seeing them getting fitter and stronger was all the encouragement he needed. "I'm gonna be like those guys on the documentary," he said to Brodie as he walked in the room.

"Well that's great, Gus, I tried it but I needed my meat," Brodie said.

"An animal's body is not yours to have and you most certainly don't need it," Evie said, pissed off with Brodie for putting his dumb taste buds in front of an animal's life. Nate squeezed her hand.

"Sorry, Brodie," she said, checking herself. Nate squeezed her hand again and smiled at her. She pulled a face back and poked her tongue out at him.

He laughed. "You and Florence are going to get on like a house on fire," he chuckled at the thought of his mischievous little girl.

"Anyway," Brodie cut in, "we have a confirmed sighting of your guy, Gus, inbound for Heathrow. A Frank Porter. Does that mean anything to any of you?"

"Really? Oh my God, that's great," Evie said, flinging her arms around Nate's neck and hugging him.

"My Guy," Gus nodded, proud of his contribution.

"Your guy," Brodie said, pointing at him. "You're the man, Gus."

"Yeah, I'm the man," Gus said, getting up and shaking Brodie's hand.

"So, does the name ring any bells?" Brodie said again. They all shook their heads.

"No, never heard of him," Nate said, "I mean we are assuming it's his real name but none of us recognised the picture either."

"OK, well we will continue as usual, we don't know for sure this is our guy, so until it's confirmed we need to go ahead with caution."

"Party pooper," Evie said. Brodie smiled and left to go back to his partner.

"I take it they are happy?" Harris said, thinking it was a little premature to be celebrating.

Nate called Cassie, "How are you doing?"

"I'm OK, Nate, just plodding on, how are you guys?"

Not wanting to jinx anything he just said, "We are all OK. Your house is lovely thank you so much for this."

"Oh, it's the least I can do," she said, pleased.

"Any news on Max or do you want me to call them again?"

"No I've heard. His body will be released on Friday. They have cited natural causes. Heart failure, bloody Max wouldn't listen," she went quiet.

"Do you want me to arrange the flights?"

"No, it's fine, Tina and Daryl are on it, they are such great kids, I've paid for them to come first class with me."

"The business will pay for it all, Cassie, just let me know when to expect you. I will be at the airport waiting. No matter what."

"Thanks, Nate, love to Evie and Gus," and she rang off.

"OK?" Evie asked.

"Yeah they have cited heart failure, she is bringing him home as soon as," he replied, sighing. He missed Max, he missed his kids, and he couldn't wait to see them. "If this is our guy I can head out to see the kids. Then we can get back to getting on with our lives," he said, smiling at her and kissing the end of her nose. That was something she was looking forward to very much.

Dom and Eddie were on their way to the airport. "Have you liked your task-force role?" he asked the youngster.

"Loved it, Sir, I think I should do the firearms training for next time."

Dom laughed he loved the kid's attitude and sincerity. "Well let's not get carried away, let's see this case out first."

Eddie knew he was made for bigger things. He had been the smallest in his family of three brothers. They were all blessed with looks. Eddie hadn't been sure who he took after and, asking his mother one day when he was twelve, she had given him the news that had changed his life forever. He was adopted. They had wanted four kids and when his mother was told there could be no more they decided to adopt instead. Everything fell into place for him that day. He now knew why he felt like the outsider with his brothers. His brothers had always treated him the same as they did each other but once Eddie knew the truth he started to slip away into his own warped idea of his world.

He had been picked on at school, 'scrawny', 'puny' and 'fagot' were all names he got used to living with. He was a nerd who was into his computers, finding solace with strangers online, he had found a place where he could be anyone he wanted to be at any time. His brothers had looked out for him in the beginning but the more Eddie withdrew himself from the world the more they drifted apart. He had looked at his ugly face in the mirror and had known this must be the reason his mother had given him away. His now-mum knew no details of his previous life telling him that when he was eighteen he could request the records. He waited until the morning of his eighteenth and he did exactly that. He found out his mother's real name was Alison Turner. She had been seventeen when she had given birth to the small boy. His father was stated as unknown. Understanding his disappointment his now-mother seemed to be of no comfort. Eddie had always been a whiz kid and he used his computer skills to track Alison down. He was sure she would want to see him and welcome him back; telling him it had all been some terrible mistake. Unfortunately, the reality of his situation did not fit his fairy-tale fantasy.

Alison Turner, now Elliot, lived two towns away. He had gone to her last known address and knocked on the door. A pretty thirty-five-year-old Alison came to the door. Her blonde hair cascaded down her neck and her smile was captivating. Staring at the scrawny eighteen-year-old in front of her she asked how she could help. Eddie was just about to surprise her with his brilliant news that he was her long-lost son when a little boy came running to the door grabbing hold of his mother's leg he said, "Mamma, I'm hungry." Eddie had looked at the boy wide eyed and jaw open. She was also now looking at Eddie with her jaw open.

"Are you Alison Turner?" he asked. She looked startled.

"I haven't been that for a long time what business do you want?" she said, very edgy and half closing the door. Eddie was taken aback again and apologised, making his excuses he left. She had a son, he had not even considered the possibility that she had gone on to have more kids. He was devastated.

Alison Elliot had been totally freaked out when she saw him. She knew exactly who he was. She called her husband and asked him to come home. Worried about his wife's obvious distress he rushed home to see her. After she put Toby down for his afternoon nap she proceeded to tell her husband about the time she was raped when she was seventeen. Ben held his wife's hand and cried with her as she told him of her ordeal. She had been held at knifepoint, dragged into an alley and brutalised. Eddie had been the result of a brutal attack. She had originally decided to have an abortion but decided as it wasn't the baby's fault, she would carry to term and give it up. She now wished she had had the abortion. The thing that upset her the most was the kid's resemblance to her attacker. He threw her back down that ally with the knife up against her throat. And she was reliving the attack. Ben had wanted to call the police but Alison pleaded with him not to. "It's not his fault, Ben, he won't know. I just can't have him in my life." She had pleaded.

Eddie was mad. He started following the pretty young woman who he now knew was his birth mum. He kept his distance, following her on foot when she took her other kid to the park, and by car when she did her daily chores. He followed her for weeks, keeping records of what she wore, where she went, and he even went through her rubbish and recycling bins. He had become obsessed. Deciding he could take it no more he rang her doorbell on a sunny Saturday afternoon. He was going to confront her with his abandonment once and for all. Ben answered the door. He stepped outside shutting the door behind him. "Walk with me," he said to the scrawny lad. Obediently he followed, they walked 100 metres down the road and stopped outside the park entrance. "You need to stay away. Alison wants nothing to do with you. Will you respect her wishes or do I need to get the police involved?"

"She's my mother, I have a right to see her!"

"You have no rights here kid, she gave you life, be grateful, now leave us alone." Ben was firm and serious.

"I deserve to know the truth!" he spat out at Ben. "I have a brother in that house!" he said with spittle forming in the corners of his mouth.

Ben suddenly became furious, "You stay away from my wife and son do you hear me? You want to know the truth your dad was a scumbag weasel rapist who attacked Alison in the worst way. He held her at knifepoint down an ally the sick fuck. She saw you and she sees him. I won't tell you again. Next time I will call the police." He turned and walked off. He hadn't wanted to tell the kid but he left him no choice. He needed him to stay away from his family. Eddie was reeling. His father had been a rapist. Eddie slowly spiralled out of control believing he looked like his father so he must be like him. He stopped following Alison. He needed to reconsider his actions. He decided to join the police force. He would work up the ranks and make his mother proud, she would want him as a son when she saw his achievements. Since joining the force, he had gone to her house a few times and sat outside and watched. Until one day he turned up and the house was empty. She had abandoned him again.

***

Waiting at passport control Eddie and Dom tried to look inconspicuous. Dom nodded towards someone and Eddie saw it was the man they now knew was Frank Porter. They waited patiently until he walked through and then both approached him and they got out their badges and asked him to go with them. Frank looked confused and looked around sure they must have the wrong person.

Two airport security guards came over holding their firearms. "Come with us," one said, as they flanked him and led him off to an interrogation room.

Sitting opposite Frank, Dom looked at him long and hard. He was an odd-looking character. He had thinning hair on top and brown patches on his head. He was in his mid-fifties and wrinkled from sitting in the sun too long rather than from age. He had his fingerprints taken on a nifty little portable gadget that sent them straight into the database, if he had a record then they would find it.

"What is this about?" Frank asked.

"I think you know that," Dom replied. Eddie was standing behind Dom, arms folded.

"And who are you meant to be?" Frank sneered at Eddie. "I have no idea why you are unlawfully holding me."

"Mr Porter, do you require representation?"

"Nope."

"Well I'm going to read you your rights before we talk, Sergeant…" He said to Eddie giving him his cue to read Frank his rights.

When Eddie finished Frank merely said, "Ah so you're the bitch," and laughed. Eddie's face went red with anger. Did he not know who he was talking to?

"All right, enough," Dom said, holding his hand up to Eddie expecting retaliation.

"Mr Porter, what was your business in New Jersey?"

"That's my business. I wasn't breaking any laws."

"Why were you stalking Nate Rivers?"

"I wasn't."

"We have confirmed information from a member of staff at The Inn on the Lake that you had been paying him for information on Mr Rivers' movements."

"So?" Alex that little shit, he should have paid his ugly bitch wife a visit.

"Could you explain your interest in Mr Rivers' business?"

"Nope." This was going well Dom thought. He gave out a big sigh.

"Mr Porter, do I need to explain the severity of the position you are in?"

"Nope. From what I can see you have no evidence of any crime," Frank said quite confidently. "So, you've arrested me on what charge?"

"We are within our rights to hold you until we are satisfied with your statement," Dom said. "OK, let's do this back to the station." He signalled the uniforms to come in and cuff Frank and take him out to the car.

Frank laughed. "Oh, you guys are in a world of shit now."

"Get him out of here," Dom said. He disliked this man with a passion.

In the car following the police car containing Frank, Dom noticed Eddie was quiet. "You OK, Sergeant?" Dom asked. "Don't let him get to you, the guy's a creep. I like him for this." Eddie wasn't sure he agreed. Back at the station, Frank was taken to a holding cell. "We got a match on the prints, guv."

"Talk to me," Dom said, listening with interest.

"Frank Porter, 55 registered address 15 Hackney Lane, he's been arrested before for trespassing but that's it. The guys a fucking PI."

"Shit!" Dom said. "Get this phone unlocked and let's see what's on it." He threw down Frank's burner phone and Eddie went to work desperate to humiliate Frank like he had humiliated him.

"Any word from HQ?" Nate asked Brodie.

"Nada," he said, as he went back to trying to beat Harris's time on solitaire.

Nate went back into the kitchen. Evie was in her usual seat with a glass of wine. "I've poured you one," she said, tapping the seat beside her for him to join her.

"How you holding up?" he asked her.

"I'm with you, I'm fine," she replied smiling at him. They had been through so much in such a short time of knowing each other.

"How's the social media chatter?" he asked her.

"It's OK, you have quite a few flesh eaters saying it's a good idea to bring healthier options in as long as you don't phase out meat altogether. But it's good, there is a lot of discussion about it. This might have just done us a marketing favour," she told him. He was used to the way Evie talked about animals as food and found it endearing as she refused to refer to them as a commodity.

"I hope you're right," he said, as he raised his eyebrows at her.

"What's for dinner, Boss?" Gus said, walking into the room eating a protein bar. He had found a gym beside the inside pool so he had decided to start working out.

"I will make you something hearty tonight, Gus, you've burnt off a lot of calories today. Don't want you wasting away now do we?" he said, making fun. Evie laughed and Gus just looked at him.

"Think you're funny huh?" he said, as he turned around muttering to himself.

"He's hangry," Evie laughed as Gus turned round and poked his tongue out at them both causing them to laugh.

***

Eddie had unlocked Porter's phone and found the pictures of Evie and Nate. So he had been following them. Eddie was impressed with the picture quality and wished he had had a better phone when he had followed Alison.

"Guv," he said to get Dom's attention, "we've got proof he was following them." He showed Dom the pictures.

"Get these printed off as evidence. Where are we on calls and texts?"

"OK, so we have identified Alex the pot washer's number, I mean we are assuming it's him as his name is in the phone. There are a couple of messages asking for more money if he wants more information. The same number, so Alex had called him yesterday morning. That was the last communication with him? Anything else?"

"There is an unknown caller, several conversations took place between them spanning a three-week period, and one text message saying 'package delivered'. Whatever that means."

"It means he was working for someone, which brings me back round to the accomplice. What if he was hired by the Black Tulip to follow

Evie to New Jersey. He may be just a sleazy PI caught up amongst this."

"OK, guv but then in that case how did the Black Tulip know Evie was in New Jersey to have her followed and, if that is the case, that means Porter is not our guy and he is still out there and he seems to be a step ahead of us all." Eddie felt exhausted.

"OK, let's go at him again, give me those pictures, let's go."

Frank had been moved from his holding cell to an interview room. He was sipping coffee and he waved at the camera in the corner of the room.

"OK, Frank, it's time to talk. We've found your photos. Why were you watching Nate Rivers?"

"It's my job," he said bluntly. "I'm a licensed PI, which you already know."

"Who are you working for?"

"I can't breach client confidentiality, you also know that."

"You can if it hinders an active police investigation, so I will ask you again, who are you working for?"

"No one has died I am not obliged to give you privileged information."

"Put him back in the holding cell, see how you enjoy a night in the block." Dom got up and left.

Eddie followed him. "Why didn't you push him more?" he asked.

"Patience is a virtue young man. Let's get as much info on him as possible and let's hit him again in the morning." Dom left him and went into his office. He called Nate. "It seems our man is a PI working for someone to have either you or Evie followed. Sorry I can't give you any more than that at the moment but if you want to get Brodie to run you over to your house tomorrow then go, but he stays with you and brings you back."

Nate agreed to this and was relieved that at last he would see his kids.

Nate filled the others in with the conversation as Brodie came out of the office on the phone to his guv'nor.

"OK, so he said he's spoken to you, Nate, and you're good to go tomorrow."

Harris was surprised at this. "Does that mean they think they have their guy?" he asked.

"You've been staring at that solitaire screen too long," Brodie joked as he filled his partner in on the rest of the conversation. So they think the Black Tulip hired the PI. Now that was very interesting Harris thought.

Later that evening when they were alone, Evie asked Nate if he thought it was safe to go out tomorrow.

"I will be OK, I will have Brodie with me, you will have Gus and Harris. Don't worry, I promise it will be OK." He kissed her and she snuggled into him needing to feel his body against hers.

"I just don't want to lose you," she said, suddenly feeling vulnerable that they were going to be apart.

"You have nothing to worry about," he said, holding her tight. "I love you."

She squeezed him. "I love you," she replied. "So much."

"So much," he said, settling down to sleep.

17

Wednesday

Waking up in Nate's arms she had the sudden realisation that he was going to see Sarah today. She had that knot in her stomach of guilt and jealousy. She knew he loved her and she didn't really believe for a second that he would go back to Sarah but she still felt insecure. He had children with this woman, she would always be a part of their life. She wasn't sure how to feel about the kids. She didn't want to be a mum but she knew one day she would grow to love them all. She was just in such strange territory. "This will be the longest time we've ever been apart," she said to Nate, watching him getting dressed.

"I know, it will be weird going anywhere without you." He came over and sat on the edge of the bed. "It won't always be like this, one day we will look back at this time and it will just be a blip in our life together."

"Not too much of a blip I hope," she said, "I quite like most of it."

He kissed her as she ruffled his hair playfully. "Oh well," he said, sighing as he stood up, "I guess I had better go and face the music."

Gus was in the gym; he hadn't mentioned that there was a TV screen in the room with access to almost any channel in the world. He sat on an exercise bike watching a morning chat show. The host was having an argument with a vegan guest on his show. Gus found this so odd. Why would you be against saving the planet and living healthily? Most importantly, like Evie had told him, "If you wouldn't eat a dog then why would you eat a pig?" He had thought about that one long and hard. He had told her that eating dogs was just plain weird, she had responded that a lot of Asian countries eat dogs as part of their normal diet, just like we eat pigs as part of ours. Gus had been confused, it's not normal to eat a dog so maybe it wasn't normal to eat a pig. Evie had helped him to understand that we only love one and eat another because that is what we are conditioned to do from birth. Our parent's habits become ours to hand down.

"Once you realise, Gus, that animals are all the same, they all have emotions and family, they feel joy, fear, pain, just like us, speciesism is like racism. It's not cool."

Gus could most certainly relate to racism and Evie was right, speciesism was basically the same thing in the animal world. Humans were disgraceful he thought. He understood that killing someone that didn't want to die was wrong. Whatever the species or race. It really was simple. So why was this guy on TV arguing against it?

He left the gym and went through to the kitchen where Evie and Nate were drinking coffee and eating toast. Gus told her about the chat show.

"Gus, lots of people have different views, that particular person is paid to be controversial, don't pay to much attention to him."

"You want me to drive you today, Boss?" he asked Nate.

"No, Gus, I want you to stay here and look after Evie, Brodie is going to take me, I may need his gun as protection against Sarah."

Gus looked horrified. "I'm joking, Gus, don't worry," Nate said.

"Sometimes, Boss, I just don't know with you."

Brodie appeared in the kitchen, "Right, you ready, Nate? I've loaded the gun," he said, as Nate downed the last of his coffee almost choking.

"Sorry couldn't resist," Brodie said, having overheard the conversation, they all fell about laughing.

"Well I'm as ready as I will ever be," he said, going to Evie to give her a kiss.

"See you later," she said smiling. "Have fun with the kids."

"I will, thanks." He mouthed at her, 'I love you' and winked and then he was gone.

***

Back at Scotland Yard Frank had spent an uncomfortable night in a holding cell. This wasn't funny anymore and he was going to sue all of them. He wondered about giving up his client but he hadn't been paid up to date so that would be a bad idea. He would wait and see what the old cop and his scrawny sidekick had to say today.

Eddie had thought about the pictures of Evie that he had found on Frank's phone, she had a stunning resemblance to Alison, she had also been dragged down an alley at knifepoint, he wished he was part of her protection detail at the house, he would like to spend more time with her. He didn't have time to think like that at the moment. The guv wanted his help breaking down Frank. If the guv thought Frank was good for this it would solve a lot of problems.

Dom was carrying a mug of coffee around with him, he seemed agitated. He needed Frank to give up his client so they could either eliminate them or arrest them. It was really that simple. He called Eddie over and told him to get Frank moved to the interview room.

***

Brodie entered the postcode of Nate's house in Google maps. "I can just direct you if you like," Nate said, but Brodie said it was just as easy.

"So, does your wife know about you and Evie?" Brodie asked expecting to be told to mind his own business.

"Yeah she knows, the ironic thing is I've never cheated on her before so her coming to surprise me like that was really out of character," he said, trailing off and looking confused.

"What?" Brodie asked, "What is it?"

"How did she know? I mean she came to catch me out. She has never had reason to mistrust me so what changed?" Nate was really confused, how had he not seen this earlier? Sarah had come to catch him out in a lie because she knew.

"What?" Brodie said, frustrated.

"I need to talk to her."

Brodie wasn't sure what Nate had been getting at but realised it was pointless trying to get him to explain. As they pulled into the gravel drive of Nate's home, Rivers Rest, Brodie was impressed. "Nice," he said, taking in the tasteful country-cottage-style house.

"Yeah it's all Sarah, I just pay for it," he said dryly.

Brodie stopped the car, "How do you want to play this?" he asked.

"If you don't mind waiting here I will go and see how the land lies."

Brodie nodded and mocked saluted him. "Call me if you need back up," he shouted after Nate.

Nate opened the door to his home and heard, "Daddy! Daddy!" as his girls flung themselves at him.

"Hello my gorgeous darlings," he said, hugging them both. "I think you have both grown!" he declared. "How long have I been away? Did I miss a few birthdays?" he joked with them.

"Too long, Dad, that's how long," said the sulky teenager as he walked through the door towards Nate. He looked like Nate at that age.

"What's up, bud?" he said, trying to sound street.

"Oh God, Dad, don't try and be cool," Mike said, giving his dad a hug.

"You all right, boy?" he asked him.

"Yeah I guess, Mum's in the kitchen."

"Oh goody, what mood?"

"Usual, so be careful."

"Thanks, son," he said, ruffling his hair, "I can count on you to have my back," he said, teasing him. The girls had already lost interest in the conversation and had gone back to the playroom. "Mike, there is a man outside called Brodie, he's a friend of mine, can you go see if he wants anything to drink while I go and see your mum?"

"Sure, Dad, good luck."

Nate thought he would need more than luck to get through the day. He walked through the spacious house; he stopped at his office and opened the door to look in. He went over to his desk and wondered if Sarah had been through it looking for proof of another life. It wouldn't have mattered if she had he had nothing to hide here.

"Hello Sarah," he said, when he looked up and she was standing in his office behind him. She shut the door and went to the window. Looking out she could see Mike talking with a stranger.

"Who is that?" she asked.

"That's Detective Brodie."

She looked at him. "Why are you with a detective?" she asked. "Are you or your slut in some kind of trouble?"

Nate rubbed his head and sighed. "Sarah, I'm not going to talk to you if you are going to talk like that." She held her hands up as if to say OK. "Why don't we sit?" he said, gesturing towards the sofa. She went and sat down, he took a chair from behind his desk and put it down in front of her and sat down.

"Are you coming back to me?"

"No."

"I want you to come home. We can make this work."

"It's too late for that."

"How is it too late, you barely know this girl?"

"I love her, Sarah."

"You love her?" Tears started to well in her eyes. "You haven't had time to fall in love with her."

"I'm sorry, I should never have started seeing someone while we were still married. I don't expect you to forgive me, I don't deserve it." She looked at him with pain in her eyes.

"How many others have there been?"

He looked up at her surprised. "What are you talking about?" he said, confused not for the first time today.

"I'm talking about your affairs, how many? I'm not stupid, Nate, I know," she said, looking at him shaking her head.

"Sarah, I have never been unfaithful to you in my life apart from this. I swear it on the kids' lives," he said, sitting forward. "Why on earth would you think that?"

She just looked at him accusingly. "I have never trusted you. You go away for months on end, what man can cope without the company of a woman? Be it affair or whore!"

Nate was flabbergasted; he couldn't believe what she was saying. "Sarah! I can't believe this. I have never ever even considered cheating on you before! Where the hell is this coming from?"

Sarah was furious she leant forward, "Fuck you, Nate! Just fuck you!"

Nate, for the first time in his life was so utterly astounded he actually didn't know what to do. He stood up and walked to the window. "Have you always felt like this?" he asked.

"Really, Nate? What woman wouldn't think her husband was playing away from home the amount of time you're away." She put her face in her hands.

Had he really got their relationship so wrong? He had honestly thought that Sarah was behind him.

He was devastated, he went to her and crouched down pulling her hands away from her face he said to her, "I am so sorry, I never realised you felt like this. Why did you never say anything, why didn't you trust me?" He was crying now, he felt like his whole relationship had been a lie. "I thought you trusted me. I mean, I know I've proved you right now but I can't believe you always felt like this, why did you never say anything?"

"I was scared you would leave me. I thought if I let you have your fun you would always come home to me. I knew something was different with you that's why I did what I did. I thought you were going to come home and support me, it was my time!" she broke down sobbing.

"What did you do Sarah?" he asked, suddenly becoming worried.

***

"OK, Frank, enough is enough. We want the name of your client. Either you are part of a bigger conspiracy to stalk and terrorise a young woman or you are caught up in something you don't realise. It's time to talk."

Frank laughed. "So this is about the pretty young woman, Evie, and her stalker," he said, totally throwing Dom off his game.

"What do you know about that case?" Dom asked.

"What, the Black Tulip? I mean really is that the best you could have come up with? Please!" he said. Dom and Eddie looked at each other.

"Frank, are you the Black Tulip?" Dom asked.

"Please, wrong question," he laughed enjoying himself. They had no idea about anything. "Are you working for the Black Tulip?" Dom tried redirecting the question.

"I don't know what you are talking about I am a PI."

Dom sighed and looked at Eddie who looked fit to burst. "OK, let me ask you a different question, how do you know about the Black Tulip as it is not public knowledge?"

"Aha!" Frank said, pointing at Dom, "That, my friend, is the right question to ask." Frank was playing with him. Dom was beyond frustrated.

"You know I can charge you for obstruction to justice, I have a search warrant ready to go, we will turn your house upside down, you smarmy piece of shit!" Dom finished by banging his fist on the desk.

"Temper, temper!" Frank said, laughing.

***

"What did you do Sarah?" Nate had become serious and more persistent, he had hold of her arm still, she snatched it away from him.

"You're hurting me let go!" she shouted at him. He let go and stood up. He rubbed his head. "Stop fucking about, Sarah, and tell me what did you do?"

***

"It was the wife," Frank said.

"The wife?" Dom questioned.

"Aha, the wife. It's always the wife, or the husband it's classic behaviour." Frank threw his arms in the air dramatically. "Don't you get it, Detective? Obviously not," he said, looking at Dom's confused look.

"The wife hired me to follow the husband and catch him in a lie," he declared opening his arms and bowing his head like some kind of mad preacher. Dom's mouth dropped open, "And there it is," Frank said, "you finally got it." He was laughing now.

"How did you know about the Black Tulip?" Dom pushed on.

"You better tell your monkey what's going on he looks a little confused," Frank said, pointing at Eddie. Eddie went for him and Dom stood up and stopped him.

"Back down, Sergeant!" he demanded, stopping Eddie in his tracks.

"I know about the Black Tulip because I have contacts in the force. Ones that I will never give up to you."

It was Dom's turn to laugh. "Oh really, well there are only a handful of people who know about the case so it won't be hard to find out!" he said, still reeling from what he had just learned.

***

"Sarah talk to me!" Nate demanded.

"What do you want me to tell you? You son of a bitch! That I hired a private investigator to follow you? That he sent me pictures of the two of you? I know all about your dirty little secrets with her!" she seethed.

Nate was taken aback. He wasn't sure which way was up, this was spinning out of control. He had believed in his marriage and he now found out that his wife had never trusted him, now she was telling him she had hired a PI to follow him? This was insane. "Sarah, what are you talking about?"

"Oh come on, Nate, you're not that fucking naïve, are you? I hired a PI to follow you. He sent me pictures of you, he left me a whole fucking file about that bitch at my hotel. I know all about her stalker and that you are screwing her!"

Nate closed his eyes. His head really hurt. He felt like he had gone ten rounds with Mike Tyson; he could hear Evie saying, "Mike Tyson is vegan you know." And then she would smile her sweet smile.

He pulled himself together and shook the thought off. "Sarah, who leaked information to the Morgan Stanley Show? Was it your PI?"

"Yes, I mean what kind of a chef doesn't eat meat, you complete freak! Anything to get in little miss perfect's pants!"

He closed his eyes again trying to remain calm. "And the tulip delivered the day after we saw you?"

"Guilty as fucking charged!" she said, holding up her hand. Nate opened his eyes and looked at her. He did not know this woman at all.

***

"So, let me get this straight, Frank," Dom said, "Mrs Rivers hired you as a PI to follow her husband?"

"Fucking right and the rich bitch owes me still."

"So that is why she made the unannounced visit to the hotel?" Dom questioned.

"Catch the fuckers red handed," Frank said, smiling.

"And you gave her the information, I mean the copy of our police file to Mrs Rivers is that correct?"

"Finally, it all clicks into place," Frank mocked, staring at Eddie.

"So, you sent the black tulip to the hotel to rattle Evie?"

"Oh no, that bad-arse idea was all Rivers' bitch wife. She has a mean streak that woman!" he said, screwing up his face.

"Jesus fucking Christ, what a mess," Dom said. "OK, write it all down, don't leave anything out and you'd better hope Mrs Rivers corroborates your story."

***

Nate walked out of the room and straight outside where Brodie was still chatting to Mike. They both stopped talking when they saw his face. He pulled his phone out and called Sarah's dad. "Peter, it's Nate. You and Betty need to come over to the house immediately and stay here with the kids. No, I can't explain just get in the car and come now please or I will be taking them with me." And he rang off.

"Dad," Mike said, "what's going on?"

What was he meant to tell his son? "Mike, your mum has done some things she shouldn't have and she's going to need you to be strong and look out for her, OK? It's not important right now what she's done, but she is going to have to speak to the policc."

"Nate?" Brodie questioned as his phone rang.

Nate walked over to Mike and hugged him hard. "I love you and your sisters more than you will ever know. I want you to go and stay with your sisters until Grandpa arrives, OK?"

Mike knew not to push it and he went inside.

Brodie was talking to the guv. "Fuck," he said, as he rang off. He looked at Nate. "The PI guy…" Brodie started.

"I know, was working for my wife."

Nate and Brodie waited until both Peter and the police had arrived before they headed back to Harringdon Manor. Nate briefly filled Peter in and a squad car came to take Sarah to the station for questioning.

"Can we go back now please," Nate asked Brodie after he had seen his kids again, assuring them Mummy would be back soon. He would not press any charges against her, he knew if he had been more aware of his marriage things would never have got to this state. He hoped Evie would understand. Brodie and Nate rode in silence for a while.

"You OK, Nate?" Brodie finally asked.

"I don't know how to feel, truthfully, I feel I failed my wife, my marriage, my kids, Evie, I mean if it wasn't for me she would have never received that stupid black tulip."

"Hey man, you can't beat yourself up, you've done everything you can. The issue here is that Evie's stalker hasn't been found and we don't know if he's gone dormant or what. I mean he may have just disappeared like he did with that other girl."

"We can hope," Nate said. "But it will never be over for Evie if he is not caught." He knew he had to go back and explain to Evie that this was all his fault. Where would he begin?

They arrived back and were buzzed in through the gate. Evie came running out and threw herself at him. "You've been gone so long I was so worried," she said, before kissing him. "I'm sorry it's been quite a day, let's go inside and talk."

"Yeah, crack open the whisky," Brodie said, with no humour in his voice.

Sitting at the kitchen island, Nate and Brodie explained the developments of the day. Harris didn't speak, which was unusual, Brodie thought.

Gus sat and listened, sipping beer. "Whoa dude, that's so messed up," he said, shaking his head. "I knew something wasn't right with that lady, shit, sorry Boss, no offence." Gus was worried he had upset Nate.

"It's OK, Gus, I just wish I had seen it coming." He looked at Evie who hadn't said anything. "Evie?" he said, taking her hand.

"Are the kids OK?" she asked.

"They are fine, are you OK?"

"Of course," she said, trying to put on a brave face. "I mean I'm not going to lie how frightened I was when I saw that tulip but this is no one's fault, Nate. Sarah is unhinged. I don't blame you."

"I feel responsible for it all," he said, looking down. "I drove Sarah to this, I put you in danger."

Evie stood up and put her arms around him.

"Nate you can't blame yourself, this is not natural behaviour. If a wife is worried about her husband's fidelity she talks to him, she doesn't hire a PI."

"She's right you know, bud," Brodie said. "You can not blame yourself for your old lady's actions."

But Nate would always feel he was to blame.

"Harris, you haven't said anything," Brodie said to his unusually quiet partner.

"Just taking it all in, like the big man over there said, it's messed up," he said, tipping his beer bottle towards Gus.

Gus tipped his back. "Amen brother," he said.

***

Dom and Eddie waited for Sarah to arrive at the station. They took her through to the interview room and took her statement. After which they went back to see Frank.

"The lady corroborates your story, Mr Porter, so you are free to go as Mr Rivers is not pressing charges."

Frank stood up and said, "I think you guys owe me a fucking apology."

"Don't hold your breath, you creep," Eddie said, as Frank was ushered out of the room.

"Well said, Eddie," Dom commented knowing his young protégé was dying to kick Frank's ass.

***

It had been a long day. Evie and Gus had made a curry for dinner and they ate in relative silence. Nate soon excused himself. Evie left him for a bit and went and sat with Brodie who filled her in again on the events of the day.

"He is devastated, Evie, he trusted her and she had betrayed his trust long before he met you. She is a proper piece of work that one." Evie felt horrible for Nate, she thanked Brodie and followed after Nate.

When she went into their room he was sitting on the floor at the end of the bed. The TV was on but he wasn't watching it. She sat down beside him and put her arm around him, he looked at her and sobbed as she held him and cradled him in her arms.

18

Thursday

Dom and Eddie arrived at Harringdon Manor; Nate and Evie were sitting in the garden drinking coffee. Eddie went through to the security room while Dom grabbed a coffee and went out to them. "Mind if I join you?"

"Of course," Evie smiled as Nate got up to shake Dom's free hand.

"How are you kids holding up?" he asked.

Nate sighed and shrugged. "I feel totally responsible for unnecessarily frightening Evie while wasting valuable police time and resources because it turns out I don't know my wife at all." Evie took his hand. "It's not your fault, Nate, you can't hold yourself responsible for this."

"Evie is right, Nate, you couldn't have known." Dom put his mug down, "What a lovely place this is," he said, taking in the landscape.

"It's not half bad," Nate replied. "Cassie is bringing Max home tomorrow."

Dom nodded, "Good."

"I've arranged for the undertaker to meet us at the airport. His brother is organising the service and he has agreed to let Cassie host the wake here at Harringdon." Dom nodded taking it in.

"Is there a date at all?" he asked.

"It's provisionally booked for Monday. Harry wants his brother buried as soon as."

Dom again nodded. "Yeah I expect he does."

"What happens now, Dom?" Evie asked. "We don't know if I'm at risk or not anymore."

"True, true." Dom sighed, the adrenaline of the last couple of days had worn him out, what he could really do with was a holiday. "I think I will be happier to keep a detail with you for a bit longer. What's happening about Sarah?"

Nate rubbed his head at the mention of her name. "I've got my solicitor coming over this afternoon to talk about legalities and divorce which will be fun. I'm hoping, as I didn't press charges against her, that she may be more open to discussions." Evie doubted she would back down but she hoped so for Nate's sake.

"And what about Evie?" Dom asked.

"What do you mean?" Nate was genuinely confused.

"Is Sarah going to do an exposé on you?"

Nate hadn't thought about that. He rubbed his head again, "I just don't know. I asked her dad to ask her to stay out of the press but who knows what she will do, like I said, it turns out I don't know her at all." Nate looked at Evie and she smiled at him a reassuring smile. "I've spoken to head office, my PR guys are putting a statement together in case. My statement acknowledges that I have had extra marital activities and that I will be looking to divorce Sarah. I intend to take all the blame. I have left Evie's name out but I doubt it will take long for it to be all over the media, I don't think it will affect my reputation as a chef. People soon forget anyway."

"Yes, I am worried about Evie," Dom said, pondering his options to protect her.

"It might be OK," she said. "It might draw the stalker out, if he doesn't know that I've got protection, it might all play in our favour."

"It might, Evie, or it might backfire. We are going to have to play this by ear. The less you both go out the better, Evie, I think you should stay here for the time being."

"I'm going to Max's funeral," she said with the determination Nate knew could not be challenged.

"I'm not going to argue with you about it, if you go, you are having security, end of discussion," Dom responded to her.

"OK sure, of course," she said.

"Nate, I will take you to the airport tomorrow," Dom said, standing up to go. "I need to go home, I've slept in the office for the last few days, Mrs Detective thinks I've left home," he said, making Evie laugh.

She got up and hugged him. "See you later," she said, as he turned to leave.

Molly, the housekeeper, found Gus in the gym watching TV. "You know you're not going to get fit like that," she said, trying to be stern and not smile.

Gus looked at her and gave her a wide grin, she was kind of pretty, she was also very skinny almost angular. "Don't you eat much?" he asked.

This time she couldn't help smiling, she had liked Gus when they first met, he was like a big bear with no bite. "I don't have a big appetite I must admit," she spoke more softly. Gus liked that, after all, at the end of the day they were both the hired help, she didn't need airs and graces around him. "Cassie phoned she has requested that you pick her and her two companions up from the airport if that is OK."

"Sure, it's what I'm here for," he said, grinning.

"If you have finished, erm, working out," she said, raising one eyebrow, "then I will take you to the garage. She asked you to bring the Range Rover."

Gus was on his feet and switched off the TV. "Awesome let's go!" he said, feeling unusually comfortable in her company.

Meanwhile, in the security room with Brodie and Harris, Eddie was telling them all about the interview with Porter and Rivers' wife. "You should have seen the guv, he was epic," he said, excited to have someone to share with.

Harris looked at him and frowned, "You don't get out much do you kid?"

Eddie was taken aback with that comment, how would Harris know what he got up to? He had spent his spare time trying to track down his birth mother, Alison, but he couldn't tell him that or that he liked to follow her. "I do, I just haven't been in on that kind of interrogation before," he said, sulkily.

Brodie looked at Eddie, "Don't be so touchy, Sergeant, Harris is just playing with you."

Eddie tilted his head to the side to look at Brodie. Who were these people to him? Nothing. One day he would be the boss of them all. He laughed. "Of course," he said, making fun of himself to them. "I am like that sometimes." Feeling like he was superior and they were too stupid to realise. Dom yelled out for him and he left.

"That's a weird one right there," Brodie said, observing Eddie's behaviour.

"You can say that again. A right oddball, not sure what the guv sees in him." Harris replied before resuming his game of solitaire.

***

Alfie Cartwright was extremely well spoken; Nate greeted his solicitor with a firm handshake. Evie was in the kitchen when they walked through. He wore an expensive well-fitted three-piece suit and he walked like he had a metal rod up his back. He had slicked his hair to the side with gel and he looked very official.

"This is Evie," Nate said, as Alfie shook her hand more softly.

"Pleasure," he said with a nod, understanding the reason his client was in his predicament. "Shall we go through to the office?" Nate suggested leading the way.

Evie asked if he would like a tea or coffee but he opted for a glass of water instead. Taking it through to him, she put it on the table and left closing the door behind her.

"Sorry about this, not my office, shall we sit in the comfy chairs?" he said, heading towards the window that looked out over the grounds. Nate could see the gardeners outside, they hadn't thought it fair to cancel them, after all, Molly had vouched for them.

"So, Nate, what trouble have you got yourself into, old boy?" Alfie said, with a grin thinking of the pretty woman he'd just met.

"Where to start," Nate said, rubbing his head. "I want to divorce Sarah."

"You know that in itself will cost you a small fortune. Is there definitely no chance of a reconciliation?" Alfie asked.

"None."

Alfie was quite taken aback by the firm blunt answer. Nate told Alfie the trauma of the past week. Alfie hadn't realised until Nate had finished speaking that he was literally on the edge of his seat listening. Settling back in his chair he held his hands together in front of his face holding his fingers to a point tapping his nose. "It's a shame you told her you would not press charges, we could have used that as leverage," he said. "But if she's adamant she won't divorce you then we need to make her an offer she can't refuse."

"She can have the house and the cars. I'm prepared to keep paying as I am for her expenses, housekeeping, whatever you want to call it, until the kids leave home. Then she can have a settlement. You put something together for me, I can't deal with her. Will you go and see her?"

"Once we have a proposal I will certainly go and see her but I don't advise me going alone."

"Don't worry, I will make sure her dad is present as well, he's living there for the time being, I don't want her alone with the kids at the moment. I don't trust her."

Alfie nodded, "I tell you what, why don't you let me draw up your proposal and maybe another for you to consider. Also, your girlfriend, Evie, I don't like to play devil's advocate but are you completely sure her interest isn't monetary?"

Nate's head jerked up. "Are you serious? Did you not hear what we have been through?"

"Yes, of course, but you pay me a lot of money to look after you and your business, Nate, I'm doing my due diligence. I hope if you plan to take further steps with the young lady you will let me draw up a prenup."

Nate just looked at him. "I know you're looking out for me but that won't be necessary," Nate said, standing up to say the meeting was through.

"Of course, early days for that, I'm sorry I shouldn't have mentioned it. I will get the paperwork drawn up and emailed to you." Alfie shook Nate's hand and told him not to worry he could see himself out.

Walking back through the kitchen he said goodbye to Evie and acknowledged Brodie who had come in for a sandwich. I hope you're right, Alfie thought, knowing he wouldn't be the first celebrity to get his fingers burnt in such a way.

Evie went into the office and sat in the chair opposite Nate. It was still warm. "OK?" she asked. He shrugged still annoyed at Alfie's mention of a prenup and Evie's intentions. He had not for one second considered Evie was after his money. Why would he have said something like that? He was thinking of all the times they had been together, it was a mutual thing he was positive, he didn't need these stupid ideas put in his head.

"It's going to be an ongoing battle for a while."

She stood up and went to him; she folded herself into his lap and put her arms around his neck. "It will be OK, Nate, we will get through this."

His heart turned over as he looked into her eyes, there was no doubt in his mind that she loved him, she kissed him softly and tenderly. She felt his excitement and got up and locked the door, she walked over to him as he was undoing his trousers, she knelt down between his legs and took over from him.

"Let me," she said, taking hold of him. His breathing became laboured as her very touch was driving him mad. She took him in her mouth and he stroked her hair, put his head back against the chair and moaned while she worked her magic and he forgot all his troubles.

***

Cassie was all packed and ready to leave tomorrow. They would be meeting the coroners at the airport and they would be able to attend when Max was loaded on the plane. How had it come to this? Tina and Daryl had been a breath of entertainment in a place where Cassie thought she would never smile again. Their constant banter and bickering kept her amused. They were like spoilt siblings fighting for attention all the time. Cassie had never had kids. She thought that she would never regret her decision but in truth, now, she was older and alone again in life, she found that she did actually have regrets. Maybe it was because she was lonely; she missed a family, grandchildren running around playing in her garden. There was no point feeling sorry for herself now. She had to get through the next week and then, she decided, she was going to take a long vacation.

Tina had also packed and was in Daryl's room watching him put his bag together. "It's so awesome we get to stay at Cassie's house!" Tina said excitedly. "Evie says it's amazing, indoor and outdoor pools, gym, tennis courts there is even an entertainment room with a bar in!"

Daryl was finding Tina's excitement infectious. "It's going to be such fun! We will be back together, the three musketeers!" he said, clapping.

Tina stopped smiling. "We must remember why we are going there, Max died after all, we mustn't seem too excited."

"Perlease darling," Daryl replied. "The reason we are going is sad but there is no reason we can't enjoy our trip, we are flying first class for heaven's sake!" He dramatically put his hand on his heart like he might faint. "This is going to be a real adventure!"

Tina messaged Evie asking if she was coming to the airport, Evie had said no but she couldn't wait to catch up with them. She had asked Tina to go to her room and pack her a few things as she had left more empty handed than she had arrived.

Back in the UK Evie was looking at clothes suitable for a funeral. "Is it all black?" she asked Nate as she scrolled through the web pages.

"I guess so," he replied, "I will have to go home at some point this weekend and get my suit and some more clothes. I wish I had thought to do it the other day."

"Why don't you ask Mike to pack a few things in a case and see if Peter will bring it and the kids over?" Evie suggested.

Nate looked at her and smiled. "That's why I love you, you think of everything," he said, kissing her.

She smiled and kissed him back feeling that electric chemistry as their lips touched. "I think I'm just going to order a few things in, I can always send them back," she said, putting clothes in her virtual basket.

***

Sarah was still in a state of shock. Not only had she had the humiliation of being taken off to the police station, she now had the creep Porter chasing her for the rest of his money. If he thought for one minute he was getting a single penny out of her then he was very much mistaken.

Her mother had tried to understand what she had done but couldn't get her head around the fact that her daughter had hired a private investigator in the first place. "What you did to that girl was wicked." Her mother had scolded when she had confessed about the black tulip. It was not right; her mother should be on her side. Her father had been more diplomatic. He had told her that, although he couldn't condone what she had done, he did understand why she'd behaved the way she had. Had everyone forgotten that she was a wronged woman here? She would not let this rest. She would find a way to humiliate her husband and his slut before this was over. She had every intention of going to Max's funeral and she would walk hand in hand with her husband. This was by no means over.

Peter and Betty were in the playroom with the girls who were happily unaware of the situation. "I'm worried about her, Peter, she seems unstable." Peter thought the same thing. His daughter's actions had been bizarre and very much over the top. "I'm not sure what we can do except be here for the children," he replied. He was furious with Nate for his behaviour. He had never in a million years pegged him as cheater. "How could he do this?" he said. Betty looked at him.

"It's not really surprising the amount of time they spend apart," she said. "What marriage could survive that?"

"A normal healthy one," he retorted. "We have been together fifty-two years and we never strayed."

That's what you think, Betty thought, remembering her office romance that lasted six months. What they don't know and all that… "Yes dear," she said, "we are very lucky. Changing the subject, Mike says he wants to go to the funeral but I'm not sure it's a good idea." She sighed, "death is no place for kids."

"He's sixteen, love, the boy's an adult in today's world, we should let him decide."

As if his ears were burning Mike walked in. "Hey Gramps, hey Grandma," he said, "Dad just called, he has given me a list of things to get him, clothes and stuff and he asked for some cash out his office, can you come with me Gramps just in case Mum loses the plot if she catches me?"

Peter looked at Betty. "See, even he thinks she's losing it," he said, getting up to go with Mike.

"Gramps, Mum lost it a long time ago, you guys are just catching up," the sixteen-year-old adult said. "Oh, and please can you take it and us over to Dad's so we can see him otherwise I'm going to get an Uber."

"Nice bit of blackmailing, kid, which parent did you learn that one from?" Peter said, shaking his head. "Betty love, can you tell Sarah the plan, you better stay here when I go, not sure she should be alone."

"Coward," she muttered under her breath.

Mike packed clothes and Peter went and got the cash for Nate, he assumed it was to help pay for the funeral but he didn't know.

Sarah was listening to her mother. "It will be good for the kids to be out the house for a while and you and me can have some girl time," Betty said, trying to make it sound like fun.

Sarah was past caring. "As long as they don't see her!" she seethed at her mother.

"OK dear, I will tell your father that," Betty said, wishing she was taking the kids instead of babysitting her daughter.

Nate came into the kitchen smiling happily. "Peter is bringing the kids over, I've just texted him the address."

Evie was thrilled for him. "Should I stay out of sight?" she asked.

"No, of course not, I will introduce you as a friend, I mean Mike's not stupid but the girls will be clueless." His phone rang again. "Billy!" he said, sounding happy. "I know, I know, that's brilliant, no of course not, Mum is too old to make the journey but I can't wait to see you. OK, OK bye," he said, ringing off. "That was my older brother, he is coming to Max's funeral, he will be here Saturday. Looks like we are going to have a full house."

Evie smiled, enjoying seeing the happy Nate again even under the terrible circumstances that were bringing his family together.

"And I'm going to meet most of your family," she said, "nervous much!" she laughed.

"Not all of them, my sister, Chrissie, can't make it but you will get to meet her soon enough." He went over to her and she stood up as he hugged her. "I hope Cassie doesn't mind if he stays here. I mean it's not like there isn't room."

"I'm sure she won't mind, the worst thing for Cassie would be to be alone right now."

Brodie had overheard the conversation and said, "I'm not protecting more people, that's beyond my job description."

Evie laughed, "You will like Cassie, Brodie. How's Harris doing? He's been in an odd mood the last couple of days."

"Yeah, he's missing home, family man, don't worry he's sound," he said, but the truth was his partner's odd behaviour had also been worrying him.

Peter arrived at Harringdon later that day. Nate went out to greet his kids. Shaking Peter's hand, he said, "Thanks for this, how is she?"

Peter shook his head at him, "She's not good, Nate, I'm surprised at you, I never thought for a second you would do the dirty on her."

Nate was ashamed, "There is more to it than that. We haven't been right for years. I'm sorry I've disappointed you."

Peter knew it wasn't all Nate's fault, he knew how difficult his daughter was but having an affair was the worst kind of betrayal. Nate took the kids into the kitchen followed by his father-in-law who was curious to meet the woman who had ended his daughter's marriage and reduced a world-class chef to a plant-based moron.

The girls were in awe of the size of the kitchen. "Daddy this is bigger than anything I have ever seen!" Florence said.

"That's because it's a castle you duh-duh brain," answered Trudie. "And you must be the princess," she said, looking at Evie and her blonde hair.

Florence looked at Evie. "She's not a princess, stupid pants, she doesn't have a crown duh-huh," she said, pulling a face at her sister.

"Elsa doesn't wear a crown and she's a princess," came the retort.

"OK, OK, kids, enough already," Nate said, laughing, "This is Evie, she is a friend of mine, say hello."

Evie was captivated by the girls, they were beautiful with their mousey hair in tidy ponytails trailing down their backs. They were not identical but they were wearing the same outfit. "Hello Evie," Trudie said, holding out her hand like she saw Daddy do to Gramps.

"Hello princess Evie," Florence said, going over to give Evie a hug.

Taken aback, she bent down and hugged the little girl back. "Well hello you two, it's lovely to meet you both, you are just as pretty as your daddy told me you were," she said, smiling. Gus walked in with Molly and there was a chorus of, "Gus! Gus!" from the girls as they forgot Evie and ran towards Gus.

"Hey, my little bandits!" he said, as they both stood on one of Gus's feet, each with arms around his waist so he could walk with them attached to his legs. Molly laughed, Evie was watching, laughing.

Noticing his son staring at Evie, Nate said, "Evie, this is my son, Mike. Say hello, Mike." Mike was still staring at Evie. Nate clipped him round the head playfully. "Oh yeah sorry, it's nice to meet you."

"You too," she smiled.

"Boss, can we take them round the grounds?" Gus asked, referring to Molly and himself. Wondering when that had happened Nate said, "of course," as they all disappeared.

Peter walked over to Evie who was standing awkwardly chewing the inside of her mouth. "I'm Peter, Sarah's father," he said, nodding at her. "I'm going to join the kids for a tour," he said to Nate and walked off.

"Well that wasn't too awkward," she said to Nate.

He hugged her, "You did brilliantly, the kids think you're great."

"Hmm, not sure about Mike though," she said, and Nate laughed.

"He's a sixteen-year-old lad who just met a beautiful woman that's all," he said, being able to read his son. "I'm going to go and join them, are you coming?"

She smiled and said, "No you go on, spend time with them I'm going to fix some food for later." He kissed her and went out to find the kids.

Brodie came out of the security room. "All OK?" he asked Evie who was chopping up vegetables.

"Yeah it's a lot to take in," she said. "It's strange, I know Nate the man, but I'm meeting Nate the father, it's all a bit out there at the moment."

Brodie pulled up a chair sitting at the island where she was working. "It will get easier," he said, stealing a carrot.

Nate was walking with Mike. "You OK, Mike?" he asked.

"Yeah Dad, she's hot."

"Mike!"

"I don't blame you, Dad, I mean not because she's hot but Mum's a handful, I know," he said, pointing to himself.

Nate put his arm around his son's shoulders. "You know it's nothing to do with you guys don't you?"

"Sure Dad, Mum is always moaning about you to me. It's so boring, why do you think I get stoned?"

Nate laughed. "We need to talk about that as well, my lad," he said, ruffling his son's hair.

After Peter had left with the kids, Nate felt regenerated. "At least I have some clothes now and more importantly my funeral suit."

Evie had never had an item of clothing that was just for a funeral. "Is Mike coming to the funeral?" she asked.

"He said Sarah was planning on coming, I've asked Peter to ask her to stay away but I can't stop her. If she comes it will be better if Mike is there with her." That was all they needed on top of an already horrid day was for Sarah to turn up.

Gus appeared. "I'm picking Cassie and the kids up tomorrow," he said, referring to Tina and Daryl. "I've been telling Molly about how nice your cooking is."

Evie had been surprised to see Molly smiling earlier. She was such a serious woman. She looked at Nate and then said, "Would you like to ask her to join us tonight?"

Gus's face lit up. "If that's OK, Evie, I'd like that."

Gus went off to find Molly smiling to himself.

Sarah was pacing, waiting for her father to return with the kids. After the girls telling her they had met a princess she sent them off with her mother. "You let them speak to that woman!" she said furiously at Peter who just looked at her.

Mike said, "Mum, she's OK, if Dad's going be with her we are going to have to get to know her."

She walked over to him and slapped him across his face leaving a red mark.

"Sarah!" Peter shouted, "what the hell is wrong with you?"

"She's psycho that's what's wrong with her!" Mike said, rubbing his face running up to his room. He didn't want them to see him cry.

"So help me, Sarah, if you ever lay a hand on those kids again I will take them off you!" Peter turned and walked out.

Sarah stood there for a minute before she went into the bar and found a bottle of expensive vodka. She took it to Nate's office; sitting behind his desk she poured herself a glass.

At Harringdon, dinner had been a success, Molly drank beer, who knew? And even Harris seemed to be more like his normal self. After a very long day, it was the perfect wind down. Tomorrow was going to be a difficult day with Max arriving, so everyone made the most of the relaxed evening.

19

Friday

There was a sombre feel to the house today. Dom arrived and had coffee and a catch up with Brodie and Harris. "We will reassess the current situation after the funeral," he told them. "Let's get the next few days done."

Brodie was quite happy where he was. Living alone, he was now enjoying company and his role as a protector. Harris seemed to be struggling more, he hadn't expected his partner to miss home to the point when he asked him if he wanted time out.

"Of course not," he replied.

"Fair enough, I just thought it might do you some good, you seem pretty quiet these days." Brodie shrugged.

"It's eating all this vegan food, Brodie. I mean, a man needs his meat."

Brodie laughed. "No fucking way, man! I thought you were missing your old lady but you're missing your steak!" He found this hysterical. "Say something if it bothers you that much."

"I can't, I thought we would only be here a few days and it would be OK, is it bad to say I'm looking forward to the funeral so I can get something decent to eat?"

This made Brodie laugh harder. "You know I've actually realised I feel a lot better from all this plant-based food," Brodie said. "And look," he said, pulling at his trousers, "I've lost a few pounds already."

"That's because you're not getting the protein you need, it's not natural," Harris replied sulkily.

"Dude you need to watch that documentary Evie showed Gus, it's really is a game changer." He walked off chuckling to himself. He hadn't told anyone but he sat and watched the documentary on his Netflix app on his phone. He had been converted enough to want to give it a serious go, after all, if a world-class chef says there is something in it then it must be worth considering.

Gus and Dom headed out to the garage. "I'm looking forward to driving this bad boy," Gus said, stroking the Range Rover Vogue Autobiography. It was black with tinted windows. "This is the bomb," he said. Cars had never impressed Dom, but maybe, he thought, it was because he could never afford something as luxurious as this.

"It's sure nice, Gus, it suits you," he said, making Gus grin from ear to ear.

Evie and Nate came out. "I wish I could come with you," she said to Nate kissing him.

"Me too, but we won't be long, I think Harry is meeting us at the airport. He's going to go with Max to the funeral home." Nate hadn't seen Harry in years neither had Max. It was an estranged relationship but a friendly one.

"Let's do this," Dom said, getting in the car.

Nate kissed Evie again and she watched Dom drive off in his unmarked police Audi and Gus in the Range Rover. She went back in the house and started making dough as she had decided to prepare pizza for everyone tonight.

It had been a traumatic journey for Cassie. When she watched Max's coffin being wheeled into the plane she felt it looked like an oversized piece of luggage. Tina and Daryl had been standing either side of her, supporting her in more ways than one. "Come on Cassie, let's board and get settled in, there is nothing you can do here." The journey was luxurious if non-eventful. Tina decided she was going to have to find a rich man to settle down with, Daryl agreed wholeheartedly. Landing back in the UK, Cassie was grateful it was at least a sunny day. They were escorted off the plane and taken to a room where Nate, Dom and Harry were waiting. Having already said their hellos and condolences to each other, Nate made a beeline for Cassie and gave her a big hug before introducing her to Dom and Harry. She had cried when she saw Harry, he resembled Max, though he wasn't quite as podgy. Nate gave both Tina and Daryl a hug and thanked them both for looking after Cassie.

"Evie is so looking forward to seeing you all," Nate said.

Harry left with Max's coffin and followed the funeral car back to his brother's next resting place for the time being. Dom had decided to go with him and had invited him to his home for dinner. Harry was grateful not to be alone. Tina fist-bumped Gus, which he found amusing for a white chick but still annoying.

Cassie went to Gus and he engulfed her with a big bear hug. "I'm glad you're home now, Molly has been worried about you." Wondering how Gus had broken through Molly's stern exterior she was looking forward to catching up on the gossip. Nate rode in the front with Gus as they filled each other in on the last few days. Nate had asked if his brother was good to stay and, as he expected, it was of course Cassie's pleasure. Nate had texted Evie when they were a few minutes away and she was at the door waiting for them with Molly as Gus pulled the car to a halt.

Tina jumped out and ran and hugged Evie, Daryl smartly pushed her out the way before Evie got the chance to hug Cassie.

"I was so worried about you," Evie said, as Molly came over and gave her employer a hug. Gus took care of the bags and showed the latest guests to their rooms. Molly went into Cassie's bedroom with her and shut the door. Tina looked at Evie who just shrugged. Everyone decided to shower and change before dinner so Evie went downstairs and joined Nate in the kitchen. He had opened a bottle of wine.

"I feel like the family is back together," she said to him. He kissed her nose and smiled.

Refreshed, the friends gathered in the kitchen. "This place is amazing," Tina marvelled, "I mean, I know you said it was big but this is just, wow."

Brodie walked in and caught Tina's eye. He introduced himself as detective Brodie and called Harris out to say hello and meet the new houseguests. "He is cute," she said quietly to Evie.

"Really?" she said, surprised, as Brodie was quite a bit older than Tina.

"Mmm," Daryl added, "very tasty." Causing the two girls to laugh.

Cassie entered with Molly and was pleased to see everyone had made themselves at home. "This is nice," she said. "Max would have loved this, all together and no work in sight." They all laughed.

Brodie went over and shook her hand followed by Harris, "Our condolences and thank you for the generous hospitality."

"Nonsense, thank you both for keeping my friends safe. Let's have a drink," she said.

"My kind of girl," said Evie holding up her glass of wine. "I will drink to that!"

Nate looked at her and said, "Evie, you will drink to anything." Causing them all again to laugh.

They had quite a production line for their dinner, Evie and Nate rolled out the dough passing it on to Gus who put the tomato sauce on top, who then handed them to Cassie and Tina to add the toppings, finally going to Daryl to add the cheese. Molly was in charge of oven operations.

Harris thought it was strange putting cheese on the pizza, as he knew cheese was not vegan but he was glad and he thoroughly enjoyed his food. "That was great thanks," he said, wiping his mouth and drinking a mouthful of beer. "But I'm confused that you put cheese on, I thought you guys didn't eat anything from an animal?" he asked.

Evie laughed. "It was vegan cheese silly, it's good you didn't even realise, just goes to show the perceptions of the brain. You thought it was 'normal' cheese, so that's what you tasted." She was pleased to be able to show that actually everything can be substituted without causing harm to an animal.

"Oh right," he said, feeling he had been robbed of the one good thing he thought he had eaten. "It's been a long few days," he said, as Brodie chuckled.

Cassie decided to turn in quite early. It had been a long, mentally draining week for her and she was looking forward to the comfort of her own bed. Daryl, Tina and Evie moved to the sofa in the kitchen to be more comfortable.

"I can't believe all this drama!" Tina said, "Who would do such a thing? That's so horrible," she said, referring to Sarah and the black tulip.

Daryl, on the other hand, said he was not surprised. "Women have hormones, it messes their sensibility up completely!" he declared.

Tina whacked him playfully. "Hey, enough with the hormone thing, how the hell would you know?" she retorted.

Evie laughed. "I kind of agree with him a little," she said, playing devil's advocate. "I mean sometimes when I'm hormonal I feel like I could wipe out all the animal eaters in the world and not care."

Daryl nodded and looked at Tina, "Exactly my point!" he said. "Can you imagine being the woman in charge of a country and you're hormonal so you say, oh fuck it, and press the red button?"

Evie laughed but Tina got very serious with him. "I suppose you think women shouldn't hold the same jobs as men as well." She threw back at him.

"I think a woman has every right to the same job as a man but how is it fair a woman gets maternity leave for so long when a man only gets a couple of weeks?"

"To be honest," Evie said, "I like having a door held open for me and I would always choose to be an actress instead of an actor. I've never understood that, I mean it's a masculine feminine thing not an equality thing. Actress sounds far more pretty."

Daryl sighed. "Well what would I be as a gay feminine man?" he queried.

"Well you're a man so you would be an actor."

"I'm a man who associates with my feminine side so technically I could also identify as an actress. Anyway, you're missing the point, Evie darling, women want to be equal, not feminised as 'pretty'."

"I don't know what you two are chatting about, actresses are so last decade they are all actors now so your conversation is pointless."

They both looked at Tina as Brodie came over having listened to their squabble. "I don't understand this binary thing, I mean, that's messed up," he said, looking at Daryl.

"Why are you looking at me? I identify as a gay man not 'us' or 'they'."

"But that's my point, everything has to have a label nowadays. Why can't we all just be people, why do people need to 'identify' as anything. We lasted hundreds of years like that why change now?" Brodie shrugged and sipped his beer.

"Just because we used to do it doesn't make it right," Evie said to him. "Times change and the world moves forward in a different direction, hopefully for the better, Brodie, it's all part of our evolvement."

"It just confuses the hell out of me. We soon won't have anything male or female, everything will be unisex or whatever it is that covers all the identities in the world now." Brodie was old school. "As far as I'm concerned if you have a penis you're a guy, if you can have a baby you're a girl. I do understand people feeling they are born into the wrong gender body and wanting a sex change. I mean I can get my head around that."

"I don't know what you all think you're chatting about." They turned around to look at Gus. "You kids know nothing about anything if you ain't black. Slavery was wrong yet we are still persecuted because of the colour of our skin, even today," Gus said. "You all put labels on yourselves, and say it's your right to be accepted as what you identify with. Try identifying as a person of colour." They said nothing.

Nate came over, "What on earth are you lot going on about?" he asked. "Live and let live, who cares as long as everyone is happy."

"What he said," Evie said.

Brodie shrugged. "I don't know man, kids today," and he went off to find Harris. Gus also shrugged. He was wasting his time trying to make these guys understand. He looked over and Molly was giving him a 'good for you' smile. He smiled back.

"Well I'm going to turn in, I need my beauty sleep," Daryl said, getting up, "coming, Hun?" he said to Tina.

"God yes I'm hanging." She hugged Evie and said, "night," and off they went still bickering.

Nate sat on the sofa with Evie. "Those two never stop," he said, amused by their banter.

"I know they can get a bit full on sometimes," she said, resting her head on his shoulder. "Shall we go up to bed?" he said quietly to her.

"Mmm, yes please," she said, as he got up and helped her to her feet.

Inside the room he kissed her softly, she stepped away and took her top off, he watched as she stripped down to her black underwear, looking at her body with hunger in his eyes. She took off her bra as he took in her perfect breasts and hard nipples. He watched her as she slid her hand down the front of her panties while stroking her other hand over her breast playing with her nipple. It was too much for him. He went to her, taking his t-shirt off, he kissed her forcefully as he stepped forward pushing her towards the bed. He took her panties off, knelt down and kissed her navel, she fell back on the bed as he opened her legs and buried his head between them.

Evie, now aware of the additional houseguests moaned as quietly as possible. He was driving her mad to the point she stopped him and said, "I need you now."

He stood up and stripped the rest of his clothes off as she lay on the bed touching herself provocatively, he was so hard it hurt. She gazed over his toned body, he was driving her crazy standing there watching. He was so aroused he had to go to her.

As they became one, he kissed her neck as she tipped her head back, "Oh Nate," she sighed, as he thrust deeper inside her, this was unlike anything she had ever experienced before as he looked into her eyes they both came, she knew she would never let him go.

20

Saturday

There was a lot to get ready for Monday and there was an air of urgency about Cassie as she organised her house. She had spoken to her caterers while she was still in the States. Between her and Molly they had everything sorted. Cleaners were coming today; caterers and service staff would be here Monday morning after setting up on Sunday. The flow of people would be ushered through to the entertainment room where the quadruple doors opened half the room out onto the grounds. It was an ideal house for entertaining, Cassie just wished it could be like the old days, full of happy people celebrating an occasion instead of sad people at a wake.

Evie found her walking around the entertainment room lost in memories. "Cassie are you OK?" she asked.

"Yes dear, I just miss him." She dabbed the corners of her eyes with her tissue. "I just wish things had turned out different that's all."

Evie went to her and gave her a hug. "We are all here for you."

Cassie smiled at her, "You're a sweet girl Evie, Nate is lucky to have you." Evie knew Cassie hadn't thought much of Sarah from comments she had made and she was glad to have friends who supported their relationship.

Tina came in followed by Daryl. "There is a delivery girl," Daryl said, "I think it's the clothes you ordered." He'd seen Evie's name on the bag.

"I'd better go find something to wear," she said, leaving Tina with Cassie.

"Come on, darling, I will help you choose," Daryl said, leading the way.

They went into Evie and Nate's room. Shutting the door behind him, Daryl looked around at the size of the room. "My God this is even bigger than my room," he said, with his hand on his chest.

Evie grabbed the bag that Tina had brought back for her and started to unpack. "I need to get a bikini so I can go use the pool," she said out loud.

Daryl was opening her packages that had been delivered and got the three outfits out. He hung them up and looked at them. There was a trouser, shirt and jacket outfit. "Hmm," he said with his finger on his lip concentrating, "I don't like that." He touched the next outfit feeling the quality. "Darling we have to get you to shop more expensively, this material is tat," he said, referring to the plain black dress. "And it's so old fashioned!"

She watched him, her eyes squinted like she was trying to figure out what he would say about the last item.

"Oh dear," was all he said as he packed them back up in the bag. "Throw these away perlease," he said, dramatically.

"But I need something to wear, Daryl, it's a funeral not a fashion show."

"Evie, enough!" he said, holding his hand up to stop her. She was a little taken aback. "You are the girlfriend of Nate Rivers, you can not buy twenty-pound outfits anymore. You have to keep up with the fashion and you have to learn your new place in society."

"Which is what?" she said.

"I've just told you, you are Nate Rivers' girlfriend. Do you think he wears twenty-pound suits from Top Man? No, his clothes cost hundreds, if not thousands," he said, expecting it to all make sense to her.

"Well, in that case, I will have to re-educate him on the value of money," she replied.

"You love him right?"

"Of course!"

"Then you need to look right for him. I mean you could wear a bin bag and he would love you but you need to be classy, sophisticated. You're not working to live now, you don't need to count the pennies."

Evie knew he was right but it was going to take some getting used to.

"I need to earn my own money I don't want to let Nate support me." Neither of them had noticed that Nate was standing in the doorway.

He had gone up to find Evie and had heard them talking. He wished Alfie Cartwright was here to hear what he just had. He opened the door and they both looked startled when they turned round and saw him.

"You are both right," he said. "Evie, you are my girlfriend and my co-worker. Once all this is over we will talk contracts and wages. But in the meantime, you are also my girlfriend and I want you to feel free to spend whatever you need."

Daryl looked relieved. "I need to go shopping now and get Evie a dress for Monday, you trust me don't you, darling?" Daryl said.

Evie shrugged and nodded. "I guess so, something plain though, I don't want to draw any attention to myself."

Nate smiled knowing it wouldn't matter what she wore she would turn heads. "Here take this," he said to Daryl, taking his credit card out and handing it to him. "Get Gus to drive you and help him get a suit." Daryl was more than pleased.

"Fabulous! See you later, darling," he said, as he went off to find Gus.

Evie went over to Nate and put her arms around his waist. "I don't want to be a kept woman," she said.

"And you won't be but you can't stop me from wanting to spoil you now and then," he kissed her nose and smiled at her.

She moved her hands up to touch his face. "I love you," she said.

"I love you too," he replied, as she kissed him.

***

Harris was staring at the security screen blankly. Brodie had gone to make a sandwich. He had bought that line about the food, he couldn't let Brodie know what was really troubling him. He thought about Eddie. He was such an openly strange man yet he seemed to think he was normal. People like Eddie freaked him out. He wasn't sure why the guv had taken him under his wing. Harris was bored of having to pretend to care for these people. He didn't actually miss his family even though he always said he did to his wife. She was the perfect wife. She looked after the kids, she cooked and cleaned and ironed all his shirts. He really couldn't have done any better. He was empty though, he had a lack of feelings towards his wife and that was something that he had to learn how to fake. She was wife material and she had produced children. Job done. The kids were both under six and he could take them or leave them, most days preferring to leave them. Another relationship he had learned how to fake. He had always observed people and their actions and he learned how he should behave in society. He had wondered in the past why he was devoid of feeling. He envied Brodie and his bachelor approach to life. If he had to do it again he would be more like him but without the temper. When they were first partnered, Brodie had been a live wire ready to explode at anything or anyone. Harris soon taught him how to act chilled and calm. He was a good teacher, he hadn't seen Brodie blow up for a while. He was a calming influence on his partner. So why is life so empty? He wondered.

Daryl found Gus polishing his new favourite toy. "Hey man," he said to Daryl who then explained he needed a ride. Gus was a bit annoyed, as he had polished the Range Rover when they got back and he would have to redo it now.

"Sure thing, anything for the boss," Gus said, wanting to make it clear who he answered to. He liked Daryl but sometimes he was so bossy Gus wasn't sure how Tina put up with him. He had enjoyed the company of Molly the last couple of days, however, she was busy getting ready for Monday and Gus hadn't seen much of her today. He felt like he wanted to buy her something but he didn't know what or why really.

"Gus, we need to get you a suit for the funeral and maybe some other clothes, Evie said you left with next to nothing, I've been given artistic licence by the boss and it is all on him!"

"Sweet," Gus said, smiling. First class, now this, he could get used to this way of living.

Molly was in her element organising things for Monday. She had everything under control. They had over 200 confirmations for the wake and Cassie had spoken to Harry and they had agreed that close friends and family only at the service but to have a more open house for the wake.

She had hired her normal security company to aid on the day making sure only people on the guest list were allowed in as she wanted no paparazzi. Dom was bringing an undercover presence as well, and Brodie and Harris would be in sole charge of keeping Evie safe. There had been some flowers delivered to the house in the morning, the first official wreath was from Dean Harper. Cassie didn't really know the man but she knew Nate and him were close. He had phoned Nate as soon as he had heard of Max's death to offer his condolences. Gus was to drive Cassie and Nate to the service and Evie and the others would follow. The funeral was not the place to announce Nate's new relationship and the overall feeling from head office had been to keep a low profile until things with Sarah had blown over.

Nate had received a text from his brother giving him an ETA. He was outside pacing, waiting to hear the roar of his brother's 718 Spyder, an awesome sounding Porsche. Billy had a passion for fast cars and fast women. He was the polar opposite to his baby brother, Nate. He had similar rugged handsome features but he was born to be in the spotlight and was always throwing his brother's name around to get into clubs and high-society parties.

"Just don't get me a bad rep," Nate had begged him, knowing his brother's thirst for fame. Billy had built up his own worldwide construction business. Success was in the boy's genes but there was only ever one happy front man. "I just don't like the fuss," Nate once told his brother.

"Bro you've got to own it," he had responded to Nate. He had never understood why Nate had decided to settle down and get married, he loved his nephew and nieces but family life was not for him. As Nate heard the car roaring down the road he called through for the gates to be opened so he could drive straight in. Coming in way too fast but slowing down once he realised he was driving on gravel, Billy tooted the horn. Evie had joined Nate who was eager to introduce her to his brother.

The car stopped and Billy jumped out running to hug his little brother. "Little bud," he said, stepping back grinning at Nate. "You look well, considering…"

He was five years older than Nate and they had grown up having a fun and happy childhood. Nate had always been the quiet one while Billy loved to play the clown. "And you must be the infamous Evie," he said, surprising her as he went over and hugged her lifting her off her feet before putting her back down.

"Oh!" she exclaimed, trying to find the floor with her toes. "It's great to meet you I haven't heard that much about you I'm afraid," she said, smiling warmly. She couldn't help but like him.

"Just as well, love," he said to her. There was a cough from the car. "Oh yeah, shit sorry, honey," he said, as he ran round to open the passenger door. An extremely tall slim brunette stepped out the car. She wore high heel stilettos, a very short and inappropriate blue dress, very heavy make-up and was covered in fake tan. Evie looked at Nate, who shrugged as if to say 'don't ask me'.

"This is Suzy, my current girlfriend," he said, holding her hand and kissing it. Neither Evie nor Nate missed the 'fuck you' glance she gave him when he referred to her as 'current'.

"It's lovely to meet you," Evie said, walking towards Suzy to shake her hand. Nate followed and kissed her cheek and welcomed her.

"Shall we go in? I will grab your bags in a bit," Nate said, leading the way.

Tina gasped when she saw the tall woman, until she realised nine inches of her was heel. Nate introduced everyone present. Cassie seemed quite happy to welcome more guests she didn't know into her house.

She walked over to Evie and said quietly to her, "You got the right brother dear." Causing Evie to try and hide a laugh. Nate took Billy in to meet the detectives who had both been fixated on the screen watching the car first then the long-legged brunette stepping out.

Evie said to Suzy, "Would you like to see your room?"

Suzy smiled, "What I would really like is to get out of these stupid shoes."

Evie grinned at her. "Likes them does he?" she said, with humour in her eyes.

"Honey, trust me, never trust a man who likes high-heeled shoes!"

Evie laughed, "Take them off and go upstairs, I will get your bag, Tina can you show her the way please?"

Evie went out to the Porsche thinking she was indeed lucky to have Nate, he might want to pay for her clothes but he certainly doesn't tell her what to wear. She got the bag out the back that she assumed was Suzy's as it was bright pink, and headed upstairs to find her.

In the room allocated to Billy, Suzy was barefoot and in awe. "Wow," she said, "This place is awesome."

"I know," Tina replied. "It's mad that Cassie lives here alone with her housekeeper!"

"No!" Suzy said. "That's criminal." She saw Evie with her bag and went over to take it off her. She said, "Thank you so much." She opened the bag and, without warning, she took her dress off and she was butt naked. Evie and Tina's eyes went wide at the same time and they looked at each other. Suzy laughed, "Ah the age of innocence," she said. "I'm a stripper by trade, escort for fun. Billy always comes to me when he needs a date. Usually though it's for parties not funerals. This is a first for me."

"So, he's paying you to be here?" Tina said, stunned, realising now why nudity didn't faze her in front of strangers.

"No, this one is a freebie. I've known Billy for years, I have made a lot of money from him, I'm not going to lie, and he is one of the sweetest clients. He's actually quite reserved and shy but I think I'm the only one who sees that side."

"Sounds to me like you are his girlfriend in a fucked-up way," Tina said, knowing she was going to have lots of questions to ask this fascinating woman.

Evie laughed and said, "You guys come down when you're ready, I will open the bar!"

"Brilliant idea," Suzy said, putting on a very expensive, very trendy tracksuit.

Evie liked Suzy, she heard the way her voice changed when she talked about Billy. There was more to it than a business arrangement. Meanwhile Billy and Nate had grabbed a beer and headed outside to be alone. Sitting at the end of the pool facing the house they could see the goings-on in the kitchen.

"So, I recognise Suzy, I mean I recognise a younger version of her," Nate said, raising an eyebrow at his brother.

Billy laughed. "There's no pulling the wool over your eyes, baby brother. It was a couple of years ago, you had a birthday party for Sarah, she was my date then as well."

Nate nodded his head. "Yeah that's right, and you got so much stick from Sarah for keeping her quiet." Billy laughed remembering. "So, have you been seeing her since then? That's unlike you not to mention it," Nate said.

Billy didn't feel like explain himself to his brother; he had more pressing matters to think about.

"Billy? What is it?"

Billy sighed, he dropped the façade and he looked shattered. "I've fucked up, Nate. I've lost it all."

"All what?" Confused, Nate suddenly sat forward worried about Billy.

"Every fucking thing, bro, I've gambled it all away. I'm in a world of shit, I owe the wrong people." Nate could hardly believe what he was hearing.

"Since when have you been a gambler?"

"Since always, I just kept it quiet, nothing high profile more under the table kind of things, card games, like I said with the wrong kind of people."

Nate was still in a state of disbelief. "What kind of wrong people Billy? The kind that will take you to court or the kind that will blow your knee caps off?" His look said it all. "Jesus fucking Christ," Nate said, rubbing his head. "Why didn't you come to me earlier? I could have helped you."

Billy smiled a wry smile. "I was embarrassed, man, you're my baby brother, besides you don't really know you've got a problem until it's too late."

Suzy and Evie came outside talking away. Suzy had changed into a tracksuit and looked a lot more relaxed than the first time Nate saw her today.

"Don't say a word," Billy said, "you are the only one who knows."

Putting his façade up he stood up. "Darling, you look as gorgeous as ever," he said, going over to Suzy and smacking her on the bum. "Come on, I will show you the grounds," he said, walking off with her.

Evie smiled at Suzy as she raised an eyebrow to her before walking off with Billy.

Evie looked at Nate. He smiled, "Come here, beautiful," he said, beckoning her to his knee.

"I like Suzy," she told him. "I think she actually likes Billy as well."

Nate was confused. "Why wouldn't she?" he asked.

As Evie told him about their conversation in the bedroom Nate listened, and at one point he nearly choked on his beer. "Oh my God, the dirty dog," he said. "He's in more trouble than I thought." She looked at him curiously.

"Don't worry about, it's boy stuff."

She decided to drop it. She knew if it was important he would tell her.

"Come on, let's go in and join the others," she said, seeing his bottle empty.

Gus was back with Daryl who had shopping bags with designer labels on. Evie promised she would try clothes on tomorrow but she just wanted a glass or two of wine and something to eat. Suzy and Billy came back in the house, Billy looked like he didn't have a care in the world. Suzy made a beeline for Evie and sat with her drinking red wine.

Nate went over to his brother, "It will be OK, let's get this funeral out the way then we can sit down and work things out."

Billy looked relieved, it had been hard for him to come to Nate begging for help and Nate had saved him from that embarrassment. "Thanks bro," he said, as Gus and Molly walked in.

"Hey Gus, look who it is," Nate said, pointing to Billy.

"Oh my, it's double trouble," Gus said, coming over and shaking Billy's hand.

"Where is Cassie?" Molly asked, "I thought she was down here?"

"Haven't seen her actually," Tina said.

Molly looked concerned and excused herself. Upstairs she found Cassie in the bathtub crying her eyes out. Putting a towel around her and helping her out the bath, Molly sat with her on the bathroom floor until she stopped crying.

"I'm OK," she said.

"I know you are," Molly replied. "You will get through this." She squeezed Cassie's hand. "Now get dressed and come downstairs, it's time to eat." Cassie nodded getting up and Molly looked at her, nodded her head once, and left.

Half an hour later everyone except Brodie and Harris were drinking and picking at finger food.

"Where are the boys with the guns?" Gus asked. Suzy looked around expecting to see a couple of fit well-toned men. He got up and went to look for them. Brodie was in the security room. "Man do you ever get fed up with playing that stupid game?" Gus said, as he saw he was playing solitaire.

"Gus it's addictive, I can't explain, I have to beat Harris's score."

"Uh-hu, well there is beer and good company out there if you care to join us. Where is Harris?" Gus asked.

"I thought he was with you lot," Brodie replied. Just then Harris came in and they both stared at him.

"What?" he said, "Can't a man go to the john in peace anymore?" they laughed and headed into the kitchen to join the others.

Cassie was again the first to go to bed. Molly went up with her and came down fifteen minutes later. "She is OK," she said to Gus as he pulled a chair out so she could sit back next to him.

Suzy was giving Billy the look and he excused them both as they headed up to bed.

"Wow, where to start with those two!" Tina said, as Daryl sat forward waiting for some gossip.

"Tina," Nate said firmly, "I'd rather you didn't gossip about my brother and his girlfriend, please."

Tina looked ashamed. "Sorry, Boss, I didn't mean any harm." It wasn't until Nate started laughing she realised he was playing her. "Say what you like I'm going to bed." He had drunk more than he had intended to while catching up with Billy. Evie said she would be up in a bit but by the time she got upstairs Nate was fast asleep. She stripped naked and cuddled up to him.

21

Sunday

Brodie and Harris were working for their money today. The house was full of people. There were flowers being delivered to brighten up the house, caterers were busy organising tables and seats for an informal seated buffet and the gardeners were called on to put in extra time. "This is mad trying to keep an eye on everyone, I'm glad we are getting extra security tomorrow," Brodie said.

Harris agreed even though he actually didn't care. Gus was polishing the Range Rover again after its journey out yesterday with Daryl. Daryl meanwhile was in Evie's room showing her what he had bought for her to wear. He had bought her a Stella McCartney fitted scoop neck dress. It came just below the knees and was short sleeved. It fitted her perfectly and it looked amazing.

"Wow!" Daryl said, "I'm so good."

Evie looked at him smiling. "Yeah it's a nice dress."

"Nice? Nice? It's stunning darling, and notice how I made sure you had a vegan designer, hmm?" Evie had to admit she was pleased about that.

"How much was it?" she queried.

"It was a steal at one thousand, three hundred and forty-five pounds," he said, without flinching. Evie's mouth fell open.

"Oh my God, how? It's a bit of material."

Daryl put his hand over his eyes and shook his head. "Darling please, you're embarrassing yourself. It is perfect for the occasion."

"OK, I trust you," she said sighing, thinking how far that money would have gone on wine.

Dom arrived with Eddie and Harry. He had persuaded Harry to stay at his house rather than book into a hotel and he wanted to run through tomorrow's operations with Eddie, Harris and Brodie. Disappearing into the security room, he was surprised to see people he did not know. "Ah guv, these are Cassie's boys, they are taking the lead on security tomorrow, means we can stick with Evie."

Dom nodded, "OK, who's in charge? Let's gather round and make a plan."

Harry was in the kitchen drinking coffee with Nate and Cassie reminiscing with stories of Max.

"I wish I had had more time with him," Cassie said, staring at nothing.

Nate squeezed her hand and smiled, she smiled back.

"Maybe on Tuesday you will come to Max's house with me, Cassie, and we can go through his things," Harry said.

Cassie was pleased to be considered part of that procedure. "I would like that very much," she said gratefully.

"Of course, Nate you're more than welcome to come over as well."

Nate nodded. "Thanks," he said, not really sure if it was something he wanted to do. It made things so final. He guessed that was what Cassie needed, closure.

Molly came in and called Cassie away to answer a few questions the caterers were asking, leaving Harry and Nate to themselves.

"I viewed Max's body yesterday," Harry said, surprising Nate. "I needed to say goodbye, as did Dom." He looked down at his hands.

Nate had been trying to keep his friend's dead body alive, that was how he had seen him the last time. He did not feel the need to see him again.

"That's understandable," he said. Harry had not married either; he lived with another middle-aged man back home in Norfolk. Harry was gay but he had never come out, choosing to keep himself to himself. Max had told Nate he felt sorry for him and wished he would just let himself be free and live openly and happily. It was a shame to hide something that, in this day and age, was openly accepted.

Evie had just taken off her unbelievably expensive dress when her door opened. Smiling, as she expected it to be Nate, instead Eddie came in. She grabbed the dress holding it up to cover her body, but he stood there looking at her.

"What are you doing in here?" she asked.

"Security check," was all he said, still looking at her. He was creeping her out.

"No one has ever done a security check in here before," she said, annoyed.

"The house has never been so busy before," he said, still staring at her.

"Get out please." She was feeling very uncomfortable.

He gave her a final look over and left.

Evie went to the door and locked it. She phoned Nate who answered the phone, "Hey, beautiful," he said, and then his expression changed and he excused himself and ran upstairs. The door was locked so he banged on it, "Evie it's me what's happened?" She opened the door and flung herself at him.

Nate was fuming. He hugged Evie and waited for her to get dressed. He took her hand and they went downstairs. Eddie was standing in the hall with Dom talking to Harry. Nate did not miss the way Eddie had looked at Evie as they were coming down the stairs. Nate let go of Evie's hand and surprised everyone as he went for Eddie, who he caught totally off guard. Nate had his arm under Eddie's chin and backed him up against the wall.

"Nate!" Evie said, as Dom and Harry went over to try and pull him off.

"What's your fucking problem, you perv," he shouted in Eddie's face. Eddie just turned his head to the side so Nate's spit didn't go in his mouth.

"Nate!" Dom shouted, "Let go!"

By now Tina had come out of her room and ran to stand next to Evie.

Gus had heard the commotion and seen the two men on Nate and ran over and started pulling them off. "Get off of him!" Gus yelled at them. Dom let go as did Harry. Nate still had Eddie up against the wall.

"Boss, Boss!" he said louder the second time. "You want me to do that for you?"

Nate looked at Gus. "He was perving on Evie!" Nate shouted in Eddie's face pushing him harder up against the wall. Eddie was so scrawny he had no weight behind him to push back. Gus took Nate's arm and moved it from Eddie's neck releasing him.

Eddie rubbed his neck and said, "You fucking idiot."

That was it, Gus had him by the neck lifting him off the ground. Dom was watching and told Nate to do something. The look Dom saw in Nate's eyes unnerved him.

Still looking at Dom, Nate said, "Put him down, Gus." Gus immediately did as he was told. "Get him out of here and don't ever bring him back."

Harris and Brodie had been watching from the kitchen entrance. "Wish we had popcorn," Brodie said, making his partner chuckle. "Should we go and help Eddie?"

"Nah," said Harris. "The guv's there, he can deal with it."

Dom told Eddie to wait in the car. Hands on his hips, Nate stood his ground and stared at Dom challenging him.

"What the hell Nate?" said Dom. Evie came down the rest of the stairs and stood in front of Nate separating the two men. Facing Dom, she put her hands on his chest and said, "Detective, he was in my room, he wouldn't leave and I was undressed."

Dom stepped back, "What?"

She told him what had happened. Brodie looked at Harris and raised an eyebrow. Harris knew the scrawny freak was bad news. He was undisciplined, unlike Harris who was always in complete control of his actions.

Evie turned round and cupped Nate's head in her hands looking into his face, she had never seen him like this before. She put her arms around his neck and felt his tension start to fade. Dom went over to Brodie and told him to keep him posted on what was going on in the house and he marched out to join Eddie and Harry who were both waiting at the car.

"Get in!" he said angrily to Eddie. He had wasted his time on this kid and he was angry. Dom dropped Harry off at his house, which was on the way back to the station. In his office was the first time Dom had spoken to Eddie since telling him to get in the car. Shutting the door behind him, Eddie went and sat in front of Dom's desk.

"Get the fuck-up, Sergeant," Dom shouted at him, "just what the hell were you playing at?"

"Sorry guv, I did knock but I guess she didn't hear me. I left as soon as I saw her, I don't know what his problem is. I think I should press assault charges against him."

"You will do no such thing. You are off the case and think yourself lucky you still have a job!"

"But the funeral is tomorrow! I have to be there. I've done nothing wrong! You can't believe that girl over me!"

"Sergeant, you are using up my last reserve. You will return to uniform duties and you'd better hope they don't decide to lodge a complaint against you! Now get out of my office!" Eddie looked shocked. This couldn't be happening. He needed to be at the house tomorrow he couldn't be benched. Not now, he had come so far.

"Out!" Dom screamed at him making him jump.

"Yes, Sir," and he left. He would show them, they would all pay for this.

"Oh dear I miss all the drama," Cassie said, as Tina told her and Daryl what had happened. "No way man, my little bro got physical?" Billy said, coming in with Suzy.

"OMG," Daryl said to them. "Where have you been?"

Suzy tried not to blush and Billy just shrugged, "We are outdoor kind of people, went for a, er, walk."

"Yes, that's what we did," Suzy confirmed.

Cassie raised an eyebrow, Tina giggled and Daryl said, "Mm, hmm, so that's what we're calling it these days." They all laughed.

"Tell me more about Nate and the perv," Suzy said sitting down. "Is it wine o'clock yet?" she said.

"Always," said Evie walking in with two bottles followed by a sheepish Nate. They all cheered and clapped.

"What a hero, bro," Billy said, slapping his brother on the back,

"OK, you lot, stop taking the piss."

"Well I thought it was very sexy," Evie said, making him blush.

Someone wolf whistled, it was Brodie. Nate had been worried that Brodie and Harris might be pissed off that he attacked one of their colleagues.

"That guy wasn't right for this job," Brodie said, as he turned around and went back into the security room.

Gus had gone to find Molly. "I lost my temper," he told her.

"It's OK, Gus, sometimes it's what you need to do. I didn't like that one anyway, there was something very strange and creepy about him."

Gus felt reassured. He had found a true friend in Molly. "How long you gonna be in here?" Gus asked, nodding towards the entertainment room.

"Not long, I just want to see the last of them off the property then I will join you all for a beer." She stood on her tiptoes and kissed him on his cheek. His eyes went big and he touched his face where she had kissed him. She had already turned and walked off before he had the chance to react.

Evie had found a kindred spirit in Suzy. They could both sit and drink red wine like it was going out of fashion. "So, Nate's gorgeous, he seems more complicated than Billy though," she said, looking at the two brothers across the island talking.

"Do you love Billy?" Evie asked.

Suzy was taken aback. "Girl I told you I'm a pro."

"I know what you said…"

"So why are you asking me a stupid question like that?"

"Because I see the way you look at him."

Suzy shifted in her seat. "It's a complex relationship. I do care for him and I think, on some level, maybe he cares for me… but love?" Suzy was confused about their relationship in truth. He always came back to her no matter what and to her knowledge he had not had a long-term girlfriend.

"Well I think maybe there is more to it than either of you realise. Nate and I tried to deny we had feelings for each other."

Suzy looked at her and nudged her with her elbow. "So?" she said.

Evie looked at her. "So what?"

"So, is he a complete stud in bed or what? Come on girl give up the gossip."

Evie laughed, she had no intention of discussing her sex life so she just smiled and raised an eyebrow causing them both to giggle like teenagers.

"Thanks for having my back, Gus," Nate said later that evening as they all gathered together to eat.

"Always, Boss, you know that." Gus was loyal there was no doubt about that. "There was something off about that guy," Gus said, "I got a bad vibe from him." Gus hadn't been wrong about that. "When you said he was perving on Evie, I wanted to kill him."

Nate believed him and said, "Yeah me too."

Billy and Suzy had been a breath of fresh air to the house. They brought a new dynamic to the friends and new stories to laugh over. It had been a fun evening and what they all needed after the earlier events of the day, and for the day that was about to dawn on them.

22
Monday

Evie and Nate were up early. The service was at 12.30pm and there was lots to do. Caterers and waiters were already at the house as were the security firm. Brodie and Harris both wore their shoulder holsters and were drinking coffee at the island.

"It will be nice to get out," Harris said.

"I've not left the house for a week," Harris chuckled. "Yeah a trip to the cemetery sounds like fun."

"Laugh it up, mate, I'm stir fucking crazy," Harris replied, looking forward to getting out of the house. He nudged his partner as Cassie came in with Molly.

"Morning," Brodie said, "how are you holding up?" he asked Cassie.

"Morning, dears, I'm doing OK at present thank you. Molly will you be OK here keeping things in order?"

"Of course, Cassie, I have everything under control."

Nate and Evie came into the kitchen. Nate went straight over to Cassie and hugged her while Evie put a new pot of coffee on.

Nate's phone rang, it was Sarah. "Oh for God's sake," he said as he answered it.

"Yes?" he said, sounding annoyed. There was silence for a few minutes.

"I'm coming to the funeral today. We should be together to show a united front to the press."

"No." He couldn't believe she had the nerve. "I don't want you coming, Sarah."

"Well that's not your choice. Are you going to deny me my right to say goodbye to an old friend?"

Nate sighed, he knew she was right. "Is Mike coming?"

"Yes, he said if he was old enough to have sex he was old enough to decide for himself."

"Did he now," Nate chuckled. "OK, but no drama, Sarah, I mean it. I am going with Cassie and I will be sitting with her in the church."

"OK, I will behave I promise," she said, then hung up. Nate rubbed his head, God he hoped so.

Nate and Evie disappeared upstairs to get ready. Evie was standing in her underwear and Nate stopped to admire her. "You are so beautiful," he said.

She smiled at him stepping into her dress, "Can you do me up please?" she asked. He went over to her and kissed her neck as he slowly did up the zip.

"This is a first," he said, "I'm usually taking your clothes off."

She laughed and turned around stepping back. "What do you think?" Evie looked stunning. She stepped into her Stella McCartney shoes and stood in front of the mirror looking at her £2,000-plus outfit.

"Wow," was all he said.

"Do you want to know what I cost you today?" she said, teasing him.

"No," he said, laughing, "Do you think Billy buys Suzy her clothes?" he said.

Evie laughed. "Oh yes. I dread to think what inappropriate mini dress she will be wearing today."

Nate grinned. "Yup, at least hopefully she will take the attention off you, I'm worried you know," he said getting serious.

She walked over to him and took over from his attempts to make his tie sit correctly. "It will be OK, I will be with Tina and Daryl and I've got Brodie and Harris with me. You can't worry about me today. Promise me, Nate, you need to be there for Cassie." He knew she was right. They had heard nothing about her stalker. It was as if it had never happened.

"OK," he said. "But just be careful." She kissed him. "I love you so much, Evie I couldn't bear to lose you."

"Hey, I'm not going anywhere, I'm not done with you yet, Mr Rivers." She kissed him and they turned and stood in front of the mirror.

"Well I think we are ready," he said, taking her hand.

Downstairs everyone was gathered in the hall waiting for Max to arrive. The atmosphere was tense and the friends were being unusually quiet. Suzy had surprised everyone as she was wearing a very suitable trouser suit outfit.

"I do have some decorum you know," she said when questioned by Daryl on her taste.

Brodie saw Evie coming down with Nate and went over to her. "We are your new best friends," he said without humour.

"Look after her," Nate said. Brodie nodded.

The security guards had opened the gates ready for the funeral cars. Harry and Dom were following them down the drive. As the hearse came to a stop outside the front door everyone fell silent. It was a stark reminder that this was real. Molly stood next to Cassie and took her hand and squeezed it. Tears were rolling down Cassie's cheeks. There was only one flower arrangement in the hearse that simply read MAX.

Evie held Nate's hand; she wished she could be by his side today.

He turned to Evie and hugged her. "I love you," he said.

"I love you too," she replied.

He kissed her and went over to Cassie. He offered Cassie his arm and escorted her to the beautifully polished Range Rover.

"My oh my, Gus," she said, as he held the door open for her. "It looks amazing."

Nate got in the back with Cassie for this journey. They were to follow the hearse, with Dom, Harry, Billy and Suzy in the first funeral car behind them. Tina, Daryl, Evie and her two protectors were in the final car. The hearse started its slow journey down the drive with the funeral director walking in front.

"This will take forever," Daryl said.

"Don't be stupid, Daryl, he will get in when we reach the main road," Tina replied.

"You two aren't going to argue all day are you?" Brodie asked.

"What are you talking about, we never argue?" Daryl said.

"Us?" Tina questioned. Brodie raised is eyes and shook his head. Evie sat quietly looking out of the window.

Gus didn't say a word in the car. He was taking his role today like a complete professional. Nate was holding Cassie's hand in the back, "Thanks, Nate," she said.

"Don't be silly, Cassie. Max was family as are you." She smiled at him wishing she could hold her beloved Maxy one last time.

As the hearse pulled to a stop outside the church, Evie saw the small troop of reporters and paparazzi waiting to take photos of Max's coffin and the mourners. There were some mourners already at the church waiting and some had gone in preferring not to have their picture taken by the hungry press. Nate got out and did his jacket button up. Gus had Cassie's door and Nate helped her out.

"Cassie, can you say something for the viewers please," someone shouted from behind the barricade Dom had organised.

"Where is Mrs Rivers?" Someone else shouted. "Is it true Max was poisoned?"

That was it, Gus had had enough. He turned around towards the troop and said, "Enough! This is a funeral. Show some respect."

They fell silent taken aback by the driver's outburst. Nate squeezed Gus's arm as if to say thanks and turned around facing the hearse with Cassie and waited. Gus moved the Range Rover and came back to stand next to his boss. The two cars following stopped and their passengers got out and gathered round behind Nate, except for Harry and Dom who stood in line with them. Cameras were relentlessly clicking. From nowhere another black car turned up. The driver opened the door and Sarah stepped out followed by Mike. She had a single black tulip in her hand.

Mike went straight over to his dad, "I'm sorry she took my phone off me this morning."

"It's OK, son, go be with your mother." Nate turned his head and looked at Evie whose mouth had fallen open.

"That fucking bitch," Tina said quietly to Evie. Dom looked at Nate and gave him a don't react look. Nate had no intention of satisfying Sarah.

The press were shouting at Sarah. "Why are you in a separate car, Sarah?"

"How come your husband is staying at Harringdon?"

She started walking over towards Nate. She walked up to him and offered him the tulip. Nate totally blanked his wife. He was past caring about his reputation. The only thing that mattered to him was Evie's safety. Sarah turned around towards the press and shrugged.

"Mum, come on," Mike was saying to her.

She turned back round to Nate. "I suppose you think this was funny," she said to him as she pushed past him and headed towards Evie.

"Stay put, Nate, don't react. Trust Evie," Dom said.

Sarah walked over to Evie as Brodie and Harris both moved closer to her. "Here you go dear," she said, holding the black tulip out for Evie, "I think this was meant for you."

Evie looked at her straight in the eye. Brodie was waiting for it to kick off but Evie just said, "Thank you Sarah, that was very considerate of you." She took the tulip and smiled at her. "Mum! Come on," Mike said, taking his mother and dragging her away. The cameras had been rolling and pictures were taken.

Cassie had had enough. She kissed Nate's cheek and turned and went inside followed by Evie, Daryl, Tina, Billy and Suzy. As they entered the church Evie saw a few faces she recognised from the crew in New Jersey. She was glad they had come to pay their respects for Cassie's sake. Sarah had gone and sat in the empty front row. Mike was a couple of rows back he looked at Evie worriedly and mouthed the word sorry to her. Evie gave him a reassuring smile.

Cassie went straight over to Sarah and said, "Sarah dear, would you mind finding somewhere else to sit please as this is reserved for friends and family and you, my dear, are neither." Sarah looked shocked. She opened her mouth to say something but everyone was looking at her and there was a buzz of noise amongst the funeral guests, as Cassie had made sure she was heard.

"Mum, over here," Mike said, coming to his mother's aid. Sarah moved, her cheeks were flushed. Cassie was satisfied. Who the hell did Sarah think she was!

The organ started to play; it sent shivers down Evie's spine. She didn't like churches, not being religious, she felt like a hypocrite being in one. They all stood up as Nate, Harry, Dom, Gus and two funeral directors walked in with Max's coffin on their shoulders and took him to the front of the church. Placing him down, they joined Cassie in the front row. The service was short. Harry had not wanted any reading or speeches about his brother, asking that if there was the need to do that then it could be done at the wake. The men returned to pick up the coffin and took it back to the hearse. Max was to be cremated but he had wanted a church service.

"That's it then," Cassie said. "Let's go home and celebrate his life." She was eager to get away from the press.

They followed the hearse so far then they took a different direction as Gus turned off to go back to Harringdon. There were a few more paparazzi gathered at the gates of the stunning mansion and there were yet more pictures taken. Once the funeral cars had entered, security started to stop cars and check they were on the approved list. Daryl and Tina hadn't stopped talking about Sarah.

"Cassie is a classy lady," Brodie said. "I thought I was going to have to get my gun out at one point," he joked.

"Where is the black tulip, Evie?" Harris asked.

"I left it in the church. The woman is deranged."

"Well done for the way you handled it," Harris said, genuinely impressed. He had expected her to fall to pieces.

"I wouldn't give that woman the satisfaction," Evie said. She had been rattled when Sarah turned up with that black tulip. What was wrong with the woman? Daryl said it would be better to discuss what was right with her, as it would be a very short conversation, they had all laughed.

Once inside the house, Nate went over to Evie. "Are you OK?" he asked her.

"I'm fine, Nate, let's just get through today." He nodded aware that there were other mourners in the house who did not know about him and Evie. She went into the kitchen followed by Brodie and Harris.

"You can stop following me now guys," she said, "I think I'm OK here."

"OK, come on let's go see what going on in our security room," Brodie said to Harris. Evie poured herself a cup of coffee choosing not to join the others in the entertainment room for the time being.

"I suppose you're happy with yourself?"

Evie spun round to face Sarah. "How did you get in?" she gasped.

"Black car following you how do you think?"

"What do you want?"

"Are you happy that you have ruined my marriage? He doesn't love you, you're just different that's all. He will move on," Sarah said.

"I wish you would, and leave us alone," Evie replied. "I mean, how pathetic are you to bring a black tulip to the funeral. Why? The day is about Max, not you."

Sarah looked at her. "Are you fucking kidding me? That bloody tulip arrived at my house this morning addressed to me!" Sarah said, pointing to herself. "Your idea of a sick little game!" Evie just looked at her. "I didn't send it to you."

"But you knew about it!"

"No, I had nothing to do with that." Evie was pensive.

Nate came marching into the room with Mike. "What the hell, Sarah?"

Mike had gone to find his dad as soon as he saw his mum heading towards Evie.

"Why would you do that?" he said.

"What? Do what, Nate?"

"Bring a black tulip, you're so spiteful."

Sarah was confused. "Just hold on," she said.

Evie looked at Nate and said, "Sarah received the black tulip this morning."

Nate looked at her. "What?"

"It's true, Dad, I was there when it arrived," Mike said.

"She probably sent it to herself to add some drama," Nate replied hoping that was the case.

"On our children's lives, Nathanial, I thought it was you."

Nate was suddenly worried. "Shit, Mike, go and find Dom now." He had his phone out. "Who are you calling?" Sarah asked.

"Hello, Peter, just listen to me. Get the kids in the car and you and Betty get over here now. No Sarah is fine she's here with me."

He handed the phone to Sarah. "Just do it, Dad," she said, giving the phone back to Nate. Dom came into the kitchen, "What's going on?"

As Nate filled him in, Evie sat down with her coffee. Did this mean she was no longer a target? Or was this a message to warn off Nate? Her head was spinning.

"I don't understand what is happening," Sarah said.

Dom took her arm and took her over to the sofa. "Wait here," he said, and he went and got Brodie and Harris to fill them in with the latest developments.

Evie got up, her head was spinning. "I'm going to go and lie down for half an hour," she said to Nate.

"OK, darling, I will come up and check on you in a bit."

She nodded and went up to their room.

Brodie was looking at Harris. He was acting really strange. "What's up with you?" Brodie asked.

"I thought I saw Eddie at the funeral. I didn't want to say anything at the time but I'm sure he was standing with a camera with the paparazzi."

Brodie looked shocked, "Really? You sure?"

"I can't be 100 per cent but, yeah, I'm pretty sure."

Brodie got his phone out and tried calling Eddie. "It's gone straight to voice mail. 'Eddie call me back it's Brodie and it's important.'" He rang off. "You need to tell the guv. I mean you don't suppose he is responsible?"

"What you mean the Black Tulip? He's a freak, Brodie, I wouldn't be surprised." Harris said, shrugging.

Brodie went over to the guv and told him quietly what Harris had just told him. Dom looked at Harris who shrugged. Dom called Harris over. "OK, call the station find out where Eddie is today."

"On it, guv," Harris said, getting his phone out and turning away.

"Brodie, make sure security at the gate let Peter in straight away. At least everyone will be under one roof and easier to protect for the time being."

Harris came back over. "Eddie has been AWOL today." They all looked at each other.

"OK, let's think about this, let's say Eddie is the Black Tulip, it's possible what happened yesterday with Nate triggered him to escalate," Dom said.

"Or," said Brodie, "he is not the Black Tulip but he sent it to Sarah to get at Nate after he attacked him. I mean he knows the case inside out." Dom looked thoughtful.

"I like him for this," said Harris. "I've always said there is something wrong with that man." That was something neither of them could deny.

"I will get the task force to do a background check. In the meantime, keep trying to get hold of him." They nodded and left.

"I will go and do a sweep of outside," Harris said, disappearing.

"I will alert security," Brodie said, also disappearing.

Dom looked for Nate. "Where did your dad go?" he asked Mike who was standing over his mum.

"I don't know, I think he's gone to wait for Gramps."

Dom headed to the front door and found Nate, arms folded, staring down the driveway. "Nate," Dom said, Nate turned round and looked at Dom then looked back down the drive. "I just need my kids to arrive. Once they are here I will be able to think straight."

"I've had a unit dispatched to your house." Nate nodded.

"Thank you. They shouldn't be long now if he did what I said. Maybe I should call again."

"No, he is probably driving let me speak to dispatch and see if there is any news." Dom got his phone out and made a call.

"It's OK, they are here," Nate said smiling, running his hands through his hair. The car stopped and the girls jumped out running towards their dad. He scooped them both up and hugged them.

Peter helped Betty out the car and they started towards Nate. "You look a mess, son," Peter said, referring to Nate's messy hair; he had also lost his jacket and his tie.

"A bit scruffy, Nate, for a funeral," Betty commented.

Mike came out and, relieved to see his sisters were OK, he took them into the kitchen where Sarah was waiting for them. Nate filled Peter and Betty in on the events.

"So you think this crazy man is stalking our daughter now?" said Betty.

"I don't know what's going on, Betty, but it's better to be safe than sorry."

Peter agreed but he was cross with Nate for bringing this to his own house. "If you hadn't got involved with that girl this would never have happened."

Nate already felt responsible enough.

"That's not going to help the situation now," Dom said to Peter. "If you could come into the kitchen please."

The newest members of the house gathered around the sofa area. "This is a lovely place," Betty commented.

"Thank you," Cassie said, staring at the unfamiliar faces. "Nate has explained the situation; I would like you all to feel at home. Except you, Sarah, you are not welcome, however, I invite you stay with your family." She turned and went back to see her guests.

"What was that about?" asked Peter.

"I will fill you in, Gramps," Mike said.

Billy and Suzy came into the kitchen and there was a chorus of, "Uncle Billy! Uncle Billy!" as the two girls went running over to their uncle.

"Rug rats! You've grown!" he laughed bending down to hug them both.

"Hey, Uncle Billy," Mike said as he strolled over and held his hand out to shake his uncle's hand.

"What's that?" Billy said, slapping his hand away and pulling his nephew in to hug him. "How you doing, boy?" he asked.

"I'm OK, it's just those two," he said, referring to his mum and dad. Billy laughed as he ruffled his hair.

"Here, meet Suzy," he said to Mike. The girls were already engaged in conversation with her. Billy watched her chatting to them, she was playing along and he saw her slightly differently, a small glimpse of a woman who could have been a mother. He shook that image off; he had been around Nate too long.

Seeing Sarah, he decided to go and say hello. "Hello Sarah," he said, as she offered him her cheek. "Betty," he said, jovially giving the older woman a hug.

"Oh really!" she said, loving the attention.

"Peter, good to see you," he said, shaking Peter's hand. "Sorry to catch up under these circumstances, hey hang on, what are you all doing here?" He had seen Sarah and Mike at the funeral.

"Ask your brother," Peter said, and turned away. Billy went off to find Nate and find out what was going on.

***

Evie was curled up on her bed sleeping off her headache. She was emotionally exhausted. He came into the room quietly so as not to wake her. She looked so peaceful. He got on the bed and cuddled up to her. She snuggled up as he spooned her from behind. She had been through so much; he stroked her hair and moved his hand to stroke her breast. Even in a black funeral dress she was stunningly attractive. She moved a little as he moved his hand down her thigh to her leg finding the hem of her skirt he tried to put his hand under her skirt but the material was to tight. She rolled over slightly into him so it was easier for him. He moved her knee open as he slid his hand up her thigh until he reached her underwear. He felt between her legs rubbing her through her panties. She moaned and opened her legs wider and she reached up to touch his face. That was the moment she knew that the man lying with her on the bed was not Nate Rivers.

Evie's eyes flew open as she struggled to move but he had already placed his hand over her mouth as he moved on top, sitting on her. Evie tried to fight but he had her pinned, he moved his arm under her chin pushing down on her neck. She was stronger than he had expected her to be.

"Don't fight me," he growled at her but she kept struggling, she managed to bite his hand and he snatched it away and slapped her hard before she had a chance to scream. "You fucking bitch," he said, returning his hand to her mouth and pushing down on her neck harder. She could feel the force of his slap and her head started to feel giddy and she felt as though she was blacking out, she tried desperately to stay alert but as she felt the wave of blackness washing over her she pictured Nate's face and hoped she would get to see it again and then it all went dark.

Moving quickly, he jumped off her, he had thought that would have been easier but he had not practised the move so he was just pleased she was out. He knew he had to move quickly before someone came to check on her. He grabbed her arm and hoisted her over his shoulder almost falling over with the effort. She was heavier than she looked but then she was a dead weight. He had played this scenario out in his head so many times but he had never imagined it would be so difficult. Watching it on TV it always looked so easy. He readjusted her on his shoulder and headed for the door. Slowly opening it ajar he was careful not to let Evie fall. He looked and saw no one so he headed out of the bedroom along the hall to the opposite end of the main staircase. There was a gap between the last two rooms and a door that he opened and entered. It led to the original staff back staircase that was no longer in use from what he could tell. It was possible the housekeeper was the only one who even knew it existed.

He went slowly down the stair bumping Evie's head a few times down the narrow winding staircase. He reached the ground floor and could hear people the other side of the inconspicuous door, he carried on down further and, as the stairs came to an end, he opened the door of the wine cellar and went in. The wine cellar was almost the width of the kitchen and entertainment area above, he hurried on through, he was getting tired and she was getting heavier. He had to find the momentum to get to his destination. At the end of the room there were steps leading to the outside cellar doors that would have been where the deliveries would come in. He had already left them open so he headed up them and put her down with a thump at the top. He closed the doors and put the padlock in place.

He picked her up finding it even harder as she was on the floor and a lot lower. He made a grunting noise as he managed to get her back into position. This wasn't as much fun as he imagined it would be. He knew where the black spots were for the cameras and, staying against the wall before darting out across a small grass area, he took refuge behind a tree. From here he made his way along his carefully pre-planed route towards the stables. There were ten stables in the block and a reasonable sized barn that was used for hay storage and there were an additional five stalls inside along with a tack room and food storage bins. A staircase in the corner led up to the groom's quarters above. He took Evie upstairs to the open-plan living quarters. There were four single beds one side of the room with a kitchenette area in one corner and a seating area, which led off to a basic shower and toilet room. There had not been working stables here for the last ten years and the room was dusty and smelt mouldy. No one had been in here for years except him.

He dropped her on the first bed and stretched his arms above his head then down to touch his toes. He ached and wished he had done some gym training before his task. He cable-tied her wrists together and then her ankles. With the rope he had prepared, he then tied her wrists to the top of the bed on the metal rail and then her ankles to the bottom of the bed. She looked like she was ready for medieval torture stretched out on a rack. He sat on the edge of the bed for a second before gagging her and placing a blindfold on her. When she awoke she would have no idea where she was. He looked at her lying there helpless and laughed, he would be back soon for some fun.

***

Nate had been talking to Gus asking him to be extra vigilant. "I'd better go and check on Evie," he told Gus leaving the kitchen to head upstairs.

Billy caught him, "Hey bro, what are your old lady's folks doing here?"

Nate filled him. "Can you keep an eye on the kids for me, Billy?"

"Hey, sure man, don't worry, the girls love Suzy!"

Nate laughed, she was quite something he had to admit. Right now he would love to curl up on the bed with Evie and sleep the rest of the day away. But for now, he would be content to just see her. He opened the door as quietly as possible and looked in. She wasn't on the bed so he went to the bathroom and knocked on the door, no answer, he opened the door and the bathroom was empty. He got his phone out and rang her, he could hear her phone, it was in the room, he searched around heading towards the ring tone, he knelt down and looked under the bed. He could see her phone so he reached for it. He was confused now, he stood up and looked around the room trying to find an explanation. She always had her phone on her, he noticed something else on the floor he hadn't spotted earlier, he picked up the leather wallet. And opened it. It was Sgt. Eddie Thompson's official police credentials.

Nate felt like his world was spinning out of control. What the hell were Eddie's credentials doing in this room? Evie said he had stood in the doorway and not entered the room the other day but how else could they have got here. As the terrible truth dawned on him he became frightened not for the first time today. He ran down the stairs two at a time and crashed into Gus in the kitchen. Everyone looked at him.

"It's Eddie," he said, panic stricken as he handed Dom the wallet. "It was in my room, as was Evie's phone, she's gone, Dom, he must have taken her."

Dom had hold of Nate's arm as if he was holding him up. "Slow down," he said.

"Evie has gone." He repeated.

"That's impossible," Harris said, "we have more security today than we ever had."

Hearing what was going on Billy went straight to his brother's side.

"Get the firm's guy out here," Dom said to Brodie, who went into the security room.

"What's the commotion?" the bald-headed security man asked.

"Radio your men, alert them we've got an intruder amongst us, how the hell did this happen?" Dom shouted.

The bald-headed man went back into the security room to radio his men. When he came back he looked worried.

"What is it?" Dom said.

"There have been quite a few people who have left. They weren't instructed to check leavers," he told Dom.

Dom was beyond fuming. He had introduced Eddie into the task force, he felt totally responsible for this.

"It's my fault," Nate said. "This is because of the other day, he can't have been the Black Tulip all along could he?" he looked at Dom.

"I don't know, Nate, as far as I know he knew nothing about the case until I brought him into it."

"How did that come about, guv?" said Harris, who knew something was not right with Eddie from the start.

Dom frowned and said, "My God, he came to me and offered his help, how could I have been so stupid."

"Guv, you weren't to know. I'm going to call it in," Brodie said.

"And get a couple of units here," Dom said.

Gus had gone over to Nate. "It will be OK, Boss, we will find her I promise," he said.

The bald-headed man stayed in the security room running through the video in case anything had been missed. Gus, Brodie and Harris started a search of the house. It was so big that there were rooms where the doors hadn't been open in weeks.

Nate went over to Sarah. "I'm going to ask Dom to get you escorted back home and have a unit stay with you until this is sorted out. I think he has what he wanted, I don't think you are the target. He was messing with me sending you that tulip."

Sarah tried not to look smug, what did she care if his slut went missing and was never found again. He might even come home.

"Dad, I want to stay with you and find Evie."

"No, son, I need you at home looking after things there for me. I'm relying on you to help Gramps look after the girls," Nate said, wanting his children out of the line of danger.

"But it's possible he's taken her somewhere, Dad, he could have driven out with her in the boot or something," Mike said, desperate to be with his dad.

"There will be security footage if that's the case, Mike, please I need to know you are all safe."

"Mike, your father is right," Billy said, turning to Nate, "I will stay with them and make sure they all get off safe, go find your woman." Billy held his brother's frightened gaze. "It will be OK." He hugged Nate, took Suzy's hand for reassurance and turned towards his extended family.

Cassie and Molly had come through to the kitchen after being alerted by the commotion. "Where are Tina and Daryl?" Dom asked.

"They are catching up with colleagues," Cassie said. "What should we do?" she asked.

"I'm sorry, Cassie, but we need to get people to go, they will need to be checked out at the gate but the fewer people here the better." She nodded; today hadn't turned out the way she had expected.

Nate had joined the search of the house; he was beside himself with worry. Tina and Daryl came to find out what was going on and Tina covered her mouth with her hands, eyes wide. "Oh my gay God," Daryl said, stepping back against a kitchen unit for support.

Suzy opened a bottle of wine.

When the backup arrived, Dom saw Nate's family out first leaving with two uniforms who were ordered to stay with them until further notice. The guests were being filtered out, as were the caterers, all vehicles were being searched. Nate rubbed his head when he found the last door he had entered was yet another empty room.

"Shit," he said.

Harris and Brodie had no luck either. "Let's get outside," Harris said to Brodie.

"Harris," Brodie called after his partner as he headed out, "it's not an excuse to shoot him." Harris smiled. "As if," he replied loving the idea of putting a bullet through the smarmy shit's head.

"Suzy, stay here in the kitchen, I'm going to find Nate."

"Wait!" she said, jumping down off the stool going to him. "Be careful Billy, I like having you around."

He moved closer to her. "Oh yeah?" he said, putting his arms around her waist smiling at her.

"Well sometimes," she said, smiling back. She stopped smiling and looked at him, she touched his cheek with her hand, and she was seeing something in his eyes that she hadn't seen before. He had a vulnerability about him, a need for reassurance. She kissed him, "Be careful."

He nodded wondering why his stomach was turning over.

There were police all over the grounds. Harris headed towards the stable block. He opened stalls and headed round to the barn. He looked inside. It was a mad space, more stalls and a room with framed pictures on the wall that looked like different horses and their owners from over the years. Harris wasn't keen on horses. As far as he was concerned horses were dangerous unpredictable creatures that could turn superman into a quadriplegic. No thank you, not for him. He left the barn, as he had to keep looking.

Upstairs Evie had slowly come round. If she thought she had a headache earlier she was wrong. Her head was throbbing. She couldn't move or see, she was gagged and was totally disorientated. She could smell musky odours that she couldn't place. Her heart was pounding; she had never been so terrified. She tried to move but couldn't, tears stung her eyes she couldn't open. I'm not dead, she kept telling herself, at least I'm not dead.

Brodie met Harris outside the stables. "I've checked in there," Harris said.

"He's long gone," Brodie replied. "We would do better to get the woods out back searched." At the front of the house Dom was coordinating with backup to search the grounds. "We've searched, guv, there is nothing, he must be off the property," Brodie said. Dom concentrated an immediate search of the outside perimeter. Nate and Gus were back in the kitchen "Anything?" Nate said to Gus as he shook his head.

"Sorry, Boss nothing."

Dom had a call from the station. "There is news on Eddie, it turns out a restraining order was put into play by his birth mother who resembles Evie somewhat but it wasn't flagged," he said, looking at a worried Cassie. She couldn't believe this was happening.

How had the police missed this? Eddie's background check had come back clean originally. "Find out if he has spent any time in Wales," Dom said to Brodie. He needed to tie it all together, he needed to know if Eddie was a copycat or the Black Tulip. Either option scared Dom for Evie.

"Gus I'm losing it," Nate said, grabbing hold of his friend for support as his legs started to give. Gus held his boss up and helped him to a seat. Nate felt like he wanted to throw up. His stomach was in knots.

"You gotta hold it together, Boss, for Evie's sake. She's gonna need you." Nate knew Gus was right and he pulled himself together.

"OK, let's find Dom and see what is going on," Gus said.

Billy appeared glad to have found them. "No luck?" he said.

"Nada," Gus said, as they went to find Dom.

Up in the groom's quarters, Evie heard someone open the door. She was so frightened. He came over to the bed and sat down.

"Evie, Evie, Evie," he said, looking at the helpless woman. "Not so clever or superior now are you?" he said. He touched her face and she tried to pull away. "Now that's not friendly is it." He told her, "Be still or I'll hurt you." She froze terrified to move. He ran his finger from her gag down her neck; she tried not to flinch as he drew a line down her body with his finger. He stopped at her breast and squeezed it before continuing the imaginary line down her dress through her belly button stopping on her pubic bone. He had tied her ankles together so he couldn't open her legs. "It's OK," he said, "We will have plenty of time to get personal later." He took her blindfold off so she could see him. Her eyes darted around trying to make sense of her surroundings. She noticed a bed on the other side of the room and she saw a body. She made a noise, she was worried it could be Nate. The body was covered and up she couldn't see who it was.

"Look at me," he said to her. She drew her eyes back to him. "Watch," he said, as he undid his trousers and pulled them and his pants down round his ankles. She looked away and that angered him. "I said watch bitch." She obeyed as she watched him masturbate. "You're next," he said, as he ejaculated. Wiping himself down with an old sheet he pulled his trousers back up enjoying the fact he had made her squirm. She knew she would die before she let him anywhere near her. He left again without blindfolding her this time. She struggled to try and get loose but it was useless.

Tina, Daryl and Suzy were in the kitchen along with Cassie, Molly and two armed police officers. Gus, Nate and Billy had gone into the security room. "Anything?" Nate asked the bald-headed man.

"Nothing, I can't see he's left. He must be around here somewhere."

Nate looked at Gus, "We should check outside, it's possible the others missed something." He knew he was probably wrong, but not able to sit and do nothing.

"Please be careful you three," Cassie said. Nate went over to her and hugged her. Molly looked worriedly at Gus who gave her a reassuring smile, Suzy and Billy looked at each other, something had changed between them but he did not know what.

Back in the groom's quarters he returned to Evie. "I'm not sure how much time we will have together before you will meet your maker. Such a shame it has to end that way for you," he told her. She looked at him pleading with her eyes. "What's that?" he said, referring to her muffles as she tried to communicate. "If I take this off you'd better not scream or I will put it back on and hurt you, OK?"

She nodded and she knew she would have to be very careful. He took off the gag and she gasped for breath. "Thank you," she said.

He looked at her. "Are you going to behave and do as you're told?"

She nodded. "If I give you what you want will you let me go?" she asked.

He smirked. He knew whatever happened he would have to kill her and burn the stable block down. He had it all planned out. It was his only way to get out of this.

"Of course, Evie, don't fight me and I will let you go." He lied.

She nodded knowing he was lying. "Why don't you untie me?" she said.

"I'm not that stupid," he replied.

"How can I take my clothes off if I'm tied to a bed?"

He thought about it. She was right, he was going to have to undo her to be able to violate her. He could feel himself getting excited. He went to the bed and sat down. He stroked her hair and then her breast. He leant down so he was close to her ear and said quietly, "I'm going to fuck you so hard, you heartless bitch."

She tried not to react. She was making this up as she went along. She just kept thinking of Nate. She couldn't bear the thought of never seeing him again.

He untied her hands from the top of the bed and she moved her arms down over her head, she was in so much pain from having been in that position for so long.

"Thank you," she said, as he licked his lips.

He got up and abruptly left. She looked around to see if there was anything she could use to cut the rope and cable tie holding her legs to the bed. She sat forward and tried to untie the rope. She couldn't. She wanted to shout but she was worried he was testing her. He was unstable, she knew that.

Outside Nate and Gus walked around the stable block. Gus was headed to the barn when Brodie appeared. "Hey, we covered that area," he said, walking off towards the house. Gus looked at the barn, then turned and followed Nate round the side of the house.

He reappeared in the room and untied Evie's feet so she just had the cable ties. She looked at him holding her wrists out towards him. He took his gun out and showed her it was loaded. Holding it with one hand he cut the cable ties with the other using his knife. She was free. Her eyes darted towards the door and he waved the gun at her. "Aha," he said, as he sat in a chair opposite the bed obstructing the door.

"Who is in the bed?" she asked referring to the covered body.

He shrugged, "A wank stain on society," he replied. "Now strip."

She didn't know how to put him off any longer so she stood up and tucked her hair behind her ears. She pulled her dress up over her panties and stepped towards him, his eyes were fixated. She went over to the chair and straddled him sitting facing him. He held the gun under her ribs just to let her know who was in charge. He had discarded the knife and had one free hand, which he placed on her thigh moving it round to feel her buttock. She bent in towards his face and touched his cheek with hers. She put her arm around his neck hoping to reach the knife; she could feel he was hard. She slid her other hand down the front of his chest moving herself a little so she could reach underneath where she was sitting and feel him through his trousers. She went to grab the knife with her other hand when he pushed her off so she fell on the floor in front of him. He stood up and pulled his trousers and pants down and sat back down beckoning her over. She was on her knees and she went to him, the gun pointed at her head. He didn't see the knife she had managed to grab and she was desperate to distract him. "Suck bitch," he told her. She went to him and took hold of his erection and before he knew what had happened she held the knife up to him as he whacked her across the face with the gun. She jabbed the knife forward just hoping to hit anywhere as he stood up and kicked her in the ribs. She dropped the knife and was curled on the floor gasping for breath. She had heard something crack, she was burning all over, she couldn't isolate the pain she just knew she couldn't breathe properly.

Nate and Billy had returned to the kitchen with Gus.

"What is it, Gus?" Molly asked him.

"I dunno, I just got this weird feeling something ain't right out there," he said.

Dom was on the phone as Brodie walked in. Dom's face drained of all colour.

"What is it, guv?" Brodie asked.

"Where is Harris?" Dom asked.

"He was here a minute ago why?" Brodie said.

"I have had confirmation that Eddie has been stationed in London for the last two years and there is no way he was in Wales when Carrie Jones was being followed."

"So, he's a copycat pissed at Nate for the other day," Brodie said. Dom looked at him.

"What is it, Dom?" Nate said.

"Harris was covering sick leave in Wales matching the same dates Carrie Jones said it began and ended." There was silence.

Brodie laughed, "You're not serious guv?" But his face told him it was no joke. Nate looked at Gus who looked just as confused at him.

"But that doesn't make sense. He's always seemed the most normal amongst us," Nate said in disbelief.

"It makes sense now," Brodie said.

"What does?" Dom said.

"Harris was always doing perimeter checks, he knows where all the camera black spots are he's a fucking expert on the grounds." He slapped his forehead. "Why didn't I see it sooner?" he said out loud.

Dom was already on the radio when Brodie stopped him. "Harris has a radio, we can't warn him."

Gus turned to Nate and said quietly, "I got a bad feeling, Boss, I think we should check the stables again. Brodie said Harris and he had checked them, but that was before."

Nate nodded, "OK, let's go." They turned to leave.

"Where are you going?" Dom said.

"We are going to check everywhere Harris said he had checked," and they left. Billy went with them; he didn't know these people as well as Nate but Nate had seemed genuinely surprised by the revelation.

"Nothing was strange about the dude?" he asked.

"It makes no sense at all," Nate replied.

Evie had managed to catch Harris's leg with the knife but it was only a graze. He pulled his clothes back on and grabbed her by her hair. He pulled her head up and then slammed it down on the floor. She was dizzy and she could see blood and not much else as it was pouring down her face. She grabbed the knife again and blindly thrust it towards him. She felt the resistance as it jabbed into flesh and he yelled. Hitting her again as he fell forward with the knife half sticking out of his side. Adrenaline kicked in as she ran to the door and he tried to grab her as they both ended up tumbling down the stairs to the bottom of the barn. She couldn't feel pain anymore she just knew she had to run. Nate, Gus and Billy had come round to the stables when they heard the thud.

"What was that?" Nate said.

"The barn!" Billy shouted as Evie came crashing through the door landing on the ground. Nate was shell-shocked. She was in a heap on the ground thrown through by Harris. She was covered in blood, he shouted, "Evie!" as he started towards her but Gus was holding him back. "Get the fuck off me, Gus, what's wrong with you?" Nate shouted.

Harris had a gun pointed at Evie's head.

Dom and Brodie came racing round the corner and stopped when they saw the scene in front of them. Evie was half sitting trying to hold herself up and Harris had his revolver at her head. Nate held his hand up towards Harris and started walking slowly towards him.

"Boss!" Gus said.

"Nate!" Billy shouted towards him.

"Don't move another fucking step, lover boy, or I will shoot her."

He stopped and looked at Evie. She was begging him with her eyes to go, she couldn't be responsible for anything happening to him.

"Nate," she managed to say. "Please," she was sobbing now. She was more frightened of what Harris might do to Nate than she was for herself but she was so relieved the body upstairs had not been his.

"Harris, please," he begged, "just let her go, please."

Brodie had his hand on his gun under his arm.

"Don't do it, partner," Harris said to Brodie.

Evie managed to stand up. She looked like she had been involved in a multi-car pile up.

"You son of a bitch," Nate said, tears starting to obstruct his view.

Harris took hold of Evie's hair and pulled her head back towards him, he was holding her as a shield, with the gun still pointed at her head.

"Bring a car round and let us go," Harris said.

"And how far do you think you will get?" Dom asked him. "It's over, Harris, there is no way out of this."

Evie tried to move and he pulled her head back, Nate moved forward. Harris pointed the gun and a shot rang out and Gus tried to move his boss out the line of fire. Nate spun round as the bullet hit him in the shoulder. Gus managed to catch him as he fell.

"Noooo!" Evie screamed, trying to break free of Harris's hold to go to him, she hadn't seen where the bullet had hit as she felt the gun pointed back at her head.

Billy was on the floor next to his brother. "Nate," he said, as Nate tried to focus on him. "Stay still, buddy," he said.

Harris still had the gun pointed at Evie's head. "I will fucking do it," Harris said, spitting everywhere as he tried to hold Evie. "Bring me a fucking car or it ends here," he demanded.

"Please, Harris, let me go," Evie begged him, looking towards Nate who was still on the floor with Gus and Billy kneeling over him.

"Evie?" he said to Gus.

"She's still here, Boss, hold on." He sat Nate up so he could see Evie. He smiled at her the best he could as she cried.

Dom looked at Brodie.

"We can't let him leave, guv, we need to end it now," he said. Brodie reached for his radio.

"Don't do it, partner," Harris said.

"Hey, bud, you want a car? I've got to radio it round." Brodie shrugged, "It's up to you man, I get a car round here or you've got to walk her round the front of the house where there are a lot of people, most of them looking for Eddie so you still have the upper hand."

Harris thought about this. It was true they had had no reason to suspect him; they were still looking for Eddie. "When they find him he won't be able to tell them much," he laughed. Evie knew now whose body was upstairs.

"Why?" she gurgled with a mouth full of blood.

"He was my scapegoat. Weird little fucker, he was so keen to meet me here the poor gullible bastard. So desperate to impress." He chuckled.

Nate was looking at Evie, he mouthed the words 'I love you' to her. She looked at him and smiled the best she could, her face was covered in blood and salty tears, some of which had dried hard on her face.

"Please, Harris, please just let me go," she begged.

Gus and Billy helped Nate to his feet. His shoulder hurt, but seeing Evie covered in blood he was more concerned about her.

"Hey, man," Gus said, putting his hand in his pocket and pulling out a set of keys. "I got the black beast round there," he said, gesturing behind him. "You know where it's parked I can go bring it now for you."

Harris considered this.

"What are you doing, Gus?" Nate said, "He can't leave with Evie." Nate sounded desperate. "It's OK, Boss, trust me," he said quietly.

"OK," Harris said, weighing his options up. He didn't really see any other choice. Gus nodded and jogged off round the corner. He stopped a few feet from the Range Rover and looked up at the camera. He just hoped someone was watching.

The bald-headed guy saw Gus waving at the camera, "What the?" he said. Realising he was trying to tell him something he called the two armed detectives into the security room. "Can we let him know we see him?" said the older of the two men.

"Sure, I will flash the recording light on and off."

"Do it. Let's go," the detective said, running out the door.

Gus saw the flashing and then the two detectives appeared. Gus filled them in quickly. "I'm going to go round back, Lewis," the detective said to his partner. "You go in from the side," he added. His partner, Coats, nodded and headed off.

"Gus you can't go back," Lewis said, "he can't get the car."

"I know but I can't leave them round there alone, I'm going back," he said, and started to walk off.

"Shit," Lewis said, deciding Gus was going to have to take his chances as he ran round the back of the house signalling officers to follow him.

Gus Walked calmly back round the corner with his hands held up.

"What the fuck?" Harris said.

"It won't start I'm not even kidding you, brother, I couldn't even work out how to open the lid," Gus said.

"Do you think I'm stupid?" Harris said, pulling harder on Evie's hair.

"Well yeah," said Gus. At this point everyone looked at him in disbelief.

"What did you say?" Harris said, flabbergasted at Gus's audacity.

"Well, come on man, you're trying to kidnap a woman from a house that's crawling with the old bill, I mean that seems pretty stupid to me," he said, and started laughing.

Nate's mouth fell open. Dom looked at Brodie, eyes wide.

Gus walked forward, "I tell you what, man, you let Evie come to me and I promise I will make sure they kill you quickly."

"Gus, what the fuck!" Dom shouted at him.

Billy felt like he was in a dream world. Everything was so surreal around him.

Evie started laughing, Nate thought she must be hysterical but she simply said, "You fucked up arsehole. Shoot me don't shoot me, you're fucked."

Nate looked at Billy, "Have I missed something? Did I blank out?" But Billy was staring at Gus, mouth open.

Brodie saw movement on the roof of the barn, realising Gus was playing for time he nudged Dom and looked at the roof.

Catching on, Dom said, "Right, Harris, you need to decide if you are coming in willingly or does it all end for you here?"

Harris was confused at this sudden change of attitude. "I'm in charge here," he reminded them.

"There is a gun pointed at your head, Harris. Let her go," Dom said. Gus had given them enough time to get into place and Harris was covered. Lewis appeared from round the back of the barn pointing the gun at Harris. Coats had climbed over the barn roof and was also pointing his gun at Harris.

"It's over," Gus said, "just let her go."

Harris looked about; he knew he wasn't getting out of this alive unless he surrendered. "OK, OK, calm the fuck down," he said. He pulled Evie close to him. "Sorry about this," he whispered to her.

Evie frowned trying to make sense of his comment as he pushed her away from him; she froze not knowing what to do.

"Evie," Nate said, as Gus started towards her.

Harris lifted the gun and shots fired out from four directions.

Nate was trying to make sense of what he was seeing. Harris was down; Lewis, Coates and Brodie had all shot him. He couldn't understand why Evie was lying on the floor in a pool of blood. His brain couldn't engage. Gus and Billy were on the floor at Evie's side. Brodie was on the radio calling for paramedics, Nate was spinning, he tried to catch himself as he fell to the ground.

Billy looked over. "No," he said, running to his brother. "He's shot, he's shot," he cried, tears flowing freely from him as he hugged his brother. Harris had managed to hit him and Evie before he hit the ground. Gus was covering the hole in Evie's stomach with his hands. She had turned back to look at Harris unsure what was her best move when he shot her. Nate was trying to crawl towards her.

"Stay still, Nate," Billy said, "don't move, buddy."

Suzy came running round the corner. She covered her mouth with her hands when she saw the carnage in front of her. She saw Billy was OK and she burst into tears. He saw her, he had hold of Nate who had passed out, Nate's head was against Billy's chest as he rocked with him holding the wound in his chest. Suzy went to him and fell to her knees holding his gaze as he rocked his brother, crying.

Brodie had found no pulse on his partner, never the less he kicked his gun away from his body. He looked down at Harris and thought of his wife and kids. "Shit," he said, "this is just fucking shit." He went over to Gus and started to check Evie over. "OK, Gus, just keep pressure on the wound."

"Is she dead?" Gus said, trying to hold back tears.

"No, she's unconscious, buddy, hold her tight the ambulance is on its way."

Dom had already got on the radio calling for another ambulance and the coroner. He stood and looked around the scene. He felt numb. How had this happened? How had it come to this?

"We've found another body, guv," said Lewis. "It's Eddie, he's been strangled."

Dom sighed heavily. He nodded. "OK, get the forensic guys here. Let's do this by the book."

Brodie went into the kitchen to let the others know what had happened. Molly hadn't realised she was holding her breath until she exhaled after hearing Gus was OK. Tina was holding Daryl and they both cried. Cassie showed no emotion. Molly knew she was in shock and hugged her.

The paramedics arrived as Brodie ushered them round the back.

"OK, Sir, we have it from here," a female paramedic said to Billy.

He stood up and Suzy went to him and held his hand while they watched them work on his brother.

"Did you want to come with?" the female said to him, Billy nodded and looked at Suzy.

"Go, I will follow you."

He hugged her before jumping into the ambulance with Nate.

Suzy went over to Gus. "Boss?" he said to her.

"He's alive, Gus, how's she?" The paramedics were loading her in the ambulance.

The paramedic said to Gus, "are you coming?" He nodded.

"I will follow," he said, knowing he wouldn't be the only one who wanted to go to the hospital. Gus and Suzy walked back to the kitchen. Molly jumped up when she saw him and ran over to hug him. He was covered in Evie's blood. She almost disappeared in his embrace she was so thin. He saw Tina and Daryl who both looked terrified.

"I'm going to the hospital, who wants a ride?" They all got up and followed Gus out to the Range Rover.

Cassie got in the front. "Oh dear," she said.

"I will wait here for you, Cassie," Molly said, looking at Gus, who nodded. The paparazzi had been going mad at the gate when they heard the shooting. No one knew what had happened or who was hurt.

Dom and Brodie were on their way to Nate's Dorking home to tell them what had happened. How was Dom going to look Nate's children in the eye if their father died? "I failed them, Brodie, I failed them." Brodie knew it wouldn't matter what he said to his guv right now so they drove in silence.

Betty took the girls off into the playroom while Dom explained to Sarah, Peter and Mike what had happened.

"I'm coming to the hospital," Mike said.

"OK, son, sure," Dom said, "we will take you."

Sarah was crying. "I'm coming as well!" she said.

"No, Mum, stay here, the girls need you."

Peter agreed and Mike left with Brodie and Dom.

"OK, now we are alone, how bad is it really?" Mike asked them.

At the hospital the friends gathered in a waiting room. Mike saw Billy and went over to him hugging him.

"Hey, little buddy," Billy said.

"What's the news?" Dom asked. Billy shook his head.

Dom suggested he took Tina, Daryl and Cassie back to the house. "There is no point everyone being here tonight."

Agreeing that there was nothing they could do he took them back to Harringdon. Gus, Billy and Mike said they were staying.

"I'm staying with Billy," Suzy said.

"I'm going to hang here, guv," Brodie told Dom.

"OK, you are all going to have to give witness statements but I will hold it off until we know how they are. I will be back in the morning but keep me posted," he ordered Brodie. "I've got a ton of fucking paperwork," he muttered as he left.

Taking it in turns to get coffee and snacks from the machine they all waited patiently. The surgeons came in together. Dr Channing spoke first. "Mr Rivers is in recovery in the ICU, the removal of the bullets was successful and he should make a full recovery. However, he will be out for the next few hours." Billy hugged Mike then shook Dr Channing's hand,

"Thank you, so much," Billy said, wiping tears away. "And Evie?" he asked.

Evie's surgeon Dr McCormick took a deep breath. "I'm afraid Miss Grey's surgery was less successful. Along with the bullet wound she had extensive damage, three broken ribs causing a pneumothorax, she has a punctured lung," he said, explaining. "Unfortunately, she also has extensive damage to her head due to the force of the beating she must have taken."

Suzy covered her mouth with her hands.

"She's gonna be OK though, right?" Gus said.

"It's too early to tell. She is in an induced coma to give her brain a chance for the swelling to go down. I'm sorry I can't give you much more than that at the moment." Gus nodded and the doctors turned and left. They sat back down. They would wait as long as it took.

23

Tuesday

Mike phoned Gramps and filled him in. "I'm staying here till I've seen Dad awake," he told him. Peter didn't argue. Betty had managed to keep Sarah at home and the girls knew nothing so far.

Suzy went over to Mike, who was standing against the snack machine. "Need some change?" she asked.

"Nah, thanks, I just want to see Dad."

She nodded. "Billy has gone to see if it's possible," she said.

Gus was asleep sprawled out on a row of chairs. A nurse had found him an extra-large scrubs top to wear as his shirt had been covered in blood. He was snoring loudly.

Billy appeared smiling, "Hey, guess what? He's coming round come on, Mike," he looked at Suzy.

"Go, I will wait with Gus." She smiled. He kissed her on her cheek and they headed off.

As Nate started to come round he remembered the exact moment he passed out, he was in the courtyard looking at Evie in a pool of blood. He could make a figure out through his blurry eyesight and, as his brother slowly came in to focus, Nate tried to sit up. He shouted the word "Evie!" but it only came out as a whisper.

Billy grabbed his shoulders, "It's OK, bro, lie down she's OK."

Nate looked scared and Billy's heart turned over. Nate lay back looking around, "What happened? Where's Evie? Mike?"

"I'm here, Dad," he said, standing the other side of the bed holding his dad's hand.

"The girls?"

"They are at home with Mum, it's OK, Dad, you need to rest."

Billy looked at Mike, "When did you become so grown up?"

"You haven't been around much, Uncle Billy." That truth hit home, he had this beautiful family and he never saw them, choosing to gallivant around the world gambling his money away.

"That's all going to change, bud," Billy said.

Nate was trying to make sense of the situation. "Thirsty," he managed to say as Mike held a glass up for him to sip out of with a straw.

"Plastic," Mike said, shaking his head. "You would think they would use paper in this day and age." Confirming to Billy that he did not know his nephew at all.

"Evie?" Nate said again.

"She's down the hall, I haven't been allowed to see her yet," Billy told him. "She is in an induced coma, Nate, they are giving her time to heal."

"Is she going to be all right?" Billy looked at Mike.

"Of course she is," he said, smiling not convincing anyone.

"I need to see her." Nate was trying to sit up.

"No, Dad, not yet," Mike said, helping Billy restrain him, "You need to be stronger, just rest, I'm going to find a nurse."

Mike left and Billy took Nate's hand and bent down so they were forehead to forehead. "I was so scared, little bro," Billy said, tears rolling down his cheek. "I thought I'd lost you." Mike came in with a nurse and Billy moved back.

"Well, well, well, look who's awake," said the nurse. She checked a few things and made some notes on his chart. "I'm going to let Dr Channing know you have decided to join us." And she left.

Dom had been up most of the night, he woke up once slumped over his desk. He had called Brodie to see if there was any change but there hadn't been so he had told him to get home and rest. Brodie had wanted to stay. He felt guilty that he had not seen his partner for what he was, a complete nut job. How had he fooled everyone? He had wanted to go and be the one to notify his wife but Dom had correctly said it was not a good idea under the circumstances. After all, Brodie was one of the three that had shot Harris.

Brodie had been home and showered, making himself a strong coffee when he phoned Dom. "I was thinking I would go to Harringdon and check on everyone," he told Dom. Dom wasn't sure if he needed to go back to the scene to come to terms with what had happened, sometimes that helped.

"OK, I'm going to head to the hospital. I've got a couple of uniforms keeping watch for the press. I have spoken to Miriam Cooper who runs Rivers Production head office. I've told her to keep this under wraps until we have an official statement. The press will have a field day with this."

Brodie knew the rumours had already got out as the press had been at the house. However, as they had no factual information, not even knowing who was in the ambulances, nothing as yet had gone to print. "OK, guv."

"Brodie,"

"Yes guv?"

"Are you OK?"

"Not sure guv, I always thought I was the fuck-up of the pair." And he rang off.

Brodie headed back to Harringdon, the security firm had gone leaving police officers manning the gates for the time being. There were a few paparazzi at the gate waiting and they snapped pictures of Brodie through the window of his Audi as he drove past. The place was still busy with forensics and police trying to make sense of yesterday's madness. As he walked into the kitchen he saw Tina, she looked awful. He went over to her and she looked at him, he put his arms around her and she broke down sobbing.

"It's going to be OK," Brodie told her. She wiped her eyes on her sleeve and asked him if he wanted coffee. Pouring them both a mug they sat at the island. "How are the others?" he asked her.

"They are like me, numb," she started crying again.

Brodie's phone rang, "Excuse me," he said, standing up and walking away from Tina. "OK, well that's a good sign. Sure, I will tell them."

He went back to Tina and said, "Hey, Nate is awake, he's going to be OK."

"And Evie?"

"She's in an induced coma which apparently is good as it's giving her body the chance to heal." He didn't tell her that they wouldn't know if she would come out of it all right or not. Tina sighed heavily. Brodie smiled at her and nudged her, "Hey, this is all good."

She smiled back, she couldn't help but think if Max hadn't died they would all still be in New Jersey.

***

Dr Channing was pleased with Nate's progress. "You were very lucky, Mr Rivers," he told him.

"I don't feel lucky," Nate replied, thinking of Evie in the pool of blood. "I want to see her."

"I don't recommend moving too much at the moment," Dr Channing said.

"Get me a wheelchair. I am going to see her."

Dr Channing didn't see the point in arguing. "We don't have a next of kin for her, do you have any contact details?" Dr Channing asked him.

Nate hadn't even thought of Evie's family. "Her parents live in Spain, I don't know where, Dom might know." He looked at Billy thinking of his own family.

"It's OK, bro, I've spoken to Chrissie and Mum," Billy said, reassuring Nate. Their sister, Chrissie, lives in Australia and had said she was getting a flight over but Billy had reassured her Nate was OK.

"You're going to have to FaceTime her soon, I promised."

Nate nodded. "Thanks, Billy, I'm glad you're here."

Billy smiled. "Me too, bro, me too, I'm going to get Gus, I know he wants to see you."

Billy and Mike went back to the waiting room.

Suzy got up and hugged Billy, "I'm so glad he's OK," she said.

Billy hugged her back, he was glad she was here with him. "Gus, if you want to go and see him, just take a wheelchair with you, he may need your help," he said, winking at Gus.

"Sure thing, Billy," Gus said, and he was off.

Gus was grinning as he walked into Nate's room with a wheelchair. "Don't worry, Boss the driver's here," he said.

"Gus, come here," he said, half sitting up to hug his friend.

"I'm so glad you're OK, Boss, I'm sorry."

"Why are you sorry? You were the one that warned the others, Billy filled me in, although it goes a bit blurry in parts," Nate said. "I need to see Evie."

Gus helped Nate to sit up and got his legs to the edge of the bed. He half carried him to the wheelchair. "My legs aren't behaving that good, Gus."

"Don't worry, Boss, you just need time," Gus said, pushing the wheelchair out of his room and heading down the hallway. He stopped outside another room and looked through the door, pushing it open he wheeled Nate in. Evie was lying in the bed. She had tubes attached to her and if it wasn't for the bruising and cuts on her face she would have looked like she was just sleeping.

"Oh my God," Nate said.

Gus was staring at Evie, he was glad Harris was already dead otherwise he would have killed him. Gus pushed him as close as possible and stood back.

Nate was crying, he held Evie's hand, "Evie, I'm here. I'm with you, I love you so much, Evie, please stay strong and come back to me."

Gus was emotional, he hated seeing Evie like this and listening to his boss was breaking his heart. He stepped out of the room.

Dr McCormick walked up to check on Evie. "What are you doing here?" he said to Gus.

Gus opened the door so the doctor could see Nate.

"You shouldn't be out of bed," he said to Nate.

"Don't you start, I'm staying with her." Dr McCormick shook his head. He didn't really see the harm but there was protocol to follow.

"When will she wake up?" he asked.

"When we bring her out of the coma," he replied. "She needs to heal, Mr Rivers, we are doing everything we can."

Nate nodded. "Thank you, whatever she needs, anything…" Dr McCormick nodded.

"She will get the very best care, don't worry. Now I need to do a few checks, can you ask your friend to take you back to your room please."

Nate and Gus left.

He took him back to his room. "Thanks, Gus."

"She looked bad," Gus said.

"Maybe a few scars for both of us," he said, wincing as he touched the dressing on his chest. "Scars are just souvenirs of your life that you never lose," Gus told him.

Dom was in the hospital café with the others. Gus joined them while Nate rested. "Well there is a lot of paperwork but the case is pretty much open and closed, it doesn't appear Harris was working with anyone. A very sick individual."

"But how does someone put on an act like that and get away with it?" Suzy asked.

"Who knows, but he did. A lot of people's lives have changed because of that man. Mine included. I can't believe I didn't see through him," Dom said, feeling responsible. "You guys should go home, get some rest and clean up. I will stay here for a while. I want to take Nate's statement if he is up to it."

Gus agreed but made it clear he was coming back later. Billy went back in to see Nate but he was fast asleep from his earlier excursion to Evie's room. "See you later, little bro," he said, as he shut the door.

Brodie was still at Harringdon when Gus brought Billy and Suzy back after dropping Mike at home. Cassie was up straight away and went to Gus and hugged him. "Brodie told us what you did. Your fast thinking and delay tactics are the reason they managed to get him."

"Cassie, I caused a shootout," he replied.

Brodie started laughing, he went over to Gus and shook his hand. "You, my friend, actually saved the day."

Gus had seen the state of Evie and his boss. He didn't feel like he should be praised. Daryl asked about Evie.

"It's going to be a few days before they know anything," Billy told them as Suzy put a fresh pot of coffee on.

Molly went over to Gus, "I'm so proud of you," she said, as she reached up to embrace him. Gus felt himself start to blush but he hoped no one would be able to tell.

Dom was sitting in a chair in Nate's room when he came round again. Dom smiled. "Oh hey," Nate said, "Evie?"

"Still the same. How are you feeling?"

"OK, tired but OK." Nate shuffled to sit up. Wincing as he went.

"Do you remember what happened?"

"Most of it until the second shot. Gus said Harris is dead." Dom nodded.

"Hmm, didn't end well. I've got men at his house today with a warrant, hopefully we will find something."

"The man was insane," Nate said, not sorry that he was dead. "Do we know why yet?" he asked.

"No, I'm hoping to find something with this search." Nate nodded.

"Have you spoken to the doctor? He asked me for Evie's next of kin but I don't know her parents' number."

Dom looked at him quizzically. "Evie's parents?" he asked.

Nate looked at him. "Yeah, she told me they lived in Spain but she didn't really talk about them."

Dom nodded. "Hmm," was all he said. Should he tell Nate the truth or was it Evie's right to lie he wondered. "I will talk to them," he said, hoping Evie would wake up soon.

"They will be beside themselves when they find out, what? What is it, Dom?" Dom was not going to be able to keep Evie's lie.

"Evie's parents are both dead, Nate." Nate looked confused.

"What? They can't be, she told me they lived in Spain."

Dom looked at him. "I can't tell you why she told you that but believe me she must have had a good reason."

Nate was so confused. Why had Evie lied to him about her parents? What else had she told him that wasn't true?

Dom could see Nate was struggling. "Nate, listen, there is nothing to worry about. Evie will explain when she can it's not my story to tell."

Nate nodded. "I'm tired," he said, "I need to sleep."

Realising Nate was trying to process what he had just learned Dom left him. "I will come back later," he said, and left.

Brodie left Harringdon and went straight to Harris's house to join the search. When he arrived, Lucy Harris was sitting in the front garden crying.

"Lucy?" Brodie said.

She looked up and stood up. She walked over to Brodie and slapped him across the face. "You shot my husband!" she spat. "You left his children fatherless!"

Brodie did not know if he had fired the kill shot or if it was an accumulation of the three shots. "I'm sorry, Lucy, I did what I had to, he was going to kill people." She wasn't ready to hear it as she slapped him again. He sighed heavily and said, "I am truly sorry." And he walked off into his partner's house.

Brodie had been here a few times for dinner, the house was warm and homely, and it was now out of character for the man who once lived here. "How's it going?" Brodie asked one of the search team.

"We have his laptop and there is a locked filing cabinet that we haven't found the key to so we may just bring the whole thing in."

Brodie nodded, "Good job guys, I will leave you to it, I'm not really welcome here." The officer looked at him sympathetically, the whole station knew what had happened, and news travelled quickly when one of your own was involved. Brodie knew people must be talking about him, how did he not see it; he'd worked so close to Harris these past months.

Billy and Gus had gone to the hospital. ICU was for close family only so getting Gus in had been a bonus. Billy went in first to check on Nate who he found sitting up staring at nothing. "Hey, you're looking better," Billy said, as he walked over to the bed and gently embraced his brother.

Nate half smiled. "How is everyone?" he asked.

"All well, everyone sends their love and can't wait to see you," Billy replied.

"What is it, Nate? Is it Evie? Is she OK?" Billy asked seeing the look on Nate's face.

"She lied to me, Billy." Billy looked confused. "Evie told me her parents lived in Spain but Dom told me her parents are dead." Billy frowned.

"Really? That's odd, but she probably has a good reason why she hadn't told you, I mean come on you've only known each other a few weeks." Nate smiled at his brother. "Your glass is always half full, Billy."

"Of course, look I've told the odd white lie, I mean look where it's got me? I've got people wanting to kill me but the point is I did it to protect people and because I was embarrassed. Don't read anything into it until you speak to her."

Nate knew Billy was right. Evie had no reason to lie to him and he couldn't believe it was for any sinister reason. "I'd like to go and sit with her," Nate said.

"That's why I brought the driver, bud!" Billy said, as he turned to get Gus.

"Hey Billy, don't say anything to anyone will you." Billy zipped his mouth and went out to get Gus.

Nate sat and talked to Evie, he hated seeing her like this but he was hoping she could hear him and take some comfort knowing he was there. "I love you so much, Evie, I don't care about your past I just want us to look to the future." It was true. He decided Billy was right, she had her reasons and he would wait for her to confide in him. There was still so much they didn't know about each other. It was unfair for him to judge her. He wondered what was going on in the outside world. At least if Evie's name came out now she did not have to fear the Black Tulip anymore. "I don't want to do this alone, you're my life now, Evie, I need you with me, without you it all means nothing." He was crying. "Please come back to me." He sobbed uncontrollably.

Later that evening Billy sat by the pool with Suzy drinking wine. "You certainly know how to show a girl a good time," Suzy said to him.

Billy laughed. "I couldn't have thought of anyone else I'd rather have here right now," he said as they chinked glasses.

"Is it really bad, Billy?" she asked him.

"What?"

"The trouble you are in."

Billy rubbed his head. "Yeah, yeah it's not good," he told her.

"Are you in danger?"

"Maybe, I don't know." He suddenly felt really selfish. "Shit, Suzy I should never have brought you here, putting you in danger."

"Me? Billy, anyone you know and love will be in danger." He knew this was true.

"I should stay away from everyone, I'm nothing but trouble."

"How much do you owe?"

He smiled, "Why you want to give me a loan?" he joked.

She slapped his leg. "I'm serious, Billy."

"Over four million, I've bled my company dry, I have no more resources. Not such a catch now am I?"

"Is that what you think of me? I've got plenty of clients I could be with right now," she said, pissed off.

"I didn't mean that, Suzy. I don't know what I mean it's just everything is fucked up at the moment."

She relaxed a bit, "I'm sorry, Billy, I overreacted. I'm just worried about you."

He took hold of her hand, "All I know is that I'm glad you are here with me now."

"Can Nate help you?"

"Yeah he can lend me the four million but how am I ever going to pay him back? My business is down the toilet with my reputation. I'm a joke. I really have nothing to offer anyone."

"That's not true," she said, as she stood up and took his hand leading him off down the garden path to a spot they had found concealed by shrubs. As she started to undo his trousers she said, "You have more to offer than you realise."

24

Wednesday

At the station they were going through Harris's files from the cabinet they had brought from his house. They had to break in, as the key was not found. There were old cases he had worked in some of the files. He had a file marked CJ and it had police reports and newspaper clippings from the Carrie Jones' case that Harris had collected over his time in Wales. Brodie couldn't help but marvel at her similarity to Evie. There was another file Dom was going through that was marked ED. This was a comprehensive file on Evie.

"Well, I've found the answer to which came first," Dom said.

"What the chicken or the egg?" Brodie joked.

"Very funny, glad to see you haven't lost your sense of humour. Evie's folder goes back to her childhood. He had done extensive research on her. He knows more than I do," Dom said, trying to take it all in. He passed the file to Brodie.

Evie's birth name had been Dawson. Born to Ben and Linda Dawson she was one of three. Evie had two brothers, twins four years older than her and they had lived in a small friendly village in South Wales. "I can't pronounce the name," Brodie said. There had been a home invasion when the intruder, already on the run from the police, had entered the house through an unlocked back door. "Jesus, do people never learn?" Brodie said, as he carried on reading. The intruder was later identified as Winston Tulip. "Oh my fucking God!" Brodie said. Dom knew the exact line Brodie was reading. "Is this for real?" he asked. "I mean I remember the case vaguely, I was a teenager." Brodie was shaking his head.

Winston Tulip was of African descent. One of the detectives on the case had referred to him as the 'Black Tulip'. Worried about the racist connotations the phrase had never made it to the tabloids. Tulip had shot Evie's parents in the head while they slept, using a silencer, he had then calmly walked into the twin's room. The two boys had also been asleep when Tulip decided to put a bullet in each of their heads. He had gone to the last room on the landing and seen the angelic little girl cuddling her teddy bear she had named Barnaby. Tulip had sat on her bed and stroked her hair. Hearing a noise, he had left the sleeping girl and headed downstairs. The noise had been the family cat who also got a bullet to his head. Tulip then opened the fridge and, pulling out a pack of cheese and a pack of ham, he had made himself a sandwich and sat down to eat. Brodie looked up at Dom who said nothing. Tulip had later been picked up by the police at a petrol station, he'd been identified by the staff from his wanted profile.

The Dawson's were not discovered until a four-year-old little girl, covered in blood from trying to wake her parents, had been found out in the street hugging her teddy bear.

After the grim discovery was made it did not take long to place Tulip at the scene. He had been high on PCP, street name Angel Dust. Tulip said he had no memory of the murders or of the reason he spared the little girl. Brodie put the file down. "Poor Evie, do you think she remembers?" he asked Dom.

"I don't know, at four maybe, I need to look at the rest of the files. I just don't know what interest Harris had in all this," he said, genuinely confused.

***

At the hospital, Dr McCormick was marvelling at Evie's recovery. "I've never seen anyone respond so quickly to the antibiotics," he said. "What is different about her?" Not being able to find any previous records on her and with no next of kin they had done the best they could with the lack of information they had. Dr Channing spoke to Nate. "It's pretty amazing the speed she is healing, have you got any idea of her medical history?"

"Evie is a vegan and doesn't take medicinal drugs by choice."

Dr Channing replied excitedly, "That is it, that's why she's responding so well, she hasn't built up any immunity, her body must be having a party," he said, fascinated.

"I don't take many drugs though, and I'm not healing as quick," Nate said.

"Ah, but yes, what you have to understand is the amount of antibiotics that humans consume through their food builds up an intolerance in the human body."

"Huh?" Nate was not firing on all cylinders yet and was finding it hard to keep up.

"OK, so let's take a cow for example, it's standard practice to load them up with drugs, animals get ill as well you know, and farmers can't afford that. The drugs are absorbed by the animal which are ultimately served up to you."

Nate felt sick. How had he been so blind to all of this? "Great," he said. "That's just lovely." Dr Channing laughed. "Yes, and it keeps us all in business fixing illnesses caused by eating habits. I need to find Dr McCormick and tell him. The good news is Evie is responding much better than anticipated." Leaving Nate with that thought he disappeared.

***

Dom handed the next file to Brodie. "So, what happened to Evie?" he asked. It turned out that due to the severity of the case and the mental damage the child might have suffered that she was admitted to a psychiatric unit for treatment. Claiming she remembered nothing they were happy and willing to believe her. Evie was given a new surname so she could start afresh and not have the stigma of the murders follow her around all her life. She was now known as Evie Delaney, a name she had picked out of the offerings. Evie was placed into emergency foster care after the hospital said they could do nothing more for the little girl but offer her ongoing counselling. With her new name she was soon lost in the system. Having no other family claim her, she started her new life.

"She had no one to look out for her," Brodie said, feeling horrible for the little girl. It appeared that Evie had behavioural problems growing up and, as her history had been sealed, she was branded a troublemaker and was bounced around from home to home. "She never got the help she needed," Brodie said, shaking his head. It was at a halfway house that she had met a lad called Josh. Two troubled young teenagers rebelling against the system they caused a riot. They ran away twice and were arrested once. Evie was sat down by a social worker who told her she had two paths in life she could take. She could continue down the trouble route or she could behave and be placed with a decent family. For whatever reason this was the turning point for Evie. She said goodbye to Josh telling him she wanted to make something of her life and left. She was placed with a middle-aged steady couple who helped Evie through her teenage years and eventually became the woman she is today. Josh had never forgiven her for leaving him in the home. "So, who is this, Josh?" Brodie asked as he was passed a photo by Dom of two kids. One was Evie, the other was Harris.

Brodie hardly recognised Evie or Harris in the photo but once he knew he could see the resemblance straight away. "He was taunting her," Dom told Brodie. "She obviously didn't recognise the adult Josh or the reference to the Black Tulip. It's like he wanted her to remember."

"It's fucked up, guv, that's what it is. How much of this do we share with her? I mean if she doesn't remember where she came from is it fair to tell her?"

"That will be ultimately up to Evie," Dom said, not knowing if he would want to know or not. "We don't know what she was told by her foster parents. But it appeared she stayed with them, settling down and getting through school and college."

"I guess we wait until she's awake."

"I don't want this being leaked to the press. I'm keeping these files under lock and key. I need to talk to my boss," Dom said, getting up.

Brodie had no one to tell. He was, to all intents and purposes, on his own again.

Brodie was struggling with the new knowledge he had. His partner had obviously come good, joining the police, having a family, why would he ruin it all for a teenage vendetta? Brodie was trying to find information out about Josh. There was no surname and it might not have been his real name. Some people are just born bad, he thought. He was going to have to talk to Lucy Harris again and ask her some probing questions on his partner's life. He just hoped Harris had shared some of his story with his wife.

Upstairs in the superintendent's office, Dom was asking for a seal to be put on this case. "She is with Nate Rivers now, she will be in the public eye enough, she doesn't need this following her around as well," Dom said, putting up a good argument. It was very rare that adult cases could be sealed but Dom explained that if it got out then the original seal of her childhood case would also come out. Agreeing that the fewer people who knew the better, the superintendent told Dom to lose the files in evidence and close the case. It was bad enough an officer of the law was the perpetrator, it needed to be shut down. Dom thanked him and left. The force didn't need any bad press and the super was preparing for a news conference, this case that was now high profile as it involved Nate Rivers. Dom had no intention of leaving the files in evidence in case it was ever revisited. He spoke to Brodie and told him that any more digging he did was to be done off the books. Keep it quiet, but he was to keep Dom informed. Brodie agreed, he couldn't stop thinking of the little four-year-old hugging her teddy bear all alone in the world.

Brodie drove to Harringdon and was greeted with a hug from Tina. He smiled as he sat with his new friends drinking coffee. "You guys are like family now," he said.

Cassie laughed, "Some kind of strange dysfunctional family!" They all fell about laughing. "But seriously, Brodie, if you ever decide you've had enough you could always go down the private security route." He nodded, wondering if Nate might have a job for him.

As if reading his mind, Tina said, "Ask Nate, then you will always be around."

Daryl looked at her. "Oh really, darling, perlease just ask him out already!" Embarrassed and annoyed Tina got up and punched Daryl in the arm as everyone laughed.

Brodie looked at her and she gave him a sheepish grin. "Yeah that would be nice," Brodie said. "I know this great restaurant owned by Nate Rivers, I think I can get a discount," he said, winking at Tina as she continued to blush.

Billy was on the phone to Nate. "They are talking about waking her up tomorrow," he told his brother.

"Will you be here when they do?" he asked.

"Of course, Nate, I will be over in the morning. Get some rest, it will be OK."

"I hope so, I spoke to head office today, they are making a joint statement with the police."

"Oh yeah what's the story?"

"Miriam said that all she was told was that Harris had suffered some sort of breakdown, I don't know, Dom is coming to see me later to fill me in but it's for the best. I don't want Evie to have to deal with the publicity."

"Well that's OK as long as everyone stays quiet about actual events." Billy wasn't sure if that was possible in this day and age.

"Well I guess everyone is being briefed, Dom said he was at Sarah's when I called him, he's handing out privacy statements for them to sign."

"Sarah's? Have you moved out already, Nate?"

"I won't ever stay there again. I can't forgive her for the lies. I will take the hit for the marriage for the kids' sake but I will never forgive her." Billy knew Nate was hurt and didn't push the conversation any further.

Dom arrived at Harringdon and joined Brodie in the kitchen. He told the friends that due to the sensitivity of the situation that the case was being closed and he needed them all to sign privacy statements.

"So we can't talk about what happened?" Daryl asked.

"It's for Evie's sake," Brodie told him. "She has been through enough. Let her start a fresh chapter in her life with Nate." Brodie wasn't sure where these feelings of empathy were coming from. Evie could tell her friends what she wanted but until then it was best not to bring it up.

"Of course," Cassie said, reading and signing the document. "We can talk amongst ourselves, there is also Harris's wife and children to think about," she said. "It will be a whirlwind in the papers and then over, they move on so quick these days."

Cassie asked who was staying for dinner. Tina looked at Brodie. "Me please," he said, smiling at her.

"Billy, can I have a word," Dom said on his way out.

"Sure, what's up?"

"I'm going to see Nate and fill him in on the situation. He knows the bare bones of it but I want to check on him anyway. Are you planning on hanging around for a while?"

"Of course, I'm not going anywhere so long as Nate needs me," he replied.

"Great, I think he will need a strong shoulder." And he left.

Not really sure what was just established, Billy went in to join the others.

"I've got wine," Suzy shouted to him.

***

At the hospital, Dr McCormick was explaining to Dom and Nate the procedure to wake Evie up in the morning. "She will wake up when she's ready but you have to understand she might be confused, there might be memory issues, we just don't know."

Nate was prepared for anything. "It will be fine, whatever she needs, however long it takes." He looked at Dom with tears in his eyes. Dom just nodded. It was going to be a long night's wait for Nate.

25
Thursday

Nate had hardly slept. What if Evie woke up and didn't remember him? Or she had brain damage. He couldn't cope with the anxiety. When morning came he was eager to get to see Evie. He had managed to get up by himself in the night, with a nurse in the room, to use the toilet so he decided he was going to walk to Evie's room. He needed to be strong for her. Sitting on the edge of the bed he reached for a crutch with his good arm and used it to hop along the corridor, he was in a lot of pain and it took him a long time, but he needed to get to Evie.

Harringdon was buzzing this morning. There was talk of Evie recovering, Billy might have led them to believe she was doing OK but he couldn't bring himself to tell them she might be altered.

"Billy, you need to be honest with these people, they are not your gambling buddies," Suzy told him.

"Ouch. I'm trying to protect them." He had complained. She was of course right. If Evie didn't wake up or was broken in any way he would have to admit he had not given them the whole story, but he wanted to give them hope. Driving over to the hospital he tried to keep positive.

Cassie had known Billy was exaggerating the facts but said nothing, except to Molly, who in turn told Gus. "I'm not going to go today," Gus said to Molly, "I don't know how to deal with it if she isn't OK." Molly had told him it was perfectly understandable and suggested he polished the Range Rover to keep himself busy.

Brodie had gone to see Lucy Harris. She opened the door and shut it again in his face. "Please Lucy, I'm trying to find out what made him do the things he did. I'm trying to help." She opened the door. "How will anything help? He is gone, his reputation's in ruins and my kids have to grow up knowing their father was a murderer."

"I'm trying to find out why, Lucy, don't you want to be able to tell your kids the truth when they are older?" She thought about that and stepped aside for him to come in.

At the hospital, Billy caught up with Nate in Evie's room. "Hey bro, I hear you've ditched the wheels," Billy said, going to hug Nate. He had managed to pull a chair up and was sitting next to the bed holding Evie's hand. "They have reversed the drugs, it's just a waiting game now," Nate said.

Billy settled into the easy chair in the corner behind his brother. "I'm here, bud," he said, as he settled in for the wait.

Lucy made coffee and they sat in the living room. "Did he tell you anything about his childhood?" Brodie asked her.

"I know he was not in touch with his parents. He said he grew up in the system which is why he wanted to join the police, make the world a better place from shitty parents like he had."

"Did he talk about them at all?" Brodie pushed.

"Not really, from the odd thing he said I believe his father was abusive to him. I asked once if it was sexual but I got shut down and never mentioned it again." Brodie felt wrung out.

"Did he ever mention any special friends? People who helped him along the way?"

"There had been a girl he thought was his kindred spirit but she had abandoned him as well in the end. I don't think he made close friends after that, I was the first person he trusted." She started crying.

"I know this is hard but did he go by any other name?"

She looked at him. "What are you talking about? I don't know what good any of this is to anyone. Can you just go now and leave us to try and heal?" Brodie knew he was wasting his time. He had learned more than expected and was sure Josh was Harris. He thanked her, apologised again, and left.

Nate was holding Evie's hand. "I can't wait to take you to Wild Rivers," Nate told her, "I hear they have a great new vegan menu." Nate heard Billy chuckle. "What?" he asked his brother.

"All you think about is food, Bro," Billy said.

"I'm a chef what do you expect?" he replied.

"Yeah but your girl is in a coma and you're talking to her about food."

"If you knew Evie you would know how much she loves her food."

Billy laughed, "I thought it was wine, like Suzy." They both laughed.

"She moved," Nate said.

Billy sat forward to look. "Are you sure, Nate?"

"Yeah I'm sure her hand just twitched." He was staring at the hand he was holding. She squeezed it. "See! Evie, Evie," he said softly. Her eyes fluttered and she made a noise. Billy stood up when he saw Nate struggle to stand. He helped him to his feet and he leaned over the bed and touched her face with his other hand.

***

Gus was polishing the Range Rover when Molly went out to find him. She had brought him a mug of coffee. "Hey thanks, just what I need," he said, taking the mug from her.

"Cassie said you could all stay here as long as you like. I think she likes the company."

"She's a fine lady," Gus said.

"Yes, she's that all right," Molly said, sighing. "I thought this was it for her, she spoke so fondly about Max. It's such a terrible shame."

"Don't be sad, Molly, Cassie is a tough lady she will get through this, besides, she has to help Nate now Max has gone. Between you and me, Max kinda ran the business for the boss, Nate made the final decisions but Max was with him all the way. He's gonna be lost now."

"He has Evie," Molly said, "She will help him."

"She has to get better first," Gus said, looking at the floor.

"Hey, Gus, she will be OK, I can feel it in my bones," she said.

"That's cold you feel in your bones you ain't got no fat on you, woman." She laughed.

"You'd better start feeding me up then," she said.

Remembering Brodie's words to Tina he replied, "I know this great restaurant in town owned by the boss, I could probably get us in for free."

She laughed and took his empty mug. "It's a date," she said, as she walked back out of the garage.

***

Nate was holding his breath as Evie slowly opened her eyelids. She was trying to focus on his face. Tears welled in his eyes and he felt like his body was on fire. He came into focus and tears started to sting her dry eyes and she tried to smile. She lifted her other hand to his face and he took hold of it and kissed it.

Billy realised he was crying too. "Shit," he said, rubbing his eyes with his sleeve. "I've got to man the fuck up." He went out of the room and left them while he went to find the doctor.

"I was so scared I'd lose you," Nate said, "I love you so much, you are my life," and he broke down. The nurse came in and asked him to step back; Nate turned round and saw Billy standing in the door. His brother's heart went out to him as he went over to Nate and hugged him as they cried.

The Doctor appeared smiling. "Welcome back, Evie!" He said to her jovially. "You have done amazingly well, young lady," he continued, helping her take a sip of water.

She tried to speak but her throat was dry, she sipped more water and, looking at Nate, she managed to say, "I love you more than food." The doctor looked confused thinking she must be muddled but Nate and Billy both laughed realising she had heard their conversation. She smiled weakly at them and closed her eyes again.

Nate asked Billy to let the others know that Evie was going to be all right. He phoned Suzy. "That's amazing news, Billy, are you OK?"

Touched that she was concerned he replied, "I'm looking forward to spending some quality time with my lady."

The phone went quiet then she said, "You might find she's looking forward to the same." He ended the call smiling. Maybe it was time he found his own happy ending, after all he had discovered feelings that he had not even realised he was capable of having.

Suzy called everyone together and told them the good news. There was hugging and crying. Tina phoned Brodie. "Hey guess what?" she said.

"You want to go out on a second date?" he said.

"We haven't even been out on a first date," she said, before realising he was teasing her, she laughed and said, "OK yeah, and a third but listen…"

"I'm listening," he said, wondering what it would be like to kiss her.

"Evie is awake, she is OK!" There was a long deep sigh.

"Thank God," he said. "That poor kid."

"Brodie, she's OK!" She repeated not knowing Brodie was picturing a four-year-old girl covered in blood cuddling her teddy bear.

Nate had sat quietly in Evie's room in the easy chair. Billy had gone back to Harringdon to celebrate with the others.

"It's going to be messy tonight," he warned Nate, "I think there will be sore heads in the morning!" Nate laughed. He could do with a drink but he wanted to wait until he was sitting with Evie and they could share a bottle of red.

The nurses had come and helped Evie to refresh and she was sitting up slightly. When they left her room, she moved herself over and tapped the bed. Nate almost forgot his pain as he jumped up cursing as he did. She laughed. "Funny is it?" he said, climbing up on the bed with her. He put his arms around her and she put her head on his chest. It felt so good to be holding her. Neither of them said a word. They didn't need to. When the nurse came in later to check on Evie she had found them both fast asleep. She smiled and left them.

Harringdon was still buzzing. Brodie had called Dom who had promised he would try to swing by for a drink but really he wanted to get home to his wife. He had not had time to process Max's death and needed to spend some time with Harry who had decided to postpone sorting out Max's house until they all knew how Evie and Nate were.

"I've spoken to Cassie," Harry told Dom. "We are going to spend the weekend going through his stuff."

Dom nodded. "I would like to join you if that's OK? I think I deserve a few days off." In truth Dom had considered his options. He wanted to talk to his wife but he thought that maybe Max's death was a wake-up call. Maybe he would consider retiring. Maybe.

Billy was trying to keep up with Suzy as she drank her wine like water. He kissed her neck and whispered something to her. She giggled and they disappeared. The others sat around the island laughing and enjoying each others' company. Every now and then Cassie would say, "Oh dear," and stare blankly ahead. These had been the longest weeks of her life.

26

After

Two months after the shooting at Harringdon, Evie and Nate had stayed with Cassie while they were both recovering. They were not alone, however. Daryl had gone back to his London home but Tina had stayed and Brodie was a frequent visitor. When he wasn't at the house, neither was Tina. Billy had bought a modest house not far from Harringdon. Nate had settled his brother's debt and loaned him the money for the purchase. "I don't know when I will be able to pay you back," he had warned Nate.

"You better come work with me then," had been Nate's answer. Suzy had categorically stated they were not living together and she was just a guest. Billy really didn't care as long as she was there. Gus had become a full-blown member of the house and keeper of the cars. Dom had not retired.

Dom had given Evie the files that he had found in Harris's cabinet. They were in a sealed envelope and he told her only to look if she needed to know and to wait until she was stronger. Up in their bedroom, sitting on the bed with the folder between them Nate asked her if she was sure she wanted to look. She told him she was. "There is something I want to ask you before we do," he said to her.

She looked at him quizzically. "Nate, what is it?"

"You know you said your parents lived in Spain…" he started.

"Yeah they do, well they are not my birth parents they are my foster parents." He smiled, relieved.

"What?" she said, smiling back at him.

"It's just something Dom said, it's nothing. How come you were fostered?"

"I guess there is still lots we don't know about each other," she said. "My parents died when I was four or five," she told him.

"Oh Evie, I'm sorry that's terrible. How did they die?"

"I'm guessing this envelope is going to tell me." She looked at him.

"You never found out or asked before?"

"I was young, I was told it was an accident," she shrugged, "I don't know, I guess I never felt I needed to know, or maybe I was afraid to find out, maybe they didn't die and they left me."

"Hmm," he said, nodding his head. "Are you sure you want to know now?"

She took the envelope and opened it. She read the file out loud stopping when she got to the bit where her parents were murdered. She put her hand over her mouth. Nate took the file from her and hugged her. "You don't have to continue."

"I want to, I've opened the can now, besides I need to know why Harris had this file and why he did what he did." She carried on reading about her brothers' murder. "I had brothers," she said through her tears.

Nate's heart was doing somersaults for her. "Oh God," he said, "No wonder they didn't tell you."

Evie didn't know how to feel, there were so many strange new emotions going through her. She came to the little girl hugging Barnaby the bear. "I called my cat Barnaby," she said. It was then she found the photograph of her and Josh.

"I had forgotten all about him," she said with a smile, glad to think about something else. "He was as lost as me. I think he had a crush on me, he tried to kiss me once. It was shortly after that we got arrested for shoplifting." She wiped the tears away. "That's where I met the first person who actually wanted to help me. She had been a lot like me, but she turned her life around and became a social worker to help kids like herself." She looked at him. "She changed my life, she saw something in me and I was ready to be a better version of me. I was so angry all the time and I didn't understand why." She trailed off. Nate couldn't imagine what she had been through.

"So what happened?" he asked.

"She found me Mary and Dan, my foster parents, they are amazing. They taught me so much, helped me through some difficult times."

"Do you think they knew about your past?"

"I don't think so, they are the sort of people who would have told me. They were both vegan."

"Aha!" he said, "that explains that!" She laughed.

"Yeah changed my life in more ways than one. They said I could go to Spain with them, but I was settled in my flat and happy in my work. Well I thought I was happy," she looked at him and he kissed her.

"You don't need to be in that world any more," he told her. "You are going to fight this a different way, you are going to help me and we will make a difference, Evie."

She loved him so much. "I don't know how I got so lucky," she said, squeezing his hand.

"I'm the lucky one," he told her.

She picked the file back up and carried on reading. When the connection was made between Josh and Harris Evie ran to the bathroom and threw up. Nate was by her side as she slid down to the floor and cried. He scooped her up, hugging her, rocking her the same way Billy had done with him when he was shot. "I'm so sorry, Evie, I'm so very sorry."

***

Cassie had found Evie's work phone while she was in hospital and had quite happily taken over the social media. She had been in touch with Miriam at head office. She had been a lifesaver for Nate dealing with the press.

"Thank you, Cassie. You will stay and continue with us won't you?" Nate had asked.

"Try getting rid of me now." She dared him cheekily.

"Well, the first job I am officially asking you to do is invite everyone to Wild Rivers on Saturday, I want to get the crowd back together to say thank you." He kissed her, "No excuses. I want them all there."

"Including Sarah?" she teased.

"Except Sarah," he said, walking off shaking his head.

Sarah had kept a very low profile. Nate had visited his old home once to hand her divorce papers and remove some of his things. "I will not give you a divorce," she had told him plain and simple. That would be his fight for another day. He had seen Mike and the girls regularly as Billy and Suzy would pick them up and bring them over. Mike had a girlfriend now, Connie. She was a nice kid and seemed to be a good influence on Mike.

He called his son. "Hey, Mike, I want you and Connie to come out with us this weekend. I'm having a get together. I will get Cassie to send you the details." Mike was excited; this meant he got to show off his dad's restaurant. It would be a long time until Mike would learn that money didn't always find you love.

Evie was also excited; she hadn't got dressed up and gone out since dinner at Rivers Rush all those weeks ago with Cassie and Max. She was also nervous. "Nate this will be the first time I've stepped out as your girlfriend," she said, worriedly. There had been many rumours and a lot of speculation on the break up of Nate and Sarah Rivers. They had managed to keep Evie's name out of the press thanks to a solid crew and privacy statements.

"It will be fine, what better way to introduce you to my adoring public," he joked. She laughed. "I can't wait to show you off," he said, taking her in his arms and hugging her.

"I'm going to need that plastic thing," she said, chewing her cheek.

"Stop that, there is nothing to be worried about, everyone is going to love you," he said, giving her his credit card.

Molly and Gus were having words in the kitchen.

"Hey what's this?" Evie said, walking in. "Molly said she is not coming to the dinner on Saturday," Gus said, with his hands on his hips. A look he learned from Nate.

"Oh yes you are, Molly," Evie said. "In fact, I was just coming to find you both. Gus can you run Molly and me into town please, we both need to buy new outfits," she said, waving the credit card. "It's on the business so let's go."

Molly shrugged and decided not to argue.

At the door, Nate kissed Evie. "Don't be long or I will miss you," he told her.

She smiled and said, "Short and sexy or long and sophisticated?"

He laughed, "I'm going to leave that up to you," he said, kissing her nose.

***

It was the night of the gathering. Tina was coming with Brodie, Daryl was bringing his latest boyfriend, Dom and his wife were coming, Harry had gone home a month earlier and declined the invitation from Cassie. Gus, Molly, Billy and Suzy were all going to be there and of course, Mike and Connie. Nate had also invited some of the top food critics and chefs in the business, along with key press and a few show business friends of old. Even his old friend Dean Harper had flown over to put in an appearance with his latest toy boy.

"I don't understand why you have invited all these people?" Evie said to Cassie.

"Look, we're hosting a come back for Rivers Productions, we are using this as an opportunity to introduce you to the business and put our name back out there. People have been wondering what has been going on these last few months," Cassie said. "And Nate wants to get us all back together after what we have all been through."

"I guess I'm just so used to hiding, now it seems unnatural to step out in public. It scares me a bit, I've never been in the limelight, this is all new for me," Evie said.

Cassie smiled, "Darling, you are going to love it!"

Evie was in the bedroom with Nate getting ready. She came out of the bathroom and stopped dead. "Wow, Nate!" she said, "you look amazing!"

He turned round from the mirror and said, "Really? It looks OK?"

Evie went over to him. "Very sexy," she said, looking him up and down.

"Evie, you can't stand there in your thong and say things like that to me," he said, referring to the bulge in his trousers.

"We have time don't we?" she said, undoing his trousers. Nate took her hand and led her to the bed so he could sit down. She knelt down and took hold of him and he moaned as she drove him to the brink of euphoria, driving him crazy until he was begging her and she took him over the edge.

Nate fell back on the bed, "Jesus," he said, "Evie, you totally blow my mind!" She laughed at him. "I know, I know it wasn't my mind you just blew," he said, laughing.

"Anyway," she said, "when did you learn to dress so snazzy?"

"Ah," he said. "A secret weapon and a bit of plastic."

"So, you sent Daryl shopping," she said, shaking her head and laughing.

"Totally busted!" he said.

She went over to the wardrobe and took out her dress. "I couldn't decide between sophisticated or sexy," she said, stepping out of her thong and into her dress. Evie had brought a silver halter-neck body fit dress that showed off every curve of her body. The dress had no material from the bottom of her neck to the bottom of her breasts showing a teasing of her olive skin. The dress swept down to her ankles but had a side split that went up past her hip.

"So you went for sophisticated and sexy," he said. "How am I going to concentrate knowing you are naked beneath that dress?" he said, feeling a heat flush over his body. Her hair was tied up off her face and she looked amazing. He went over to her as she stepped into her matching heels that brought her level with Nate. "I have something for you," he said, as he put a bracelet around her wrist. It was platinum, it had her name engraved deep into it and the letters were embedded with tiny white diamonds except for the V which had tiny green emeralds.

She looked at it, "I don't know what to say, it's stunningly beautiful," she said.

"So are you, Evie, and I love you," he told her.

"I love you," she said, and she felt tears and started to wave her hands in front of her eyes. "You're such a bird," he laughed at her flapping. "Come on, Miss Evie Delany, our chariot awaits." And he led her out of the bedroom.

Gus argued with Nate that he wanted to drive them, but Nate had insisted that everyone was getting a driver tonight and that included Gus. He was arriving with Molly. Cassie had already gone to the restaurant earlier to make sure everything was perfect. Everybody else had left and Evie and Nate were the last ones to arrive. As they pulled up outside Wild Rivers there was a green carpet underneath the canopy that led to the door. The driver opened her door and Nate offered her his hand. "I like your style," she said, noticing the green carpet. As she got out of the car cameras started clicking and flashes were going off.

"Over here, Nate."

"Give us a picture, mate." The press were calling out.

"Where is Sarah?"

"Is that your new girlfriend? Smile here, luv."

"Just keep smiling," Nate said, squeezing her hand. She walked with Nate and they stopped on the carpet turning for the cameras.

Nate waved at the press, "Thanks, guys, I will have the left-overs sent out." They laughed at him as the couple went inside.

The restaurant was packed with familiar and some unfamiliar faces. Nate and Evie made their way through the restaurant shaking hands, kissing people and smiling and waving. Evie noticed Lloyd Baxter sitting with Dean Harper and waved. Evie was glad when she saw their table was full with her new family.

"Wow, Evie, you look amazing, darling," Daryl said, introducing Tom his current love. She waved across the table at Brodie and Tina and found her seat next to Suzy. She kissed Billy and hugged Suzy. Gus and Molly were opposite, sitting with Dom and his wife and Mike was sitting next to his dad with Connie.

"This is so amazing, Mike, I need to get as many selfies with these people as possible. My Insta account is going to be mad!" Connie said to him.

Cassie was sitting next to Tina and she nodded at Nate, he nodded back. He stood up and said, "Ladies and gentlemen, if I can have your attention please." A few people stopped and looked over.

Billy stood up and wolf whistled. "Hey, rich people!" he yelled. The room fell quiet as everyone looked over towards Billy who waved and sat down.

Nate continued. "Ladies and gentlemen, my brother," he said, gesturing towards Billy as everyone laughed. "Thank you all for coming tonight, and thank you for bearing with me. These last few months have been challenging for my friends here and me. I want to take this moment to thank every one of you," he said, looking at the faces around his table. "We have been through so much together and I don't think Evie or myself would have made it through without all of your love and support, and hard work." He looked at Dom, who raised his glass to Nate. "Each one of you has a special place in my heart and a place at my table." The room chuckled. "For those of you who don't know her, I would like to introduce my partner, Evie Delany." She looked up and smiled as people craned their necks to see the blonde beauty sitting next to Nate. "Evie," he said to her, "you have changed my life. From the day I met you my life has been turned upside down." More chuckling "We have been through some challenging times."

"I'd say!" said Cassie. Nate smiled at her.

"We have lost a dear friend and we almost died." There was muttering amongst the tables. "But we have made it through and I have to tell you that you make me want to be a better person, I want to be the best I can be for you." She held his hand "You have shown me a love and a life that I did not know existed, you have taught me so much." He smiled at her and her heart turned over. "This is why I have brought all of you together tonight," he said, returning his attention to the room. "This restaurant has a new menu and it's 100% plant-based." Evie's mouth fell open, she was expecting a vegan menu alongside the original. He looked at her enjoying her confusing. "As we speak all my other restaurants are implementing the change in their menus as well. By the end of next month, Rivers Restaurants will all be 100% plant-based." There was chatting amongst the guests. "Please," he said, "please try the menu before you start complaining." More laughing. "Rivers Restaurants are moving forward towards a cleaner and kinder way of living and eating." Nate noticed Lloyd was saluting him, he smiled and saluted back. "By the end of the year, all my restaurants will be 100% vegan. We will be replacing everything that is in our establishments that is currently unethical and cruel."

Evie stood up and Nate looked at her. "Nate! Oh my God! What have you done?" she said.

"Everything I possibly could," he replied. "I told you we will fight this battle another way, we will change people's perceptions through their taste buds."

She touched his face and moved into him oblivious of the rest of the people in the room. "I love you," she told him as she put her arms around him and kissed him.

"Careful," he said quietly in her ear, "you know what happens when you touch me," he teased. She smiled and hugged him so hard. "A toast," he said. "To new beginnings and a very missed dear friend."

There was a chorus of cheers from around the room as Nate took Evie's hand. "Come with me, I've got something to show you," he said, taking her back outside. "Look up," he said, she hadn't noticed when they arrived that the name of the restaurant was in darkness. He put his thumb up and the lights came on showing off the new name of the restaurant 'EVIE'S RIVERS'. "This is your restaurant now, Evie. I want to change the world with you." She had tears pouring down her cheeks.

She nodded her head. "I would really, really like that," she said.

"It looks good, doesn't it? Our names together."

"It's a great play on words," she said.

"How about if I dropped the 's'?" he asked. Not quite understanding him, she looked quizzically at him. "I like the sound of 'Evie Rivers'."

She caught on. "Me too," she said, as they kissed passionately while the press had a field day taking pictures.

References and Resources

Stronger, Kinder, Vegan

Be Kind, It's Easy

www.retreatanimalrescue.org.uk

Vegan Animal Rescue Shelter. Charity.

The Retreat was born in 1989 out of frustration at the way the human race treats animals. A rescue centre, which would save tormented, abused, sick, injured and unwanted animals from certain death, was therefore founded.

We offer specialised care for the animals we take in. We are a not-for-profit organisation and all the Trustees and most of the volunteers being vegan.

All funds raised go to the welfare of the animals, being cared for. We also use the funds for The Retreat's facilities and where possible, animals are re-homed in permanent, loving homes. The Retreat operates a genuine no-kill policy.

Our site accommodates our main rescue centre and, wildlife hospital to deal with most animal intakes and emergencies, together with our permanent horses, cows and sheep residents.

Our Mission

The Retreat finds the continued exploitation, abuse, bullying, violence against and murder of animals in today's society totally degrading and unacceptable.

We are pressing for a more enlightened world where humans remember their dignity and show compassion and love to all others, regardless of sex, race, age, gender, disability or species.

Our Aims

The Retreat offers much needed support to all animals - farmed, domestic and wild. Our aims are to educate the public that all animals need commitment, love and respect, also that animals should be neutered to avoid more unwanted litters, and are given the care they need.

By rehoming animals we can free space to rescue more abused animals.

All the animals are given the time, veterinary care and love they need to recover before being re-homed. If a suitable home cannot be found they are never killed, they simply stay at The Retreat for the rest of their lives.

Donations are used towards animal feed, rescue and animal-specific equipment, and veterinary costs. We rescue animals that are domesticated, wild or farm within a range of 50 miles from our centre. We then look after them and help them feel safe until we find them a forever home. We have rehomed hundreds of animals so far. Animals that don't find a home stay with us here at the Retreat.

Most vegans choose to live a vegan lifestyle because they are against contributing to the suffering, exploitation, abuse, the torture and the murder of innocent lives each year.

We view the consumption of non-human animals as well as their by-products to be unnecessary and unjustifiable.

Animals have every right to live just as humans do. We take a stand against cruelty and exploitation by choosing not to consume their bodies and their excretions.

If everyone knew what happens behind the closed doors of slaughterhouses, dairy and egg farms, then we believe that the vast majority of people would easily make the connection and they would choose

- not to have animal corpses on their plates
- not to consume by-products of their excretions
- not to wear their skins

- and not to use cosmetics and other products tested on animals

Animals are not ours to use or consume.

What is more important? The life of an animal or the satisfaction of our taste buds?

We have witnessed that when compassionate people learn the horrific truth of animal agriculture, they choose to stop funding it.

Why There's No Such Thing as "Humane" Meat

There are many ways that the industries and individuals who stand to make a profit off of animal exploitation and cruelty try to hide or tame the facts about how animals are treated in captivity or before they are turned into food and by-products. Terms like "ethically sourced," "humanely raised," "free range," "cage free," and more show up on animal products to put the consumer at ease, but the bottom line is that it's not an ethical practice to kill a living being that does not want to die just so you can enjoy the taste of their body for a brief moment in time, no matter how nicely you treated them before sending them to slaughter.

Why Milk & Eggs are Not Free from Harm

A common belief is that a lacto-ovo vegetarian diet (one that abstains from meat but still consumes eggs and dairy) is a cruelty-free choice. While a vegetarian lifestyle certainly creates less of a demand for animals killed for their meat compared to a standard omnivore diet, it unfortunately is still very complicit in the crueller practices faced by animals who are used for their milk and their eggs.

No Milk without a Baby Cow (or baby goat, or baby sheep…)

Cows are mammals that, like all mammals, only produce milk as a result of giving birth. Milk is produced in mammals for only one reason: to feed and nourish their young. When a dairy cow gives birth to a calf, however, that calf may never receive the nutrients intended for them. Whether milk is produced in a giant factory farm or on a small family farm, the results are the same: a cow is forcibly inseminated and made to carry her calf to term, after which the calf is taken from her so that he or she doesn't feed on what is intended to be profit for the farmer. This causes extreme emotional distress in the mother every time the cycle happens, not to mention the physical toll of being forced to birth far more babies than she would naturally in her lifetime, stand confined on concrete floors to be milked three times per day, and fed hormones and antibiotics to increase her milk production and stop the spread of disease that these conditions cause in the first place.

The fate of the calf depends on its sex, and is horribly cruel either way: if male, the calf is considered a waste product of the dairy industry (because he will never produce milk), and may be put into veal production, where he will be kept confined and restricted of nutrients until his very early death (usually around 8 months old). If the calf is female, she will be put into dairy production as soon as her body is able to conceive, and meet the same cruel fate as her mother. The natural lifespan of cattle can be up to 20 years, but a dairy cow often will only make it to age five before no longer being viewed as profitable, and sent to slaughter. These fates are similar for other female species used for dairy, including but not limited to goats and sheep.

The Hidden Costs of Eggs

Most egg-eating folks assume that, because chickens naturally lay eggs, eating eggs comes at no harm to the hens. However, we know this is not the case. A wild hen will only lay around 10-15 eggs per year (other sources estimate 20-30), and despite being natural, the process comes at a huge physical toll on the hen's body. To meet the demands of eggs for consumption by humans, hens have been "intensively bred" and subjected to all manner of cruel practices to force their bodies to overproduce the estimated 250-300 eggs each egg-laying hen is forced to yield annually. If between 10 and 30 eggs carries a physical burden on a hen's body and reproductive organs, imagine the pain and anguish 10-25 times that production causes.

The natural lifespan of a chicken can be anywhere from 8-15 years, but an egg-laying hen often won't make it to age two before she is considered "spent" and no longer of use to the industry, at which point she will be killed. As fertilized eggs are hatched by the thousands in hatcheries to produce newer generations of egg-laying hens, naturally around 50% of the time a male chick is born. Much like male calves in the dairy industry, a male chick is of no use to the egg industry, and is considered a waste product. Male chicks are routinely collected and ground alive when they are less than one day old.

Eggs produced in these facilities are not a cruelty-free by-product for anyone involved

What about eggs from a backyard hen? While the hens cared for more as pets than as egg-laying machines in factory farms might be given some kind of improved quality of life (and in other cases, may not), eating or selling their eggs is still a basic form of exploitation. Though the day-to-day cruelty may possibly be diminished, these individuals are still being used for what they can provide for someone else, and not given bodily autonomy. Buying eggs or chicks to become backyard hens also feeds directly into the exploitative and cruel practices of egg farming that most "urban farmers" are trying to avoid in the first place, as well as perpetuating the profitability and desire of eggs.

The Retreat is open to visitors and is free to visit. Their vegan café serves the most amazing food. Please check the website for opening times and how to donate.

Be kind it's easy.

Viva!

VEGAN IS A STATE OF KIND

www.viva.org.uk

Non-profit. *Viva!* Is a State of Kind. Helping you go vegan and be a champion for animals. Experts on all aspects of being vegan.

Viva! was founded in 1994 by Juliet Gellatley, who is the charity's director.

"The most powerful action you can take to end animal suffering, protect the environment and improve your health is to go vegan. Support us and help Viva! campaign for a better world." "Taking the life of an animal who does not want to die is a profoundly terrible act and yet committed so casually in our culture. Viva! nudges, cajoles, persuades, educates - we help people question a lifetime's worth of propaganda and make it easy to go vegan. If you believe in what we do, please join us. The animals need you - unity really is strength. In the last six months alone Viva! reached about 20 million people with our Face Off campaign. And society is changing. People are increasingly accepting the benefits of veganism; the tide is turning." Juliet Gellatley, Founder & Director of Viva!

Viva! Animals

Every year, one billion animals face the barbarity of slaughter in Britain, and a further 4.5 billion fish and 2.6 billion shellfish are killed for the UK. Most animals spend their short lives in misery, imprisoned in the squalor of factory farms. Many are fully conscious when they are killed by having their throats cut.

Viva! Planet

The human appetite for animal flesh is a driving force behind virtually every major category of environmental damage – deforestation, erosion, fresh water scarcity, air and water pollution and climate change. At sea, fishing has brought all the world's oceans to the point of collapse. Yet still politicians fail to act. Millions of children in the developing world die from hunger - alongside fields of high-quality food, destined for the West's farmed animals.

Viva! Health

The science is overwhelming - vegans are healthier than meat and dairy eaters and are likely to live longer. Yet the food industry continues aggressively to promote animal products to our children, helping to destroy their health and threatening their future. With the simple decision to stop eating animals, you cease to play a part in this destruction. By supporting Viva! you are part of the fight back against cynicism, self-interest and cruelty. It is a fight for life.

Dairy is Scary

www.scarydairy.org.uk

Britain's hardest working mum.

It still surprises many to hear that in order to produce milk an animal first needs to be pregnant – it's one of the dairy industry's biggest misconceptions and it's a perpetual cycle of suffering! To meet the demands of modern high yielding dairy farming we push Britain's farmed animals to the limit.

Starting from around the age of 15 months a heifer is artificially inseminated (AI) with semen mechanically drawn from a desired bull, often a beef breed – resulting in bigger, bulkier calves that can, and often do, lead to birthing difficulties. Permanent nerve damage through problematic calving affects a mother's ability to control her back legs, so to prevent her from doing the splits and causing herself further damage, farmers shackle her hind legs together with 'hobbles' like a dangerous criminal. Although horrifying to see and certainly to hear an animal dragging around chains it is considered standard practice in the industry, as a means to keep her moving to the milking parlour in order to exploit every last drop of milk she produces.

Following a nine-month pregnancy the calf is typically removed from his or her mother within 48 hours. The industry argues that this is for the health of the calf! They say that they can better measure the amount of colostrum – a form of milk containing antibodies to protect newborns against disease – the calf drinks if it is given artificially. In reality it's simply so we, as human society, can steal all her milk for our own consumption.

The separation process is a painfully emotional experience with mother cows bellowing for days, looking for their lost babies. The female calves, or the 'replacement milking herd', are shifted to isolated hutches (think outdoor dog kennel), sometimes just metres away from their mothers. Here they'll legally spend up to eight weeks before being transferred to group housing with other young females awaiting a life sentence of suffering.

It is not uncommon however to find calves up to six months of age still living in isolation, struggling to get inside the hard plastic hutches designed for much smaller animals

If the calf is born a male he becomes a useless 'by-product', sold for cheap meat (beef as well as veal) or killed on-farm. The young calf, for example, at the centre of a 2011 Viva! Campaigns investigation into dairy farms supplying Cadbury was shot in the head on the back of a truck and his body handed over to the local fox hounds for food. He was just one of an estimated 95,000 calves that meet their end this way in the UK every year.

Having been through the process three to four times by the age of five or six she is exhausted and experiencing a complete body breakdown. The fuel her body needs to meet the demands of intensive dairy farming simply cannot be met and the reason why dairy herds are often found looking emaciated with their pelvic bones, spine and ribs almost sticking right through their skin!

Once her milk yield drops or pregnancy becomes difficult she's ultimately sent to her death, killed for cheap beef at a fraction of her natural 20 year lifespan.

The dairy cow is arguably the hardest worked of all farmed animals, forced into a perpetual cycle of dual pregnancy and lactation, confined to live more than half the year in barren sheds and fed unnatural mixtures of silage. Not being able to consume enough food to keep up with the demands of nurturing an unborn calf while still lactating from a previous pregnancy, whether zero-grazed or not, leaves her in a constant state of 'metabolic hunger'. It is therefore 'normal' for cows to draw on their body reserves to meet these requirements, resulting in a 'coat rack' appearance where her bones and spine protrude. This is an indication of malnourishment.

Being dairy-free is a natural and healthy choice. All the nutrients in milk are easily found in plant-based foods that will make you thrive and you won't miss a thing!

Many of us have been brought up with the idea that we need milk for calcium but it's nothing more than a successful ploy by the dairy industry. They provide 'educational' materials to schools, lobby the Government, organise lectures for healthcare professionals, sponsor research and pay millions for advertising to condition people to think they 'need' milk. Yet no one needs milk after weaning and no one needs the milk of another species. There's **nothing in cow's milk** that you can't find in plants, just minus all the bad fats, hormones and gluey protein.

Go Vegan World

www.goveganworld.com

Non-profit. Public vegan education organisation highlighting animal sentience and the injustice of human domination.

Go Vegan World CLG is an animal rights and advocacy organisation established as a not-for-profit company. It is founded on the notion that everyone has the fundamental right not to be owned, bred, used, harmed or killed, regardless of species. Living vegan respects these fundamental rights. Go Vegan World exists to educate the public on animal rights, to promote veganism, to dispel the myths that sustain animal exploitation, and to dismantle the legal property status of other animals. It is an advocacy body whose activities pertaining to animal rights and dismantling the legal property status of other animals do not fit within the definition of a charitable organisation in the Republic of Ireland, and it is, therefore, not a registered charity.

Why Vegan?

Other animals share our capacity to think and feel. They are aware of themselves and of the world and they value their lives. Therefore, they share the fundamental right not to be owned, used, bred, harmed or killed.

There is no ingredient in the lives or bodies of other animals that humans need for survival, health or happiness. Therefore, we use them for reasons that are trite and unjustifiable such as taste, convenience, habit, tradition, and culture.

Vegans do not use other animals for food, clothing, entertainment or other purposes, insofar as it is possible and practicable to do so. Veganism is not a matter of personal purity. It is simply the least we can do to stop harming others.

Veganism is not an act of charity. It is not about compassion so much as it is about justice and fairness. There is nothing heroic or special about vegans; they do not live abstemious lives; they merely live in a way that accords others their basic rights. Neither is veganism some distant goal, that we work towards in small stages. The goal is the liberation of non-humans from human oppression, and their full recovery from the effects of our use of them. Veganism is simply the least we can do to begin that process.

Being vegan means acknowledging and securing for others the basic rights that we demand for ourselves: the right to live free of oppression, the right not to be owned, used or exploited by another; the right not to be harmed or killed; and the right to life.

Our website will help you to become vegan, and facilitate you to play your role as an advocate for others in one of the most important social justice movements of our time.

www.goveganworld.com/download-free-vegan-guide

ANIMAL AID

www.animalaid.org.uk

Animal Aid was founded in January 1977 to work, by all peaceful means, for an end to animal cruelty.

Animal Aid is one of the world's longest established animal rights groups, having been founded in 1977. We campaign peacefully against all forms of animal abuse and promote cruelty-free living. Our vision is a world in which animals are no longer harmed and exploited for human gain, but allowed to live out their lives in peace. We work hard to bring an end to practices that involve animal abuse and exploitation, but we also take a pragmatic approach and call for measures such as CCTV in slaughterhouses, that will help to reduce suffering in the meantime. Here are just some of the ways in which we help animals:

- We carry out ground breaking undercover investigations exposing the suffering of animals on farms, slaughterhouses, and 'game bird' establishments. These frequently make the news, and our films are viewed thousands of times on social media.

- We send out tens of thousands of leaflets, booklets and other resources, exposing the suffering of animals and empowering people to help them.

- We carry out extensive political lobbying, in order to help end some of the worst suffering that animals endure.

- Our vegan pledge initiatives enable thousands of people to try cruelty-free living for a month, while getting all the support they need. Our follow-up survey showed that around half of participants in our Summer Vegan Pledge intended to stay vegan. Every year we send out thousands of free vegan packs, giving people the information they need to adopt an animal-free diet.

- Our ethical shop provides a vast selection of cruelty-free products, and we attend vegan fairs all over the country.
- We train volunteer school speakers who give hundreds of school talks and cookery demonstrations every year, educating young people about kindness to animals.
- We produce innovative resources for schools, including DVDs, lesson plans and worksheets. We provide a range of resources on cruelty-free living that are designed specifically for young people.

Our Vision

Our ultimate vision is of a world that is free from animal abuse and exploitation. Animals would no longer be harmed and exploited for human gain, but allowed to live out their lives in peace. The public would recognise and respect the rights of animals, and these would also be protected by law. All animals, regardless of their species, would benefit from these fundamental rights to life and freedom.

We recognise that this is very much a long-term vision, which will take many decades to achieve. So as well as working towards this, we also take a pragmatic approach, and campaign for measures that will help to reduce animal suffering in the meantime. In practice, much of our work brings the truth about animal exploitation to the attention of the public, and this contributes towards both the achievement of our vision and to measures that will help to reduce animal suffering in the shorter term.

Our Aims

Change the status and perception of animals, from 'objects' that can be used for human gain, to sentient individuals whose rights should be respected.

Decrease public support for practices that involve animal abuse, to the point where people would like to see them outlawed.

Decrease demand for practices that involve animal abuse, to the point where they are no longer commercially viable.

In the meantime, secure legislation that will help to prevent some of the worst animal suffering.

Veganism

Veganism is about putting compassion for animals into practise by living a cruelty-free life. It means avoiding animal suffering wherever possible by not buying or using products that come from animals, as well as not contributing to any other form of cruelty.

Challenge 22

www.challenge22.com

Non-profit advise and help on going vegan.

Challenge 22 is the flagship project of Animals Now (www.animals-now.org, formerly Anonymous for Animal Rights), an Israeli NGO established in 1994, promoting animal protection and cruelty-free living.

Challenge 22 offers participants a free, supportive online framework for trying veganism for 22 days. More than 400K people from all over the world have participated in the project since its launch in March 2014.

While similar programs around the world are based on vegan starter-kits and email guides, Challenge 22 is an interactive program that offers a unique combination of group support and personal mentoring.

How does it work?

Facebook: each mentee joins a secret Facebook group, which enables participants to share their experience and learn from each other.

Experienced team: the group is mentored by experienced vegan volunteers – culinary experts, parents, students and longtime vegans. In addition to the group support, mentees can be assigned a personal mentor, for the space to share and ask privately.

Registered dietitians: the program is supervised by certified dietitians who give nutritional advice.

Structured program: each day participants receive a small task. By the end of the Challenge, mentees are equipped with nutritional information, cooking tips and recipes that enable them to maintain a healthy, tasty vegan lifestyle.

It all happens in a very joyful and supportive atmosphere – people upload pictures of their dishes, share recipes and cooking tips, talk about their daily experience, and all in all, live a great adventure together with other people in the same spirit.

www.veganuary.com

A non-profit organisation giving advice and support.

Our vision is a vegan world

Veganuary is a non-profit organisation that encourages people worldwide to try vegan for January and beyond. During the 2020 campaign, more than 400,000 people took our pledge to try a vegan diet, while more than 600 brands, restaurants and supermarkets promoted the campaign, and launched more than 1200 new vegan products and menus in the UK market alone.

Throughout the year, Veganuary encourages and supports people and businesses alike to move to a plant-based diet as a way of protecting the environment, preventing animal suffering and improving the health of millions of people.

Our vision

Our vision is simple; we want a vegan world. A world without animal farms and slaughterhouses. A world where food production does not decimate forests, pollute rivers and oceans, exacerbate climate change, and drive wild animal populations to extinction.

Our mission

Our mission is to inspire and support people to try vegan, drive corporate change, and create a global mass movement championing compassionate food choices with the aim of ending animal farming, protecting the planet and improving human health.

Animals

For many, trying veganism is about ending their role in animal suffering. Life for most animals on a modern farm is a miserable existence. Most chickens, turkeys, ducks and geese are raised in huge warehouse-style sheds with tens of thousands of other birds and little to occupy them. They will never feel the sun on their backs, breathe fresh air or scratch in the earth.

Pigs are also often intensively farmed, which can mean being locked inside tiny farrowing crates for weeks on end. Cows on dairy farms are impregnated again and again to keep their milk flowing, while sheep are likely to be surgically impregnated to ensure high conception rates. All mothers on farms have their young taken from them, and all animals - including those reared under free-range or organic systems - end their days at a slaughterhouse.

Environment

Research is increasingly showing the link between what we eat and damage to our planet. Animal farming is a leading emitter of climate-changing gases. It provides us with just 18 per cent of our calories and yet is responsible for 60 per cent of agriculture's greenhouse gas emissions. Oxford University research shows that plant foods - including nuts and soya - have a far less damaging impact than animal foods.

The lead researcher concluded that becoming vegan was 'the single biggest thing' a typical consumer could do to help protect the planet.

Because it requires so much more land than is needed to farm plants, animal agriculture is also a key driver of deforestation. Huge swathes of trees are cleared to make way for animals to graze or to grow crops to feed to animals on intensive farms. The animals who once lived in the forest must flee or die out.

Animal farming is also responsible for much air, soil and water pollution, including causing or exacerbating ocean dead zones. These are areas where there is so little oxygen, nothing can survive.

Fish are scooped out of the ocean in their billions and fed to farmed animals including fish. And most of the plastic found in the Great Pacific Garbage Patch actually comes from abandoned fishing gear. Consuming animals contributes to this pollution and our oceans dying.

Health: Many people try vegan for a month because they want to see if it will improve their health. Decades of research links our diets to a whole array of health conditions, and suggests that vegans suffer less from heart disease, type 2 diabetes and some cancers.

Some of those who take part in Veganuary report significant health improvements in those first 31 days - from sleeping better to improved digestion and clearer skin! We can't promise everyone who takes part will see incredible health improvements but many say they do!

Every person who reduces or ends their consumption of animal products is having a positive impact, but it can be fun, too! Veganuary aims to ensure everyone who takes part has an enjoyable, exciting and eye-opening experience, and we must be doing something right! 98 per cent of participants who respond to our surveys tell us they would recommend taking part in Veganuary

When you sign-up to our 31-day pledge, you will receive a celebrity e-cookbook plus daily emails offering support, recipe's, shopping tips and nutritional information. You can sign up at anytime. The pledge is not just for January.

EARTHLING ED

www.earthlinged.org

World known liberator saving animals and the planet through vegan education and activism.

Inspirational speaker.

Ed Winters is a vegan educator, public speaker and content creator based in London, England. Winters is the Co-Founder and Co-Director of Surge an animal rights organisation determined to create a world where compassion towards all non-human animals is the norm. In 2016 Surge founded The Official Animal Rights March, which succeeded in a growth from 2,500 participants in London in 2016 to 41,000 participants across the world in 2019.

Winters has spoken at over 1/3 of UK universities and at 6 Ivy League colleges, including as a guest lecturer at Harvard University in April 2019. He has given speeches across the world, including at the University of Cambridge, EPFL, Google NYC and Google Zürich. In early 2019 he gave two TEDx talks, reaching a total of 1.3 million views online. His speech "You Will Never Look at Your Life in the Same Way Again" has over 33.4 million accumulative views online and has been given to thousands of students across UK universities.

Ethics

We consider ourselves a nation of animal lovers, they are our friends, companions and even members of our families. However, as a nation we also slaughter one billion land animals every year as well as billions of marine animals, for no necessary reason.

We are born into societies and cultures that condition us from birth into believing that animal products are normal, natural and necessary. Our societies dictate many philosophies and ideologies that we carry with us through life and in the case of animals, we are told to love some - and eat others. We have normalised behaviour that we would normally consider to be horrific, using excuses and ingrained justifications to hide behind the reality of our immoral actions.

We are indoctrinated with advertising and marketing, further reinforcing the idea of separation and segregation between species, with decades of devaluing and reducing the lives of farm animals to nothing more than commodities for human disposal. In many respects we are vulnerable to the power society holds over us, but at what point do we choose to look past what we are told and seek the truth?

Animals suffer, just like us. They feel a vast spectrum of emotions including love, joy, grief, fear and pain. The fact that animals experience pain means that they have an innate preference to avoid it. Therefore it is our moral obligation to protect them from unnecessary suffering - however we have normalised exploiting them in the trillions, profiting from their gentleness and their innocence.

The suffering that occurs in order to produce animal products is immense - and it is all unnecessary. The consumption of animal products has no necessity in the human diet and is in fact massively detrimental to our health and life longevity. Moving from an animal-based diet to a vegan diet is directly opposing animal cruelty and oppression. Every purchase we make is a vote for the type of world that we want to live in, therefore when we buy animal products, or products tested on them - we are saying that we are comfortable living in a world that inflicts violence upon animals. However when we choose the vegan option, we are stating that we oppose animal cruelty and wish to live in a compassionate, non-violent world.

LIVEKINDLY

www.livekindly.co

The leading plant-based news site.
Empowering people to make positive changes.

Kindness is simple. It's our true nature. We're firm believers in being the change we want to see in this world. For humanity, our home, and those who share it with us, we're creating new, better, and kinder choices to help us all LIVEKINDLY.

Honest

Our North Star. It makes everything we do possible. We're honouring the planet with respect and a commitment for a better today and all of the tomorrows.

Inclusive

What unites is always greater than what divides us. We embrace uniqueness and always encourage the very best in each other and ourselves.

Mindful

We lead with the awareness that who we are and what we do is only achievable through honouring our connection to the world around us.

Bold

We're working tirelessly toward transforming the status quo and creating a kinder future by leading with our hearts every step of the way.

IMPATIENT

Our world needs new food solutions, fast. We're working with urgency because kindness matters now more than ever.

Vegan Historical Figures

Albert Einstein
Albert Schweitzer
Alice Walker
Buddha
Clara Barton
Epicurus
George Bernard Shaw
Henry David Thoreau
Henry Salt
HG Wells
Isaac Bashevis Singer
Jeremy Bentham
John Wesley
Leo Tolstoy
Leonardo Da Vinci
Mahatma Gandhi
Mark Twain
Mary Shelley
Nikola Tesla
Percy Shelley
Plato
Plutarch
Pope Porphyry
Pythagoras
Sir Isaac Newton
Sir Isaac Pitman
Sir Mark Oliphant
Socrates
Srinivasa Ramanujan
St Francis of Assisi
Susan Anthony
Voltaire
William Blake
William Wordsworth

Documentaries to Watch

The Game Changers
What the Health
Dominion
Cowspiricy: The Sustainability Secret
Speciesism
Forks Over Knives
Earthlings
Land of Hope & Glory
The Animal People

Available worldwide online and from all good bookstores

www.mtp.agency

www.facebook.com/mtp.agency

@mtp_agency

Michael Terence
Publishing